Run

Caged Trilogy: Book One

by

H.G. Lynch

Published by

Crushing Hearts and Black Butterfly Publishing, LLC.

Novi, Michigan 48374

Cover by H.G. Lynch
Edited by: CLS Editing

Dedication:

To My Blue-Eyed Hero

Chapter One

** Tilly **

Run! Run, Tilly, and don't stop! A voice screamed in my head.

I ran. I ran until my feet ached, my legs burned, and my breath sawed in my lungs. I kept running, even when branches tore at my face and arms, nettles stung my bare calves, and I could hardly see where I was going for the stinging tears blurring my vision. When I fell, scraping my knees on rocks and hard dirt and gouging my palm on a jagged stone, I scrambled up and ran again.

When night began to fall, darkness descended through the woods—turning the trees to living monsters and the singing of crickets to tiny screams. I fell more often, and still, I got up and kept running. My knees and hands were stiff and caked with mud and blood, and my heart was hammering so hard in my chest, I thought it would explode. Blood pounded in my ears, my breathing rasped in my throat and my muscles flamed as I pushed myself to keep going, and then I was going down.

My foot caught on a root or branch that I hadn't been able to see in the darkness of the woods under the bare, frosty night sky, and I suddenly rolled, tumbling down a hill. Stones and leaves flew into my face, pelting, blinding, and choking me. Rocks loomed out of the spinning grey-black of the world and whacked into my ribs, arms, and legs—leaving cuts and searing pains that would turn to bruises soon enough. I might have screamed, but I don't know if I did.

At last, I stopped rolling, very abruptly, when I slammed into a tree at the base of the hill hard enough to knock whatever breath was left in me right out of my chest. I made a harsh, breathless whimpering sound, and that time, I didn't get up immediately to keep running. Instead, I lay at the base of the tree, gasping and aching. I felt battered all over, as if I'd been pelted with rocks. I couldn't tell if the dampness running down my face was from tears, sweat, or blood. My legs were on fire, my ribs were screaming, and I could barely find the energy to breathe—it just hurt too much.

I knew I had to move. I wasn't safe yet. I wasn't out of the woods—literally or figuratively. So I dragged myself upright, biting down on a gasp of pain as a twinge shot through my left leg. I was almost blind in the darkness, but the moon was out, peering through the trees and giving me just enough light to see by. I looked down at my legs and saw they were blackened with dirt, my knees smeared with blood from falling on them repeatedly. My elbows, scraped raw, weren't much better. My forearms were lined with thin slices from the whipping branches. I reached up to the throbbing spot at my hairline, and when I drew my fingers back, they were stained with dark liquid. My hair was tangled with twigs and blood and falling into my eyes. I pushed it back and saw my hand was shaking like a leaf in a high wind. In fact, I was shaking all over.

Slowly, swallowing a groan of pain, I hauled myself to my feet, stumbling against the tree that had so kindly stopped my rolling descent. Breathing hard, I tried to think. I knew I couldn't keep running, not in that state, but I had to get somewhere safe—or at least somewhere with a little cover. If I stayed there, *they* would find me…and then *they* would drag me back.

Come on, Tilly, think. Move. Think and move at the same time. You can do that much, right? I wasn't so sure, but I tried. I pushed myself regretfully away from the tree propping me up, ignoring the protests of my weary legs, and took a few unsteady steps. A sharp pain jolted up my left leg again, and I grabbed for the tree, gritting my teeth so I wouldn't cry out. *They* might hear me.

Closing my eyes, I leaned my forehead against the rough bark of the tree trunk, feeling my muscles tremble. The adrenaline was wearing off, leaving behind a numb coldness and the burning ache of my wounds. My own breathing was disturbingly loud in my ears, and I tried to calm my racing heart rate. *You need to find shelter*, my mind told me in an annoying, condescending voice, as if I hadn't already figured that out. *Well then, get moving!*

I pushed away from the tree, ready to make another attempt at walking, but then I heard a quiet sound—a snapping branch. A footfall on dry leaves. My heart jerked hard into my ribs, my stomach slammed into my throat, and I went deathly still, holding my breath. *They found me!* The thought was a panicked scream inside my skull. Every muscle in my body was tense, frozen, and my vision swam. Black trees against a navy background tilted and sparkles danced in my peripheral vision. I let out my breath slowly, silently, and took in a clean, crisp gulp of air. I strained my ears, listening, too scared to move my head to look around me.

After about a minute had passed, and I still hadn't heard anything more, I cautiously relaxed, loosening my howling muscles. My breath hitched halfway out of my throat, and threatened to dissolve into sobs, but I stuffed my knuckles into my mouth, biting down on them and tasting dirt. When I gained control of myself again, I started to move out from behind my tree. I heard another sound, like a whisper, to my left, very close. I whipped around to face it, eyes scanning the dark. The sudden movement was too much for my shock addled mind and exhausted body. The darkness rose up over my vision, and I fell again. That time, thankfully, I didn't feel it when I hit the ground. I just kept falling, falling into unconsciousness.

** Spencer **

The girl was unconscious when he found her, lying in the dirt like a broken doll someone had thrown away. In ragged shorts and a torn t-shirt, she looked like a street kid. He could see the beads of blood spilling from cuts and scratches on her arms and legs and crimson liquid matted into her pale, dirty hair from a head wound. He looked up at the top of the hill, saw the disturbed leaf litter churned up from where she'd obviously rolled down it.

Cautiously, he crept forward, sniffing the air. She smelled like blood, sweat and the acrid scent of fear. With his ears swivelling to pick up any noise, any sign of what had been chasing her, he lowered his head and gently pressed his muzzle into her side. She didn't wake up. She was so still, that if he hadn't been able to hear her heart fluttering, he might have thought she was dead.

He raised his head, his ears twitching, as he thought he heard a twig snap. Then he caught the scent of a fox on the breeze, and relaxed. He returned his attention to the girl with a chuffing sigh, knowing he couldn't just leave her there for whatever she was running from to catch up to her. Even if there was nothing chasing her, which he suspected, because he couldn't hear anything but the usual noises of the woods. There were other creatures out there that would take full advantage of an injured, unconscious girl. No, he couldn't leave her there.

Stretching out his paws, the wolf dug his claws into the dirt and began to shudder, spasms rolling through his body from his muzzle to the tip of his tail. He whimpered once before closing his eyes and thinking of anything but the agony of his bones breaking and shifting, muscles tearing and rejoining, blood vessels bursting and sealing, every cell in his body burning and changing shape. It felt like forever, but it only took minutes for the wolf to become a boy.

On hands and knees on the ground, he quaked, his muscles twitching with the after effects of the Change. His chest heaved with gasping breaths as he tried to get air into lungs that suddenly felt too small and wrong. His dulled human senses made him anxious. He couldn't hear, see, or smell half as well as in his wolf form, which was a real problem in the dark with a girl to protect. Shaking off the itchiness of his skin, he pushed himself to his feet and looked down at the girl with new eyes. With his dimmed human vision, she was just a shadow on the ground, but he could still see the paleness of her hair and skin.

For a second, he just stood there, debating what to do with her. She needed first aid to clean up those cuts, and probably water to replace the sweat she'd lost running. He could take her back to his cabin quietly. Nobody ever came into his cabin but him; nobody would have to know. But he had a feeling that she'd be frightened when she woke up, and he wasn't exactly great at calming crying girls. He was more used to them flirting with him, or avoiding him because he was scary in some indefinable way they couldn't put their fake fingernails on; it was a side effect of being a werewolf. Some humans could tell there was something different about him, and some couldn't. It didn't really matter, seeing as he avoided most people anyway, because, well, he just didn't like them very much.

But the girl…no, sneaking her to his cabin wouldn't do. If he got caught trying to slip her in, his father would give him hell for it, maybe even kick him out of the pack. He was barely allowed in the pack as it was, and that was fine, but he didn't want to push it. So he'd have to take the girl to the camp and hope Jane's compassionate nature would mean she couldn't turn the girl away when she clearly needed help.

With his mind made up, Spencer bent over and easily lifted the girl into his arms. She was light, and he could feel her ribs through her t-shirt. She hadn't been fed very well—maybe she was a street kid after all. It didn't matter who she was for now. He could worry about that later. With her hanging limply in his arms, he loped back toward camp, imagining the look on his father's face if he found out he'd brought a human girl into their den. The thought made him wince and smile at the same time.

Chapter Two

** Tilly **

Waking up, the first thing I registered was the pain in my body. My head was splitting, and my ribs creaked with every breath, but I was still breathing at least. That was a good sign.

Without opening my eyes or trying to move, I attempted to work out where I was. I was lying on something soft, there was a rough blanket covering me, and there was a strange musky scent in the air—like moss, earth, and wild animal. I could hear muffled noises nearby, voices, and beyond that, a rushing sound like water—a stream. That puzzled me and worried me immensely; the only stream I knew of was deep, deep in the woods on the very edge of town. That meant I was several miles from home, but it also meant I was miles away from *them*. I wasn't sure how much good that would do me. *They* would find me eventually.

Concluding that, at the very least, I was alive and relatively safe for the time being, I finally opened my eyes. Soft, yellow light surrounded me, and I groaned as I rolled over, blinking. The bed under me creaked, the complaint of metal springs on a foldout bed. The kind you might use for sleepovers or camping. I suppose that explained why I was in, what appeared to be, a very large tent. Across the room from the whiny bed I was lying in, there was another bed. That one was empty, but made up with a cosy looking waterproof sleeping bag and some ratty blankets. There was also a white plastic cooler, a first aid box, a gas lantern…and a little girl staring at me with wide, excited eyes.

She clapped her hands together when I looked at her, and I flinched back. *Where the hell am I?* I wondered. The little girl, who was sitting on the floor at the foot of my bed, hopped up, grinning. Her dark hair ponytails swished as she bounced from foot to foot, watching me.

Uneasy, I tried to smile at the cute little girl. Her grin widened, showing tiny white teeth. Her eyes were as dark as her hair, shining with childlike curiosity.

Sitting up slowly, so as not to aggravate my injuries, I said, "Hi there. I'm Tilly. What's your name?" Before I'd even finished speaking, the girl squeaked and ran out of the tent through the fluttering gap in one wall. I blinked, frowning. Had I scared her?

Outside, just beyond the flapping doorway, I heard a high, sweet voice saying to someone, "She's awake! She's awake! Come look, the girl's awake!"

A moment later, the girl ran back into the tent and stopped just inside the doorway, pointing at me. As another, larger figure entered behind her, I shrank back, suddenly hyper aware of the mess I was in. I probably looked downright feral. Also, I was embarrassed to be lying in someone else's bed, in someone else's tent, having obviously been taken in by some kind strangers as if I was a wounded stray cat.

The person who entered the tent behind the little girl was a boy, probably about my age. He tugged on one of the little girl's ponytails as he brushed past her, eyeing me with a small smile on his face. Nervously, I tugged the blanket higher around my neck. The boy was cute—he had curly chestnut hair that fell into sparkly green eyes, and a dimple in one cheek. He was fairly tall, a little lanky, dressed in camouflage print trousers and a khaki t-shirt that looked a size too big for his slender frame.

The boy's smile twitched wider, and I realised I was staring at him. I blushed and dropped my gaze, twisting the edge of the blanket between my fingers nervously. With my eyes on the bumps under the blanket that were my knees, I heard the rustle of clothing as the boy moved, and the low murmur of his voice as he spoke to the little girl.

"Annie, go get Sarah and tell her the girl is awake. I'll keep an eye on her until you get back."

I peeked up and saw the boy kneeling next to the little girl, Annie, who was chewing her lip hesitantly. She glanced at me, and then back to the boy, before nodding and bolting out of the tent. I assumed she was going to get Sarah–whoever that was. That left me alone with the boy. He stretched to his feet again and sauntered further into the tent, keeping his eyes on me. In return, I kept my eyes on him, until he casually sat down on the empty bed opposite me and put his hands on his knees. I waited for him to say something, but he just sat there and stared at me thoughtfully, an odd fey smile on his lips.

Uncomfortable, I cleared my throat, and not quite looking at him, I said, "Um. Hi." My voice came out dry and hoarse, and I swallowed, curling into a tighter ball. I shuddered, and the boy's eyes narrowed, but he had the tact not to say anything about it.

Instead, he said, "Hello. How are you feeling?"

His voice was gentle, and I glanced up at his face. He was still smiling, but it was a kind sort of smile. I looked away again, clutching the blanket to my chest.

I nodded. "I'm–" My voice cracked, and I swallowed again, taking a breath and trying again. "I'm okay, I guess." I was alive, I didn't seem to have any broken bones, and I appeared to have been rescued by some nice campers. It could have been worse—a lot worse.

The boy's smile faded a little and his eyebrows drew together slightly, giving me a concerned look. "You've been unconscious for nearly two days. What's your name?" he asked quietly, leaning forward so his elbows rested on his knees. A chestnut curl fell into his eyes, and he brushed it back absently, not taking his eyes off me.

"Tilly. My name's Tilly," I said, my voice almost a whisper.

The boy tilted his head, his green eyes narrowing curiously for an instant. "Tilly. Is it short for something?" he asked.

Carefully, I nodded. "It's short for Matilda. Everyone just calls me Tilly, though." I hated it when people called me Matilda. Only *they* ever called me Matilda.

Grinning, the boy nodded. "Tilly it is then. I'm Dominic. You can take you pick of shortened forms: Dom, Nick, Nicky, or my least favourite, Dick. I'm actually not really a Dick kind of guy."

His grin turned roguish, and I laughed, surprising myself. It seemed to please Dominic, and I found myself smiling back at him. He seemed friendly enough.

"Don't forget Minnie. I thought Minnie was your least favourite nickname," a dry voice stated from the doorway, and I jumped a little.

I hadn't heard anyone else come in, but a second boy was standing by the doorway. His arms were crossed over his chest, showing off more pronounced muscles than Dominic had, and he had a lazy grin on his mouth. It didn't look as friendly and open as Dominic's, but it didn't look unfriendly either. The new boy had wavy brown hair, but the same green eyes as Dominic, and I guessed they were brothers.

Dominic sighed at the other boy good naturedly. "Yes, I hate being called Minnie. That's probably why I didn't mention it to Tilly, just in case she decided to call me that."

He gave me a sideways grin. The other boy's eyes slid to me, regarding me with curiosity and pursed lips.

"Tilly, this is my brother, Desmond. He's too cool to introduce himself," Dominic said, waving a hand toward the other boy.

Desmond scoffed and unfolded his arms. Giving his brother a pointed look, he strolled over to me, and held out a hand. I stared at it for a second, and then looked up at him blankly. He raised his eyebrows into his wavy hair expectantly.

"It's a hand. You're meant to shake it. It's generally regarded as the polite thing to do when you meet new people," he said, and I scowled at him.

"You don't seem like a polite person," I said, the words rolling off my tongue before I could think about them.

Dominic laughed delightedly, and Desmond glared at me, taking his hand back and shoving it into his jeans pocket. I frowned, blushing, and realising it was incredibly rude to insult someone who'd rescued me—or was at least part of the family who'd rescued me.

"I'm sorry," I muttered ruefully. "I didn't mean that. I'm sure you're perfectly polite. It's nice to meet you." Actually, it wasn't really, and my saying so seemed to make Dominic laugh harder.

Desmond whirled on him, bared his teeth, and stalked out of the tent with an impressive growl.

I sighed. "I'm sure I just made a great first impression," I murmured, rubbing my eye.

"Don't worry about him," Dominic assured me, still grinning. "You were right. He's not very polite, but he's not a bad guy. He'll probably have forgotten about it within the hour."

I smiled again, and was about to reply, when the curtain-doorway rustled, and someone else came in. The woman was young, maybe mid-twenties, with long red hair and a bright smile. Sarah, I guessed.

16

"Hello there! Glad you're finally awake. We were all starting to worry about you. I see you've met Dominic. I'm Sarah, by the way." The woman spoke rapidly, crossing the room to my bed.

A little flustered, I nodded. Behind her, Dominic snickered.

Sarah paused, looking at me, and shook her head. She put her hands on her hips, and I noticed she was wearing a long, flaring skirt and a grey tank top. Her slender feet were strapped into beaded sandals. She eyed me with soft, green eyes, a darker, less startling shade than Dominic's, before tucking her wavy red hair behind her ear and shaking her head again as she clucked her tongue.

"Poor girl. What did you do, pick a fight with a bear? It took me hours to clean you up and bandage all your cuts and bruises. At least you're awake now. Come on. Get up. We'll get you dressed and fed, and then I'll introduce you to everybody else. They're all very curious about you, you see, and…."

Sarah wittered on pleasantly, flipping back the blankets and hustling me out of the bed, leaving me standing there uncomfortably while she rooted around in a duffle bag by the end of the bed that I hadn't noticed before .

That was when I realised I wasn't wearing my own clothes; I was clad in an oversized pink nightgown and mummified in white bandages. I felt awkward and embarrassed, uncomfortable with my scratched legs and plaster covered knees showing under the hem of the nightgown. Especially since Dominic was still sitting on the other bed, grinning at my discomfort.

Sarah returned to me, carrying a bundle of clothes, and held them out to me. I took them with a grateful smile. "Um, thanks," I murmured, "Not just for the clothes, but for, you know, bandaging me up and...everything."

The woman's smile crinkled the corners of her dark eyes. She moved as if to hug me, but stopped herself when I flinched in surprise. I bit my lip. Her smile didn't waver though.

"It's alright. You just get changed, and I'll go have Kat rustle up some food for you. It's supper time anyway. You're not a vegetarian are you?" She pulled a face as if the idea of someone not eating meat was as ridiculous to her as the notion of a lion eating with a fork and knife.

I shook my head no and she gave a satisfied sigh, saw I wasn't moving, and glanced at Dominic. He wasn't grinning now, but he was watching me thoughtfully. Heat burned in my cheeks, and I looked down, toying with the bundle of clothes in my hands.

"Eh, Dom? Give the girl some privacy, will you? Not everyone's as bold as you and the boys are," Sarah said, slightly chastising.

I cast her a grateful smile as Dominic rose from the bed, looking puzzled and a little offended. I wondered if he'd actually thought I'd just get changed right in front of him—a teenage boy I didn't even know. I supposed that maybe he'd grown up around guys, not a lot of girls, and privacy didn't mean quite as much to them.

Once Sarah and Dominic were gone, I unfolded the clothes Sarah had given me and laid them out on the bed I'd been lying in. A

18

black t-shirt that looked as if it might actually fit, a purple hoodie, which looked as if it wouldn't, and my own knee length denim shorts with the ragged hems. They looked as if they'd been washed. For some reason, that touched me, and I found my eyes welling with tears. I blinked them away and hastily stripped off the nightgown, hopping into my worn denim shorts and doing up the button with one hand while trying to wrangle my way into the t-shirt. My flimsy trainers were by the bed, so I laced them on next. Then I shrugged on the hoodie and zipped it up, since it would at least cover the bandages around my arms. My knees, coated in blue waterproof plasters, were still visible, but I'd have to live with it. I hadn't exactly had time to pack a suitcase before I had ran away from *them*.

Outside the tent, there were people everywhere, running between more large tents and the trees. Little kids were playing a game of Tag, and older kids lolled about, laughing and keeping an eye on the younger kids. There were adults too, of various ages, scattered around. Most of them were either scolding the little kids for pulling each other's hair, lining a plastic foldout picnic table with plates and cups, or tending chunks of meat sizzling on the portable grill. I stared, amazed.

I'd thought it was just one family on a camping trip, but it looked like at least four families—maybe more. I couldn't count the number of people, because everyone was moving around, busy. I stood where I was, unsure of what to do, and then someone touched my arm. I jumped, whirling, and came face to face with Dominic, holding up his hands in surrender.

19

"Whoa! You're jumpy, aren't you? Relax. Nobody's going to hurt you. I promise." He gave me a reassuring grin, and I relaxed just enough to smile back. Shoving his hands into his pockets, he looked me over swiftly and nodded approvingly. "Sorry about your t-shirt. It was kind of wrecked, so Sarah tossed it," he said.

I just shrugged. I didn't much care about the t-shirt. I'd gotten away with my life; a wrecked t-shirt was a small price to pay for that.

Dominic led me around the campsite, introducing me to everyone; it turned out there weren't nearly as many people as I'd first thought. A little over a dozen, including Dominic and Desmond. There were three toddlers: Polly, Ben and Emma. There was little seven-year-old Annie, eight-year-old Chris, blonde thirteen-year-old Marissa and her just-as-blonde twin brother Justin, and pixie faced fourteen-year-old Laura. Then there were the adults, red-haired Sarah who turned out to be Annie's big sister, Kat who was Chris, Polly and Ben's mother, Jane who was Dominic and Desmond's mother, John who was Kat's husband and Graham who was Emma and Laura's dad. Nobody had claim to Marissa and Justin, as far I could tell, but I guessed they were just tagalongs for the camping trip. Honestly, it was a lot to take in, and I doubted I'd remember everyone's names, let alone how they were related.

During our tour of the camp, Dominic and I bumped into Desmond again, who seemed to have forgotten about my insulting him earlier, just as Dominic had predicted. He turned when Dominic called his name.

"Hey, do you know where Spence is? You'd think he'd at least want to meet Tilly," Dominic asked his brother, looking as if he already knew the answer and was just a little exasperated by it.

Desmond shrugged. "Probably where he always is. What makes you think he'd want to meet her?" He cast his green gaze over me again, and I scowled at him. Oddly, it made him smile.

Dominic sighed and shook his head, chestnut curls bouncing. He didn't respond to Desmond's question, just gave him a warning look and said, "If you see him, tell him I want to talk to him."

He turned, and taking my elbow very lightly, led me back to the centre of the camp, where more tables had been set up within the circle of the tents. Most of the people had taken a seat already, and were chatting away loudly when Dominic tugged me into the clearing and sat down at the nearest end of the closest table. When I hesitated, he patted the seat next to him, and I carefully sat down, making sure not to bang my knees or elbows.

I looked around and saw that the only people missing from the gathering were Polly, Emma, Laura, and whoever Dominic had been looking for—Spence. Annie was sitting a few seats away, playing with Ben, who was banging a spoon on the table. Sarah was keeping an eye on them, and Jane was trying to shush Marissa from crying— from what I could tell, Justin had pulled her hair. Kat was filling plates with hamburgers and steaks, and Graham was tending the grill, prodding the meat every so often with shiny steel tongs. Desmond dropped down in the seat opposite mine, and exchanged a coded glance with Dominic, who frowned in response.

Before I could ask what was wrong, Kat leaned over my shoulder, her long dark braids brushing my arm, and piled a hamburger on top my plate, asked if I wanted steak as well, or bacon, and I shook my head. The hamburger was big enough that I doubted I could even finish it, let alone a steak, too.

Dominic got two burgers and three strips of greasy salty bacon on his plate, and I wondered at the amazing ability guys had to put away massive amounts of food in one sitting. Then I looked around the tables, and saw that everyone else had just as much on their plates as Dominic and Desmond, even the younger kids and women. It was like a feast. I'd never seen that much food in one place.

The smell of cooked meat and warm buns made my mouth water, and I lifted the burger off my plate and bit into it. Meat juices, soft bread, and crispy lettuce made paradise in my mouth, and I nearly moaned in bliss. It tasted so good. The only thing *they* had ever fed me was dry fish with a disgusting white sauce or baked potatoes with cheese and tuna. I used to sneak beef stew or burgers in school lunch, though, before *they* took me out of school to home school me.

"Wow. Someone's hungry," Dominic commented, nudging my elbow on the table with his.

I chewed the chunk of warm meat in my mouth, swallowed it, and hoped I didn't have ketchup on my chin or anything. Dominic was already halfway through his second burger; he'd taken off the top half of the bun and was lining up strips of bacon inside. He put the top bun back on and grinned at my look of disgust before taking a massive bite and making an exaggerated noise of delight. I snorted.

Desmond shot him a challenging look, put down his own burger, stuck the extra-rare-still-bleeding steak into it, and showed it off to his brother. "Beat that, Dom." He bit into the steak burger and red juice spilled onto his fingers.

I wasn't sure if it was ketchup mixed with meat juice, or actual blood from the barely cooked steak. I made a face as the boys engaged in some sort of eating competition.

The noise of several conversations going on, the sizzling of the grill, kids squealing and laughing, reminded me of the school canteen. Only, when I'd been at school, I'd always sat at a table on my own. Now I was sitting with two cute guys, Sarah, and little Annie. Annie had moved along a few seats, so she was right next to me, picking at her burger with her fingers. Sarah attempted to ask me about myself, how old I was, what I was doing in the middle of the forest, over the din of the group.

I feigned deafness over her last question. I couldn't tell her why I was out there, or who I'd been running away from. It would put her in danger, and anyway, she'd never believe me. None of them would. They were all so friendly and welcoming, though, that I wished I could stay there with them instead of running again, no destination in mind except for *away*.

"Spence! Knew you'd show up for dinner!" Dominic's happy voice snapped me out of my thoughts, and I turned, blinking in surprise when I saw another boy sitting next to Desmond across the table who hadn't been there a minute ago. I hadn't even noticed him arriving. God only knows how I missed him showing up, because he was downright stunning. I think I might have actually gaped, until Dominic turned to me and introduced the new boy. I slammed my jaw shut, trying not to blush.

"Tilly, this is Spencer. He's our half-brother. He's also the one who found you and brought you back to the camp."

I glanced at Spencer, at his shadowed face and hunched shoulders. Sleek black hair fell into his eyes as he prodded at a strip of bacon on his plate before picking it up with his fingers and snapping off a bite savagely, as if the bacon had personally offended him.

"Oh," I murmured, unsure what else to say. I supposed I should thank him, but somehow he didn't look like he'd appreciate it. In fact, he looked like he wanted to get away from the table and the noise as fast as possible.

At my small noise of surprise, Spencer glanced up at me, his jaw stilling as he paused in his chewing, and blinked as if he hadn't noticed me there until then. I bit my lip, shrinking instinctively under his powerful blue gaze. It was as if he was trying to figure out what I was doing sitting at the table next to his friends. I swallowed nervously, growing more and more uncomfortable as he continued to stare. The muscles under his black t-shirt swelled, his fingers tightening around the strip of bacon in his fist, and I started to think he might actually hit me. What for, I didn't know, but he certainly didn't look happy that I was there. Surely, he couldn't have been the one to take me back to the camp, to rescue me? He looked more like he wanted to kill me himself.

Dominic whistled suddenly, a sharp sound that pierced the tension, and Spencer finally looked down. I snapped my gaze to the cooling half burger on my plate, suddenly no longer hungry in the least. There were knots in my stomach, and a tightness constricting my lungs. I took a deep breath, and realised that everyone around me had gone quiet. I looked up slowly, and found many pairs of eyes on me—everyone was looking at me, except for Spencer. My gut clenched and I felt fingertips touch my arm lightly.

"Don't be scared. Ignore them," Dominic said quietly in my ear, his breath stirring my pale hair.

I shivered, ducked my head, feeling the eyes burrowing into my skull. "I can't ignore them when they're staring at me," I whispered back to Dominic.

He rubbed his knuckles against my wrist. "Just pay attention to me and they'll stop. Look, I'm a walrus!"

He nudged me, and I glanced at him to see he'd stuck two plastic straws in his mouth like walrus tusks. His chestnut curls bounced into his bright eyes and his cheeky grin made him look like a little boy. I smiled weakly, despite the uncomfortable butterflies in my stomach.

Then something small hit Dominic in the side of the head, and he yelped, the straws falling out of his mouth. I reached down and picked up the thing that had been thrown at him—a pinecone.

Desmond snickered. "Idiot," he muttered at his brother, and Dominic bared his teeth playfully.

Half the table laughed in response, and the feeling of eyes on me broke. I wasn't sure, but I thought I even saw Spencer's lips twitch. I let out a breath of relief and my stomach unclenched. I still didn't think I could eat, but I picked up my half-finished burger anyway and forced myself to take a bite, chew it, swallow, and relax.

Nobody's going to hurt you.

"So, Tilly," Jane spoke up.

I tensed, waiting for everyone to turn their attention to me again, but they didn't. Everyone kept their eyes on their own plates, but I knew they were listening.

"Where were you trying to run to, all the way out here?" Jane asked gently.

I frowned. I didn't want to talk about it. Not in front of everyone else—not to anyone.

I shrugged, keeping my eyes on my hands on the edge of the table. "Nowhere specific."

"You were running away, not running toward, then?" Jane sounded concerned and motherly.

How my mother had sounded when I was very little and I'd fallen off the swing set at the park; that was one of my only memories of her. She'd died in a car crash when I was little, both my parents had. Then I'd been adopted by *them,* and *they* had been nothing like my parents. *They* were cold and cruel. *They* forced me to do things I didn't want to do, and when I didn't do them, *they* locked me in my room for days without food or water. Or worse.

"Tilly?" Dominic murmured.

I realised there were tears in my eyes. Some people were looking at me with sympathy and pity on their faces, and others were tactfully not looking at me at all. Annie, next to me, tugged on the sleeve of my borrowed t-shirt and I glanced down at her. Her little heart shaped face was tipped up to mine, her brown eyes sad. I blinked back the tears and touched her hair lightly, awkwardly.

I cleared my throat, and forced a smile to my face. "Thank you," I said, directing my words to Jane, but meaning them for everyone assembled. "Thank you for finding me and helping me and everything, but I think I should go now. I've imposed enough–"

"Oh, no! No, sweetie, don't you worry about it! You're welcome to stay as long as you like," Jane offered kindly.

I noted that several pairs of eyes flickered sharply to her and away again, and I got the message that me staying hadn't been discussed yet. I shook my head, opened my mouth to say that I couldn't possibly, but Jane interrupted me.

"Have you got anywhere to go to?" she asked pointedly.

I shut my mouth. Hesitantly, I shook my head.

"Then you're not going anywhere. You'll stay with us. At least for now." Jane's tone brooked no argument, and her gaze slid over the rest of the crowd as if daring them to contradict her. Nobody did.

I felt uneasy and embarrassed, as if I was intruding, but then Dominic turned to me and grinned, his white teeth flashing and the dimple in his cheek flickering. He was clearly pleased.

"It looks like you're staying. You're not getting away from us that easy." He winked.

Spencer was gone—he must have left while Jane was talking to me. It was kind of freaky how slyly he just appeared and disappeared.

I smiled at Dominic. Of course, he couldn't possibly understand just how little I wanted to get away from the friendly crowd. He also couldn't know that I would have to leave very soon, if I wanted to keep from bringing down my monstrous adoptive family on him and these wonderful people. After all, humans were no match for the witches who owned me.

Chapter Three

** Tilly **

That night, I was designated to the bed I'd woken up in that morning, and Sarah took the other bed in the tent, with Annie snuggled up next to her. It turned out, it was Sarah's nightgown I'd been wearing for my two days of unconsciousness, so she let me borrow a clean one. I protested on the grounds that I could easily sleep in my clothes, but she wouldn't hear of it. So, after she'd removed the bandages on my arms, satisfied that the cuts had scabbed over nicely, I changed into the pale blue nightie she handed me.

I crawled into the springy camping bed and bade Sarah and little Annie goodnight.

Sarah, smiled. "Goodnight, Tilly," she said softly.

"Goodnight," I murmured, snuggling down into my bed as Sarah turned off the gas lantern. Darkness descended in the tent, and I spent five minutes lying there, staring into the dark, telling myself I'd never get to sleep with worries about *them* finding me swirling in my head…and then I fell asleep.

*****

"Matilda! Focus! You will do this. We need to talk to the demon, and you will summon him for us!"

I shook my head. I didn't want to do it. I couldn't do it, not again. I didn't care what they did to me, how long they locked me in my room, how long they starved me. Anything was better than summoning one of their demon lords. Anything was better than feeling the hole between Our world and Theirs tear open– black and cold and sucking, pulling at my life, ripping at my mind, begging for my blood.

"No," I squeaked.

I was shaking, sweat dampening my shoulder blades and neck. I couldn't look at any of them, so I stared at the chalked lines on the floor—a circle inside a circle, runes etched in the space between, lines crisscrossing. I hated those circles, those runes, those lines. I hated what they meant and what I could do with them. I'd never asked to be what I was, never asked for the power I had, but they exploited it whenever they got the chance. They liked the power demons gave them, and they needed my power to get it. I was just a tool they used to call up demons—a telephone to Their world. The Underworld. And every phone call came a little closer to killing me.

"No? Did she say no? You insolent little bitch! You will do it, right now. You will summon the demon, or I will put you in the Dark Room!" One of them, Olivia, snapped.

I flinched. Not the Dark Room. The Dark Room was torture to me; tiny, pitch black, no windows and no air, cages lined along the walls filled with animals for sacrifice, and tiny demons whispering

30

all the gruesome ways they'd kill me slowly if they ever got out of the cages.

The noise in the Dark Room was terrible, the smell even worse—animal faeces, stinking fur, and the sulphur of demons—but it was the feeling in the Dark Room that threatened to drive me mad every time I was stuffed into it. It felt like hell. Not in any physical way, not in any way that a human could feel, but in my bones and under my skin, it felt like flames roasting skin, jaws cracking bones, and claws raking flesh. It was a pain I felt only in the deepest part of my soul, in the darkest part of my power.

As much as I hated summoning demons, the Dark Room was worse. At least when I summoned demons, there was a chance one of them would kill me. In the Dark Room, I couldn't die. I couldn't escape, not ever

With tears rolling down my face, bile rising in my throat, I lifted my eyes to the women who had been terrorising me since I was six years old, and I felt like screaming. Instead, I said, "Okay."

*****

I woke up shaking, my hair plastered to my forehead with sweat, and I swallowed a scream. I was staring into pitch blackness, and for one terrified moment, I thought I was in the Dark Room. My heart nearly jumped out of my chest. Then I heard a soft, sleeping murmur across the room, and my eyes started to adjust. I remembered where I was;

31

it wasn't the Dark Room. I was safe. I'd escaped. I'd never have to face the Dark Room again, never have to summon another demon.

I'd kill myself before that would happen. If *they* found me, I'd take my own life before *they* could do it for me.

Suddenly, the tent seemed claustrophobic and small, as small as the Dark Room, pressing in on me from all sides. I could hear the phantom whispers of caged demons, the hissing of impatient snakes and lizards, the chatter of angry ferrets and hamsters. I could smell the ghosts of animal fear and demon sulphur. I could feel the faint sizzle of Dark magic slithering under my skin and wrapping around my limbs.

I had to get out. I had to escape.

So I did.

I slipped out of my bed as silently as I could, pausing when one of the springs creaked, and sighing internally in relief when neither Sarah or Annie stirred. I tugged on my shorts, exchanged the nightie for the black t-shirt and hoodie, and fixed my feet into my trainers. I was out of the tent in less than two minutes, without waking the other occupants.

The cool, faintly damp air hit my skin and raised instant goose bumps. A gentle night time breeze lifted strands of my fair hair around my face, and the musk of the woods banished the ghostly scents of sacrificial animals and sulphur. I tipped my face up to the clear, cobalt sky and breathed deeply, watching the silver stars twinkle in the spaces between the leaves. The soft sounds of night insects and the stream I still hadn't seen soothed me, and my heart rate began to slow. The night, the trees, the sleeping bodies in their tents, made me feel safe. Safe in a way I hadn't felt since I was six years old.

Without knowing where I was going, I walked out of the centre of the makeshift campsite and into the trees surrounding it, listening to the quiet, *feeling* the night. It sank into me, soft, dark, and as seductive as melted chocolate. The evening was still on the surface, but humming with nightlife just out of sight–fresh, wild and beautiful. I breathed it in with every breath. I absorbed it with every step, until I was wandering with my eyes closed. I didn't need to see the woods when I could feel them.

Then, a noise dropped into my trance, and my eyes flew open. I stood still, holding my breath, listening. My heart started into a gallop, words rolling through my head: *"Matilda! Focus! You will do this!"*

No. No, no, no. Don't let them *have found me. Don't let* them *ever find me. Please.*

The noise came again, and I flinched at the way it broke the quiet of the woods, loud and unnatural as a gunshot amidst the chirping crickets and rustling leaves. It came again, and again, until I realised what the sound was and where it was coming from. *Plink...plink...plink.* It was the sound of stones being tossed into water. Someone was at the stream.

Without thinking about it, my feet led me through the trees, my senses drawing me unerringly toward whoever was at the stream. I moved almost silently, easily, through the darkness, the babbling of the stream growing louder and louder, until a ribbon of silver-black water glimmered in front of me. The light of the stars played across the ripples of water flowing over worn round rocks on the bed of the stream, and the little eddies of green algae congealing at the edges of the water where it met the mossy grass.

Plink...plink. The sound of stones dropping into the water distracted me again, and I turned, my eyes searching the stream banks for the source of the noise. I spotted him easily, perching on a large boulder that sat half-in and half-out of the water. He had one leg tucked up to his chest, the other dangling over the side of the rock, his bare foot in the water and the hem of his jeans leg rolled up to his knee. One hand was cupped, holding a collection of stones, while the other tossed with careless precision. I watched him throw three more stones, each one landing in exactly the same spot, the ripples echoing outward before being distorted by the current.

In the darkness, his black hair was a shadow, his torso blending with the background in a black t-shirt. His face and arms were visible enough, pale smudges on the night air.

Somehow, I knew he knew I was there. He didn't look at me, he didn't speak to me, but I knew he sensed me watching him. I didn't *feel* it. I couldn't feel people like that. I could just tell.

Slowly, measuring every step, I made my way over to him and sat down on the grass next to his rock. I folded my legs, tugged the sleeves of the hoodie over my hands, and I watched him throw stones into the water, one at a time, always landing in the exact same place.

Plink...plink...plink. And then, finally, he spoke. "What are you doing out here?" Spencer asked, his voice low and quiet, a velvet murmur in the night time air. He threw another stone. *Plink.*

I shrugged, looking down into the water at my distorted reflection. I studied my pale hair, which someone had kindly brushed for me while I was unconscious, the small scab at my hairline from where I'd gotten cut during my tumble down the hill, the smear of a purple bruise across my left cheekbone, and my steady grey eyes that seemed to reflect colour without ever absorbing it.

"Couldn't sleep," I said simply.

"No? Did she say no? You insolent little bitch!" The voice from my nightmare hissed in the back of my mind.

I pushed it away. I was free now. I had escaped. For now, that was enough to make the nightmare settle into a dark box in my mind, like a panther settling into its cage, waiting for an opportunity to strike at the hand that fed it.

"You shouldn't wander about the woods at night," Spencer said. "You never know what might be lurking around." *Plink.*

I glanced up at him, his face turned away to the water. I studied the sharp angle of his cheekbone, the curve of his eyebrow under the scrappy black hair, the line of his jaw. His posture was casual, and though only his hand moved as he flicked stones into the dark, swallowing water, there was a restless air to him. As if he wanted to be doing something else, somewhere else. Still, he looked more relaxed than he had at dinner. He looked more natural sitting on the large rock under the stars than he had surrounded by people and plates. As if he was more at home in the woods, as part of the night.

"I think I can handle myself," I stated quietly, turning my gaze back to the burbling stream. The breeze tickled the back of my neck, and I shivered, curling into a tighter ball.

Spencer looked at me, scowling. His blue eyes caught a glint of light, turning them oddly golden for a second. If I hadn't flicked my eyes back to him the second he twitched, I wouldn't have seen it—a trick of the light, but a strange one.

"If you're cold, why don't you go back to camp." It wasn't really a question, more like a thinly veiled command.

Okay, got the message, asshole. You don't like me. Though it's not as if I invaded your family vacation by choice. You're the one who brought me here!

I wanted to say it but didn't. I'd gotten good at keeping my sharp tongue and my temper under control these last eleven years. It was better than having a Silence Spell put on me. So instead, I stared at him for a second more, watching his jaw strain, his muscles tense. Having made my point, I got slowly to my feet, brushed off my knees, and walked back into the trees toward camp.

Just inside the trees, I paused and turned, peering at him through the branches. He hadn't moved an inch, but he was rattling the stones in his hand agitatedly. His head was bowed, his broad shoulders solid under his t-shirt. I'd done a good job of pissing him off, and I hadn't even done anything. Fine. He could dislike me, he could hate me if he liked. I wasn't staying there much longer anyway. Tomorrow night, maybe the night after, I was going to take off. I didn't know where I'd go, but I'd go.

With the decision made, I turned and started walking again, putting my back to the hostile boy at the stream. I had only taken a few more steps when I heard a sound like rain. He'd thrown the rest of his stones into the stream at once. *Plink, plink, plink, plink.*

I smiled.

** Spencer **

After Tilly walked away, he stared at the stream for a long moment before launching his pebbles into the water in frustration. He hadn't meant to make her leave. He'd only meant to ask her why she was outside, not send her away. She'd said she couldn't sleep—but most people when they couldn't sleep counted sheep or got a glass of water. They didn't wander around in the woods in the middle of the night. Not that he was judging, seeing as he was there at the stream almost every night. He liked it there, especially at night. It was quiet, solitary. Still, he hadn't minded Tilly's interruption. He wanted to talk to her. Ever since he'd found her in the woods, he'd been curious about her, and he'd only gotten more curious today.

He'd been surprised, and a little bit glad, to see her at the dinner table. He'd half been beginning to think she wasn't going to wake up, that she'd hit her head hard when she tumbled down that hill and maybe had brain damage. He wasn't surprised, though, to see her next to Dominic. Minnie was the kind of guy that everybody liked, and when Spencer had first brought Tilly into camp when she was unconscious, his curly headed half-brother had been particularly concerned. It was just his nature; Spencer thought he got it from his mother. He certainly didn't get it from his father.

Our father, he thought.

Spencer knew he didn't have the compassion gene, but then, he had a different mother. That was the main reason for his being on the fringes of the pack, instead of a full member, but he preferred the fringes anyway. What he didn't prefer was Frank, his dad, treating him like crap, as if he was half-wolf just because he was only half-pack. It wasn't his fault his mother had run away with him before he was even born. She'd chosen to leave Frank for a reason, and Spencer totally understood why.

He shook his head, knocking away the thoughts. He didn't often succumb to self pity, but he supposed the long day had worn him out a bit. He really wished he hadn't driven Tilly away; he could have used the distraction right now. He wanted to talk to her, find out who she was, and it struck him as odd because he never really wanted to talk to people—except sometimes his half-brothers. For a moment, he wondered why Tilly should be different, and then came to the only good conclusion. She wasn't pack. She wasn't one of them, she didn't know him, so she couldn't ostracise him for his mother's betrayal of his father. If she hated him, she hated him for himself, not for his mother. And that was strangely refreshing.

A little part of him didn't want her to hate him, but he pushed that little bit away, chalking it up to curiosity and nothing more. He didn't need a friend. He didn't want a friend. Maybe a night time companion to sit by the stream with him in the dark hours…? No. He was being stupid. Maybe he was just tired.

With a sigh, Spencer got to his feet, and then paused, lifting his face to the sky. Just a sliver of a moon. He felt his spine flex, the wolf inside him wanting to come out and play, and he wanted to let it. But Tilly might not be back at camp yet, or maybe she'd just gone to walk somewhere else. If he went running around as a wolf, she might see him, and then there'd be trouble. No, he'd just have to stick to two legs, but he wouldn't go back to camp. He was too wound up to sleep, now. So instead, he turned and walked along the mossy bank of the stream, following the silver line of water through the darkness until the sun began to stain the sky in hues of pink and blue.

** Tilly **

"Did you sleep well last night, Tilly?" Dominic asked me after breakfast.

"Yeah, I slept okay," I lied, shoving my hands into my pockets. I saw Dominic's eyes narrow, as though he could tell I was lying, but he didn't press it. I wondered if Spencer had told him I'd showed up at the stream in the middle of the night. Now that I thought about it, I wondered why *he'd* been out that late.

Dominic and I were taking a walk along the stream that morning; I'd wanted to get away from the many prying eyes all watching me and wanting to know how I'd ended up out there all battered and bruised. Even when I wasn't looking, I could feel them watching me, even the kids.

They were perfectly polite and friendly, but I got the sense that, aside from Dominic, Jane, and maybe Desmond, none of them really trusted me. Like I was some sort of murderer on the run, and I was going to kill them all in their sleep. It didn't matter. Whatever they thought, they could put it to rest soon. I needed to get out of there before *they* came hunting for me again. If I hadn't put a No Tracking Spell on myself long before I ever ran, *they* would have already found me and dragged me back.

It was peaceful walking with Dominic. He did most of the talking and didn't question me—much. Sometimes I fell behind, because he had longer legs, and I was always stopping to admire the little flowers by the stream or watch a leaf floating down the current like a little green boat. Dom never complained, and he never snapped at me to hurry up. He just waited for me to catch up, and slowed his stride to match mine whenever I started to fall back.

In the sunlight, the stream was sparkling and clear, and I could see the smooth pebbles at the bottom. Rays of sunlight danced across the ripples, and misted through the trees, covering the woods with a hazy glow. Wildflowers waved in the breeze, splashes of pink, white, and yellow, and mushrooms sat like corpse pale toads in rotting trunks and piles of moss.

It was all so beautiful and relaxing, and for a while, listening to Dominic talk and smiling when he laughed, I could forget…everything. I was just me, Tilly, going for a walk with a cute boy. It was that simple, and I didn't want it to ever be over.

But eventually, we turned around, though I noticed Dominic walked much more slowly heading back.

When Dom and I finally arrived back at camp, everything was in chaos. Laura, holding Ben and Emma in her arms, was running about after Chris and Justin, trying to round them up. Jane, looking worried and harried, swept past with Marissa in tow. Marissa looked as solemn as ever, but there was fear in her wide hazel eyes. I heard someone calling Kat's name, and either Chris or Justin yelling indignantly as Jane caught hold of them.

The boys were tense beside me. Dominic had his lips pressed into a hard line, and Des was leaning forward slightly, his nostrils flaring. "What's going on?" he asked.

Sarah floated up to Laura, taking Ben away from her as he squirmed unhappily, still wailing. She reached down and took Annie's hand, and Annie hugged her leg, burying her face in Sarah's hip. Ben's wails quieted to whimpers, and Laura gave Sarah a tight, grateful smile.

"Thanks," she said breathlessly, shifting Emma on her hip and bouncing her gently. "It's Spencer. We don't know where he is and there's…" Laura's voice trailed off as she caught sight of me over Sarah's shoulder.

Sarah glanced back at me, as if she'd forgotten I was there, and let go of Annie's hand to take Laura's elbow, drawing her away.

Over her shoulder she called, "Dominic, look after Tilly. Des, go and find your mother so she knows you're safe. She'll fill you in." Then she and Laura disappeared into a tent with the kids.

Desmond didn't waste a second in obeying her order, and took off into the camp in search of Jane, leaving me and Dominic the only still pieces in a riot of panic. I turned to him, wanting to say something, but his hard expression made me swallow whatever comment I'd been about to make. His green eyes were narrowed, scanning the area as if he expected an attack, and I had to wonder if all the panic was really necessary over Spencer being missing. Somehow, I couldn't see him getting himself into any kind of danger he couldn't handle, definitely couldn't see him getting lost. He'd probably just gone for a wander to a quiet place to be alone and forgotten to come back.

Looking lost without Chris on his tail, Justin stumbled past us, and Dominic reached out, nudging his shoulder with his knuckles to get the boy's attention. Justin turned around, his eyes the same hazel as his twin sister's. He looked like a clone of Marissa, only with shorter hair and sharper features.

"Justin, what's going on? I heard something about Spencer being gone," Dom asked the kid.

Justin shrugged, his mouth turned into a sulky frown. "John saw a hunter in the woods and nobody can find Spencer. They're worried he might get shot because he changed–"

"Okay, got it." Dominic held up a hand, giving Justin a very stern look.

42

Justin blinked innocently, looking confused, and then shrugged again.

Dom asked, "Did Graham and John go to find him?"

The kid nodded, his dirty blonde hair flopping into his eyes. "Yeah, but I'm not worried. Spencer can handle himself. He's totally kick ass." Justin lifted his chin defiantly. He shoved his hands into his shorts pockets, and I almost smiled at his obvious attempt at Spencer's manner.

Dominic snorted, rolled his eyes. "Look, find Chris and go play in one of the tents, keep out of everyone's way. I'll let you know when we find Spence, okay?" Justin nodded and Dominic mussed his hair. The kid scampered off, and Dom sighed. "That kid hero worships Spencer, and I don't have the heart to tell him Spence isn't someone to worship," he said, half to himself.

"Why? What's wrong with Spencer?" I found myself asking.

Dominic grimaced. Instead of giving me an answer, he just shook his head, looking somewhere between exasperated and sad. I was about to mention that I'd spoken to him last night and he seemed like a very…*reserved* person, but Dominic changed the subject.

"I'll be back in a minute. I need to check something with Kat. Will you be okay here for a bit? You can wait for me in one of the tents if you don't feel safe out here." He didn't wait for a response. Instead, he took off through the camp with amazing quickness, loping gracefully between tents and tree roots.

I stood for a few moments staring after him, chewing my lip thoughtfully, before deciding that I really didn't want to just hang about when I could be doing something useful—like helping look for Spencer. Asshole or not, if there was a hunter going about with a gun, he could accidentally get shot. Or maybe not so accidentally, if he irked the hunter the same way he'd irked me last night. Whatever my personal opinion of the guy was, it didn't matter. I couldn't let him get himself shot, just because he was stupid enough to go wandering when there were hunters out looking for deer.

It would upset Dominic, I thought, using that as my excuse.

Decided, I turned and slunk away into the trees, wishing for the first time ever that I could sense people the way I felt my surroundings. It would be so much easier to find Spencer that way. I'd just have to feel for a cold spot of boredom and mild irritation.

As I walked, searching, the trees tugged at me to listen to the whispers of their leaves. I tried to ignore them, but the tugging became stronger, and I paused. The camp was way behind me now, out of sight, and I couldn't hear the stream anymore. The trees loomed up around me, endless pillars of bark holding up a roof of leaves, talking to me in a way that didn't need words. I closed my eyes and listened, letting the leaves tell me what they wanted to say. My heart rate slowed and the world dimmed out of focus until I could feel what the trees were telling me.

My eyes flew open and I ran, letting my feet guide me to where the trees wanted me to go. I stepped over roots and leapt over a fallen tree, avoiding crushing a rabbit's warren. My body knew the terrain, even if my mind didn't.

I made it to where the trees had directed me, just in time to see a gruff man with a greying beard and an orange cap pointing a shotgun at a large, tar-black wolf. The man had the gun raised to his shoulder, his finger on the trigger, his lined face set with concentration though the trembling of his gun betrayed his fear.

The wolf—*Holy hell, an actual wolf!*—was huge, its hackles raised, its massive pointed teeth bared in a snarl that was so low and continuous I felt it in the rattling of my ribs as much as I heard it. The wolf was angry, its lupine body coiled and ready to attack. I knew that, the second it started to move, the man would pull the trigger.

Without thinking, I threw myself in front of the wolf, spreading my arms to shield it. My heart pounded loudly in my ears as I stared down the barrel of the shotgun, and distantly, the rational part of my mind screamed at me. I ignored it. I couldn't let the man shoot an animal. I remembered, as a kid, when my mother had taken me to the zoo and shown me the wolves in the enclosures. I remembered her saying that it was monstrous to lock up such a beautiful animal, that the only thing worse was hunting them for their pelts or as prizes to be hung on a wall. I didn't have time to reminisce though, because there was a man pointing a gun at my head and an angry wolf less than a foot behind me.

Yeah, not your smartest move, Tilly.

The hunter jerked, his narrow eyes widening under his bright cap. He was wearing a plaid shirt with ratty jeans, heavy workman's boots, and an old green fleece coat that clinked when he shifted, telling me he had ammo in his pockets. He looked startled by my entrance onto the scene, then angry because I was blocking his shot, but he didn't lower the gun.

"Get out the way, girly! You trying to get yourself killed?" he rumbled, bushy brows pressing down over his eyes. His mouth was a thin line, half-hidden under a rusty moustache and a month's worth of beard. He didn't look like the kind who'd shoot a girl just to get at an animal, but I knew better than to underestimate what people could do when they were properly motivated by fear and power. He had the gun after all.

The wolf, behind me, growled loudly and the pressure to scream rose in my throat. I could feel the wolf's hot breath on the small of my back, damp and heavy through my t-shirt. The backs of my legs felt vulnerable, the air hitting my bare calves and ankles. My hands shook as I raised them, palm forward, toward the man with the gun.

"Put the gun down, sir. Please, put the gun down," my voice trembled.

The man scoffed, then spit on the ground toward me. "You crazy, lass? That's a wolf you're trying to protect! The minute I put this gun down, it's gunna rip us both to bits. Get out the way before you become its lunch." The hunter shook his head, but his gun didn't waver.

I heard, felt, the wolf take a half step closer to me, so close its nose brushed my hip. I gritted my teeth, refusing to flinch. It could probably smell my fear, but it wasn't the wolf I was really scared of, it was the man with the gun.

I held my ground. "I'm not moving. I won't let you shoot it. It won't hurt either of us, if you just put the gun down. You're scaring it, that's why it's snarling at you. Put the gun down, and it won't hurt anyone." I tried to use a reasonable voice, but I sounded more as if I was pleading. The man scoffed again, and I felt my fear curdling into anger, adrenaline making it harder to control my temper.

The wolf's muzzle nudged my hip again, and I glanced down at it reflexively. Its large head bumped me, its golden eye looking right at me. It nudged me again, and for a second, I thought I understood what it wanted—it wanted me to move out of the way. It was trying to push me aside, out of the way of the gun. I stared at the wolf, amazed, and then heard a soft click. I turned just in time to see the hunter flipping his shotgun closed; he'd been reloading it. It hadn't been loaded before, but now it was, and he was pointing it at the wolf's head next to me. His finger twitched on the trigger, his hands steadier than before, his tongue caught in the corner of his mouth as he took aim.

Fury boiled up inside me, and before he could pull the trigger, I lashed out. Not physically, but with my power. I'd been taught to never, never lash out that way, that I could kill someone if I did. At that moment, I didn't care. I wanted the hunter to die. What right did he have to murder an animal just because he had the fingers to pull a trigger and it didn't? What right did he have to kill something just because he *could*?

Fire sparked along my nerves. The power blasted out from my body with enough force that I stumbled backward, nearly losing my footing—Newton's Third Law of Motion, I guess. Across the clearing, the orb of white light slammed into the man with the gun, knocking his shotgun from his hands. As it twisted from his grasp, his finger jerked on the trigger and a shot rang out deafeningly loud, startling the birds from the trees with terrified shrieks. The shove of power sent him sprawling on the ground, clutching his chest breathlessly. His cap fell off his head, and I saw his eyes showed white all around. He was gasping and staring at me in horror, as he scrambled to his feet and took off, forgetting his gun and cap. He fell over a tree root, and then was up and running again, glancing back all the way, until he made a swerve and was out of sight.

Breathing hard, I realised I had fallen to my knees and my palms were sweating. My heart raced, my fingers itched with aftershocks from the power, throwing tiny white sparks into the leaf litter. Distantly, I hoped that wouldn't be enough to make them catch on fire, but it was a numb thought. I was in some sort of shock and didn't even remember the wolf until it circled around in front of me, huge, sleek and black as midnight. It stood several feet away from me, eyeing me warily through reflective golden eyes, its head tilted a little as if it was trying to work out whether or not I was edible. I was suddenly too tired to care if it wanted to eat me. I wanted to lie down somewhere quiet and rest for a while.

Through the trees, I heard voices yelling and quick footsteps crunching in the dirt. Everyone back at camp must have heard the gunshot. It was still ringing in my ears—or maybe that was my own blood.

"It came from over here!" Desmond's voice was close by.

I tried to stand up, keeping my eyes on the wolf, but my legs felt like noodles. A wave of dizziness swept over me and I groaned, planting my hands into the dirt, so I wouldn't face plant and get a mouthful of leaves.

The wolf's ears pricked up at the sound of running feet and calling voices, shouting for Spencer and for me—they must have found I was gone too—but it didn't take off as I thought it would. It stayed where it was, watching me. I tried to return its gaze, but the edges of my vision were turning grey, and I felt exhaustion crawling over me. My eyes slid shut, but I could still hear.

"Over here!" Desmond shouted.

"Oh my God, Tilly!" Dominic, sounding worried.

"Is she okay?" someone else asked in a concerned tone.

I could hear others mumbling to each other; nobody mentioned the wolf. I wondered if it had finally run off.

"Did she get shot?" another voice, female, questioned.

"No."

That was Spencer; I recognised his quiet, dark voice amidst the panicked murmurs.

"No, she's fine. Probably just got scared and passed out," he said.

I heard a gentle mutter of sympathy from Jane. Dom was murmuring by my head, not talking to me, but to the others. I couldn't be bothered with listening to what he was saying. I wanted to slap Spencer for his comment.

Got scared? Screw him. Why the hell I'd went out there looking for him in the first place was beyond me. All it had gotten me was a near miss with a wolf and a bullet, and a snarky comment.

Arms slid under me, lifting me off the ground, and I knew without having to pry my lazy eyes open that it was Dominic. His voice was louder in my ear, his steady breathing on my cheek, and he lifted me as if I weighed no more than a rag doll, though I supposed I really didn't weigh much. I was too tired and weak to bother being embarrassed at being carried like a small child, so instead, I relaxed into Dominic's gentle arms as he walked with sure, easy strides. I let myself fall asleep, knowing I was as safe as I could be for now.

Chapter Four

** Tilly **

I woke up back in Sarah and Annie's tent, with a blanket draped over me. I had a flash of déjà vu from the day before, waking up in the same place in the same way. Only that time, I wasn't wrapped in bandages, and instead of Annie, it was Desmond keeping a check on me. The tent was dim, making me wonder how long I'd been asleep, and if Desmond had been watching me sleep the whole time. His green eyes were fixed on me intently when I blinked mine open, and he let out a chuckling sigh of relief, pushing his wavy dark hair out of his face with one hand.

"The princess awakens. You seem to have a habit of passing out in the woods. Next time, try making it to a bed first." He grinned.

I glared at him. Opened my mouth to tell him I didn't pass out, then realised I couldn't explain what had actually happened without telling him I'd blasted some hunter with my power. *Yeah. So not happening. Better to let them all think you're a scaredy cat than a crazy person.* So instead, I just intensified my glower until Desmond noticed it and held up his hands defensively.

"Okay, sorry! How are you doing? Hungry I'm betting. Dinner should be ready really soon."

I blinked. "Dinner? How long have I been–"

"Out? Uh, little over four hours. Spencer said–"

I didn't want to hear what Spencer said. I wanted to take a branch and ram it down Spencer's throat, so he couldn't say anything else ever again. "Oh, so you found him, did you? Where was he? Hiding in a cave?" I snapped before I could rein the words in.

Desmond's eyes widened and he looked surprised by my outburst. He pressed his lips together, though I could see his mouth twitching at the corners, a sure sign he was trying not to laugh.

"Um. You don't like Spence much, do you?"

He said it as if he understood perfectly. I'd expected him to maybe be angry with me for bitching about his half-brother, but he just looked amused. I shook my head.

"Not really. Sorry." I wasn't really sorry. It wasn't my fault his half-brother was an anti-social caveman. But Desmond really didn't look too offended, and I couldn't muster up any guilt for disliking a guy I barely knew. I got the impression it would be worthless to even try to get to know him, even if I wanted to—which I didn't.

"Yeah, Spencer is kind of hard to like sometimes. He's not a bad guy, he just…prefers his own company, I guess. But you seem to be getting along with Dominic okay, and Annie likes you. She got kind of upset when we brought you back to camp unconscious again. What happened out there anyway? We heard a gun go off and thought…" Des trailed off, a small line denting between his eyebrows.

He was sitting casually enough, on the edge of Sarah's bed with his elbows on his thighs, hands dangling between his knees; but

52

there was something strained in the set of his shoulders and jaw that made me worry. Had he, or someone else, seen me use my power? God, I hoped not. No, nobody had been around when I'd done it, I was sure. Only the wolf and I doubted it was telling.

Thinking of the wolf reminded me, and not completely unintentionally avoiding Desmond's question, I asked, "The wolf. Did anyone else see the wolf?"

The question made Desmond's spine straighten, though he tried not to show it, and I swallowed, confused by his reaction.

"Wolf? What wolf? There are no wolves around here, Tilly." He looked at me as if I was crazy, but I wasn't buying it.

I pushed it. "Yes, there is. There was. That's what the hunter was shooting at. I jumped in front of it, so he wouldn't kill it, and then…" I bit my lip, unsure how to continue without explaining why the hunter had run off, but it didn't matter because the look Des was giving me made it clear he thought I should be locked up in a loony bin. I shook my head, frustrated. "I swear there was a wolf. It must have run off before you guys arrived." It was the most I could say, but despite his expression, I knew he believed me. He just wouldn't admit it. I didn't know why he'd lie about such a thing, but I couldn't see any way to ask without annoying him, so I let it drop, feeling foolish and irked.

He shrugged, effectively signalling the end of the discussion anyway. "Maybe it did run off, but I didn't see any wolf. Anyway, dinner will be up in ten. Just grab a seat when you feel up to eating."

53

With that, he got up and left, the muscles in his neck tight the whole time until he disappeared out of the flapping fabric doorway.

I sat for a moment, staring at my hands and scowling. Really, I wasn't that hungry, and I didn't feel up to facing more questions about what had happened in the woods. Also, I didn't want to run the risk of seeing Spencer at the dinner table, because I'd be too tempted to lunge across it and strangle him. I opted to sit up and spend some time meditating instead. Mediating was good for lots of things, mostly for releasing stress and anger. I'd been doing it for years now, and I was practised enough that I could meditate almost anywhere.

My adoptive family, the coven of witches, had insisted I do two hours of meditation every day since I was eight years old, telling me it was a way of focussing one's power, making it stronger. I used the meditation session to relax and felt the anger and confusion drain away from me. I slowed my breathing, listening to each breath passing my lips, and feeling the steady rise and fall of my chest. The life of the woods outside the tent pawed at me, and I let it in, feeling it purr as it met my magic and moved through my body. I even managed to forget about the beautiful black wolf…

Sometime later, I opened my eyes again, feeling peaceful and refreshed, and the black wolf was the furthest thing from my mind. Once again, upon opening my eyes, my gaze was met with green ones. That time, it wasn't Desmond, and I immediately broke into a grin that matched Dominic's. The dimple in his left cheek smiled with his mouth. I noticed a smudge of dirt on the knee of his jeans, as if he'd been kneeling on the ground at some point—and remembered he'd probably had to kneel to lift me up when he'd carried me back to camp. I wanted to thank him, but seeing as he'd thought I was unconscious at the time, I thought it might be awkward, so I settled for a standard greeting.

"Hey," I said casually, untwisting my legs from the lotus position and stretching them out. My knees gave a satisfying pop, and I made an *mmh*-ing sound in appreciation. Boneless after stretching, I flopped down on my belly on the bed and sighed contently. Dominic chuckled, a sound much less sarcastic than his brother's snickering laugh.

"Were you *meditating?*" Dom asked in a tone of disbelief, raising one eyebrow into his curls.

The tent was getting dark, filled with a hazy grey light, and there was a crisp coolness to the air that told me it was probably late evening. I'd been meditating for hours, no wonder I felt so comfort drugged. Beyond the thin tent walls, crickets sang and an owl hooted softly, asking the endless, unanswerable question *who-who?* Maybe owls were perpetually confused. Maybe that was why they only came out at night, unlike normal birds. Who knew? Hey, maybe that was what they were asking!

I sniggered stupidly at the thought, and Dominic gave me the same '*Are-you-crazy?*' look his brother had given me earlier—only, when he did it, it didn't annoy me. I wasn't sure why exactly, maybe it was just because Dom wasn't trying to act as if I was crazy when he secretly believed me. But I thought it was something more than that—I just liked Dominic better. He was funnier, cheerier, less sarcastic. Plus, he didn't eye me as if I was a fine steak the way Desmond did, or glare at me as if I was a disgusting beetle crawling along the ground the way a certain other person did.

Pushing that thought out of my head before it could kill my good mood, I mock scowled at Dominic. "Yes, I was meditating," I said it like it was a challenge. "Do you have a problem with that, Minnie?" I recalled Dominic saying he hated that nickname, so I grinned when I used it.

He shook his head, sighing and chuckling at once. "Only Spencer usually calls me Minnie. Everyone else calls me Dom, but he likes to take the piss out of me."

I snorted, rolling my eyes before I could resist the temptation. "Sounds like a real nice guy," I muttered, then bit my lip anxiously as I realised Dominic might not take my comments as well as Desmond had. That was one thing I did like about Des, though. He seemed to appreciate frankness, or at least, didn't rebuff me for it. I'd spent so long keeping my opinions and snarky thoughts to myself; I kept expecting to get in trouble for letting them out. I had to keep reminding myself I was free now.

"He's Spencer; he is how he is." Dominic shrugged, as if that were a both an explanation and an excuse for Spencer's bad attitude. Then he gave me a wry look from under his cap of curls. "So…meditation, huh? Is that why you missed dinner?"

I shrugged awkwardly, not wanting to lie. Meditation wasn't the reason I didn't go to dinner. It was just what I'd done after deciding not to go to dinner for various other reasons. "I wasn't hungry anyway," I said, pushing myself off my belly. The camping bed groaned at me, and I huffed at it. It wasn't like I weighed that much.

"You must be hungry now, though, right?" Dom asked.

I thought about it, and then nodded slowly. "A little bit, I guess."

He laughed. "A little bit? You haven't eaten since breakfast!"

I wasn't sure how to respond to his tone of incredulity, like he'd never heard of anyone going without food for so long before, so I just shrugged. He shot me a sideways grin as he stood up and held out his hand.

I stared at his outstretched fingers for a moment, noting that he still had dirt under his nails and his knuckles were chapped. Cautiously, I put my hand in his. and he helped me to my feet. His fingers were cool and dry, gripping mine gently, and he didn't let go once I was standing.

He smiled a little crookedly and jerked his head toward the tent door. "Come on, let's get you some food. I can show you that thing I wanted to show you earlier while we're at it."

I let him lead me out of the tent, and saw the sky was turning the colour of molten lead. I hoped it wouldn't rain. I didn't think the tents would be much defence against a downpour and the resulting mud. A group was gathered around the foldout table, apparently playing a card game. Jane was bouncing Polly on her knee. Marissa was holding Emma with one hand and a fan of red-backed cards in the other, which Emma kept trying to pry away from her. I couldn't tell what they were playing, but it could have been blackjack. I could hear Desmond laughing as John grumbled, shaking his head.

Dominic tugged me on, and we slipped out of the camp without being seen. Shadows clustered thickly under the leafy canopy of the trees, and flowers closed up their bright petals for the night. Mushrooms glowed with sickly pale light, and streams of sap gleamed on the bark of the tree trunks. The ground was springy with moss and decaying leaves under my trainers, and the woods seemed to be sighing as the nocturnal wildlife peeked out from their burrows with shining eyes. A little part of me panicked as he pulled me deeper into the trees, walking parallel with the stream. It wasn't that I didn't trust Dominic—I did. Mostly. As much as I could trust someone I had only met yesterday. It was just that I had a creeping sensation rolling down my spine, which made me think we weren't entirely alone. But then, it could have just been the scare I'd gotten earlier that had rattled me. After all, nearly getting shot could probably do that to a girl.

We walked for a short while, with Dominic pointing out different kinds of flowers and informing me what medicinal purposes they could serve. I didn't have the heart to tell him I already knew many of the plants and their medicinal values, since I'd used lots of herbs and plants in spells and rituals *they* had made me perform. I listened to him talk, just enjoying his company and the sound of his voice, and letting my eyes wander over him while his eyes wandered over the flowers. Aside from the ones I saw on the street when I went to pick up stuff from The Witch's Den—a little store on Main Street full of odds and ends, herbs, spices, incense, tarot cards, and books on Wicca and Pagan rituals—I hadn't been around a lot of guys since *they* pulled me out of school. I was curious.

Dom was walking a little ahead of me, having dropped my hand a while ago, and he was chatting away animatedly. He was tall enough that he had to duck under branches quite frequently, but slender enough that riddling between the trees seemed easy for him. He slid through the woods with a casual, almost absent kind of grace, as if he'd walked the path a hundred times and could have done it in his sleep. In the darkening shadows under the boughs, his chestnut curls looked almost black. I noticed that, though he had to weigh nearly twice what I did, he barely made a sound as he walked, whereas my feet crunched on dried leaves and branches with every step. For all the length of his long legs, he wasn't clumsy or gawky, and there was a subtle aura of strength about the way he held himself, despite his lean musculature.

He was still talking, his voice soft in the growing darkness. "…is really good for fevers when you make it into a tea, and I know you're not listening to a word I'm saying anymore. And if you keep staring at me like that, I'm going to get the wrong idea." His tone was amused as he came to a halt and spun round on his heel to face me.

He was grinning, his teeth flashing white in the shadows, and his eyes surprisingly bright. He blinked, and they dimmed, his lashes falling light on his cheekbones as he narrowed his eyes at me in a wry, knowing look. It took me nearly a full three seconds to register what he'd said, and then felt my cheeks grow hot.

I looked down, embarrassed I'd been caught ogling. "Oh," I squeaked, unsure what else to say.

Dominic laughed, and came back toward me, his footsteps freakishly quiet on the carpet of leaf litter.

"Don't worry about it. I was joking. but if you're going to stare at guys around here, try to be sly about it. We can tell when we're being watched. And, here's a tip for you for dealing with Spencer: Don't look him in the eye too much. He doesn't like it," he advised sagely, and I nodded slowly, frowning.

"Is that why he looked like he wanted to kill me yesterday at the dinner table? Spencer, I mean. Because I was staring at him?" I asked.

Dominic paused, and then nodded. "Yeah. He gets a bit testy when people stare at him." I thought about that, and then scowled.

Before I could say anything else, Dominic grinned abruptly and said, "Here we are." He flourished a hand grandly.

I followed his gaze, and felt my mouth drop open. There, in the middle of a good sized clearing, was the biggest oak tree I'd ever seen. It was huge. Towering above the other trees, its leafy roof spread out over the whole clearing, thick boughs spanning twenty feet and twisting up and around one another like pythons. In the spaces between the branches, I could see it went up and up, seemingly endlessly, as if you could reach heaven if you just kept climbing. The trunk was massive, as thick around as five of the smaller trees put together.

Soft green moss crawled over the heavy, looping roots that protruded from the ground like natural seating. Vines of ivy twisted around the trunk like waxy green tinsel, and spots of white lichen sprouted here and there. Bells of pink foxgloves clustered around the roots, crowding together with delicate snowdrops and sweet baby's breath. Sprays of daffodils and blue bells fanned out from the tree, a flush of colour. Strung from low branches and nestled in the winding ivy vines, there were little gas lanterns, like the ones I'd seen back at camp. They glowed with tiny white flames, lighting the clearing with a warm pearly glow and casting mysterious shadows into the higher boughs.

Just below the grand tree, there was a picnic set up, spread out on a tattered crimson blanket. A small, woven wicker basket perched in the centre of the blanket, and a little red squirrel sniffed around it curiously, its bushy tail twitching. The bright clearing was like a shining jewel in the midst of a field of coal.

I gaped for an eternity before I was able to tear my eyes away and look at Dominic, who seemed pleased by my reaction.

"Don't worry. It's not supposed to be, like, romantic or anything. I just thought you might like to see it," he said, suddenly shy, rubbing the back of his neck nervously with one hand.

I beamed at him, and impulsively threw my arms around his waist. He jolted in surprise, and then gently patted my back, his laughter rumbling in his chest.

"I take it I was right then," he chuckled.

I stepped back quickly, blushing. "Sorry," I said, realising what I'd just done. "Yes, you were right. It's beautiful. Thank you."

I wanted to say more, but a lump was rising in my throat, and I had to swallow before it dissolved into ridiculous tears. It was just that…it was the nicest thing anyone had done for me since I was six. I guess I'd forgotten what it was like to have someone do something nice for me. I'd forgotten what it was like to have a friend. The only friend I'd had since I was a little kid was Tamara, the checkout girl at The Witch's Den. We chatted every time I was there, but we never saw each other in any other settings, since I was rarely allowed out of the mansion, and when I was, I was escorted to ensure I didn't run off.

Not now, I reminded myself, *you're out now, and you never have to go back.*

That was only now starting to sink in as I watched Dominic saunter over to the picnic blanket, scare off the squirrel, and turn to smile at me. His hair was washed with light from the hanging lanterns, making it shine the colour of copper. For a second, his eyes seemed to flash strangely, but when I wandered over, he looked perfectly normal—and excited. Like a little boy showing a friend his new toy.

He folded himself neatly on the ground, and gestured for me to do the same. I lowered myself onto the blanket; it was rough under my hands. Dom started pulling stuff out of the wicker basket. He took out fresh apples, strawberries in a plastic carton, and raspberries and brambles that I suspected he'd picked from the bushes growing naturally in the woods. Then he dug out a spray can of whipped cream and two bottles of water. I laughed at the satisfied smirk on his face as he popped the lid off the whipped cream and shook the can. He tipped his head back and squirted the foamy cream into his mouth, pointed the can at me, and I squealed, holding up my hands defensively. Swallowing the whipped cream, Dominic laughed at me.

"I'm not going to attack you with it, relax. Have some. It's one of man's greatest creations," he said with the air of someone who also thought pizza and wireless internet were some of man's greatest creations.

I snorted, took the can from him, and squirted some into my mouth before tossing the can back to him. I *mmm*-ed in delight and Dom threw a plump pink raspberry at me. It hit my collarbone and threatened to fall down the neck of my t-shirt, but I caught just in time and glared at him.

"Didn't your mother ever teach you not to play with your food?" I teased, picking up a bramble and aiming it toward his head. He dove for it and caught it in his mouth, grinning as he chewed.

He pretended to look thoughtful for a moment, and then shook his head. "Nope. My mother has definitely never told me not to play with my food. She has, however, told me not to make a mess with my food. Completely different, and completely pointless. I eat like an animal." He growled playfully to emphasise his point.

I rolled my eyes, trying not to laugh as I bit into a sweet, juicy strawberry. It was cool and delicious. I tipped my chin up to look at the sky, but the foliage of the oak tree was too thick to see through. Instead, I sat and watched an owl hunching high in the leaves, looking half-asleep the way owls always seem to.

I could feel Dominic watching me, but I didn't take my eyes off the owl as I asked, curiously, "So, where do you actually live?" Town was several miles away and there was only one school, but I couldn't remember ever seeing him or his brothers there before I'd been yanked out. Surely, I'd have remembered him, right? Unless he lived somewhere further away, and went to a different school.

From the corner of my eye, I saw Dominic pause and tilt his head, as if he was considering how much to tell me. Then he lifted a hand, holding half a strawberry between his fingers, and pointed to the east of us.

"That way," he answered simply, and I shook my head, glancing at him sideways.

"No, I mean, where in town?" I clarified, looking for a little more detail than the general direction. For all I knew, he could mean he lived in a city forty miles in that direction. That would suck. At least if he lived in town, there was a chance I might see him again—seeing as I was leaving. I couldn't hang around much longer without *them* finding me.

Dominic hesitated again, and then shrugged, half to himself. "We don't live in town. We live in the woods. We've got cabins about a mile that way." He pointed with the strawberry again, considered the little fruit, and then popped it into his mouth.

"You...don't you go to school or anything?" I asked, examining a shiny black bramble. I'd never actually tasted brambles before. I put it in my mouth, bit down on it, and bitter juice burst on my tongue. I decided I didn't like brambles, and picked up a raspberry next.

"Oh, aye, I did. All of us did," Dominic murmured around a mouthful of fruit, tossing an apple from one hand to the other as he spoke. "But then my dad pulled us out to home school us. Said it would be easier, because we always take a few days off school when there's a full moon. It's...kind of a family ritual thing. All the others do it too."

Home schooling, I understood. Though, I doubted normal kids like Dominic were taught the best way to make a Truth Serum, or how to read the Casting Sticks. "Like a...cult thing?" I wondered.

Dom shook his head, curls flickering in the lantern light. "No, nothing like that. Just...it's hard to explain." His mouth made a funny line for a moment, his face scrunching as if he was confused about something, but then his expression smoothed out. He squirted a dollop of whipped cream onto his apple, then licked the cream off, and took a bite of the apple.

I eyed a large, abnormally shaped strawberry as I thought of my next question. "So, why camping then? If you already live in the woods?" It seemed a bit redundant to take a vacation just a few miles from home. Not that I'd ever been on vacation, but I knew enough of the normal world to realise that most people chose to go to hot countries or theme parks for vacations.

Dominic continued to chew slowly, for so long that I thought he hadn't heard my question, but then he answered slowly, "We're just sort of keeping away from home for a couple of weeks while my dad works something out with the, uh, neighbours. The fighting can get pretty loud and it upsets the little ones when–" He stopped talking abruptly, and cast his eyes up toward the massive tree, like he'd already said too much and wasn't going to say any more on the subject.

We sat in an awkward silence for a moment, before I asked, "So…what's Spencer's problem?" After I said it, I wished I hadn't. I needed to stop bitching about his brother, but I couldn't help it. The guy got under my skin, and he'd barely said ten words to me. There was just something about him.

Dominic didn't seem to care about my snarkiness. He sighed, his mouth turned down at the corners. "Our dad…he really is great, but he doesn't always treat Spencer the same way he treats me and Des," he said carefully, tugging on one of his curls.

I frowned. "Why not?"

He hesitated again, biting his lip as if he was unsure how much to tell me. I got the feeling there were things about his family— about all of the people I'd met at the camp, really—that they didn't want me, or any other outsider, to know. It made me anxious, but I could hardly begrudge them their privacy and their secrets, when I had so many of my own.

Finally, Dominic seemed to decide it was okay to tell me about Spencer, and he leaned forward with his elbows on his knees, keeping his voice low as if someone might overhear, though we were about half a mile from camp.

"You know I told you Spencer's only my half-brother?" He started, and I nodded. "Well, a few months before he was born, his mother ran away from our dad. Then she got really ill and died when he was a toddler. One day, someone just left him at our front door. We don't know who, or how they knew who the baby's dad was, but someone did and they just left him there for us. So my dad took him in, and he's been with us ever since. But…I think my dad sometimes forgets it isn't Spencer's fault his mother ran away. I think he really loved her, and when she left, it kind of broke his heart. So he's kind of harsh to Spencer sometimes." He shook his head, frowning.

"Spencer doesn't help himself, though. You've seen how he is. He's…distant from the rest of us. He likes to go and hide in the woods, and he stays there for hours. He always comes back but..." Dominic paused, sighing, and turned to gaze into the darkness beyond our little dimly lit clearing, staring at something I couldn't see. There was sadness in his green eyes, shadowing them, and a softness to the shape of his mouth that told me he loved his half-brother, despite Spencer's distant attitude.

When he spoke again, his voice was so soft I barely heard it, and he kept his eyes on some spot in the trees, as if he was talking to

Spencer himself. Quietly, he murmured, "Sometimes I worry that the next time he goes off alone, he won't come back."

Chapter Five

** Tilly **

For the second night in a row, I woke up out of a nightmare while the moon was still up.. I jerked awake so violently that I nearly toppled over the edge of the creaky camping bed. I caught myself just in time and clamped a hand over my mouth as I squeaked, not wanting to wake Sarah. Thankfully, she was quite a heavy sleeper, so she didn't twitch, even when the bed protested my getting up out of it at oh-god-no o'clock. It was time for me to leave.

I'd only half undressed before flopping into bed, so I pulled off my borrowed nightie with my shorts still on underneath, and tugged on the black t-shirt and hoodie. As I laced up my trainers, my hands finally stopped shaking from the nightmare, but there was a cold spot just under my sternum and a knot in my stomach. I felt bad about leaving without as much as a thank you and goodbye. I knew Dominic would worry about me when he woke up tomorrow morning and I was just gone. I didn't even really want to leave, but I knew I had to. That wasn't my place, and if I stayed, I risked *them* finding me there and hurting those nice people just for helping me. I couldn't risk that. So I gathered my resolve and slipped out of the tent, leaving Sarah sleeping soundly.

Outside, the night air was sharp with a chill, but it felt good against my damp neck and forehead. Pausing, I looked around the camp, at the cosy tents pitched in a circle, and the foldout table in the centre. Inside each of the tents, slept people who had probably saved my life by taking me in when I was injured and letting me stay there for two days after I woke up. Good people, friendly people. Dominic. I hoped that, wherever I ended up when I got the hell out of there and as far away from *them* as possible, I might meet more people like these.

Yeah, I should be so lucky, I thought with a mental eye roll. So far, my life hadn't exactly been made up of lucky moments, but I could always hope.

Feeling a pang of guilt and sadness, I turned away from the tents and headed into the thick darkness of the trees. Everything was still and quiet, the only sounds were the murmuring of leaves in the cool breeze and the babble of the stream. The trees seemed to close in on me like a protective guard as I walked, tall and kind. Ferns brushed my ankles, curling round my legs as if trying to stop me from leaving. The moon was just a slice of silver in the pitch-black sky. It lent a milky glow to the leaves and illuminated my path just enough that I didn't trip on roots or fallen branches, since I couldn't afford to tune out and let the woods guide me. I needed to stay focussed, already knowing there was at least one wolf out there somewhere and it could come back for me at any time. I didn't know why it didn't eat me the first time, but I wouldn't be holding my breath for a repeat of that consideration if it found me again.

At some point, I decided, not entirely consciously, that my safest bet of finding a way out of the woods was to follow the stream. I don't know why I thought it, but I ended up walking along the side of the stream anyway, watching it swirl and twinkle in the moonlight and listening to its soft mumbling rhythm. The breeze, scented with wildflower fragrances and the musky, indefinable perfume of the woods, stirred my hair around my face, the pale strands catching the light so they looked almost silver.

I wasn't sure how long I'd been walking, maybe twenty minutes, when I got the feeling I wasn't alone. It started as a tingling across the back of my neck, and rapidly progressed to full out shivers juddering up my spine, the hairs on my arms prickling warningly. Telling myself there was nothing there, I tried not to panic. I kept walking, breathing steadily, but the feeling grew stronger with every step. I realised I couldn't hear the hum of the stream anymore for the pounding of my blood in my ears. Forcing myself to stand still and relax, I closed my eyes and let a little of the trees' calming energy seep into me.

Then I opened my eyes and slowly turned my head to see what, if anything, was following me. At first, I didn't see it—it was so dark. I thought it was just another shadow, but then it moved. I bit down on a gasp as a sleek, jet-black wolf slunk out of the trees just a couple of metres away from me. It was the same wolf from earlier that day, I was sure of it.

Without a gun pointed at my head, I could fully appreciate the beauty of the beast. It was large and powerful looking, with a healthy shine to its pure black fur, and it moved with the silent, liquid grace of a predator. Its gold eyes fixed on me, and I set my shoulders back, trying to look as big as I could—not that it mattered. If it wanted to eat me, it would eat me, and no amount of posturing would deter it.

There was still just enough of the woods' energy flowing into me that I wasn't panicking. Yet. I should have been, but I wasn't. I was fascinated. The wolf was so beautiful, and it was just standing there, staring at me with oddly gentle golden eyes. It didn't look angry or hungry, and didn't look as if it would attack me. It seemed to be…waiting for something.

Mustering whatever courage I could, I let out my breath slowly and raised a hand, flat with the palm up, toward the wolf. Its ears twitched, it cocked its head, abruptly turned, and took off—loping into the darkness between the trees with eerily silent movements.

I waited several minutes for it to come back, maybe with reinforcements. When it didn't, I finally relaxed, letting go of the energy I'd been pulling from the woods around me. The second I let that go, my heart jerked and spluttered, as if it had been held back from the start of a race and had to catch up. I stood for another minute, breathing hard, willing myself to stop trembling. The adrenaline in my veins finally started to abate, and I shuddered once, violently, before taking a tentative step forward.

"Where are you going?"

The sudden voice made me jump, and I shrieked as I spun around, my newly settled heart rate kicking up again. Adrenaline gave a short, sharp burst through my blood, and I squeezed my hands flat over my chest as if I could hold my heart inside that way. In the darkness, it took me a moment to spot who had spoken. I wasn't in the least surprised to see Spencer leaning against a tree with his dark head slightly bowed and his arms folded, hiding in the shadows under the boughs.

I glared at him. "Goddammit, Spencer! You scared the hell out of me!" I snarled.

His eyes flashed up to mine, icy blue. I thought I saw the corner of his mouth tilt up. I curled my hands into fists, shoving them back into my pockets, so I wouldn't be tempted to hit him.

"Good. I'm glad I scared you. I already warned you there were dangerous things out here at night."

I swore there was a hint of amusement in his voice. He pushed himself away from the tree with one fluid movement, and stalked toward me with his hands in his jeans pockets. I lifted my chin and met his icy stare defiantly, which seemed to tick him off. He set his jaw and narrowed his eyes to cold blue slits.

"And I told you I could handle myself," I said sharply, refusing to take my eyes away from his, although his glare was piercing enough to make me uncomfortable all the way to my toes.

He shifted his weight a little toward me, a tiny, but inherently menacing movement. I instinctively rolled my weight back half a step, but I didn't take my eyes off his. The freaky thing was, he didn't blink. Not once. My eyes were starting to sting, but he looked as if he would stand and glower at me all night without blinking at all.

In the end, I blinked—I had to—and he seemed to take it as a victory. He eased his weight back fractionally, no longer imposing, but still unmistakably immovable. I had no idea what kind of mind game he was trying to play, but I didn't want to play it. I wanted to leave…or, I had wanted to leave until he'd showed up. Suddenly, I felt oddly compelled to stay there and find out why exactly he'd come after me.

He gave me a wry, knowing smile, and I nearly choked on what I'd been about to say.

"Yes," he said quietly, in a strangely intimate voice that made me shudder from head to toe. "Yes, I'd say you can handle yourself okay," he murmured, tilting his head as if he was eyeing me up for a fight…or for something else.

My face grew hot, and I looked down swiftly so my hair screened my face. I did not like him one bit, and I really wanted to know why the hell he'd stalked me out there. Just to scare the bloody blue hell out of me and engage me in a staring competition? No, he wouldn't waste his time talking to me unless he had a reason.

Spencer dropped his gaze to the shivering stream and dipped his toes into the water, spreading ripples. It was the first time I'd noticed he was barefoot, and I wondered if that was why I hadn't heard him coming up behind me.

"Were you leaving so soon? Without even saying goodbye?" he asked, his tone mocking.

Though he didn't look at me, I saw the corner of his mouth curl upward, a flash of blue showing under his half-lowered lids. Just for a moment, I thought there might have been a note of something else under the mocking, but then he cut his eyes to me under his lashes, and I decided I was imagining things.

"I don't see how that's any of your business," I replied sharply, crossing my arms like a sulky twelve-year-old. I hated how petulant I sounded, but it was petulance or violence, and I didn't think Dominic would appreciate me knocking his half-brother into the stream.

Spencer withdrew his foot from the water slowly, his annoying half-smile dying. Seeing only his profile, I couldn't read his expression, and when he spoke, I couldn't quite figure out his tone either.

"It's my business because I'm the one who saved you. I could have left you there, unconscious, for the wolves or whomever you're running from to find you." He still didn't look at me, but his jaw tensed. Even standing still, he looked defensive and agitated.

I stared at him for a moment, trying to work out if he really could have left me there if he hadn't been overwhelmed by a single moment of sincere humanity. He was just impossible to read, but Dominic and Desmond had both said Spencer wasn't a bad guy, he was just distant.

Giving up on trying to figure out the level of his detachment from human feelings, I asked, "Why did you?"

He looked at me, blinked, and frowned. "What?"

I almost smiled at having apparently caught him off guard with my question. "Why did you save me instead of leaving me there?"

His frown deepened, his expression darkening. He looked away from me sharply, raising his foot as though he might stick it in the water again, and then hesitated. "Because," he said in a low, thick voice, "I'm not a monster." He kicked the water, sending up a spray of glistening drops that caught the moonlight.

"Why are you leaving?" Spencer asked suddenly, his narrowed eyes fixed on my face and watching me intently.

It made something inside me quiver, whether with fear or something else, I couldn't be sure. I swallowed and looked away, glancing down at the silvery stream. Under the surface, there was a small white stone shining, out of place amongst the darker pebbles.

I knelt as I spoke, so I wouldn't have to look at Spencer, but I could still feel his gaze burning cold on the back of my neck. "I'm leaving because this isn't my place. It was…kind of you to save me, and for your family and friends to look after me, but I can't stay here. I'd rather leave before I wear out my welcome."

I reached into the water, the liquid coldness of it shocking the nerves in my fingers, and grasped the little white stone. Pulling it out, I saw it wasn't plain white after all; there was a swirl of pale blue on it, and inside the swirl was a freckling of gold. It looked like something precious that someone must have dropped. I doubted they'd be coming back for it, so I decided to keep it.

I dried my hand on my shorts, and when I looked up, Spencer was still staring at me. It was disconcerting. I glared up at him from the grass, rolling my new pebble across my palm.

"Anyone ever tell you it's rude to stare?" I grumbled.

Spencer blinked, his expression smoothing out. His mouth curved up in an approximation of a smile, and he said, "No, I don't believe anyone ever has."

He hesitated a moment, then sank down to the grass next to me, and half-turned away from me toward the stream. His black hair seemed haloed with the silver light of the moon. I saw past my dislike of him for just long enough to remember he was amazingly attractive, and he couldn't be all bad—he *had* saved me and brought me to the camp.

Then he glanced at me sideways, a flicker of blue under his lashes, and said, "You're not very bright, are you?"

The moment of generous thinking toward him was over, and I glared at him, stung by the insult. "And what makes you think that?" I asked, my voice biting. How would he even know? That was the longest conversation we'd had, and we hadn't exactly been discussing Pythagorean Theorem.

Spencer raised one eyebrow, just a fraction, effectively expressing what he thought of my having to *ask* why he thought I was an idiot. "You're leaving a safe place, with nowhere to go, no food, no money, or anything but the clothes you're wearing, in the middle of the night, and you honestly expect to get somewhere. I'd say you could make it five more miles before you'd break an ankle or get eaten by something."

He seemed amused by the idea of me getting eaten. I was starting to think it wouldn't be enough to just push him in the stream. I should hogtie him first, and then push him.

"I'm not stupid. I was going to make a trip into town. I have a friend there who could help me out," I said, suddenly thinking of Tamara. I don't know why I hadn't thought of going to her before, but it seemed like a good idea. I'd have to swear her to secrecy, but she'd already known I'd been planning on escaping the witches, because we'd talked about running away together for ages. She wanted to escape her alcoholic stepdad and go to a real city with more than one bookstore.

"Town, huh?" Spencer murmured, looking caught between smugness and laughter. He lifted a hand, and without looking away from the water, pointed backward over his shoulder. "Town's that way."

Oh yeah, he was smug. I gritted my teeth, feeling a wave of embarrassment at my own inept sense of direction turning my face red. Of course I'd been going the wrong way, why had I even thought that going by the stream was a good idea in the first place? Not a clue.

I sprang to my feet, angry, humiliated and feeling despair rushing up to me. If I couldn't even find my way out of the woods, how would I ever take care of myself in the real world? I'd probably end up living under a bridge with a hobo named George and his ugly dog Maxwell.

Tears prickled my eyes, and I turned away from Spencer to scrub at them, refusing to let him see he'd wounded me. He was such an ass, but he was right, too. Where was I going, in the middle of the night? I was *going* to end up in a ditch as a wolf's chew toy.

A hand touched my shoulder lightly, and I jumped, whacking the hand away. "Don't touch me!" I snarled, glaring at Spencer through tear blurred eyes.

He was developing a nasty habit of creeping up on me like that, and I didn't like it. If a human could sneak up on me, I didn't stand a chance against my creepy adoptive family, who had all sorts of Stealth Potions and Sneaking Charms at their disposal—half of them made with my power. *Dammit!*

Three feet away, Spencer stood with his hands up, palms toward me, as if I was a wild animal that he was trying not to frighten. There was no mocking or coldness in his face, and the way his hair fell into his eyes made him look younger, gentler. "Relax, Tilly. I'm not going to hurt you," he said quietly.

I believed him, just as I had believed Dominic when he'd said nobody would hurt me. I thought it might have been the first time Spencer had called me by my name. He eased a step toward me, and I went still, wondering what he was doing. A breath of air lifted fine strands of dark hair around his face, brushing them across his brow and cheekbones. His eyes stayed steady on mine, and he kept his hands where I could see them. Another step toward me, and he was close enough to touch me, but he didn't. He just stared at me evenly, unmoving, until my heart began to slow and my tears subsided.

Then, in a very soft voice, he said, "Sit down a minute. You're shaking."

I did as he said and sat down, slowly, watching him the whole way to the ground. He lowered himself down with me, keeping his eyes on mine, and then we were sitting together on the grass, his knees almost touching mine but not quite. The woods had gone still, as if they were holding their breath.

Spencer held out his hand to me, uncurling his fingers to show the pretty white stone I'd picked up gleaming on his palm. I hadn't realised I'd dropped it. Hesitantly, I reached out and plucked it from his hand, curling my own fingers around it so tightly my knuckles turned white.

"Thank you," I murmured, not sure if I meant it for more than just the pebble. The half-smile, genuine and not in the least sarcastic, on his face made me think he understood that.

"So," he said quietly, leaning over to reach into the stream, "are you still planning on leaving?" His tone was carefully neutral. When he took his hand out of the water, he was holding his own pebble between his fingers; an irregular grey stone with speckles of white and silver in it.

I thought about it for a moment, chewing my lip, and then nodded slowly. "Yes…." I said.

Spencer's eyebrows drew down. He opened his mouth to say something, but I cut him off.

"But not yet," I added, allowing myself to give him a tiny smile.

He relaxed a little, almost imperceptibly, and I had to wonder just how neutral he really was about the idea of me leaving. Tipping his head down, so his inky hair flopped forward and hid his eyes, he watched the grey pebble as he rolled it from palm to palm as if it were mesmerising.

For a while, we just sat there in silence, him rolling his pebble around in his hands, me listening to the cool shushing of the stream. The sliver of the moon moved across the endless blackness of the sky, tugging the stars along with it. A leaf fluttered down from a nearby tree, spinning and twirling until it landed in the stream and was carried away on the gentle current. The trees hummed in their silent way, calling the night-creatures slinking through the shadows and vines. I didn't realise I'd been meditating until Spencer's voice broke me out of it, snapping me back to myself.

"Why did you save that wolf today?" he asked, and I blinked. For a second, his shape was a blurry shadow and his eyes shone gold out of a morphed face. I blinked again and my vision cleared. He was looking at me with blue eyes in a handsome, pale face. His expression was blank, uncurious, but his eyes…there was something sharp and serious enough to cut in the blue orbs. It took me a moment to process his question, and then I frowned.

"How did you know I…?" I couldn't finish the question.

His eyes flickered, though he didn't look away or blink, and my throat closed up for a moment around an inexplicable second of panic. I breathed out, letting the moment of fear pass. Even though he hadn't moved, there was suddenly something in Spencer, in the intensity of his gaze and the coiled way he was sitting, that made me feel like…like prey.

He was waiting for me to answer, and for a minute, I wasn't sure what to tell him. Why had I save the wolf? Because…it was just a wolf. It was an innocent animal, it didn't deserve to die. More than that, it was a *wild* animal. It was free, the way I was trying to be. It was strong, beautiful, and free to run as far and as fast as it wanted. The wolf could run the way I wanted to run. I couldn't explain that to Spencer, not really.

"I saved it for the same reason you saved me," I said softly, meeting his clear blue eyes, "I'm not a monster."

The next day, Dom and I went for another walk along the other side of the stream. I liked hanging out with him without the clamour of a dozen other people around us, and it felt good to get rid of some of the pent-up energy that had been building in me over the last couple of days I'd spent mostly sitting around camp. Staying in one place, while knowing the witches were looking for me, was making me agitated. I thought again, very briefly, of leaving. But I discarded the notion quickly, telling myself that Spencer had been right. I had nowhere to go, no food, and no money. Even if I could go to Tamara, I wouldn't, because that would risk bringing *them* down on her head, and she didn't deserve that. She knew what *they* were, but she was purely human. No way could she fend *them* off if *they* wanted answers from her about where I'd gone.

Also, a little part of me—okay, a pretty big part of me that was growing even as he grinned at me and chased me through the trees— didn't want to leave Dominic. He was my first real friend, aside from Tamara, and as much as I didn't want to bring the witches down on him and his friends and family, I found I wanted even less to leave them all. What they had there, what they had brought me into willingly and kindly, was the closest thing to family I'd known since my parents had died.

After walking up and down the stream, Dominic and I were almost back to camp. The dull green of a tent came into view beyond the shielding leaves of the trees, and he pulled me to an abrupt halt, cutting off my joke midsentence. I jerked when he grabbed my arm, his fingers surprisingly tight, and turned to face him, scowling.

"Dominic, what is—" I didn't get to finish my question.

He held up a hand for silence, and I bit my tongue. His head was tilted as though he were listening to something I couldn't hear, like when Desmond had been following us the day before, but his narrowed eyes were directed toward camp.

My heart hiccupped nervously. Did something happen in camp? I didn't know. I couldn't hear…wait, yes I could. Voices. Not just the normal mutterings and laughter of the camp, but a new voice— male, loud, and strong. I couldn't make out words, but the tone was unmistakable: The guy was in charge somehow, and he wasn't happy.

I looked at Dominic again, opening my mouth to ask who it could be, but he'd gone very pale, and his grip on my arm was tightening almost painfully. He'd become very, very still. I touched his hand on my arm gently, not trying to pry it off, but trying to make him aware of how hard he was gripping— possibly hard enough to bruise. Not that I couldn't handle it. The witches had left me plenty of bruises before, but I thought he might feel bad about it later.

"Dom? What's—" I murmured softly.

He whipped his head round, fixing his green eyes on me. He put a hand over my mouth, glanced toward camp, and then took his hand away carefully.

He leaned in very, very close, so close I could smell the fresh, musky scent of him like leaves, dirt, and salt. My stomach jumped into a knot, and I felt his breath tickle the hair by my face as he whispered in my ear.

"Stay here. Don't make a sound. Don't move until I come back for you."

Before I could ask questions, he loped off toward camp and out of sight. Mildly stunned, and extremely confused, I leaned against the nearest tree and waited for my stomach to relax. Chewing my lip, I wondered who was in camp and what was going on. The man was angry about something.

About me? I wondered. *About me, an outsider, being in their camp?* The thought made me feel guilty and nervous. I should have just left the previous night, instead of listening to Spencer. Even if he was right, I should have stuck to my principles and gone before anyone could get into trouble for their misguided altruism.

Thinking of Spencer, I hadn't seen him all day. Maybe he was avoiding me. Maybe he'd known the man was coming to camp and knew he'd be angry if I was there. Maybe he'd been hoping I'd be in camp when the man arrived and he would kick me out on my ear. So many maybes, and I couldn't get answers without knowing what was going on in camp.

Biting my lip, I peered around my tree, eyed the distance to camp, and stepped out carefully, wishing I had Spencer's ability to creep around silently like a cat. My first step was silent, so I took another, and another, and then…*snap*. A twig I hadn't noticed cracked under my foot, and I froze, holding my breath. The voices in camp paused for a second.

Please don't let me get caught, I thought, half-praying to the woods. Thankfully, the voices resumed, and I let out my breath slowly, heart jumping. I couldn't go any closer without risking standing on another twig or getting caught in a branch, but I still couldn't make out what was being said properly.

Cursing mentally, I tried to strain my hearing, desperate to know if they were talking about me. If I closed my eyes and tilted my head the way Dominic had, it helped a little, but I still couldn't— *Pop*.

"…can't be here, Jane, you know that! You'd risk our safety to protect one little girl?" The angry man's voice, the voice I didn't recognise.

I almost gasped, but clapped a hand over my mouth. I could hear them perfectly, every word as clear as if they'd been standing five feet in front of me, not twenty-five feet. It was as if someone had burst a bubble around my head, and I could hear better, much better.

Then I realised what was happening. The energy of the woods was shifting, it had pushed its way into my power, but somehow not into my body. Pulsing close to my skin, like an aura, it was amplifying my hearing. I listened to what was going on in camp, trying to pick out the voices.

"...doesn't belong here! She has to leave!" Angry man yelled.

I sensed more than heard others shifting in discomfort, and wondered how many of them were there. Maybe the whole camp was gathered.

"But Frank, she has nowhere to go. We can't just send her packing and hope she can find her way out of the woods. She was running away from something... someone. Whoever they are, she's running from them for a reason–"Jane's, airy voice was compassionate and pleading.

Frank—I assumed Frank was the angry man—cut her off. "Even more reason she needs to leave! If whoever she's running from comes looking for her, we're in trouble, and I won't have this family in danger just because one silly little girl ran away from her mummy and daddy."

"Frank, the girl...she's alone, and scared, and she hasn't noticed anything strange so far. I think if she did, she'd turn a blind eye to it, convince herself it was her imagination. She's a teenager, not a little kid. Too late to change her worldview now without some serious proof," Graham's gravelly voice insisted patiently.

I wanted to snort at his logic. *My* worldview? So what if they had some weird cult thing going on? I had magical powers, and I could summon demons. If anyone's worldview was going to be disrupted, it would be theirs, but I hoped to avoid that at all costs.

There was a pause, a sense of uncertainty, and then Frank spoke again, sounding much calmer. "Who found her? Who brought her to the camp?" he asked.

His question was met with an uneasy rustling of people who didn't want to answer. I could imagine the nervous glances flitting around the crowd of gathered campers. Then, just when I was beginning to be sure that nobody would tell him, someone finally spoke up.

"I did. I brought her to camp."

Spencer. It wasn't hard to recognise his voice. He still spoke quietly, his voice low and dark, but there was no nervousness in it and no pleading like in the other voices. He sounded as if he was issuing a challenge, and I felt the awkward, anxious tension from thirty-feet away.

"You," Frank said, his voice scarily flat. "I should have known it'd be you."

I could have sworn there was a note of disgust in that flat tone, and I remembered what Dominic had told me. *"Our dad…he really is great, but he doesn't always treat Spencer the same way he treats me and Des… I think my dad sometimes forgets it isn't Spencer's fault his mother ran away."*

Oh. Something in my brain clicked, and I finally understood. Frank was Dominic and Desmond's father—Spencer's father. He was in charge of the…group, cult, whatever. That explained everyone else's nervousness…except maybe Dominic's. He'd looked downright scared before he'd taken off toward camp. But

87

then, I could understand that too. Nobody liked getting in trouble with their parents...or adoptive family. I just hoped Frank didn't punish his kids anything like the way the witches had punished me. It hadn't always been the Dark Room or starvation, they had a birch cane that worked just as well.

"Well, explain yourself, Spencer. Why did you bring the girl to camp?" Frank's tone was still flat, but even I could hear the anger under the surface.

I flinched at the question. It was almost the exact question I'd asked Spencer the night before. *Why did you save me instead of leaving me there?*

I expected Spencer to give Frank the same answer he'd given me, to tell him that he wasn't a monster and couldn't just leave an injured girl in the mud, but he didn't. There was just silence.

"Speak up, boy! Come on, answer me," Frank snapped, his voice no longer flat, but energized with something like cruel amusement. As if he was enjoying Spencer's...what? Fear? Anxiety? Discomfort? I couldn't imagine Spencer scared or anxious.

"I don't know," Spencer said, his voice even quieter.

Somehow, the quieter he spoke, the darker he sounded. Not scared, not ashamed, but not openly hostile either—just a chilling kind of calmness. I was glad, right then, that I couldn't see his face when he used that voice. He was intimidating enough when it was just the two of us talking by the stream, when he was relaxed.

His father didn't seem too worried about his son's shadowy tone. "You don't know? You've endangered us all, and you *don't know why you did it?*" the man's voice rose almost to a roar.

I heard one of the kids—maybe Annie—squeak fearfully. Meanwhile, the practical part of my brain was ticking over Frank's booming words. *Endangered them? Endangered them how?* Did he think I was secretly an escaped lunatic with a knife and a box of matches in my back pocket? Or maybe he meant I would endanger their…way of life, or whatever.

"Frank, please—" another voice, male, maybe John spoke up.

"No, I won't have her here. It's too dangerous for us," Frank insisted.

"But she's only—"

"It doesn't matter who or what she is. If she finds out—"

"But she won't!"

"And if she does? What then? She'll run screaming and tell the whole town—"

"No, she won't," Spencer's smooth, quiet voice sliced through the louder ones like a knife cutting warm butter.

Things went silent again for a moment, and I found myself leaning toward the camp. My feet were rooted to the spot, but my eyes desperate to *see* what was happening, see everyone's expressions, see *Spencer*. I couldn't tell from his voice if his words were a threat or a promise.

Sounding curious, Frank asked, "And how do you know that?"

There was a tiny pause in which I just *knew* Spencer was shrugging. His tone when he answered seemed to confirm it—casual and disinterested, to match the shrug I couldn't see.

"Just a feeling. Call it…instinct." He weighted the final word with some meaning I couldn't understand.

Someone cleared their throat, and I recognised Dominic's voice next.

"Dad, I agree with Spencer. I think we should let Tilly stay. I don't think she's any danger to us."

He sounded much less certain than Spencer had, but coming from Dominic, it seemed to convince Frank. His next words, at least, weren't a command for my removal. Quite the opposite.

"Let me see the girl," he demanded.

I snapped upright, no longer swaying toward the camp and the drama unfolding there. A moment before, I'd been dying to see what was going on, but now I really didn't want to. I didn't want to face the angry man who wanted me gone from his camp, because he thought I was dangerous somehow. What if he took one look at me and booted me out, and told me never to return and never speak of his family and friends to anyone? What if Dominic and Spencer got into trouble for defending me?

"What?" Dom sounded confused, as if he couldn't understand why on Earth his father would want to see me.

I wasn't sure how I felt about that. It probably wasn't a good sign, and it certainly wasn't reassuring.

In a gentler tone, Frank said, "I want to see the girl for myself. Bring her out of wherever you hid her. Yes, I know you, Dom. It's okay, son. I just want to see her."

The way he spoke to Dominic was so different from the way he spoke to everyone else, especially Spencer, that I thought I might be starting to understand why Spencer was so distant from everyone. If his own father treated him like an unworthy misfit all the time, of course he'd want to hide out from everybody. I could sympathize with him. I'd spent most of my time at school trying to blend into the shadows, covering the bruises on my legs the cane had left and hiding the bags under my eyes, put there by nights made sleepless by nightmares and worries. When you felt like no good, you didn't want to face people you thought were better than you.

"Tilly!" Dominic's voice called into the trees.

I heard his crunching footsteps coming toward me. With a pop, whatever bubble of force that had been allowing me to hear the voices in camp abruptly burst. I sank back against a nearby tree, leaning against it, trying to look casual, and picking at the leaves on the branches as if I was totally bored. By the time Dominic found me, I was certain that my expression betrayed nothing of what I'd overheard.

I looked up curiously as he walked toward me and smiled at him. "Hey, you're back. I was starting to think we were playing Hide and Seek again, only you weren't looking for me very hard." I managed to sound just a little bit hurt, and I pouted sulkily to add to the effect.

My heart was hammering on my ribs, and I had the sudden urge to flee as he reached out a hand to take my elbow, but I stayed put and let him tow me away from the tree. He was smiling, but I knew it was only for my benefit, so that I didn't worry. I was worried anyway.

"It would be a very bad game of Hide and Seek, considering I told you where to hide in the first place," he said, his voice a little too cheery.

If I hadn't already known there was something wrong, I might have started to suspect right about then, but I didn't let on.

"Yeah, is there a reason you decided to make me stand in one place for fifteen minutes? Because, just to let you know, I get bored very easily." I tried to sound flippant and wasn't sure I pulled it off, but Dominic glanced at me sideways, a hint of a genuine smile making his dimple flicker. I relaxed a little—just a very little bit.

We were almost back to camp, and Dominic's smile died, but his fingers stayed light on my elbow. "You can meditate for two straight hours, and yet standing on your own for fifteen minutes bores you? You aren't right in the head, you know that?" he said with a half-hearted grin.

I shrugged. He was more right than he knew, and way more right than I was comfortable with admitting to myself.

"And, just to warn you, don't be scared. You're about to meet my dad, and he looks a lot scarier than he is. Just…avoid eye contact."

I remembered he'd given me the same advice for dealing with Spencer. What was it with these people and eye contact? When I thought about it, none of them really looked me in the eye for more than a couple of seconds at a push. Not even Desmond, who seemed more than comfortable to eye the rest of me for as long as he pleased. Only Spencer ever held my eyes…those piercing blue eyes of his…

However, as Dominic led me into the centre of the camp, Desmond didn't leer at me at all. His gaze was steady on my face, but not quite meeting my eyes. He was hovering next to his mother, holding Chris's hand on his other side. Annie, clutching Sarah's skirt, peeked out at me, her brown eyes wide and sad.

Everyone was there, gathered together between the tents, leaving the circle in the middle clear. Well, not entirely clear, because standing in front of one tents was Spencer. He looked as distant and cool as ever, not even glancing at me. In fact, he was somehow not looking at anyone, but staring through them toward the trees.

Next to Spencer was a tall, broad shouldered man with unruly red hair and a handlebar moustache over a thin mouth, a fuzzy orange beard coating a strong jaw, and fine wrinkles around steely grey-green eyes that I only glimpsed before I shot my gaze downward, as per Dominic's advice. He was, in short, scary.

Aside from Spencer, every pair of eyes was fixed on me as Dominic drew me to a halt in front of his father—who loomed over me by about a foot. I wasn't short, but I wasn't tall, and the guy

93

made me feel like a dwarf. I kept my head down, partly out of respect and Dominic's advice, and mostly because I was too scared to look him in the face. My shoulders were hunched, and I had my back to Spencer, but I still felt the back of my neck prickling with his gaze. At least Dominic was still by my side, though he'd let go of my elbow.

"You must be Tilly. Oh, don't worry, girl, I won't bite. Come on, let's see your face," Frank said pleasantly, his voice almost as tender as when he'd been speaking to Dominic.

Perfectly friendly. If I hadn't heard him yelling just a minute before, I'd never have guessed he was even capable of raising his voice. Not wanting to seem disrespectful, but mindful of Dominic's advice, I raised my head just far enough that he could clearly see my face, keeping my eyes on the buttons of his shirt, which wasn't hard because my eyes were on level with a spot just above his collarbones.

I waited for him to speak, my hands clenched behind my back so only Dominic could see them, and feeling nervous dampness on the back of my neck. I felt like a defendant waiting for the jury to proclaim me innocent or guilty.

Behind me, I felt Dominic shift a little closer, just a fraction of an inch. Whatever expression was on his father's face, it was making him uneasy.

Frank's voice was utterly unchanged when he spoke again. "So, Tilly, Spencer tells me he found you in the woods. What were you doing out there? Hiding from someone?" his tone was gentle, compassionate.

The questions seemed appropriate enough from a concerned adult looking to help a lost kid. But they weren't questions I wanted to answer, not to a stranger, especially not in front of everyone in the camp. I wasn't quite ready to spill my heart to a scary man who really didn't want me around, and a whole group of people I barely knew. Most of all, I didn't want Spencer to know. I don't know why I was so bothered about *him*, of all of them, knowing things about me, but I was. Maybe it was because he scared me almost as much as his dad did.

I swallowed against the dryness in my throat, and murmured, "I was running away." I sounded like a silly, scared little girl.

I could feel the weight of everyone's eyes on me, their attention lying heavy on my shoulders. Two sets of eyes felt particularly intense—the man in front of me, and the boy far behind me. Frank and Spencer. For all their disdain of each other, I wondered if they knew how much they were alike in body language. It was as if they were both coiled a little bit tighter than the rest of them.

"Running away from whom? Where are your parents?" Frank asked.

I shook my head, hesitated before choking out the words, "Dead. My parents are dead."

The pause was brief, but heavy. My lungs felt tight, constricting. I didn't want to be standing there, answering those questions. I wanted to run, run away from there and those people, who suddenly seemed strange and prying. I wanted to run away from my past. My legs ached to do it, to take me away as fast as possible. I forced my knees to lock, and gripped Dominic's fingers hard enough to break them. He didn't try to stop me, didn't even twitch.

"So who are you running away from?" This time, it wasn't Frank who asked. It was Spencer.

I felt him move up behind me, and I tensed. Instinctively, I bristled at his nearness and his soft tone. "None of your business," I spat through gritted teeth, my stomach lurching.

I sensed him smiling at the back of my neck. "I thought we already had this conversation," he said, his voice low and surprisingly intimate, as if we were the only two people there.

My fingers tightened further on Dominic's, and I heard Spencer make a small chuffing noise that wasn't quite a laugh.

Dom's voice spoke in my ear, almost a whisper. "You don't have to answer him if you don't want to. It's okay." To Spencer, he said, "Spence, I think you should take a step back. Before she tries to bite your head off." Dominic sounded as calm and cheery as if there wasn't a crushing amount of tension in the air.

I wondered for a second what the rest of the group thought of the interaction, my obvious dislike of Spencer, and his comment. *I thought we already had this conversation.* I could practically hear the speculation going on inside their heads.

Then Frank interrupted, chuckling, apparently amused. "Well, it'd be interesting to see her try, but Dom's probably right. Back off a bit, Spencer."

Spencer backed away, though I could still feel his eyes on my neck, and I got the impression that he wanted to rip my throat out right then. I swallowed, forcibly loosened my grasp on Dominic's fingers, and sighed silently.

"Does that mean Tilly can stay?" Dominic asked quietly.

A moment of hesitation, then, "Yes, she can stay. For now. But Dominic, you're in charge of taking care of her."

As if I was a pet, not a person. I was too eager to get out of there, and too relieved that I wasn't being tossed out on my ear, to take offence at it.

"Okay," Frank said loudly, and the tension snapped, everyone shifting their attention to him, instead of me. "Everybody pack up! It's time to go home!"

Chapter Six

** Tilly **

As it turned out, 'home' was a collection of pretty wooden cabins not all that far from where the group had been camping. The cabins were large and spaced far enough apart that my first impression was of some sort of holiday resort dumped in the middle of the woods. You couldn't see one cabin from the next, but a short stroll in any direction would bring you to your neighbour. Each of the cabins had neat little porches out front, and a set of small steps leading up to them. Aside from the glass windows, you'd have thought they'd had just grown out of the ground naturally, they were so quaintly organic looking. Trees clustered around them, wildflowers pushed up against the walls, and strings of ivy wrapped the porch banisters.

 The last cabin on the tour—and it had been a tour, because Dominic had been quite zealous about showing me around—happened to be Dominic and Desmond's. For some reason, it surprised me to find that they had their own cabin, as opposed to living with their parents. I supposed when your kids' home was just a five minute walk away from any of the adults' cabins, it was hardly a big deal to let them live alone. Silently, I wondered where Spencer lived, seeing as Dominic hadn't mentioned anything about him sharing the cabin with him and his brother. It wouldn't surprise me in the least if Spencer had his own cabin. I couldn't imagine him sitting eating breakfast cereal and watching Friends reruns in the morning with his brothers.

"Ah, home sweet home. It's not really big or fancy or anything, but it's lovely all the same." Dom grinned at me, sweeping an arm wide to present his cabin.

Desmond, behind me, snorted and pushed past both of us, loping up the steps. They creaked faintly under his weight. He paused at the door, presumably unlocking it, though I hadn't seen him take out a key, and the door swung open easily. Desmond stepped inside and slammed the door behind him without looking back at Dominic and me. He appeared to be sulking. Was he unhappy that I was being allowed to stay with the group?

Dominic shook his head, curls twisting in a faint breeze. Slithering shadows cast a pattern on his face from the late afternoon light coming down through the leaves. "Don't worry, it isn't you he's upset with," he said, as if reading my mind. His eyes darted to me, impossibly bright and glinting in the softening sunlight. "I think he's actually annoyed at Spencer for his attitude toward dad earlier. Des is all about respecting our father, and Spence is all about, well, *not* respecting anyone." He sighed, smiling ruefully.

I looked up at the cute cabin, with its gently sloping roof covered in fallen leaves and the friendly looking shutters, painted cobalt blue and swung wide open, inviting. It was beautiful, the kind of place I'd always wanted to live. The kind of place my mother had promised me, when I was small, that we would live one day. Then she'd gone and died, and I'd spent the last eleven years in a big, cold manor house on the outskirts of a new town.

I just knew my mother would have loved it there in the woods. I felt a deep, searing pain in my chest, a deeply buried grief I hadn't felt in a long time. I'd gotten used to pushing it down, because it hurt too much to think about. The memories were bearable, so long as I didn't have to *feel* them. My eyes stung with tears, even as a wistful sort of smile curled my lips.

"Tilly? You okay?" Dominic asked quietly.

I blinked back my tears, turning to him with a soft smile. I nodded at him. "Yeah, I'm okay. Just…thinking about my parents. They would have liked it here." Saying it aloud didn't make my lungs constrict and my throat burn the way talking about them in front of everyone else had. I didn't mind telling Dominic so much. His kind smile eased the small ache in my heart like a balm on a burn.

"Well, how about I show you to your own cabin?" he said, splitting into one of his cheery smiles. He reached into his pocket and pulled out a shiny gold key with a little blue fob in the shape of a crude wolf, or maybe it was a fox.

I stared at it glinting in his hand. "I get my own cabin?" I asked, amazed and excited by the prospect.

He nodded. "Yup, your very own, all to yourself. There are actually three free cabins you could choose from, but I thought you might like the one closest to mine and Desmond's. It's not as big as the others, but hopefully you'll like it just the same." He shrugged casually, starting off into the trees behind his cabin.

The cabin Dominic led me to was just barely out of sight of his. In fact, I could see the glow from the windows of his cabin in the fading daylight, a faint smear of light through the trees. It was, as he'd said, smaller, but plenty big enough for one person, even two people. The outside was a little run down, probably because nobody used it. The blue paint on the shutters was faded, there were nests of cobwebs over the door and windows, and one of the boards on the steps looked rotted through. But still, my own cabin! Privacy!

When you lived with witches, who could unlock your door with a flip of their wrists when they felt like it, privacy was practically nonexistent. The tent I'd been sharing with Sarah and Annie was hardly private either. A cabin with four walls, a roof, a door that locked and nobody could open unless I chose to let them in, it was a home, however temporary. I didn't care what it looked like on the outside, or the inside.

Metal jingled by my ear and I flinched in surprise, turning to Dominic, who was rattling the key by my face. I meant to glare at him, but instead I was grinning. I threw my arms around him, only the second time I'd really hugged anyone in a long time, and both times it had been him.

He didn't seem so surprised by my embrace that time, and he ruffled my hair, chuckling. "Glad you like it. Wait until you see inside," he said.

I didn't let go. I must have been crushing the air out of him, but he didn't complain. He just let me hug him until I got myself back together enough to pull away.

Then he gave me an odd look, soft and considering. I smiled shakily at him and wiped at the stupid tears that had escaped my eyes, feeling my face redden. "Sorry. I just…." I shook my head, unsure how to explain how much all of it meant to me. Not just the cabin, or him defending me to his father to let me stay, but his friendship. I'd have to find a way to make it up to him, do something for him—maybe for his half-brother, too. Spencer did save me, and he did sort of defend me. Sort of. In his quiet, strange way.

Dominic was still giving me that indecipherable look. "You don't get a lot of kindness, do you?" he asked it very gently.

I felt my eyes fill again, and pushed away the tears. Swallowing, I shook my head. "I ran away for a reason," my voice was barely a whisper.

Dominic nodded, sighing, and took my hand. He squeezed my fingers lightly. "Come on, I want to show you inside. How do you feel about portraits of birds?" He let go of my hand and moved up the steps to the cabin door, batting away streamers of cobwebs and probably really, really angering the spiders.

I was about to follow him up the steps when the fluttering of a small bird in a nearby tree caught my attention. It was a little blue tit, with a white mask on its face and a crown of soft blue spilling down its back. I smiled at the cute little birdie, and very slowly reached out my fingertips to see if it would come to me. The movement startled the bird, and it chirped sharply before taking off in a flutter of blue and gold feathers. I was staring at the spot it had vacated, a little disappointed, when I noticed something through the clustered branches—another cabin.

I could only glimpse it in small puzzle pieces, and I leaned forward, pulling a few branches out of my way to get a better look. It was dark and even more run down than the cabin I was going to be living in. There were no lights on, and shadows gathered thick around the porch. The railing had been smashed or had rotted away, and just a couple of drunken posts remained to show there had ever been a railing at all. Yet, there were no cobwebs over the door, and the locks—more than one, I noted—all appeared to be brand new, shining brass in the darkening woods.

"Tilly!"

I jerked and spun around when Dominic called my name, and saw him leaning forward over the porch railing of my cabin, looking concerned and a little panicked. Had he thought I was going to wander off into the trees or something?

With a final glance at the possibly abandoned cabin, I walked back to my cabin and climbed the little wooden steps. The top one creaked quietly, and then I was on the porch, with Dominic looking at me with laser-like green eyes. I hadn't realised how dark it had gotten until then. His face was entirely in shadow, and the trees surrounded us in total darkness, but for the shine of light from his and Desmond's cabin a little ways away.

"Is that other cabin over there abandoned, or is it used for something?" I asked, innocently curious, pointing in the direction of the dark cabin.

Dominic's mouth tightened for a second, and his normally cheery face set into a surprisingly serious expression. It made me wish I hadn't asked. Slowly, he shook his head, but it seemed to be a warning rather than an answer to my question.

"You can't go near that cabin. You hear me, Tilly? Never go near that cabin. It's…not safe. If you hear or see something at night that scares you, stay inside and lock your doors. The woods are dangerous at night. You never know what could be lurking out there."

I nodded, stunned and a little scared by his seriousness. "You know," I said carefully, "Spencer said the same thing. About the things lurking."

I couldn't tell what his reaction to that was, because he turned away and began unlocking the door with his head bowed and shadowed by darkness and his curls. He turned the handle, handing me the key, and the door swung open. A puff of stale, musty air swept out, and I sneezed. When Dominic glanced back at me, he was grinning again, as if he hadn't just warned me in a stone hard voice not to leave the cabin at night. He flipped a switch on the wall, and the dark cabin lit up with a warm orange glow that had me blinking against the brightness.

When I stopped squinting, I could see the whole cabin, and my lips parted in amazement at the perfect, adorable décor. The living room was open plan, pouring out into a kitchen at the far end of the room, behind a high breakfast bar ringed with tall, wooden chairs. The clean white fridge nestled between a clunky stove and the Cyclops that was the washing machine. A dining table ringed with elegant chairs took up most of the space in front of the kitchen, which was on the left side of the room. The living room, on the right, was comprised of a low, comfy looking brown leather sofa in front of a cheery stone fireplace filled with damp, rotting firewood. The place was lit by a plainly shaded bulb over the dining table, and one over the dust matted red rug in front of the fireplace. There was another bulb, bare and unshaded, over the kitchen. Dominic went to touch the wall next to the microwave, and the kitchen bulb lit up, making the silver sink shine through its coat of dust.

At the back of the room, next to the kitchen, there was a narrow hallway, and Dominic led me down it, his footsteps stirring the dust on the floor. I realised what he meant by the comment about bird portraits. The hallway was hung with several of them, photos and paintings of ducks in flight and sparrows perched on branches, one of an owl scowling at the camera from its hole in the trunk of a tree, and a cute one of a red-breasted robin hunkering on a frosted twig. I kind of liked the pictures, even if birds weren't my favourite creatures on the planet. There was something pleasant about the framed birds, like little watchful friends there to keep me company.

Three doors lined the narrow hallway, and Dominic paused at the first one, twisted the handle, and pushed open the door. "This is the first bedroom. It's the bigger one of the two," he explained, showing me into the room with a sweep of his arm.

The room was painted in a neutral beige colour. The bed was a double, stripped bare and covered with a ragged sheet to protect it from the dust. Next to it, there was a small nightstand with a lamp that looked as if it had been carved from a hunk of wood, the bulb hidden by a plain brown, square shade. Opposite the bed, there was a sturdy wooden bookcase with a handful of books leaning in one of the shelves. I went over and ran my fingers over the spines, brushing away the dust. I picked up one of the books and flipped it open, curious. The first page was a table of contents, so I kept flicking until I came to a page with a photo of a wolf on it.

"Hey, Tilly, come look at this!" Dominic said.

I turned, closing the book, but he wasn't in the room. Putting the book back on its shelf, I frowned before spotting the open doorway in the wall, not the one we'd come in through. I peered around it, and found Dominic standing in the middle of a small, walk-in wardrobe. Poles set in the walls ran from one end of the room to the other, hung with dozens of empty coat hangers. There were a few pairs of jeans, a couple of skirts, a handful of t-shirts, and a hoodie hanging up.

"Clothes Sarah has outgrown", Dominic said.

The walls were bare wooden paneling, and the floor was covered in thick, dusty-pink carpeting. A single naked bulb swung from the ceiling, illuminating the small space.

I grinned. Dominic walked back up to my end of the room and closed the door, trapping us inside. Suddenly the small cosy space seemed dim and intimate. I swallowed, nervously wondering what Dom's intentions were, but he wasn't looking at me.

There was a door opposite the one I'd come in by, and Dominic flipped open the sliding lock on the inside of the door and pushed it open. The door led into the other bedroom, which was painted a pale, powder blue with the window in the west wall right above the bed. There was a dressing table against the east wall, next to the door that, presumably, led out onto the hallway.

"The bathroom is across the hall, and you can take your pick of whichever bedroom you feel like sleeping in. Hell, you can take turns sleeping in either one if you feel like it. The bedding and pillows are in the walk-in wardrobe, and I think there are some old board games somewhere in there, too." Dominic hovered with his hands in his pockets while I examined the room.

I decided I wanted to sleep in the room with the wood paneling, so Dominic helped me root out the clean bedding and tossed the pillows to me while I straightened the duvet and blankets. Then he found a sweeping brush and attempted to sweep the dust off the floors. He was useless at it and kept putting his feet in the piles of dust he'd gathered, so I took over and handed him a ragged yellow duster and a can of polish I'd found under the sink in the bathroom. He was much better at dusting, though I told him he didn't have to help me if he didn't want to.

He insisted, and I got the impression he would use any excuse to hang around a little longer, as if he didn't want to leave me alone in the new place. So we cleaned the little cabin as best as we could, both getting quite a bit of dust on our clothes in the process, and then sat down at the dining table with a game of Snakes and Ladders from the walk-in.

"Bugger, another snake!" Dom muttered glumly as he slid his coloured plastic piece back to the bottom of the board again. His luck with the dice sucked.

I laughed, picked up the dice, shook it, and threw it. It skittered across the table and landed on five. Grinning, I shifted my plastic piece five spaces to the little yellow square marked **100.** I smirked, wriggling gleefully at my victory.

Dominic put his head down on the table, groaning. "Damn that snake! You hear me snake? Damn you!"

I giggled. "I won."

He lifted his head, glaring at me. "I know. I got that."

I grinned wider. "I beat you."

"Remind me why I wanted you to stay?"

I paused, batting my lashes and looking as sweet and innocent as I could. "Because I'm just a lost little girl who needs a fwend?"

He pulled a sarcastic face, his curls falling into his eyes. "Ha, ha. You're lucky you're pretty, or I'd toss you out on your ass." His glare changed to something warmer, and he hitched one eyebrow up a few millimeters.

My mouth had suddenly gone dry. I leaned back in my chair, pressing my lips together anxiously, and Dominic dissolved into laughter, shaking his head.

"Relax, Tilly. I'm kidding," he said, misunderstanding my expression.

I slumped, glaring at him. "You're mean," I stated sulkily.

"Really? Normally, I'm told I'm quite charming." He gave a cute little smile that made his dimple stand out.

I snorted, and he scowled. Then, he sighed, leaned back in his chair, and crossed his arms over his chest. He glanced around the room, looking for something, and his eyes fell on the clock over the sink in the kitchen. It was after eleven at night. I hadn't realised it was so late; no wonder my eyes were starting to get itchy.

"I guess I should get going," Dominic said, sounding none too thrilled about it. Then again, maybe he was just tired.

"Yeah," I muttered, just before I was overtaken by a yawn.

Dominic got up from the table, and I hauled myself out of my chair, stumbling over my feet. He tried not to laugh and failed, chuckling tiredly. Somehow, we both made it to the front door, and Dominic stepped out onto the porch, paused, and turned to say goodnight. He opened his arms wide, and it took my exhaustion addled brain a whole three seconds to work out what he was doing. I smiled and stepped forward, hugging him weakly, and he patted me on the head.

"Goodnight, Tilly."

"Goodnight Dom," I mumbled. I waited until he was at the bottom of the steps, fading away into the darkness, before closing the door and fumbling to lock it. Then I fell into my new bed, made up with soft clean sheets that smelled like mildew and lilacs, and fell asleep fully dressed.

That night—for the first time in days, weeks, maybe months—I slept soundly, without a single nightmare.

** Spencer **

Lying in bed, with his hands folded behind his head on the pillow, Spencer stared at the dull grey ceiling of his bedroom, his mind elsewhere. Actually, his mind was on the cabin he could just barely see through the trees if he looked out the window. He was thinking about Tilly, though he knew he shouldn't have been, but he couldn't help himself.

He'd seen her lights go out a little over an hour ago, and he'd spotted Dominic leaving, and the sight had made something hot and nasty crawl up his throat. It had taken him almost half an hour to identify the feeling as, absurdly, jealously. He was jealous of the time Dominic spent with Tilly, and the realisation of how late it had been before he'd bade Tilly goodnight, left a slightly sick feeling in Spencer's stomach. The idea that maybe Dominic had gotten closer to Tilly than he'd realised, that he and Tilly had been up to something in that cabin, gnawed at him.

Of course, it was natural that he should be jealous. It was in the nature of the wolf inside him to want to fight for the girls of the pack. The problem was that Tilly wasn't in the pack. She wasn't a wolf, wasn't even a remote possibility for a mate, not to mention that relationships with outsiders were strictly prohibited. So he shouldn't have been jealous. If Dominic was getting it on with the new girl, he was risking his own neck. It was no skin off Spencer's nose if Minnie got himself in trouble with daddy alpha. Yet…he was still jealous.

With a growl, Spencer shook his head, trying to dislodge the thoughts from his mind, but other thoughts popped up that weren't any better for him. The way Tilly had stared him down that first night at dinner, her grey eyes steady and unafraid. The paleness of her hair under the moonlight as she'd sat on the bank of the stream with him. The way she'd thrown herself in front of him to save him from being shot by that hunter—so brave and selfless, ready to put herself in the firing line just for a dumb animal that could have eaten her for her attempt at heroism.

Of course, *he* was that dumb animal, and he had enough presence of mind as a wolf to know not to eat people, but she didn't know that. In her mind, she'd saved a wolf. In actual fact, she'd saved Spencer's life, and he couldn't let that slide. Maybe it was time Tilly found out who he was—what he was—so she wouldn't do something so stupid again.

No, he thought, shaking his head again in agitation. He sat up, running a hand through his inky hair. *I can't tell her. Frank would kill me*. His lips twitched at the idea. *Frank would try to kill me*, he corrected. Normally, when a kid said something like that, they didn't mean it literally.

In Spencer's case, it was literal. If he told Tilly about the werewolves, as the alpha, Frank would be duty bound to kill him for it. He doubted Frank would have any issues with that. Spencer had been a thorn in the alpha's side since he'd been dumped on his front step when he was a toddler, but secretly Spencer doubted Frank was capable of killing him, physically. His father was a big man, extremely strong, but he was getting old. Years of Changing and living in the woods were taking their toll on him.

Spencer, while not as big or as strong, was smarter and faster than most of the others. If it hadn't been for Frank's loathing of him, Spencer ought to have been third, maybe even second in command of the pack. Instead, Dominic was the second, and Des was the third. Not that Spencer minded. He liked his position at the bottom of the pack just fine, but it was the principle that annoyed him.

Status doesn't matter to Tilly, and she'd still never choose you over Dominic. She's probably already drawing hearts around his name and daydreaming about his stupid dimpled grin. Spencer frowned. He didn't usually dislike his half-brothers as much as he disdained everyone else, but at the moment, he kind of hated Dominic for being so bloody likeable. The irony of that didn't escape him.

Heaving a sigh of frustration, Spencer rolled out of bed and went to push up his window, letting in the cool night air. The fragrance of something purely night time, like moonlight and shadows made tangible, wafted into the room. He took a deep breath of it, letting it work through his body to soothe his claustrophobic wolf. The animal inside him rumbled appreciatively, stretching languorously as it woke up. His wolf wanted to run, to be out in that night air, hunting badgers and deer through the bushes

Spencer pushed it down, feeling his skin prickle with the phantom feeling of fur, his muscles rolling pleasurably. He grinned, feeling his teeth grow sharp and long. That was the feeling he loved best, just before a Change, when his body trembled with the desire to be on four legs, and the wolf inside him panted to be released.

Pushing the window open further, he couldn't hold onto the feeling any longer, couldn't hold himself back from the edge of the Change. He grabbed the windowsill and swung himself easily through the open window and out into the cool, dark night. He landed in an easy crouch, sprang up, and started running without even missing a beat. He ran as fast as he could on two legs, hurling himself over roots, vines and logs—laughing wildly as the wolf inside him howled in delight.

The wolf pushed to the surface, and he stumbled, falling to his knees as spasms wracked his body, half-pain and half-pleasure as he turned his mind to Tilly to ignore the sounds of his bones breaking. The adrenaline of the Change was blissful and reckless, and burning through his veins like a drug. The thought of Tilly, a female who was to be fought for and won, coveted and prized, made his wolf purr. His wolf liked her, despite the fact she wasn't one of them,

113

despite the way she always tried to stare him down without knowing she was staring down the wolf and not the boy.

Fur spread over his skin like black oil, soft and warm, his jaw stretched into a muzzle, his nails elongating into claws, and a long brushy tail sprouting from his coccyx. His shorts tore off him, scattered bits of fabric fluttering to the ground like fallen leaves, but he was already running again—kicking up dirt from his hind paws and panting with his tongue lolling out from his jaws.

His furry ears twitched and swivelled, following the sounds of squirrels darting up trees and foxes retreating to their dens to avoid the bigger predator. The moon was a half-coin shining in the black sky, smiling down at him. With a chuffing laugh, Spencer put his head down and ran faster. He moved further and further from his cabin, further from his dad who didn't want him, the pack who didn't accept him, his happy half-brother, and the strange girl with the mysterious magic power to knock a full grown man on his ass. He ran without looking back, and hoped that, someday, he could just keep running and never go back.

Chapter Seven

** Tilly **

It was after noon before I finally hauled my lazy, sleepy butt out of the cosy, cosy bed. The bright sunlight speared into my eyes the second I opened them, because I'd forgotten to close the curtains in the bedroom before I'd tumbled into bed. I rolled out from under the soft blankets, groaning, and somehow found my way to the bathroom, the smooth floorboards cool under my bare feet. At least I'd taken off my shoes and socks at some point.

The bathroom was a small, wooden paneled, white tiled room with cold tile flooring and a maroon bathtub. There was also, much to my disgust, a mirror over the sink. I happened to catch sight of myself in the silvery glass when I looked up from splashing cold water on my face, and nearly scared myself stupid with my own reflection. Not a pretty picture.

"Ugh," I muttered, gazing despairingly at the mirror. For the first time, I saw what a mess I really was. My fair hair was greasy, there were blue smudges under my hazy grey eyes, a small brown-red scar marked the place just at my hairline where I'd hit my head when I rolled down that hill, and there was a fading greenish bruise across my jaw.

Dominic had been flirting with me last night? Was he blind, or just unbelievably kind?

Feeling disgusting and itchy, I stripped and stepped under the showerhead protruding from the wall above the taps. I breathed a sigh of bliss as the hot water washed away the griminess on my skin. A shower had never felt so good in my life. I lathered my hair with shampoo I'd rooted out from the cupboard under the sink, where I'd also found some razors, a toothbrush, and guys' shower gel. I popped the lid on the shower gel, sniffed it, and decided I could live with smelling like a guy. It was better than smelling like dirt and sweat.

I spent far longer in the shower than necessary, reveling in the hot soapy water, and after shaving my legs carefully, I sat down in the bathtub under the spray of the water and meditated, letting the energy of the woods beyond the walls pulse in and clear the foggy hunger headache from my skull.

Once I was dried and dressed in a pair of jeans and a t-shirt from the walk-in wardrobe, I wandered into the living room just as someone knocked on the door. With my damp hair dripping over one shoulder, I took the key from the dining table where I'd left it and unlocked the door. I was unsurprised to see it was Dominic behind the door, grinning at me, his own curly hair looking frayed and damp, as if he too had just stepped out of the shower.

However, I was surprised to see him holding a white plastic bag in his hand. He lifted it up to show me, his grin widening.

"Special delivery. Thought you might want breakfast, or lunch, considering it's now nearly one in the afternoon. You're not exactly an early bird," he commented, nudging past me into the cabin.

I laughed, closing the door behind him, and he dumped the plastic bag on the counter in the kitchen. He turned and flashed a charming smile at me.

"By the way, you smell like a guy. Is it weird that I like it?"

I couldn't tell if he was kidding or not, so I ignored his comment and stalked over to see what he'd brought in the plastic bag. I leaned my elbows on the breakfast bar as Dominic pulled things out of the bag and spread them on the countertop. A carton of eggs, tomatoes, a bottle of milk, a tub of butter, a bottle of orange juice, a box of Choco Pops, and of course, a pack of salty bacon rashers. Always with the meat. My mouth started watering just looking at the food lined up in front of me. Dominic, noticing my awed expression and laughed.

"Oh my God...Dominic, I love you," I said dramatically, hoping he didn't take it the wrong way.

Predictably, he didn't. He just beamed wider and flipped open the egg box, pulling out two eggs. "Baby, you only think you love me. You *will* love me once you've tasted my scrambled eggs."

With a flick of his wrist, he tossed one of the eggs into the air, and I gasped as it soared back down, but he caught it lightly and held both eggs in one hand while he rooted around for a frying pan. I took a seat on one of the tall chairs behind the breakfast bar and watched in fascination as he moved around the kitchen, finding various pieces of kitchenware and preparing food with half-absent motions, all while chatting to me about his disastrous trip to the store with Kat.

117

"…and then the kid started screaming, and his mother tried to calm him down, but the brat just wouldn't shut up. When she tried to give him his bottle, he shook it and squirted it everywhere, and I, the innocent bystander, got soaked in baby milk. The mum, of course, got upset and tried to apologise to me, but I just walked up to the kid in the trolley and growled at him, and he shut right up. Dropped his bottle onto the floor, so I picked it up and handed it to the mother, and she was like, 'Oh my God, thank you! I haven't been able to get him to settle all day.' I just shrugged and walked away, but it's hard to look cool and heroic when you're dripping milk from your hair," he explained, his eyes on the tomato he was chopping.

I sipped the orange juice he'd poured, smiling bemusedly while he cooked. It felt strange to have someone else cooking for me like that, in a pleasant, friendly setting. Normally, when *they* cooked for me, *they* just thrust a plate into my room and came back to collect it an hour later.

Tearing my mind away from dark thoughts, I refocused on the cute boy making me breakfast in the sunlit cabin, and the delicious smell of bacon frying next to the tomato slices under the grill making my stomach rumble. The golden light coming in through the windows caught in Dominic's curls, turning the strands a bright red-brown. His dimple flashed when he caught me staring at him, my chin resting on my palm.

"Admiring, are we, Miss Tilly?" he said, half-turning from the pan of scrambled eggs.

I tilted my head. "Maybe. Actually, I was just thinking that I've never had a boy make me breakfast before. It's a new experience. I like it."

Dominic flicked me a look under his lashes as he poured the scrambled eggs onto a plate, and I realised I was flirting with him. I blushed, ducking my head. I didn't mean to flirt, I didn't want to give him the wrong impression. He was just so easy to be around, and I hadn't spent enough time around guys to know how to act with them. Hopefully, he'd understand I was just playing about.

I was already in so much trouble without adding a possible boyfriend to the mix, especially since I knew I couldn't stay there forever. At some point, I'd have to move on. The thought made my chest constrict painfully, as if I'd been punched, so I shoved the idea aside brutally. I wouldn't think about it right then.

Dominic slid a plate in front of me, and I inhaled the warm scent of the scrambled eggs, crispy bacon, and grilled tomatoes. Scooping up the first bite of scrambled eggs, I chewed while he grabbed a plate for himself, piled food onto it, and stood at the counter to eat it.

Swallowing the eggs, I looked at him and said, "You were right, Dom. I love you. And you are totally making me breakfast every morning from now on."

He just beamed at me, and I smiled back, thinking that when I did leave, I was going to miss him most of all.

When I woke up in my dark room that night, I didn't know if I had been woken by a nightmare or the stifling heat. I groaned, feeling sweat on my skin, and rolled over to stare at the ceiling, rubbing at my eyes. I glanced at the clock on the nightstand, and its little glow in the dark hands told me it was almost four am. I'd only been asleep for a few hours, but once I was awake, I wasn't tired enough to go straight back to sleep. I tried, though, pulling off my t-shirt and socks and closing my eyes, I was still too hot. I tossed and turned for a few minutes, before giving up. I sighed, sitting up, and went to the bathroom to grab a glass of water. Even after drinking the whole glass in one go, I was still roasting. I didn't know what else to do, so I went to the walk-in wardrobe and found a clean t-shirt, pulled it on and retrieved my trainers from the front door.

Once I had the key in my hand, I remembered Dominic's serious warning not to go out at night, no matter what, but Dominic didn't know about my power. He thought I was a harmless little human girl, and I wasn't. Whatever was out there, I could handle it. Even if that black wolf came back for me, I was pretty sure I could take it. I just couldn't stay in the cloying heat of the cabin anymore. I shoved the key in the lock, twisted, and heard it click open. I stepped out into the wonderful crisp chill of the night air and sighed in relief as it slid over my overheated, damp skin.

Locking the door and tucking the key into my bra, I loped down the steps as quietly as possible. I watched for the light of Dominic's cabin, but the woods were dark and still. The quiet was broken only by the gentle *who-who?* of the owl, and the whisper of the breeze through the boughs of the trees. I couldn't hear the babble of the stream and didn't know which direction it was from there, but I decided to look for it anyway. I imagined the feel of the cold water flowing over my skin, and I started walking, brushing the strands of pale hair that flew into my eyes back behind my ears.

As I walked, the soft dirt muted my footsteps, and I avoided the twigs and crispier leaves. I wandered, directionless, but with a target in mind, somehow instinctively knowing where to go. Soon enough, I heard the pattering rhythm of the stream bubbling over rocks, and I moved faster, catching my hair in branches and my jeans on bushes, but I didn't care. I just wanted to get to the stream and feel the water, listen to it so it could wash away the dark worries as I thought.

When I reached the water, I saw I wasn't alone. I was unsurprised to see Spencer there at the stream. The slight tightening in his posture said he knew I was there, but he didn't look up.

He did, however, speak. "Couldn't sleep again, Tilly?" he asked with just a hint of mocking in his voice.

It banished my nervousness, and I stepped forward, joining him next to the stream. I sat down in the grass, hesitating only a moment before beginning to unlace my trainers. "Too hot. Thought I'd get some fresh air," I said as curtly as I could, setting my trainers aside with unnecessary care and then sliding off my socks.

He was looking at me, and I felt oddly exposed, as if I'd taken off my t-shirt instead of just my socks. Unnerved, I rolled up the hems of my jeans and plunged my feet into the water. The shock of the icy water enveloping my feet up to the ankles made me gasp, but I swallowed it, and the smooth water flowing over my toes began to soothe the uncomfortable heat on my skin. I sighed in relief.

"Hmm…me too. It's definitely warm tonight," Spencer said, tipping his head back to the sky, a smile curving his mouth.

I shrugged casually, and murmured, "I guess so." I splashed my feet in the water a little, watching the waves ripple out around my ankles.

Spencer glanced at me, blue eyes flashing and his smile widening, as if I'd said something funny.

I scowled at him, confused. "What's so funny?" I mumbled, unnerved. I didn't know what it was, but something about him just threw me off balance, even when he wasn't saying anything. I tried not to notice that he actually had a really nice smile, when he did deign to use his mouth for something other than pouting or snarky remarks.

His t-shirt was dark green, rather than black, and again he wasn't wearing shoes. He sat on the grass with his legs folded, leaning back on his hands. My eyes automatically traced the curve of his body, and he noticed, his eyes flicking over my body in return.

"What's funny is that I can't tell if you genuinely hate me, or if you're just pretending. It's…" He paused, searching for the right word.

"Annoying?" I pitched unhelpfully, giving him a bland smile.

His brow furrowed, and he shook his head. His eyes caught the glint of the water. "I was going to say *unnerving*. I'm normally pretty good at reading people, but you…you I don't understand," he said it while looking at me as if I were a puzzle he couldn't quite put together, but he sounded like it surprised him that he couldn't figure me out.

I was glad he couldn't. I doubted he'd be so calm and composed if he knew I could raise demons and knock full-grown men on their asses. Once again, I shrugged casually, thinking of the irony. He thought I was unsettling, yet he was the most unsettling person I'd ever met, and that included the witches.

The witches were scary and cruel, but I knew where I stood with them—I was dirt. With Spencer, I had no idea if he hated me, scorned me, liked me, or anything. He barely spoke to me. I never saw him during the day, but for some reason, I kept finding him there at the stream. I didn't mean to look for him, my feet just sort of took me to him.

"You're not good at listening to advice, are you?" Spencer said abruptly.

I turned to glare at him. He just seemed more amused by my glower than anything else. I kind of wanted to hit him—again.

Curling my fingers into the grass, I asked in a sharp tone, "What do you mean?"

He tilted his head again, blinked, his eyes strangely flat for a second, like the stare of an animal considering whether something in front of it was prey. I swallowed nervously. I really didn't want to become this guy's prey—whatever that would entail.

"Well, both Dominic and I have warned you that it's dangerous to be out here at night by yourself, and yet here you are. Again." He waved a hand toward me in a sweeping gesture, his expression an odd mix of curiosity and exasperation. At least he didn't look irritated. That was a mild improvement.

I lifted my chin, kicking at the water a little viciously and soaking the hems of my jeans. "And I told you, twice now, that I can handle myself. Also, I'd just like to point out that I'm not alone. You're here…for whatever that's worth." I tacked on the last bit under my breath, but I suspected he heard it anyway. He didn't comment on it, though. His face lost all its humour, and I thought I'd managed to annoy him again after all.

In a low voice, he said, "How do you know I'm not what you need protecting from?" His eyes were steady on my face, but I couldn't meet his gaze.

"I don't," I said quietly.

My answer seemed to please him in some obscure way, and he smiled slightly, nodding as he turned his gaze back out to the twinkling stream. "Good. Keep that in mind, Tilly."

I wanted to ask what he meant by that, suddenly a little scared, but a breeze swept past us, raising goose bumps on my arms and lifting the hair around Spencer's face. He abruptly went still and as tense as a rabbit in the sights of a hunting dog. I saw his throat move as he swallowed, and suddenly he was on his feet, so quick I hardly even saw him move.

He seemed to remember I was still there, looked down at me for a second, his eyes hidden by his hair flopping forward. "I have to go. You should go back to your cabin. Now," he said tersely, barking out the words like a command. Then he turned and ran into the trees, eerily fast and silent, blending into the shadows like smoke.

Startled by his sudden departure, and most definitely annoyed by his command, I stubbornly stayed exactly where I was. I did take my feet out of the water, though, because I was shivering, and I didn't think it was just because of the cold water or the breeze. Distantly, I wondered if I was actually scared of Spencer. At what point did unsettled turn into scared? Where was the line in the sand that separated one from the other? Was it before, or after, a guy subtly threatened you?

How do you know I'm not the one you need protecting from? If anyone else had said it, I would have thought they were flirting. When Spencer had said it, it had sounded like a threat. Maybe it had just been his dark voice, and the way his eyes had glinted when he'd said it. Maybe he'd thought he was being alluring and had just failed. I doubted it. Spencer struck me as the kind of guy who knew exactly how to seduce a girl.

I shook my head, mentally smacking myself for even thinking about it. It was stupid. I didn't even like the guy, and if I really was scared of him, how could I possibly be attracted to him? Plus, just like with Dominic, I knew a relationship would be a bad idea, almost impossible, since I was leaving eventually.

Yes, I told myself sternly, *I am going to leave...just not yet. Not quite yet.* And anyway, if I was going to even consider a relationship with any of those boys, it should be with Dominic. It *would* be with Dom. Again, it was pointless, because I was *leaving*.

Fed up with my own frustrating, circling thoughts and quite cold, I wrestled my socks onto my damp feet, shoved on my trainers without bothering to lace them properly, and stood up to brush grass off my jeans. I heaved a sigh and walked back into the trees, hoping I could remember the way back to my cabin. I hadn't been paying attention to which direction I'd taken I was regretting that as I wandered between spidery branches and clumps of waving ferns, trying to recognise something familiar in the gnarled trunk of a beech tree or the half-crumbled log lying on the ground next to a patch of sleepily drooping snowdrops.

Just when I was starting to think I really was lost, I heard something that made my panic level rocket up several notches. A growl. The low, guttural growl of a large animal, like, oh I don't know…a wolf? My heart jammed into high gear, pounding like the hooves of a racehorse on the track, and I froze. Around me, the woods had gone even more silent than before, and even the muted hooting of the owl had ceased. My eyes roamed the darkness, looking for a slinking shape or crouching shadow. I heard the growl again, ending in a high whine, as if the creature was in pain, and I realised the sound wasn't as close as I'd first thought.

Before I knew what I was doing, I was running through the trees, feeling ferns and branches whip at my arms and legs. I had a sickening flash of déjà vu from the night I'd run away from the witches. Terror slamming into my ribs and tears slicking my face, I pumped my legs desperately to get as far away as I could as fast as I could.

The howl of the wolf sent chills skittering up my spine, and brought me back to the present with a jarring jerk. I pushed leaves out of my way, twigs scratching my palms, and I realised I wasn't running away from the howling—but toward it. The wolf was in pain. I had to help it. Somehow, I knew, I just *knew*, it was the black wolf. The wolf I'd saved from the hunter the other day, and I had to save it.

Up ahead, I saw a flash of light and a snarl erupted through the trees. I picked up my pace, bolting into a small clearing and nearly slamming into the midnight black wolf, hunched low against the ground in an aggressive, tightly coiled crouch. The wolf was so dark, I hadn't even seen it until its brushy tail whacked against my legs as I burst into the clearing. I squealed and skidded to halt, stumbled back a couple of steps.

The wolf—my wolf—jerked its head around as I bumped into its swishing tail. Its golden eyes fixed on me with what could have been surprise, if wolves could express surprise. It didn't look hurt, but a slight shifting on the other side of the clearing, made its head snapped back around.

It bared its teeth at the figure that I hadn't noticed before, its snarl ripping through the calm night air. Swallowing my racing heart, I lifted my eyes to the person the wolf was growling at…and nearly turned to run again as the copper taste of terror rose on my tongue. Unfortunately, fear paralysed me, tightening my muscles like the strings of a guitar, until they were so tight, I was shaking.

My teeth ground together hard enough that I thought my jaw might shatter, and my skin ran with goose bumps.

Oh God, Oh God no, please no, I begged silently, tears springing to my eyes reflexively. I breathed in short, choppy gasps that verged on hyperventilation, but I couldn't tear my eyes away from the woman on the other side of the clearing.

She was tall and slim, with frost pale hair even lighter than mine, a sharp feline face, and glass green eyes. In most peoples' opinions, she would be seen as beautiful, but I knew better. Just under that flawless skin and angular face, there was a soul as black and viscous as tar.

In my eyes, she was ugly, hideous. She was a merciless smile, a slapping hand, and a whip sharp voice of command. A nightmare. My nightmare, or at least one of them. Her pale green eyes fixed on me, cold and vicious, and her rosy lips parted in a deceptively enchanting smile. A flare of triumph showed on her face, and I swallowed, every cell of my body pulling at me, telling me to run. I wanted to, but my feet were rooted to the spot, and I knew she knew it.

Her voice, almost a whisper, sent ice into my bones as she said, "Hello Matilda."

Chapter Eight

** Tilly **

At the sound of my full name coming from her lips, I flashed back to the hundreds of times she'd said it before. The times she'd commanded me, berated me, threatened me, and taunted me. Always calling me by my full name, knowing how much I disliked it. I could feel her magic, prickling and icy, slithering along mine, searching for a way into my head and into my will. The feeling made me nauseous, made me want to fall to the ground and retch, but I locked my knees and held her malicious gaze, while she tried to break me down into pieces she could cart off.

Through the tightness of fear clotting in my throat, I choked out in a rasping voice, "Hello Olivia."

The woman who had adopted me when I was six stared back at me with savage delight, while the wolf between us continued to bare its fangs. It was no longer snarling, but its hackles were raised and its ears flattened back against its skull, and I prayed it stayed where it was. I felt safer with my wolf there, confident that it wouldn't attack me. After all, Olivia was the greater threat here.

"I see you've found yourself a pet. Nice guard dog. It tried to attack me just before you showed up, and when I smacked it with a Deflection Spell, it just came back for more. Stupid animal, really," Olivia said with a tone of disgust, glaring at the wolf. She shook back her perfectly straight blonde hair and planted her hands on her hips, returning her gaze to me. "Maybe not as stupid as you, though, Matilda. You shouldn't have come to rescue your little pet dog, but then you've always been too softhearted when it comes to animals." She sighed.

I couldn't think of anything to say, so I kept my mouth shut and my eyes on her, waiting for her to strike.

Seeing that I wasn't going anywhere, she took a step forward, and my wolf growled at her again, a sound so rough and loud it made my ribs rattle. Olivia pursed her lips, eyes narrowing at the wolf, and the growl cut off in a whine. I didn't know what she was doing to it, but the sound of the wolf's whimpering unthawed me from my fear enough to drop to my knees next to it. I threw my arms around the animal's neck, pressing my shields out and encompassing the wolf in the warding that had protected me so far. I knew it wouldn't hold up for long, not when the witch was so close. I lifted my head to glare at the woman, who was smirking thinly as if my show of affection for the wolf were both amusing and contemptible to her.

"Stop it! Leave the wolf alone!" I snapped, the words leaving my mouth before I could stop them. Being away from her influence and the influence of the birch cane had made me careless and mouthy, and I waited for the sting of a slap that never came. Olivia stayed on the other side of the clearing, but the wolf stopped whining, its sides throbbing as it panted.

With shaky legs, I got to my feet again, my fingers knotted in the wolf's silky black fur for support. Emboldened by the fact that she hadn't yet crushed me or Cursed me, I glared at the cruel woman. "I'm not coming back. I am never coming back. I won't be your slave anymore. I'd die first!" I yelled, my heart beating in my throat, and my stomach jammed into my mouth.

I was shaking all over, but I'd meant what I'd said. I couldn't go back to being a witch's tool, sinking my soul further into the depths of the Underworld with every demon I summoned, feeling the burning pain of a demon sucking at my mind and power. I shuddered.

Olivia tilted her head to the side, her smile turning patronizing. I ground my teeth. I hated that smile so much. It was the smile she'd used every time I threatened to run away, warned her I'd get revenge one day for all the pain she and her sisters had put me through, and every time I'd told her I'd kill them all.

Every time, she smiled like that—like I was a child throwing a tantrum—she'd locked me in the Dark Room. Not just to punish me, but to weaken me, because we both knew I could do it. I could kill her if I got angry enough, if I ever let my temper truly get the better of me. If my power ever consumed me, I could do terrible things, and I might never find my way back to who I really was. While there was Light in me, the part that let me feel the gentle energy of the woods and use it to protect myself, there was another part that was Dark, the part that allowed me to summon demons. The Dark part of me relished the idea of killing the bitch in front of me, but the Light part shivered at the thought of killing anyone or anything and shrunk from the idea of letting my temper control me—making me as angry and cold as the women who'd raised me.

I will not be like them. I won't ever be like them, I swore it, over and over in my head, just as I had done for years. I was determined to be better than *them*. I was determined to be good, even if it meant letting *them* live. However, I would not go back to being *their* link to the dark side. I would kill myself rather than be the conduit to allow demons into our world.

"Oh, Matilda, did you really think you could hide forever? Did you really think we wouldn't find you? And now, do you think I'm just going to let you go? You won't kill yourself, and we both know it. So why don't you just come with me now, and you won't even be punished. My sisters will be very glad to have you back, and we can forget this ever happened," Olivia said sweetly.

I stared at her in disbelief and laughed out loud, bitter and cold. Olivia's green eyes widened in surprise, her mouth thinning to a hard line.

I looked her in the eyes, and I said, "Go to hell, Olivia, and take your bitch sisters with you. I'm not your little slave girl anymore. I'm free."

Olivia's eyes narrowed to slits, and I knew a second before she moved what she was going to do. A flare of light burst out from her fingers, electric and snapping, enough power to paralyze but not kill. She lifted her arms, ready to throw it at me, and I sucked in air, my chest constricting. I couldn't move fast enough to get out of the way of the blast, and if it hit me, it would all be over.

She would drag me back to the manor and make sure I couldn't kill myself. She'd cuff me to my bed, have one of her sisters watching me at all times, and she'd drug me to keep me docile. She'd done it before. I'd be helpless, trapped in a living body, but not really alive. The vision of it all passed before my eyes in the split second before Olivia swung her arms forward and launched the glowing magic straight at me.

I stood, already paralysed by fear, as the light hurtled toward my face. It shone blindingly bright, but I couldn't look away, couldn't even blink. I tensed for the impact of all that power slamming into me...and then, I felt something else crash into me from the side, knocking me down at the very last moment. The flare of power shot right past me, so close that it fried the ends of my hair as I was flung aside by a wall of fur and flesh slamming into my hip. I hit the ground hard, scraping my right arm from wrist to elbow, my head smacking into the dirt hard enough that I saw stars for a moment. My teeth clamped on my tongue, and I tasted blood, making me gag. Pain burst behind my eyelids, and I lost my breath.

Above me, the wolf was growling ferociously. I heard Olivia hiss a curse at the beast, heard her footsteps crunching as she tried to run, but the wolf pounced. Regaining my sight through the haze of stars, I saw it leap off me and fly through the air toward her. A slick shadow against the sky, it disappeared into the trees. The sound of growling and snapping jaws faded, and I was left lying on the ground with agony hammering through my skull and a burning in my arm. But I was alive. I'd have some bruises, but I was more or less okay.

I sat up slowly, swallowing the wave of nausea and dizziness, and pulled myself to my feet carefully. Gasping and trembling, my hair falling in tangles into my eyes, I clutched my sore arm to my chest and turned away from the clearing. I was halfway back to my cabin when the tears came, blurring my vision and making it impossible to see where I was going. It didn't matter, because I could see lights ahead of me. The commotion had woken people, and I could hear voices calling into the darkness, most of them shouting for Spencer. At the time, I was too tired and scared to find it strange that they would automatically think it was Spencer in trouble. I slipped through the trees around the edge of the lights, creeping through the branches as quietly as I could, and I made it to my cabin unseen.

Trancelike, I pulled the key out of my bra, and tried three times before finally getting it into the lock. Once inside, I closed the door and locked it, put the key back on the dining table and kicked off my shoes. I shuffled to the back of the cabin, found a first aid kit under the sink in the bathroom, and cleaned the dirt from the scrapes up my right arm. I sprayed the raw skin with antibacterial stuff, taped it up with gauze, and returned the first aid kit to the bathroom. I undressed mechanically and slid into the bed in my underwear, pulled the duvet over my head, curled my knees to my chest, and cried myself to sleep.

** Spencer **

Furious, Spencer snarled, teeth snapping, as he lunged after the witch. He dove through the trees and over rocks and roots, even as the roots reared up like living vines to trip him or snag his paws, and rocks lifted from the ground and pelted him. The jagged edges of the stones bruised his sides and clattered against his legs and thorny bramble bushes caught his fur and tore it painfully as he ran, but he kept going. Growling and gnashing, his paws thudded rapidly on the dirt.

The wolf was slathering, thirsting for the blood of the woman who'd dared to harm his female. It didn't matter that Tilly wasn't really his, not in the least, or that she wasn't even a wolf. His wolf had decided she was his, and therefore, he had to protect her. The woman, the witch, was an outsider threatening what was his, and he wanted to rip her apart and tear her flesh from her bones. The thought might have made Spencer recoil in his human form, but then again, maybe not. In his wolf form, he enjoyed the hunt, the chase, the pounding of his paws on the ground and the working of his muscles pumping, the phantom taste of blood already on his tongue and teeth.

A root lashed at his side, opening a small slice in the skin under his fur, and his growl stuttered, but his stride didn't. Only when rocks began flying into his eyes did he start to slow, but he was still bent on blood, seeing the agile figure of the fleeing witch weaving through the darkness ahead of him. He could smell her terror from there, on the wind, the acrid stench of fear like that of rotting meat and fungus. The scent filled his nostrils as they flared, and he barked, a savage sound of delight. He was catching up to his prey, but still she was somehow ahead of him, rocks and roots slowing him down. She shouldn't have been that fast.

With another bark, one more of frustration, he shook his head and launched himself over a small ditch. It was small enough that the witch had jumped it nimbly, but he pushed off with his powerful hind legs and threw himself through the air, soaring toward his target. And There was a flash of light, bright and blinding as a star in the darkness under the trees' leafy boughs, and a weight slammed into his chest, wringing a breathless, startled yelp of pain from his jaws.

He hit the ground hard and awkwardly, blind from the flash, and rolled across the dirt before finally coming to a stop. He scrambled to get up, twisting to get his legs under him, but by the time he regained his footing, the witch was already gone. Vanished, no doubt some magical witchy trick. Spencer bristled from head to tail, growling his frustration and anger that his prey had escaped.

Instinct told him to go back to Tilly. He'd just left her in the clearing, and he wasn't sure if she'd been hurt or not. He had to go back and check, he had to protect her. Watch over her if he could, in case the damn witch came back, but he couldn't go to Tilly in that form.

Slicing his tail through the air, Spencer stretched out his paws, feeling his muscles burn and his fur rippling, waiting for the surge of adrenaline that would allow him to Change, but it never came. He shuddered, rolling his ears back and forth uneasily, but nothing happened. His body stayed wolf. The witch had done something to him. She'd spelled him, and he couldn't Change back.

For how long? Forever?

Normally, the thought would have excited him, at least for a while, because he loved being a wolf. But he had to see Tilly, and while she was recklessly stupid about getting close to the big black wolf when she was scared of other things, he wasn't sure she'd be so willing to throw her arms around his neck when he went stalking around her cabin on lookout duty.

The brief, very human image of Tilly throwing her arms around his neck if he walked up to her cabin door in human form made him shudder again, but in a different way. The image was gone as quickly as it came, imagination like that being strange to the wolf brain. But he still knew he had to Change back, and he couldn't. He barked in anger at what the witch had done to him, at his own failure to kill her. There was nothing he could do, except make sure Tilly was safely in her cabin. He could do that without being seen, at least.

Slinking through the trees, Spencer snapped at every creature that dared to stray across his path, from an innocent little squirrel, to a brown hedgehog that curled up into a tight, prickly ball. When he arrived at Tilly's cabin, he carefully stuck low to the ground, keeping in the shadows, and got right up to the cabin wall under one

137

of the windows. He didn't know which room was her bedroom, so he had to try three times before he found the right window. He knew instantly that it was the right one, because he could hear crying coming from inside. His wolf wanted to growl, fearing she might be hurt or scared, but he kept it silent.

Instinct warred with the little human logic he retained in that form while he paced outside the window. The human part of him wanted to go in and comfort her, maybe hold her, but his wolf wanted to stay there and patrol her cabin. Since he couldn't exactly knock on the door with his paws, he settled for staying under the window, laying his head on his paws. The moon was still hanging high in the sky, but it didn't seem inviting, it was frowning down on him sympathetically. Annoyed, he turned away from it and listened to Tilly's sobbing until it faded, and he knew she was asleep just beyond the glass.

** Tilly **

The next morning, I felt steadier. So Olivia knew where I was. The fact that she'd come alone made me hopeful that she hadn't told the others yet. While I was in the shower, being hopeful, I imagined my wolf had caught up to Olivia before she could get back to her sisters. A not so little part of me hoped the wolf had torn her apart. I had faced the woman who had been in charge of my imprisonment and torture, and I had come away alive, with my soul intact. I hadn't let

138

my temper, my Darkness, win. I hadn't killed her. I could only hope the wolf had done it for me.

Still, being alive was a small victory. Maybe Olivia had come alone because she hadn't bet on me being so difficult. Maybe she'd thought she could just zap me and bring me back to her sisters. If the others knew where I was, they'd be coming soon, and even my wolf couldn't protect me then. I wouldn't be able to protect myself. If the others knew where I was, even leaving right that minute wouldn't protect those around me. I'd possibly just sentenced them all to death, but until the witches came, I had to act normal.

I made an omelet for breakfast, poured myself a glass of orange juice, and was trying to convince my nervous stomach it needed food, when Dominic knocked on the door of my cabin. I glanced at the clock, surprised he was already up. It was only a little after eight in the morning.

I called to the door, "Come in."

The door groaned open and Dominic's curly head poked around it, grinning. His grin dropped though when his eyes fell on the bandage covering my right arm from wrist to elbow. His eyes widened in concern, and he let the door close behind him as he rushed over to the dining table.

"Tilly, what happened? Are you okay?" He came around the table and reached for my arm.

I shook him off. "I'm fine. I just fell in the shower, cut my arm on a razor." I shrugged, mildly surprised at how easy and natural the lie sounded on my lips. I barely tasted the omelet as I scooped the last bit into my mouth and got up from the table, shooing Dominic out of the way. I walked over to the kitchen, dumped my plate and fork into the sink, and glanced at him over my shoulder. "You want anything? I can cook up another omelet in a heartbeat, if you want."

Dominic shook his head, his eyes still on my arm. He'd gone a little pale, and his mouth was pressed into a line. His throat moved as he swallowed, his hand absently reaching up to tug on a curl.

"No, it's okay. I already ate. You fell in the shower? Are you sure you're okay? Maybe I should take a look, make sure—"

"No," I snapped, a little too sharply.

Dominic's mouth tightened further, his eyes flicking up to my face. I shook my head, sighing.

More softly, I said, "No, it's fine. I'm fine. It wasn't deep. I just don't want to get any dirt in the cut or anything." He still looked pensive, unconvinced, so I strolled over to him and put a hand on his arm. I smiled at him. "But thank you for asking anyway. I'm sure your first aid skills are as good as your cooking. If I break a leg or something, you'll be the first to know." I felt bad, flirting with him to distract him.

He still didn't look entirely convinced, but he let it go. He smiled back at me, and tipped his chin up. "Well, I am an exceptional cook," he said.

I laughed, glad we were changing the subject, and rolled my eyes. "You're also humble," I muttered sarcastically, turning the taps so hot water began to fill the plastic basin in the sink.

Dominic nodded haughtily. "Just another of my awesome traits," he said. "Right alongside being a total gentleman, whose willing to do the dishes for you." He came around to the sink, grabbed a dishtowel, and tossed it to me, rolling up the long sleeves of his dark blue t-shirt.

I shook my head. "I can do it. It's okay."

He hip bumped me away from the sink, grinning, and nodded pointedly toward my bandaged arm as he picked up the bottle of green washing up liquid and squirted it into the basin, covering my plate and glasses in bubbly green slime. "You'll soak your bandage. I'll wash, and you can dry." He turned off the taps, snagged a cloth, and plunged his hands into the soapy hot water.

I sighed and leaned against the countertop, eyeing him as he scrubbed the dishes. His chestnut curls were falling carelessly over his brow, brushing the tops of his high cheekbones, and I noticed how fair his skin was in the early morning light. The muscles of his forearms swelled as he splashed his hands about in the bubbly water, totally relaxed and casual in ragged jeans and an oversized t-shirt. His eyes flashed toward me and back to the frothy plate he was swiping at with the cloth. His dimple flickered as he tried not to smile.

A faint sweep of pink touched his cheekbones and he hunched his shoulders uncomfortably. "You're staring at me again," he observed, handing over a dripping plate without looking at me.

I took it carefully, began rubbing the dishtowel over it, and shrugged. "I wouldn't say I was staring per se…" I knew I'd been staring. I really had to learn not to do that. But I just occasionally got glimpses of him at certain angles, or in certain lights, that reminded me he was actually really cute. Not devastatingly attractive like Spencer was, but certainly cute enough.

He smiled again, his shoulders loosening. "You were totally staring. Is there something you want to tell me, Tilly?" he asked playfully, his smile turning mischievous.

I felt a flutter deep in my stomach and nearly dropped the plate I was drying. *Whoa.* I blinked, surprised by the feeling in my gut, and doubly surprised that *Dominic* had caused it. He glanced at me sideways as I fumbled with the plate, his eyebrows rising a millimeter or two, and I felt my cheeks heat up. I bit my lip, putting the thoroughly dried plate down on the countertop with undue care just as Dominic handed me a glass. His fingers brushed mine as I took it, and the fluttery feeling came back. The slippery glass slid from my suddenly trembling fingers, and I gasped. With amazing reflexes, Dominic's hand shot out and caught it. He didn't even look. His eyes were still on my face, which was flaming.

Confused by the butterflies in my stomach, I pulled my hand back slowly, staring at my fingers as if I'd never seen them before. "Sorry," I muttered, scrunching the dishtowel in my hands. I kept my eyes on my bare toes, not able to force myself to look at him quite yet, but I heard him put down the glass.

"Don't be," he said quietly, and I looked up.

I clamped down on another gasp. He was closer than I'd realised, just inches away, and his green eyes were glowing with a warmth that made the butterflies in my stomach turn into bats. He was so close, I could smell the scent of leaves and soap on his skin, the sharp tang of oranges from his shampoo.

"Huh?" I squeaked, wincing internally at how stupid I sounded.

Dominic's mouth tilted up, but there was no cute dimple. He didn't look cute anymore. He looked…he looked more like Spencer. I could see the features they shared, the features their father had given them, in the slope of his nose and the shape of his eyebrows, in the way his lashes shadowed his eyes as he lowered them to look down at me.

Dominic lifted a hand, his fingers brushing mine where I was clamping the dishtowel hard enough to tear it in half. I tried to take a deep breath as a slow heat spread from my fingers along my arm and down into my stomach, but the air tasted like fresh ferns, oranges and something far more intangible.

"I meant, don't be sorry," he said, his voice husky as his fingertips trailed up my un-bandaged arm.

It took my hazed, distracted mind far too long to work out he was talking about the glass…or maybe he wasn't. From the look on his face, I couldn't be sure.

I realised he'd moved us without me even noticing. My back was against the edge of the counter, and he had one hand braced against the edge of the sink, blocking me in on one side, while his other hand continued to glide up my arm. My heart pounded in an unfamiliar rhythm, not with fear or exertion.

143

Dominic's fingertips slid up over my shoulder, up the curve of my neck, and rested against my jaw, tipping my face up a little. My eyes went to his mouth, and his lips twitched in response. His body was barely an inch from mine, leaning over me, my chest brushing his with every rapid breath I took.

I knew he was going to kiss me, and I was filled with equal parts longing and anxiety. It was Dominic for God's sake, my *friend*. I didn't like him that way…did I? How would I know? I'd never even had a crush before, but maybe that's what the nervous warmth jittering through my gut was.

Dominic started to bend his head to mine, leaning in so his body pressed against mine from hip to chest, and I closed my eyes, lifting my chin instinctively. I felt the ghost of his breath on my lips, then the light pressure of his mouth just barely touching mine. A soft spark clicked in my stomach, a shudder rolling through my spine as my lips parted, trailing in a shaking breath. The hand he'd been holding the sink with came up and pressed flat against the small of my back, holding me to him. The pressure of his mouth increased, still chaste but testing, asking permission for more.

I don't know whether or not I would have granted him permission, because just at that moment, the door to the cabin burst open and we sprang apart. As I jerked away, my elbow caught the glass Dominic had set down on the counter and knocked it to the floor. This time, his reflexes weren't quite fast enough to snag it before it smashed into wet, sudsy shards on the wooden floorboards. I guessed he was just as dazed as I was, but he recovered faster than

I did, spinning around to see who had intruded onto our moment so violently.

Blushing, I raised my gaze to see Desmond, thin-lipped and unhappy, standing in the doorway with one hand on the handle. His eyes were narrowed on his brother, but his wavy hair was windblown, and his clothes were slightly rumpled, as if he'd been running through the trees to get to us.

The two boys stared at each other, Des glaring and Dominic innocently, and I got the feeling they were having some sort of silent discussion I wasn't a part of. Seeing that they weren't going to loop me into the conversation, I cleared my throat. Desmond glanced at me and frowned, a line of embarrassment forming around his mouth. He looked back to his brother as if he couldn't stand to meet my gaze.

"Dom, have you seen Spencer? He's missing again, and after last night, we think he might be—" Desmond shot me another glance and jerked his head toward the door. "Can we talk outside?" he asked his brother in a vaguely pleading voice.

I blinked, offended that he would come bursting into my cabin without knocking, interrupting me and Dominic, and then try to exclude me from whatever he'd burst in to say.

Irked, I put my hands and my hips and glared at him. "So Spencer's gone again, huh? Anybody check by the stream, 'cause he seems to end up there a lot." Actually, I was a lot more worried than I sounded. Desmond had mentioned something had happened. I knew what, but I didn't see how it would relate to Spencer being

145

gone, unless he'd run into Olivia before I had. Olivia wouldn't have hurt him unless he gave her reason, though, so maybe Spencer's disappearance was totally unrelated—just Spencer being Spencer. But what if it wasn't? What if he'd run into Olivia, and she'd done something to him? What if she'd—no, she wouldn't have killed him. I hoped.

Desmond made a noise of either irritation or shame, and his eyebrows tilted up. He looked beseechingly at Dominic, who was standing with his arms crossed and his sleeves still rolled up, though he'd dried his hands. He looked concerned, and his lips pressed thin.

"Dom, please?" Des jerked his head toward the door again.

I resisted the urge to snap at him.

After a second of consideration, Dominic glanced at me apologetically and nodded briskly. "Sorry, Tilly. I'll talk to you later, okay?"

I didn't reply, but Dominic nodded to himself as he and Desmond left, shutting the door on their way out.

Once they were gone, I let out a deep, uneasy breath and leaned forward, clutching the edge of the counter opposite me. With a groan, I laid my head down on the cool countertop and folded my hands over the back of my skull, grasping handfuls of hair between my tense fingers.

"Damn!" I spat, not sure if I was cursing about Dominic kissing me, or the possibility that Spencer was missing because he'd run into Olivia. I felt faintly sick, I was developing a throbbing headache at my temples, and I wanted some time to work out what the hell I was thinking in kissing Dominic back. Stupid, stupid move. I couldn't let him get that attached, especially not now that the witches probably knew I was staying there. The closer he was, the closer they all were, the more danger they were in. I had to keep Dominic at a distance, but the idea of pushing him away made me feel terrible, so I shoved the idea aside for the moment.

First of all, I needed to go find Spencer—again—to make sure Olivia hadn't turned him into a frog or something.

Slipping out my bedroom window, so Dominic and Desmond wouldn't see me if they were still hanging about out front, I headed into the trees. I kept a watchful eye out, knowing others were probably out there looking for Spencer, too. I don't know why I was bothering, seeing as I was probably the last person who would be able to find him, but I felt like I had to try. I felt responsible in a way. If Olivia had gotten to him, and he was somewhere in the trees, hurt, it would be my fault. Olivia never would have been anywhere near the cabins if I hadn't been there.

I knew I should have left before! Now it's too late. They *know these people helped me.*

Shaking the thought away, I focused on scanning the area around me, listening for sounds of someone hurt, cries for help, or anything that might tell me where Spencer was. I was listening so hard that I forgot to pay attention to where I was putting my feet, and I tripped over a raised tree root, toppling onto my hands and knees. With a hiss of surprise more than pain, I pulled myself to my feet again and wiped my hands on my jeans. I looked up, and then I saw it.

Straight ahead of me, barely visible through the branches, my wolf was slinking back and forth, apparently pacing. I watched for a moment, a sigh of relief lifting from my chest. I hadn't realised, until then, that I'd been worried about my wolf. I was ridiculously glad that Olivia clearly hadn't maimed it. Though, I did have to wonder if my wolf had killed Olivia. It was a dark thought, but one I kind of enjoyed, if only for a moment.

Then I was moving toward my wolf, not quite sure what I planned to do, but wanting to make sure it really was my wolf, and that it really was okay. Something was bugging it. Wolves didn't normally pace like that. In fact, did wolves ever pace? I didn't know. It made me anxious, watching it.

The closer I came, the more anxious I became. The ebony wolf had stopped pacing, and was standing perfectly still. I could see it wasn't alone—there were two men facing it, both holding guns. I felt a wave of déjà vu sweep over me, and as I stepped up beside my wolf, I even recognised one of the men as the guy I'd scared off the other day. Apparently, he hadn't gotten the message after all, and he was back for more. He flinched, though, when I stepped into view. The guy next to him was taller, bulkier, and his eyes narrowed on me, jaw clenching.

"Neil, that's her! That's the crazy girl!" The shorter man, the one I'd knocked on his ass, said to the big guy. He cringed when my glare fell directly on him.

The tall guy, dressed in much the same way as the short guy, but with a red cap instead of orange, and a green jacket, eyed me with one lip curled scornfully. He made an unimpressed noise. "She don't look so tough, Jack. And we're not here for her anyways. We're here for the wolf, and unless Little Miss Tree Hugger there wants to get her head blown off, she's not going to get in the way this time."

I bristled at the indirect threat, and so did my wolf. The wolf bared its fangs, a low rumbling growl building in its chest. I put my hand on its soft fur, feeling its ribs vibrate under my fingers.

"If either of you as much as twitch, if you even think about raising those guns, I'm going to make you regret it. So how about you just walk away now and leave the nice little wolf alone. Jack is it? Yeah, you. You know what I can do. Maybe you can convince your friend it's in his best interest to leave now." I planted my hands on my hips, drawing myself up as tall as I could. My fingers were still hooked in the wolf's bristling fur, giving the impression I controlled it and could set it loose on them at any moment. I didn't and couldn't, of course, but after the night before, I suspected that if either of them raised their guns toward me, my wolf would tear them apart before they could pull the trigger. My wolf protected me, and I could only assume it was because it remembered I had saved its life.

Neil, the tall guy, barked a gruff laugh at me. "Get out the way, little girl. This wolf needs to be put down." He raised his shotgun, levelling the barrel at my wolf's head.

I remembered the terrifying feeling of staring down that barrel, less than a pound of pressure on the trigger was all that stood between me and a bullet to the brain. I still moved in front of my wolf, even as a cold knot of fear clotted in my throat. The tall guy looked a little surprised at my boldness, but like his partner before him, he didn't lower his gun. Jack, the short guy, however, was backing away slowly, trying not to attract my attention.

I shook my head, curling my hands into fists so they wouldn't see them shaking. "I'm not letting you shoot the wolf, so you might as well just leave."

The tall man grunted and pulled the trigger. I jumped, a scream catching in my throat as the bullet skimmed past the air inches from my head and exploded into the trunk of the tree behind me. With wide eyes, I stared at him, heart galloping. My knees wobbled, and there was a ringing in my ears. My wolf pulled against my grasp on its fur, snarling viciously, and Neil stumbled back a step from its snapping, slobbering jaws. His aim didn't falter though, and he tried to shoot again before I could get in front of the wolf. He missed, but only barely. My breath was wheezing in my chest, and it took me too long to jump in front of my wolf again, my mind too stunned by the fact that *the guy had nearly goddamn shot me*.

Fury rising up over fear, I narrowed my eyes at the tall man, feeling the rush of power building up inside me. He reloaded his gun, snapped it shut, and re-aimed. The sound of it clicking broke my fragile hold on my temper. The power shot out of me like a stone from a slingshot, hurtling straight toward the hunter. A bright ball of electric light, pure power, slammed into him before he could utter a yell.

With a thud, he hit the ground, skidding back amongst the leaves until he hit a tree headfirst. There was a blackened patch on his shirt where the power had burned him, his eyes were closed, and his jaw slack, but his chest was still rising, slightly and erratically. He was alive but unconscious. His gun lay in the spot where he'd been standing, where he'd dropped it.

After a moment of consideration, I started to move toward it, figuring I might need it at some point. I'd never used a gun in my life, but at least if I had it, they didn't. One less weapon for the idiot hunters to use against my wolf. I wasn't letting anyone hurt him.

Suddenly, another shot rang out, startling birds from the trees and making me drop to my knees hard, my hands covering my head. After a moment of panicked gasping and certainty that I'd been shot, I realised I hadn't been. Tentatively, I looked up, uncovering my head, and my eyes fell on the man slumped against the tree. He was still unconscious, and his gun still lay three feet away from me. Confused, I looked around, and I spotted a bright spark of orange darting away through the trees—the short guy's cap.

I'd thought he'd run off before, but he hadn't, he'd been circling round for a better shot. I knew he hadn't missed, because I could hear my wolf whimpering. Terror clutched at my heart with ice cold fingers, and I whirled. My wolf was lying on the ground, thrashing, strangled plaintive wails and yelps emitting from its throat. The leaves under it were pooling red with blood. The bastard had shot my wolf.

Without thinking, I dropped to my knees next to the wolf, forgetting about the huge claws and snapping teeth that could tear me apart in seconds. I knew it wouldn't hurt me. With shaking hands, I felt over its fur, wet and sticky with blood, for the bullet hole. My hands were shaking so badly, I don't know how I found the wound, but I did. I willed my hands to be steady, taking deep, gasping breaths, in time with the wolf's heaving sides. Feeling panic and shock setting in, I knew I needed to delay them, so I could get this done.

I let the tugging fingers of the energy around me seep into my body, smoothing out the jitters in my nerves and steadying my hands to only trembling a little. Then I gulped a breath of air tainted with musky wolf and the tang of blood, and shoved my fingers into the wound. The wolf whimpered, a soft breathless howl escaping its jaws, but it held still and didn't try to rip my head off. Gagging, I felt around in the wound, pushing my fingers deeper into the warm, liquid mess of blood and flesh, until my I brushed something hard and surprisingly cold. I bit my lip hard as I fought to grab hold of the slippery bullet. It squirmed out of my fingers, and I tried again. Finally, I got a good grip. Carefully, slowly, I eased the bullet out, and it emerged from the wolf's flesh with a sickening wet slurping sound. Letting out a long breath of relief that sounded more like a sob than a sigh, I tossed the evil, mashed bullet into the leaf litter as far my trembling arm could throw.

I still had one hand on the wolf's side, and the minute the bullet was removed, the wolf spasmed violently. The bloody fur under my hand rippled, melting away into skin, and I gasped, jumping to my feet in shock. I backed away from the writhing animal as its bones cracked with wet popping sounds, as loud to my ears as the gunshots, its body deforming and shrinking, limbs reshaping, sleek black fur rolling away into pale human flesh. It was all over quickly, but it felt as if it took an eternity before the gorgeous, injured wolf gave way to a gorgeous, injured boy.

The boy shuddered, rolling up onto his hands and knees, shaking with racking coughs. He spat blood and slumped back in a half-sitting, half-lying position, bracing his hands on the blood soaked leaves. I stared, breathing hard, numb except for the painful trembling taking over my muscles. The boy looked up at me from under dirty black hair sticking to his forehead with sweat, gazing with frantic, but perfectly human blue eyes. He was naked, and one side of his chest was smeared with a gory coating of crimson blood from the shoulder down. There was no visible wound for the blood to have come from—the bullet wound had already healed.

Somehow, I found, I still had the capacity to be embarrassed by his nudity, even if he wasn't. I looked away quickly, my throat working. Looking down, I saw my hands, limp by my sides, quivering and soaked in blood to the wrists. The wolf's blood. Spencer's blood. It was on my jeans and my t-shirt, and somehow, it had gotten into the ends of my hair. I was covered in blood. I might have felt better if it were at least my own.

Spencer lifted a hand toward me, opening his mouth to say something, but I flinched back, stumbling over a root and falling against a tree. I slid down the trunk, scraping my back on the rough bark and not caring, and then I sat there, staring at my hands. I couldn't look at Spencer. He didn't move again, didn't try to talk to me or explain. He just sat across from me and watched as I shook.

I closed my eyes.

I must have zoned out for a while, still awake but not really there, lost in the darkness behind my closed lids and still trembling. Distantly, I was aware of people around me, moving and yelling, some just talking, maybe talking to me, but the words were meaningless in my ears. I felt someone lifting me, and I was too tired to protest. My limbs flopped like a badly jointed doll's, and I felt the gentle rocking of footsteps under me. It was a relaxing motion. Combined with the exhaustion of shock and adrenaline wearing off and the kind waves of energy from the woods pulsing into me, it was enough to lull me to an unconsciousness filled with nightmares and the sounds of cracking bones.

Chapter Nine

** Tilly **

I rolled over, raising a hand to block the sunlight streaming in through the window and prodding into my sensitive eyes. My limbs were achy, my stomach was twisted with hunger, and I had a monster headache. Groaning, I looked down at myself and found I was lying on top of the covers on my bed, dressed in dirty bloodstained clothes. Images flashed through my head, each one making me feel sicker by the second. The hunter pointing his gun at me and my wolf, and then him lying unconscious at the foot of a tree. My wolf thrashing on the ground in pain as blood seeped from a wound in its shoulder. The wolf shuddering violently after I pulled the bullet out, bones snapping and reforming, fur replaced by flesh, blood on bare skin, and rabid blue eyes staring at me…

Spencer. He was a…*oh god*. He was a werewolf. *Oh God*. My wolf wasn't a wolf. Spencer was my wolf. He'd saved my life. In fact, he'd done it twice. He'd taken me to the camp when I was injured and unconscious, and he'd knocked me down when Olivia had tried to paralyse me with that blast of power. The annoying, mysterious, distant boy I'd sat by the stream with in the middle of the night was a goddamn werewolf, and he'd saved my life.

It really shouldn't have freaked me out as much as it did. I'd always known werewolves existed—hello, I was a witch. I'd raised demons. I knew people who could see ghosts. Of course there were other supernatural creatures out there. It wasn't really that weird…except that *it* was. It was incredibly weird, because I knew better than to assume Spencer was the only one. Werewolves stuck together, just like real wolves. They formed packs like real wolves. So the odds were, the slightly eccentric people I'd been living with for a week were all werewolves. It wasn't a cult—it was a pack.

It explained a lot of things. Like Dominic's advice about not looking Frank or Spencer in the eyes, Frank's reluctance to let me stay with them, and the way they all seemed to move so fast sometimes. Hell, even why they ate so much meat. Why they lived out there in the woods. All the little things I'd been turning a blind eye to, because I was just grateful to have a place to stay away from the witches and amongst people who treated me as, well, a *person*, opposed to a tool or a slave. If I thought about those little things, it all made sense, and I wanted to kick myself for not seeing it sooner.

It's amazing how ignorant a person can be when they don't want to know something. I'd always thought normal humans were stupid that way, passing off strange occurrences like cold spots in empty hallways, strange sounds in the night, and things falling when nobody touched them. All of that stuff, passed off as coincidences or just random inexplicable events. None of them ever thought there could be something there, something happening, that was outside the realm of what science told them was possible. And I had become the one who'd been wilfully ignorant.

156

Another, totally inappropriate thought popped into my head. *I kissed Dominic this morning. I kissed a werewolf.* The thought made me giggle, not entirely sanely, either. It made my head hurt, and I flopped onto my back, pressing my hands over my eyes, trying to stop the giggles before they could turn into sobs.

I gasped, my stomach turning over and over as my breathing hitched ever closer to hyperventilation. Determined to control myself, I forced myself to let out a slow breath, letting in the gentle energy of the woods that was stroking at my aura. I took a few deep breaths, the energy working through me, soothing my headache and nausea, easing the shaking in my hands. I carefully lowered my hands from my eyes and stared at the beams of light striped across the ceiling.

"I'm okay," I whispered to myself, "I'm okay. Everything is okay. Just keep breathing and you'll be okay." I took another deep breath, held it for a moment, and let it out again. My mouth was dry, and I really wanted a glass of water. Sitting up, I swung my legs over the side of the bed, thankful that I didn't feel dizzy, and I stood up. I sat back down a second later.

Okay, actually, I kind of threw myself backward onto the bed, scrambling across it, gasping. My eyes were wide, and my heart had jammed into my throat, because there was someone else in the room with me, and I hadn't noticed him until that moment.

Sitting on the floor with his back against the closed door, Spencer watched me with wide, startled eyes. He held up his hands, palms toward me, in a nonthreatening gesture. "Whoa! It's okay. I'm not going to hurt you," he said, not moving from where he sat. His hair was damp, and he was fully dressed again, obviously having showered to get the blood off him.

I got a quick image of him lying in the dirt, naked, and I blushed hotly. Swallowing, I looked away from him. My hands were shaking again. Spencer chuckled suddenly, a soft and slightly embarrassed sound. When I glanced at him, I saw he was tugging at the end of his t-shirt, the first nervous thing I'd ever seen him do. His eyes were on my shadow, cast across the floor by the sunlight slanting through the window.

Another first, I thought. Spencer couldn't meet my gaze.

Before, I'd thought he just enjoyed making me uncomfortable by staring at me, but now of course I knew better. I'd looked him in the eye, and to a wolf, that was seen as a challenge. He'd just been trying to outstare me, to show he was dominant. No wonder everyone had freaked at dinner the first evening I was in camp, with the way I'd cavalierly stared back at Spencer.

I was surprised he hadn't gone wolf and rolled me belly up a dozen times by that point, and that was a really bad way to put it. Belly-up. Combined with the image of Spencer naked, it put things into my head that absolutely didn't belong there. *Oh God*. My face was on fire, and I knew he could see it. I cleared my throat and turned to face out the window, rolling up the glass to let the breeze in, pretending I needed fresh air. I just needed something to cool my face and the sudden, uncomfortable burning in my gut.

"It's good to know what makes you more uncomfortable: Werewolves or nudity. Apparently, it's nudity," Spencer commented from across the room, snickering. There was a lilt of amusement in his voice.

I gritted my teeth, taking deep, deliberate breaths of the cool, fresh afternoon air. The smell of bluebells and oak leaves filled my lungs. "Technically," I muttered, not turning my face away from the window, "it would be nude werewolves that make me particularly uncomfortable."

Spencer snorted, and I could practically feel him rolling his eyes. "I'd apologise for making you uncomfortable, but, well, I'm not really sorry," he said.

I finally turned to shoot him a glare. He grinned at me, and I was startled by how boyish it made him look.

"And I'm willing to bet you're not sorry either." He twitched his eyebrows meaningfully.

I counted to three to rein in my annoyance before asking, confused, "What?"

He tilted his head to the side, the same way my wolf had after I'd saved it from the hunter the first time, when it had stood there watching me as if trying to figure me out. Then I remembered my wolf and Spencer were one and the same, and I repressed a shudder. I didn't want to think about that just yet. It was too horrifying.

There was something distinctly animalistic in his mischievous eyes as he asked, "Did you like what you saw?"

I counted all the way to ten, paused, and counted to twenty. I wanted so badly to glare at him, but my face was burning again. Knowing what he was, I didn't dare taunt the wolf inside him, so I turned my head away, feeling embarrassment and anger sour on my tongue. He was toying with me, and I didn't like it.

My fingers clenched on the window frame. "Why are you here?" I snapped.

He didn't answer for a long moment, and I had to look over my shoulder to check he was even still in the room. I knew how freakishly quietly he could move—stealthy and silent like the predator he was. He was still sitting on the floor, but he'd lost his grin. All signs of amusement were wiped off his face, and I settled with my back against the wall, satisfied that he was done joking—for the moment. There was a line between his brows, which were drawn together pensively, and he scowled at a spot on the floor hard enough that it should have spontaneously combusted under his glare.

"Dominic thought it would be better if I talked to you when you woke up. He said it might be easier for you to handle the whole werewolf thing if I explained it, rather than if he did. I guess his logic was that it'd be easier to hear it from someone you disliked, than to hear it from a friend you'd trusted."

I almost thought there was something bitter in his voice, but it could have just been resentment that he'd been nominated to give me The Werewolf Talk. The breeze from the window behind me blew my hair forward, and I tucked it back impatiently, huffing in irritation. I really needed a hair bobble, or a ribbon, or something.

Spencer's mouth twitched as the breeze blew my hair forward again, and I grabbed it in my fist, twisting it into a rope over my shoulder.

"Bloody hell, it's hard to have a serious conversation about supernatural creatures while my hair is in my face," I grumbled.

Spencer looked at me as if I was crazy, with his eyebrows raised into the mess of his black hair. "You know, most people would be quite terrified to be in the same room as a werewolf," he observed, narrowing his eyes thoughtfully.

He did that tilting his head thing again, and I shrank away from his knowing gaze. "Yeah, well," I mumbled, absently braiding my hair. "I'm not most people."

Spencer smiled wryly at that. "Yes, I know." He rolled to his feet smoothly, and opened the bedroom door a crack, indicating, with a jerk of his head, that I should follow him. "Let's go for a walk and we can talk properly."

My fingers paused halfway through my braid, and I bit my lip, pressing myself into the wall at my back anxiously. It wasn't that I was scared of him. I knew perfectly well that he wouldn't hurt me. He was my wolf, after all. I cringed when I thought that. Spencer was not *my* wolf. I got the feeling Spencer didn't belong to anyone, maybe not even the pack.

He'd unnerved me before, and that feeling of unease around him hadn't been reduced any by my newest discovery. What if I pissed him off and he wolfed out and tried to eat me? What if the pack had decided I was a liability and Spencer had been sent to lure me into the woods and leave me there? Or worse, to kill me?

I understood why Frank had said I was dangerous. My knowing about them meant I could—probably should—go screaming '*werewolf*' through the town. That could only end badly for them, even if nobody believed me. Someone would still have to investigate the woods if I started claiming I'd been taken in by crazy people who turned into wolves. They'd no doubt think I'd been abducted by strange woodland people, and that there were wolves running wild where there shouldn't be.

Yes, I'd definitely be a liability…if I weren't a witch, unlikely to go yelling *wolf* when my kind had been burned at the stake because some punk ass kid went yelling *witch* to the townsfolk.

"Or," Spencer said, pulling me from my thoughts. He was watching me with a half-concerned, half-amused expression. "Or we can go out the window if you'd like?" He lifted his hand off the door handle and gestured to the open window, which I happened to be practically pushing myself out of backwards with how hard I was digging myself into the wall.

I blinked and shook my head. "I think I'll stick with the door," I muttered, sliding off the bed and walking toward him with some effort. My instinct wanted me to stay as far away from the wolf as possible, even though he was in human form, even though I knew he wouldn't hurt me, and even though I hadn't been that afraid of the wolf since I'd saved its—*his*—life from that hunter the first time.

Something inside me was finally realising how much danger I could have been in before. I'd been inches away from a wolf with huge teeth and claws, I'd put my back to it, I'd had my arms around its neck when Olivia had tried to put a spell on it. On *him*. I was having trouble accepting that my wolf and Spencer were the *same bloody thing*, because that meant I'd saved *Spencer's* life.

I remembered something he'd said the night after I'd saved the wolf. *"Why did you save that wolf today?"* I had thought, then, that it was weird he knew I'd saved a wolf, when the others had all been furiously denying they'd even seen one, but I hadn't wanted to ask how he knew. Now I knew how, and I also knew why he'd asked. He'd wanted to know why I'd saved *him*.

I paused at the door, eyeing Spencer, and then motioned for him to go first. It was funny how I'd trusted him at my back in wolf form, but as a boy, I didn't like having him where I couldn't see him. That had nothing to do with his being a werewolf, so much as having to do with the fact that I couldn't be sure he wasn't checking out my ass. After all, he was still a teenage boy, and that was something I *couldn't* forget.

"Also," Spencer added, "you might want to get changed first." He gestured to my bloody clothes, and I grimaced.

"Right."

Unsurprisingly, after I'd changed into clean clothes and washed the blood off my hands, Spencer led me to the stream. Walking through the trees, I hadn't seen anyone else, and I suspected they may have been avoiding me until Spencer had had a chance to explain everything. I was a little stung by Dominic's assumption that I'd be less freaked out having Spencer explaining it to me than himself. Did he think I'd be scared of him? Resent him for misleading me?

Really, I just wanted to hear him tell me himself that he was a werewolf. If he could have the guts to tell me to my face that he'd lied to me, I could forgive him for making me think he was a normal human boy. But then, I was being hypocritical. Dominic didn't know I was a witch, only Spencer knew that, because he'd seen me use my powers. That thought freaked me out. Nobody except the witches had ever known about my powers before.

Spencer and I sat on the mossy bank of the stream, under shafts of warm afternoon sunlight that sparkled and swam on the crystal clear water. Trees shook their leaves at us, like scolding parents shaking their fingers, as if what we were talking about was not allowed to be discussed. I couldn't help but feel that it probably wasn't, and wondered if Spencer had permission from his father to tell me all about their little secret, or if he'd just used Dominic as an excuse to be the one to tell me. From what I'd seen of their relationship so far, I got the impression Spencer would do anything to piss off his father. The guy had daddy issues. I didn't judge. I had parent issues too, if you could classify my legal guardians as any form of parents.

"It's not as painful as it looks. The first few times you Change, it's agony, but once you learn to block out the pain, it's not so bad," Spencer explained, twirling a leaf by its stem between his fingers. He was stretched out on the grass on his side, propping his head in his hand. His t-shirt rode up a couple of centimetres, flashing a line of fair, smooth skin, but I determinedly kept my eyes either on his face or on the stream. We were having a serious conversation, it wouldn't do for me to get distracted, but damn it was hard to concentrate. Werewolf or not, he was stupidly good looking.

I nodded thoughtfully at his answer, watching a sparrow hop along the ground on the other side of the stream, amongst a patch of foxgloves and buttercups. "Okay. Well, obviously you don't just Change on a full moon. Can you Change any time you want, or just at night, or what?" I asked.

The full moon was in a few days. Would they all wolf out and try to eat me? No, no, of course not. Spencer had made it obvious that they had more self-restraint than that. He hadn't eaten me when he had the chance, so I had to assume the others wouldn't either. Hopefully.

Spencer shook his head. "We can Change whenever we like, but it's easier nearer the full moon. Well, actually, it's just harder to contain around the full moon, hence why Frank pulled us out of school. He didn't want us wolfing out on our classmates. There are things that can trigger the Change, like anger, or if we feel threatened. Bullies were a big problem at school. I think if Frank hadn't pulled us out, I probably would have gotten kicked out for fighting. I don't take kindly to people beating on my friends." He palmed the leaf he was toying with and curled his fingers around it, crushing it. I felt sorry for whoever had thought to bully Spencer or his pack mates.

"Wow. Okay. Would it really offend you if I said I wasn't surprised? Because you do have the whole, um, dark and dangerous bad boy vibe going on. It's a little scary sometimes." I leaned away from him, watching him clench and unclench his fist around the leaf, mashing it to a pulp. I actually got up and moved away when he grinned abruptly, showing unnaturally long and sharp teeth. "That right there is exactly what I'm talking about. Scary."

He laughed, his fangs melting back into normal teeth. It was a surprisingly un-sarcastic laugh, and it startled me into grinning back. He finally gave up on pulverising the leaf and dropped it to the ground, a mangled mess of green bits, and used his leaf-blood-stained fingers to beckon me back over.

"Get back over here. It's hard to have a conversation when you're fifteen feet away from me."

I scowled at him. "Maybe I'm just afraid you'll bite me or something."

His grin turned mischievous. "Trust me, if I was going to bite you, you'd know it."

I blushed, but slowly made my way back over to him. I sat down a few feet away from him, and he snapped his teeth at me playfully. I flinched, and then I felt stupid for flinching, so I leaned over and punched him in the arm.

"Have I mentioned that I don't like you?" I muttered, glaring at him.

He shrugged. "I know. Most people don't like me. I'm not exactly a people person," he admitted it unapologetically, as if he

166

really didn't care what I thought of him. He probably didn't. I was just an outsider, after all, an invader into his pack.

"You're an animal person then, I'm guessing?" I said.

He rolled his eyes at the bad joke, but his expression grew serious. He looked at me, eyes locking on mine, and I couldn't look away, even though I knew I should. His eyes were just so blue, so intense. It was like looking into the heart of a storm, trying to see the stars through the clouds and rain and flashes of lightning.

"I'm a werewolf," he said slowly, tilting his head. His eyes narrowed. "But what are you?"

The question took me by surprise, and I bit my lip. What was I? I called myself a witch, but what did that really mean? There were so many different kinds of witches. Witch was such a broad term, but most witches couldn't summon demons, and I knew that. No normal witch—no *good* witch—could summon something from the Underworld, because their power came from the Earth, and the Earth wouldn't allow them to bring something into her realm that could destroy her creatures, her life. I called myself a witch, because I wasn't sure what I really was. It seemed like the simplest answer, but I'd read enough textbooks and grimoires to know that if I was a witch, that wasn't all I was.

I frowned, tearing my gaze away from Spencer's, so I could look at my hands folded in my lap. I shrugged. "I...I don't know. I've never really thought about it before. I always just accepted my powers are part of me. I spent most of my time just trying to work out *who* I am." It wasn't entirely true.

I had thought about it many times, I'd just never found an answer that made sense. Honestly, I didn't think it mattered all that much. I could do what I could do, and knowing why I could do it wouldn't change anything, except my perception of myself and my parents. I mean, what if I found out I was part demon? What if my dad had had demon blood? That would explain why I could raise creatures from the Underworld. If one of my parents was something from the dark, I didn't want to know. I wanted to remember them the way I thought of them now; loving, kind, and happy.

Spencer looked confused. "What do you mean?" he asked quietly, pushing himself into a sitting position mirroring mine. He leaned closer, putting his elbows on his knees, as if what I was saying was fascinating to him.

I smiled at him a little ruefully. "It's hard to know who you really are when everyone around you is telling you that you're just a tool to be used." I didn't think he could understand what I meant, since he at least had his dad, however strained things were between them.

But his expression held both sympathy and understanding. He looked away from me, out over the tops of the trees. "If it's anything like being told you're only a part of the pack because you're bound by blood to the alpha...must suck," he said.

His voice was flat, but there was sullenness in the twist of his mouth that made me want to take his hand in comfort. I kept my hands to myself, drawing up my legs and laying my chin on my knees, holding myself together in a protective ball.

I stared at the stream flowing over the rocks, sunlight shining over the surface, making it shimmer like glass. I wished I could float away on it, drift away to somewhere that the witches would never find me, somewhere quiet and beautiful, far away from there. Far away from *them*, the Dark Room, the birch cane, the demons, and the nightmares. Anywhere.

"Spencer?" I whispered.

"Hmm?" he murmured distractedly.

"That witch you saved me from? Olivia?"

He glanced at me, nodding slowly. "She was one of the people who adopted you, wasn't she?" he asked gently.

"Yeah," I sighed.

He nodded again, his face darkening. "I can see why you ran away."

My lips turned up in a sad smile at the corners. Then it faded. "You chased her off. Did you...is she..." I bit my lip, unsure how to ask without sounding evil myself. But I needed to know, I needed to know how much longer I could be safe before *they* swooped down on me like a hawk on a mouse.

Spencer grimaced, his lips becoming a flat, angry line. Gold flashed in his eyes. "I didn't kill her. I would have, but she cast some sort of spell on me. It slowed me down, and then I couldn't Change back to human form, right up until I got shot..." He shook his head violently. "It was a silver bullet. It broke the spell, but...if you hadn't been there, I'd probably have been dead by the time the others found me. So thank you."

169

I wasn't sure what to say, so I just stayed quiet for a long moment, and then something occurred to me, and my eyes widened. I turned to Spencer, who was scowling at a spot in the stream as if he was waiting for the water to boil. "Spencer, you said it was a silver bullet? Those actually work on werewolves?" I was familiar with the concept from movies and books, but I'd never put any credence in the idea.

"Yes, silver bullets work. Silver is poisonous to us. So is wolfs bane, surprisingly enough."

I felt a thrill of ice go down my spine, and I whispered, "Why would the hunters be using silver bullets?"

Spencer's jaw clenched so hard, I thought he'd break his teeth. His eyes blazed gold, terrifying to see wolf eyes in a human face, and when he spoke his voice was half-growl. "Because, somehow, they know about us. Someone told them, maybe even hired them to take us out."

"It wasn't me. I swear, I would never…" I rambled, shrinking away in fear of the animal I saw gnawing under the surface of his skin.

He shook his head again, and when he looked at me, his eyes were back to their normal, cool blue. "I know it wasn't you. It would make no sense for it to have been you anyway. You saved me. You threw that hunter fifteen feet into a tree. By the way, that was sort of awesome." He grinned swiftly, but the smile was swallowed by the dark, roiling anger in his eyes. "No, you didn't do it, but that witch I chased probably did. Her name's Olivia?" He scoffed, "She'd better not come back here."

I shivered, hugging my knees. I wasn't sure that the threat of one werewolf would keep Olivia away. I wasn't sure a whole pack of werewolves would keep her from coming after me. If she was hiring hunters to kill the werewolves…I was just as screwed as they were. They were going to die just for helping me, when they didn't even know what I was. I was going to go back to the Dark Room and demons trying to rip my soul out, all because the witches liked power, and selling demons on the Ghost Market—the supernatural Black Market—was a lucrative business.

I couldn't go back to it, I couldn't, but I didn't want to kill myself either. Suicide was the lesser of two evils, but in just the short week I'd spent with Dominic, Desmond, Sarah, and little Annie…I'd gotten to know what freedom felt like. What life could be like if I was free, and I didn't want to give it up.

"Tilly," Spencer said softly.

I glanced at him, realising with a jolt of shock that he'd moved closer to me. Close enough that I could smell his scent—wilder than Dominic's sunny scent of fresh leaves and shampoo. Spencer smelled like rain in a storm and the smoke from a bonfire.

He raised his hand hesitantly and touched my face, his fingertips sliding over my jaw, drawing sparks along my skin. I was finding it hard to breathe, hard to think. He was just so *close*, and my body was prickling as if I was standing next to an open flame, a roaring fire. I thought I could see the stars through the storm in his eyes.

171

Almost a whisper, he murmured, "Tilly, you are *not* just a tool."

My breath caught, and my eyes stung, my throat swelling shut under the pressure of tears that I refused to let show. I feigned a smile. "How would you know? You've only known me a week, and night time excursions excluded, you've barely spoken to me." My voice came out as a choked whisper, the lump in my throat clogging the words and distorting the tone, so I sounded hurt rather than teasing.

He sighed, his eyes flicking down, dropping his hand from my face into his own lap. He looked ashamed. Then he shook his head slightly, muttering something under his breath that I didn't catch, and looked up at me again with bright eyes.

"I know because you saved my life," he whispered.

That night, I tossed and turned in my bed, the day's events playing over and over in my head. Surprisingly, the thing that stuck in my mind most wasn't finding out that Spencer and Dominic and everyone else were werewolves; it was the way Spencer had looked at me by the stream when he'd whispered that I'd saved his life. His soft voice was the last thing I thought of before I finally fell into an uneasy, restless sleep.

*****

I dreamed I was running. Running through the trees in my nightgown, my bare feet hitting the dirt. Running away from the evil cackling and hissing voices, the echoes of whispers promising to catch me and punish me, to throw me into the Dark Room for weeks, whip me with the birch cane until my skin flayed off my body.

The threats breathed from the trees, the ground, and the soulless black sky. All around me, the voices floated from the darkness. The dark pillars of the trees blurred past me as I ran, the branches whipping at my hair and arms. The voices followed me, chasing me. The cold night air rasped in my throat. My leg muscles burned as I leapt over a fallen log, landing on a pinecone. My ankle twisted, spines of the pinecone digging into the tender arch of my foot, and I went down to my knees, scraping them along the ground.

"Matilda! Matilda! There's no use running, Matilda! We'll find you!"

"Come out, come out, little lamb! We're going to kill your Big Bad Wolf!"

"You can run but you can't hide from us, Matilda!"

The cruel laughter bounced off the trees and rose shrilly into the night sky, morphing into the howling of wolves unseen. Twigs snapped behind me, and suddenly, there was hot breath on the back of my legs. A breathless scream caught in my throat as the strong, ferocious jaws of a wolf clamped down on my leg. I threw out my arms, pain shooting up my leg, as the sharp teeth dug into my calf, tearing at the muscle.

I fell forever, never hitting the ground. Just falling, falling, falling into blackness.

Chapter Ten

** Spencer **

If there was anything Spencer hated more than being dragged out of his bed, it was being dragged out of his bed by his father. But that's exactly what happened that morning, and he'd worn a scowl perpetually since he'd been shaken awake to find Frank's bearded face looking down at him disapprovingly.

All Frank had said was, "Get up, boy. You're coming with me and Dominic. Move it."

There hadn't been a whole lot of choice about it, so Spencer had grudgingly rolled out of bed, gotten dressed, and resisted the urge to point out—for the hundredth time—that he loathed being called *boy*, seeing as he was nineteen and no longer a kid.

Still scowling, he stood at the entrance to the *Buck and Bullet*—the local pub where hunters particularly liked to hang out—with Frank and Dominic. He'd told his father that the hunter who'd shot him had used a silver bullet, and the alpha had come to the same conclusion as Spencer had—someone was hiring hunters to kill the wolves.

Thankfully, there were two things that his father always believed him on. One was pack safety issues, and that he would never challenge the man to become the alpha. Spencer was certain that if Frank had had even the slightest inkling that Spencer might want to be alpha, the *boy* would have been out of the pack in a heartbeat. Spencer couldn't imagine wanting to be alpha. He'd much rather be a lone wolf.

Dominic sighed, looking up at the big, wooden sign over the door to the bar. The pub's name was engraved into the faded, rotting wood and painted blood red. There was a depiction of a buck's head between two crossed shotguns, the bar's emblem, on the large, stained glass window to the right of the door. Through the doorway, Spencer could see it was dim inside the bar. Wooden booths were lined with greasy brown pleather, and tall stools sat at the long bar at the far end of the room, behind which were rows and rows of bottles of alcohol. There weren't many people in the *Buck and Bullet*, except a couple of guys in orange caps up at the bar.

"I hate hunter pubs," Dominic muttered, tugging on one of his auburn curls.

Frowning, Spencer silently agreed with him, but if they wanted to find out who had hired the men to hunt wolves, they had to talk to some of the hunters. It would be easier to do when the bar was quieter, before everyone got too drunk to form coherent sentences.

Frank grunted. "Hate them if you like, but we've got work to do. Both of you, let me do the talking and keep an eye out. You know how it goes."

Spencer noted that the man's steely eyes rested particularly on him, though he'd said *both of you*. It was always like that. Spencer didn't bother to point out that he rarely spoke when he didn't have to anyway, because Frank already knew it.

Dominic just nodded, gave a final tug on his curls, and settled on his serious face—the one he used when they were doing something important or when his wolf was close to the surface.

Spencer was still scowling, so he just stuck with that, knowing full well that the only reason Frank had brought him along was because he trusted Spencer's instinct. Well, that and his ability to be intimidating, even to men twice his age. Dominic was there because he was Frank's son.

They walked into the *Buck and Bullet*, Frank first and Spencer last, and went straight to the bar. Dominic wrinkled his nose for a second, but smoothed out his expression quickly. With his bright curls and lanky build, he looked far too young to be in a bar, but his eyes were sharp, scanning the place for threats.

Spencer couldn't blame the kid for wrinkling his nose. The pub stank of sweat, beer, blood and gunpowder. It was choking to wolf senses, even when they were in human form. Just one of the many reasons Spencer rarely went to bars and pubs. He preferred to lose his troubles in the pounding of his paws on the dirt and the wind whipping through his fur as he ran, than to drown them in a cold bottle of Bud.

Frank took a seat at the bar, a couple stools down from the hunters in the orange caps, and Dominic sat down on his right, away from the hunters. With an internal sigh, Spencer hooked a stool down from Dominic and leaned his elbows on the bar. Ignoring Frank and Dominic, the bartender—a buxom woman most likely in her early thirties with dyed black hair and a lined face—looked up from arranging glasses under the bar and came to him first. She smiled at Spencer, showing a missing incisor, and he didn't smile back.

"What can I get you, honey?" she asked, drumming her long, painted nails on the polished wood.

Spencer opened his mouth to reject the offer, but then he thought that might look suspicious. With a smirk, he said, "Scotch, if you please." He felt Frank glaring at him down the bar, and he ignored it.

"Coming right up, sweetie" The bartender dropped him a wink and moved off to grab a bottle of scotch. She poured his drink and slid it in front of him. He began to reach into his pocket for cash, but the woman shook her head at him. "This one's on the house, so long's you promise to come back. We don't see a lot of younger lads in here." She gave him another toothy grin before sauntering down the bar to Frank, leaning forward to give him a good view of her considerable cleavage. To his credit, Frank didn't even glance at her chest as he ordered a bottle of beer.

Spencer snorted, lifted his drink, and caught Dominic glaring at him. He raised an eyebrow.

"What?"

Dominic shook his head, making his curls bounce. "I hate you sometimes, you know that?" he said, but his lips quirked into a grin.

Spencer doubted his statement, simply because he doubted Dominic was capable of hating anyone—though, if he were to hate someone, his half-brother would probably be a likely candidate.

With a shrug, Spencer said, "You've only got another year, and then you can drink as much as you want."

The younger boy frowned.

Their attention was redirected when they heard Frank speaking to one of the orange cap wearing hunters.

"…heard there was a wolf going about those woods. Dunno if I believe it, though. I mean, it's been decades since there've been wolves around here."

The hunter, a grizzled man with greying brown hair peering out from under his ugly fluorescent cap, was frowning as he tipped the neck of a brown bottle to his lips. Frank had his hand curled lightly around his own bottle, looking deceptively calm and indifferent. Only Dominic and Spencer knew how much he wanted to Change and rip the hunter's throat out with his teeth. They knew, because they wanted to do the same thing. Well, Spencer did anyway. It was hard to imagine Dominic killing anyone, but the tension in his shoulders and back was definitely of a violent nature.

The hunter Frank was speaking to put down his bottle and shook his head. "There are wolves in there alright. I've seen them," he said. He had the rough, gravelly voice of a chain smoker.

Frank's fingers coiled more tightly around his beer bottle, but his voice and posture remained the same—casual, disinterested, non-threatening. "Them? There's more than one? You're talking bull," he scoffed, lifting his beer bottle to his mouth.

Spencer saw a muscle tick in the alpha's cheek.

"Nah," The other hunter at the bar leaned forward, joining the conversation. "He's telling the truth. I've seen the wolves too. There was a couple broads who came in here the other night saying they'd pay good money to anyone who'd go out shooting the wolves who've been prowling 'round their manor house. Me and a few other blokes took them up on it, went out the next day with shotguns. The women, they give you the ammo for it, too." Hunter number two grinned, adjusting his cap. "'Course, I'd have shot the damn beasts for nothing if it meant getting to know those women a bit better, if you get what I mean." He chuckled, and his friend chortled.

Frank did a good job of making a snarl look like a grin. Under his breath, Dominic made a disgusted noise, and Spencer just took another sip of his drink.

And we're *the beasts*, Spencer thought with a frown. *They kill animals for sport, money, and an attractive woman. Wolves kill for food, not for pleasure.*

"So who're these fine women, then?" Frank asked, his fingers deceptively loose on his brown bottle.

Hunter number one shrugged. "Dunno exactly. Just know they were good looking, and they live in some fancy ass house on the edge of town. Didn't ask too many questions. But they said they'd be back here at the end of the week to pay anyone who could prove they'd shot a wolf."

Spencer ran his tongue over his teeth, feeling the unnaturally long fangs hidden under his top lip. The hairs on his arms bristled, anger pushing his wolf closer to the surface. Listening to the men cavalierly talking about killing his family and friends was pissing him off, and if he didn't get out of there soon, the hunters were going to have a wolf to shoot right there in the bar.

"Excuse me," Spencer muttered to nobody in particular, sliding off his stool and storming out of the bar. He felt Frank's glower on his back for a brief moment, and heard him mutter something to Dominic. Spencer was out of the bar and halfway down the empty street before he stopped walking and leaned against the wall of a butcher's shop. He didn't look in the window, knowing the sight of meat would only rattle his wolf more.

Dominic caught up to his half-brother and hesitantly leaned against the wall next to him, tugging on his hair. Spencer had his hands in his pockets, his head down, glaring at the cracked pavement and the moss growing between the uneven slabs of concrete.

They were both silent for a long few minutes before Dominic spoke. "So...assholes, right?"

Spencer nodded. "Aye," he growled. "Assholes."

Dominic chewed his lip nervously for a moment, then said quietly, "Did...were either of those guys...you know, the guy who shot you?"

"Wouldn't be standing here if they were," Spencer said softly. "I'd be killing the bastard."

Pressing his lips thin, Dominic nodded slowly. He was still tugging at his hair. Spencer wanted to tell him to quit it, but he didn't. The silence grew uncomfortable between them. Dominic fidgeted uneasily, but Spencer just stood, not entirely disliking his half-brother's discomfort. Sometimes, Spencer thought Dominic was scared of him, but it wasn't fear exactly that Minnie exuded.

Suddenly, Dominic spoke again, and managing to surprise Spencer. "So what do you think of Tilly?" the curly headed boy asked, smiling under his curls.

Spencer didn't want to talk about Tilly. He spent enough time thinking about her without having to talk about her too, especially to Dominic.

Aloud, Spencer groaned. "We're not going to have a brotherly bonding moment here are we? 'Cause if we are, I'll need to go get another drink." He tipped his head back against the stone wall and closed his eyes. Behind his lids, Tilly smiled at him, her grey eyes bright and thoughtful.

Dominic laughed, snapping Spencer out of his thoughts. He opened his blue eyes and fixed them on his half-brother, who was grinning.

"I was just wondering, because she doesn't seem to hate you quite as much now. Weird, considering she knows about the whole werewolf thing now. You'd think she'd hate you more, hate me too, but she doesn't." There was a tone in Dominic's voice, somewhere between awe and incredulity that Spencer didn't want to hear. But Dominic kept talking. "She's a weird girl, though, isn't she?" It wasn't really a question.

Spencer bit his tongue. *You have no idea how weird she is, Minnie. I know how weird she is, and I know she hasn't told you. I wonder what that means*, he thought.

He wanted to say it, wanted to tell Dominic that Tilly wasn't just a weird human girl, but he liked that Dominic didn't know. He liked that he was the only one who knew Tilly's secret. So he kept his mouth shut and stared past Dominic down the street to the bar, where Frank was just emerging onto the pavement.

"Did she tell you I kissed her?" Dominic asked quietly, a shy smile curling his mouth. He'd bowed his head, and was tugging on his curls again.

Once again, he'd managed to surprise Spencer, though he really shouldn't have been surprised. He'd suspected, after all, that there was more than friendship going on between Dominic and Tilly. But the bite of jealousy dug deep, and his wolf snarled, raising the hairs on the back of his neck like hackles prickling. Dominic looked so damned happy with himself, too. For the first time he could remember, Spencer wanted to hit his cheerful half-brother.

Just then, Frank walked up to them, looking just as pissed off as Spencer felt, though for a very different reason. "Let's go. I need to talk to Bob and Graham. And then I need to talk to the whole pack. We have a problem, and until it's handled, I want you two and Desmond to be on the lookout."

He glanced at Spencer, who looked as calm on the outside as ever. But inside, he was thrumming with the need to let out his wolf and kill something—a rabbit, a squirrel, a hunter. It didn't matter what it was. He just wanted blood.

As if he knew what Spencer was thinking, the alpha grimaced. "Spencer, no more Changing without my permission. That's an order. I can't have you running around as a wolf when there are men with guns looking for wolves to kill. You hear me?" Frank said sternly, his steely glower heavy on Spencer, pressing down on him with the weight of a command from his alpha.

It was difficult to fight—not impossible, but difficult. He didn't fight it…for the moment. He bowed his head, lowering his gaze and nodding once, sharply, unable to speak for fear his voice would come out as a growl. He hated to be ordered. He couldn't stand the idea of having to ask Frank's permission before Changing, of being refused the Change just because there were some idiots with guns going around the woods. It made fury rise, hot and thick, in his throat, but he swallowed it. He took solace in the fact that he didn't plan on obeying his alpha's order for long.

** Tilly **

"What the hell?" I said to my reflection in the mirror. Confused grey eyes stared back at me from under a nest of pale hair that looked as if it had been whipped into knots and jewelled with crumbling leaves as accessories. There was also a thin red line across my forehead, as if I'd scratched myself in my sleep—which might have been possible if I had long nails. I didn't. I was in the habit of biting my nails when they started to get too long, because long nails annoyed me.
In addition, the soles of my bare feet were black with dirt. I had no idea how I'd gotten so filthy just lying in bed. I hadn't even left the

window open, so it wasn't as if leaves could have just blown in and miraculously buried themselves in my hair.

Flipping on the shower and waiting for the water to heat up, I pulled my nightshirt over my head, and a curled green leaf fell out from between my breasts. Dropping the nightshirt to the floor, I stared at the little green leaf, then bent to pick it up. I examined it curiously, frowning. I had the sudden nasty idea that I'd been pranked. That one of the boys had decided to toy with me while I slept, and the leaf in my cleavage had been their calling card.

I shook the thought away quickly, mostly because it was too mortifying to think of. I knew Dominic at least would never do that to me—but I wasn't so sure about Des or Spencer. But no, I refused to believe it. Werewolves or not, they wouldn't dare. There was another explanation. I just didn't know what it was yet.

"Maybe I'll come up with the answer in the shower," I muttered to myself doubtfully, glancing in the mirror one last time before the steam fogged up the glass. I stepped into the hot spray of water and tried not to think about Spencer.

And here I thought I was sworn away from boy trouble. Apparently, with the decision to stay there, I'd stopped resisting the idea of having 'boy trouble' and it was already creeping up on me. I sighed and began working on the leafy nest of my hair.

After breakfast, I went to find Dominic, but instead, I ran into Sarah—who looked more than a little surprised that I was still willing to talk to her, knowing what I did. She was decked out in dozens of clinking bangles and a pair of beaded flip-flops under a swirling black skirt. Her red hair was pulled back into a simple ponytail, making her face look sharper and her dark green eyes look wider.

"Hi, Sarah," I greeted her with a smile, and she turned from her game of tic-tac-toe with Annie.

Her bracelets chinked as she laid her hand on the table. "Oh, hi, Tilly. Um, how are you doing? I mean, with…the new information and everything? I hope you're not freaked out," Sarah said, looking at me worriedly.

I shook my head. "I'm okay. I know none of you would hurt me—well, I'm not sure about Spencer. I think he got a kick out of scaring the hell of me." I grinned to show I didn't really mean it. In a strange way, I trusted Spencer most of all.

Across the table, Annie chewed on the end of her pen thoughtfully, before marking an X in one of the empty boxes on the page. Her face lit up, and I grinned, seeing she'd gotten three crosses in a row. She looked delighted by her victory. I nodded over Sarah's shoulder, and she glanced back at the game board scribbled on the paper, shook her head at her little sister in defeat.

"Looks like you got beat, Sarah," I said, winking at Annie, who giggled.

Sarah sighed. "Yeah, third time in a row." She smiled fondly at her little sister.

Annie beamed proudly, her round cheeks glowing faintly pink, her brown eyes bright with pleasure. I laughed.

"I guess you're looking for Dominic, huh?" Sarah asked, twirling a loose strand of hair around her finger. I nodded. She pursed her lips for a moment, looking thoughtful. "I think he said he was going somewhere with his dad and Spencer—but Desmond's around here somewhere if you want to hang out with him. Or," she added hastily, seeing my expression, "you can have the next game against Annie. Maybe you can beat her, but I warn you, she's a sore loser. She gets all pouty." Sarah splayed a hand at the fresh sheet of paper that Annie was drawing a tic-tac-toe grid on.

The little girl looked up, scowling."I do not get pouty," she said.

I started to draw out another grid for the next game, but a shadow fell across the page, and I looked up with a smile, expecting to see Dominic. I blinked in surprise as Spencer loomed over me, looking all dark and brooding as usual, only somehow more so. I opened my mouth to ask him where Dominic was, but he spoke first, his voice brisk and serious.

"We need to talk. Now."

Startled by the look on his face, I just nodded and stood up. Next to me, Sarah touched my arm, making me hesitate. I looked at her, confused, but she was looking at Spencer—pouting.

"Spencer, that's no way to talk to a lady," she said, chastising.

Spencer glanced at her, his mouth quirking, and she smiled at him playfully. It made me want to knock out some of her perfect teeth, which surprised me, because I wasn't generally a violent person. I wasn't normally jealous either. I had no right being jealous.

Smiling thinly, I said, "It's okay. If he needs to talk to me, he can. Just as long as he remembers his manners." I hated the sickly sweet tone to my voice, and hoped Sarah couldn't hear the bitter edge to it.

Sarah's smile tightened and she flipped her hair. "I'm sure he will," she said, then turned back to Annie, who was watching the whole exchange with a small frown, as if she didn't understand what was happening.

I turned back to Spencer, who appeared to be trying to hide a smirk, and he gestured for me to follow him. Scowling, I did.

Spencer led me to the stream, and sat down on the boulder he'd been on that first night I'd found him there. He stretched out his legs, his heels resting on the grass, and I sat down next to the boulder. He looked down at me with a pensive frown, his eyes shadowed by his hair.

Unerringly, I stared right back at him, curious and impatient, waiting for him to say something. He didn't. He stayed silent, and I ran out of patience.

With a sigh, I asked, "Where's Dominic?"

He blinked, his frown deepening. "He and Frank are giving the rest of the pack orders regarding the hunters wandering around the woods with silver bullets." His jaw tensed and he looked up into the trees.

The sunlight filtered through the leaves, creating dancing patterns on the dry brown dirt. Reflections from the water sparkled on the grass like fireflies darting between the blades. The sky was a washed out, pale blue, with wispy grey clouds moving in across the treetops. The slight bite to the wind was a hint that autumn was just around the corner.

"The witches hired the hunters, didn't they?" I asked quietly. I knew Olivia would have told the others where I was by then, and they would try to get me back however they could. I didn't know how they knew the people protecting me were werewolves, but it didn't matter. It just mattered that they knew, they wanted the werewolves dead, and it was my fault.

Without looking at me, Spencer nodded. "I think so. The men don't know what they're hunting, though. The witches supply the bullets, and the men just want their money, so they don't ask questions." He pulled one of his legs up to his chest and clasped his fingers loosely around his knee. His eyes moved as he stared into the trees, and I spotted the little red squirrel he was tracking. I wondered if he was considering grabbing lunch.

I frowned. "You haven't told Frank or the others that you know who's hiring the hunters?"

He glanced at me, and shook his head. "If I told them, they'd want to know why the witches were after us, and then I'd have to tell them about you. It isn't my secret to tell, and if Frank knew you were the reason we're being hunted, he'd hand you over in a heartbeat." Spencer's eyes flashed gold, and his upper lip peeled back over his teeth. "I won't let them hand you over to the witches, Tilly," he said, his voice so dark it was almost a growl.

I shrunk back, swallowing nervously, and I asked in a small voice, "Why not?" His words made my heart flutter a little faster, not entirely with just relief, and I couldn't be sure if he could hear that or not. I hoped not.

His expression changed, but his eyes remained the strange gold of a wolf's. Meeting his eyes was like staring into the heart of the beast inside him. It made a prickle of fear run over the back of my neck, and I bit my lip.

"I told you," he said roughly, "I'm not a monster." Then he smiled, a tiny wry twist of his lips.

He blinked, and his eyes were blue again, but my sense of fear didn't entirely abate. There was still something primal inside me screaming that he was dangerous, and another primal part of me was screaming that it didn't care if he was dangerous.

I ignored both shrieking voices, and said, "No, you aren't. But I think you don't really care whether people believe that or not. Do you?" I saw from his face that I'd surprised him. I added, "The rest of your pack act like you should be avoided, like you're more dangerous than all of them, and you let them act that way. You don't try to interact with them or make nice with them. You just…wander around by yourself at night, all shadowy and mysterious and quiet. You act like that, and it creeps them out, but you don't try to change it."

I realised, as I said it, that I wasn't criticising him. I envied him. I wished I could hide out in the quiet night time trees and not care what anyone else thought of me. But the thing was, I didn't know how to feel about myself, so I needed other people to think I was good and kind. Otherwise, I might start to believe I was evil for the things I'd been made to do for the witches. For what I was, whatever I was, with my inexplicable connection to the Underworld. If being tied to Their World didn't make me evil, what did? If risking my life to save a wolf didn't make me good, what did?

For a long moment, Spencer just looked at me, and I couldn't tell if he was surprised, annoyed, confused, or some combination of the three. I found it disconcerting.

Then he said, "I'm not a monster, but I am a werewolf." He said it as if it explained his behaviour, his strange manner and attitude.

I understood. There was a wolf inside him, a creature who roamed the night with silent steps under the moonlight. Spencer was more wolf than person in that he reflected a predator more than he reflected the people he faced. If you put him in front of a mirror, I was sure yellow eyes and long fangs would look back from the silvery glass.

I smiled with one side of my mouth, thinking, *You're definitely something alright.*

Chapter Eleven

** Spencer **

Two days until the full moon. Just two more days, and then he was free. Two more days until even Frank couldn't stop him from Changing. It had only been a single day since he'd last wolfed out, and already his skin was itching, his muscles feeling cramped. He looked up at the slightly asymmetrical silver coin in the sky, digging his nails into the soft bark of the rotting log he was sitting on. The night smelled of shadows, moss and wild things lurking in the bushes. Spencer sighed, lowering his face into his hands. Looking at the moon only made his wolf twitchier, but even without looking at it, he could feel the pull of it calling to him.

He was sitting further own the stream than usual, mostly because he'd walked out of his cabin half an hour before, and had found himself heading in the wrong direction. Not toward the stream, but toward another cabin, the one he could see out his bedroom window. He'd gotten halfway through the trees, before he realised what he was doing, shook his head, and turned away in frustration. He didn't even know what he'd been thinking. Okay, no, that was a lie. He hadn't been thinking at all. He'd been wanting to see Tilly, to talk to her again—he liked talking to her.

Earlier, she'd surprised him. It was a rare occurrence when someone managed to surprise him, and it had happened more than once lately. But Tilly seemed to do it on a daily basis. It was both discomfiting and intriguing. Talking to her was always a little like playing chess. Sometimes he could predict what she was going to say, he thought he knew what she was thinking, but sometimes she would pull out a move that totally threw him. His conversation with her today had been one of the occasions where she'd said something that snatched one of his protective pawns away from him, leaving him feeling vulnerable.

I told you, I'm not a monster, he'd said, and she'd stared at him thoughtfully for a moment, her grey eyes uncomfortably piercing on his. Something about those grey eyes made his stomach twist and his wolf purr.

No, you aren't, she'd said slowly, her thin brows pulled down slightly. *But I think you don't really care whether people believe that or not. Do you?* It wasn't even really a question. She'd already known the answer. That had made him feel all out of sorts, because she was right. It was strange to think that Tilly, an outsider, understood him better than his own half-brothers— his own blood. His own kind.

A rustle in the trees behind him snapped Spencer out of his thoughts. He tensed, lifting his chin to sniff the air, and then relaxed. He didn't have to turn to know who it was. A small smile touched his mouth as he said, "Evening, Tilly." His voice held his usual quiet manner, despite the sudden perking of his wolf inside him at the familiar scent on the air.

There was another rustle, and then Tilly stepped out from the trees, moving past him to the stream. She hesitated on the edge of the water, and the hairs on the back of Spencer's neck prickled with the instinct that something was wrong. He frowned. He thought Tilly might step forward into the stream. She swayed slightly toward it, her toes curling over the edge of the grass. She was barefoot, dressed in just a long t-shirt that came down to her mid-thighs. Her pale hair was loose around her face, bits of leaves caught in the silky strands, and her ankles were covered in scratches. Spencer got to his feet and moved toward her, his heart beating an uneven rhythm. It wasn't quite fear, but anxiety at least. Something was wrong; he could feel it.

"Tilly?" he said softly, moving toward her cautiously.

She didn't turn her head, didn't even twitch at the sound of his voice. She just stood there, swaying, as if to some distant music that he couldn't hear. His wolf was uneasy, bristling, but he held it back. He reached out and touched Tilly's arm, but she didn't react. He shuddered at how unresponsive she was, as if he were invisible to her. Then he saw her eyes were closed and realised he was invisible to her, because she wasn't even awake. That sent sharp, hot spikes up his spine and he jerked back, a sound halfway between a growl and a whine escaping his lips as the hairs on his arms stood straight. There was something unnatural about a person walking around insensible to what they were doing.

Spencer had heard somewhere that you were never supposed to wake a sleepwalker, though he wasn't entirely sure why. With his teeth bared almost absently, he crept back to the swaying girl and waved a hand in front of her face. She didn't flinch. Behind her closed lids, her eyes were darting rapidly back and forth. It creeped him out, and he didn't know what to do. It was like staring at a zombie. No, not a zombie. In the moonlight, Tilly was all pale hair and milky skin, too pretty and ethereal to be a zombie. She was more like a ghost, lost as she wandered the darkened woods.

Then, just as suddenly as she'd come, Tilly turned and started to walk back into the trees. Her movements were slow and strange, almost clumsy. She walked straight through a patch of thorny brambles, scratching her slender legs, and Spencer blinked in surprise before chasing after her. She didn't notice him as he followed her through the darkness, making sure she didn't trip over anything or walk through more thorns. Unlike when she was awake, she was eerily quiet moving through the woods.

With a strange thickness in his throat, Spencer followed Tilly all the way back to her cabin, and watched from the bottom of the steps as she climbed up them onto the porch. She reached for the door handle, turned it, and the door swung open. Tapping his fingers against his thigh nervously, Spencer debated whether he should follow her in and make sure she didn't try to make an omelette while she was at it. He thought that would likely end badly. But to go in uninvited, while she was unconscious of her actions, felt somehow wrong, even if it was for a good reason.

The front door of the cabin closed while he was standing there uncertainly, and he settled for slipping around to the window. He peered inside, feeling just a little guilty about it, and saw Tilly walk unfalteringly from the living room, past the kitchen, and down a hallway. Frowning, he moved to her bedroom window in time to see her coming in, closing the door mechanically behind her, and getting into bed. She folded the covers over herself with sluggish fingers, and rolled over to face the window.

There were still bits of leaves in her hair. A line formed between her brows, her lids fluttering, and her lips parted slightly. Through the glass, Spencer heard her whimper, and he gritted his teeth, his fingernails sinking into the chipped paint of the windowsill.

Inside the cabin, Tilly was still again, and he watched the steady rise and fall of her chest. She was soundly asleep again, really asleep, and Spencer sighed a little in relief. Leaning his forehead against the wall of the cabin, next to the window, he felt the moon stroking the nape of his neck with cold fingers. His muscles twitched with the Change pushing at him, and he cursed Frank for his 'No Changing Without Permission' order. He wanted to break it, wanted to feel the night in his wolf form, but to break it would be to put himself further outside the pack. At that moment, the pack was exactly where he needed to be, because that was where Tilly was most of the time—in the thick of the pack, with Dominic.

If there was ever a reason for him to force himself out of his pattern of solitariness, it was to keep an eye on Tilly. He was the only one who knew her secret and about the witches who were hunting her, just as they had hired the men to hunt him and his pack. So he was the only one who could protect her, and more than that, he *wanted* to be the only one to protect her. He wasn't sure if that was his wolf or his jealousy over Dominic speaking, but either way, starting the next day, he was going to stay by Tilly's side as much as possible.

He sat down with his back against the cabin wall, and looked up at the moon. Not for the first time, he reminded himself that Tilly wasn't his to protect—couldn't be his. It didn't matter. If she was anyone's to protect, she would be his, no matter what the pack, Frank or Dominic had to say about it.

** Tilly **

For the second morning in a row, I woke up with dirt in my bed and leaves between my toes. I spent half an hour scrubbing twigs from my hair, and then changed the sheets on my bed, ignoring the sick feeling deep in my stomach. If I pretended as if I wasn't freaked out by it, maybe it would stop...and maybe it wouldn't, but at least I didn't have to think about it.

I was halfway through eating a bowl of Coco Puffs cereal while frying up bacon and tomato, when I heard a knock at the door, quiet and hesitant. I smiled to myself. I'd been expecting company for breakfast, but when I opened the door with my tablespoon in my hand, the company I received wasn't who I'd expected. Instead of green eyes and curls, I was met with blue eyes and sleek black hair. I blinked.

"Spencer?" I winced at the slightly insulting, disbelieving tone to my voice.

Spencer just smiled wryly, as if he'd been expecting that kind of reception. It was just that I couldn't imagine a reason for him to be on my porch.

He exchanged his wry smile for a mocking one, and said, "You're going to catch midges."

It took me a second to work out what he meant, and snapped my mouth shut, scowling at him. "Sorry. I'm just in shock because it turns out you can walk in daylight after all." I pulled open the door a little further, indicating for him to come in. He hesitated, his mouth working, and then came inside slowly as if he was expecting someone to jump out from behind the door and brain him with a lamp.

Glancing around the cabin warily, he said, "I'm a werewolf, not a vampire."

I watched him moving around and noted that his hands were casually folded behind his back, but they were not so casually in fists. I wondered if it was because the cabin was unfamiliar territory, marked with my scent instead of his, or because of something else. When he turned back to face me with an eyebrow slightly raised, I shrugged.

"I thought you might be both." I slid back to the kitchen, where the bacon was spitting angrily under the grill and my cereal was getting soggy. I dropped my spoon back into the bowl of chocolaty milk and stirred it around a little, while Spencer leaned against the breakfast bar, but I suddenly wasn't all that hungry. Something about having Spencer in my cabin made me nervous. I told myself it was because he was a predator, a deadly wild animal inside that skin—more deadly and wild, I was certain, than Dominic ever was.

"You saw me in daylight yesterday afternoon," he pointed out.

His eyes narrowed when I turned and dumped the rest of my cereal down the sink, but he didn't say anything about it, or ask why I was cooking enough bacon to feed a small army—or in that case, a growing teenage werewolf. I hoped Dominic didn't take it the wrong way when he arrived and saw Spencer was there.

I shrugged again, prodding at the hissing bacon with a fork. It spat at my hand, hot grease stinging my wrist, and I snatched my hand back. "Evil bacon," I muttered, and then glanced at Spencer.

He was trying not to grin.

"It was cloudy yesterday," I returned.

He just shrugged fluidly. The bacon bit me again, and I grumbled a curse. Spencer snorted, and I glared at him.

"You're the very picture of homeliness, Tilly. Dominic must be very lucky." He rolled his eyes.

I glared harder, but felt heat touch my cheeks. "What's that supposed to mean?" I asked, putting my hands on my hips. Unfortunately, I was still holding the fork I'd been prodding the bacon with and somehow managed to stab myself in the leg. "Ouch!" I lifted the fork and glared at it, before slamming it down on the countertop.

Spencer's shoulders shook as he tried not to laugh. Then there was another knock at the door and I sighed, relaxing a little. Spencer stopped laughing abruptly and lifted his head in a way that, even in human form, looked lupine. I could just imagine his ears pricked toward the door like a dog's, but the look on his face said his tail wasn't wagging.

I patted him on the head as I walked past, and he shot me a piercing glower. I smiled back blandly.

"Down, boy. It's only Dominic." I had my hand on the door handle when I thought I heard him say something like, "That's what I was afraid of." I guessed I'd misheard.

I pulled the door open, grinning, and Dominic beamed at me for just a second before his expression went south. He lifted his chin slightly, and I knew he was sniffing the air, either for the bacon, or for the other wolf in my company. He had pretty much the same expression Spencer had, so I supposed it wasn't the bacon he was smelling. I blew out my cheeks noisily and Dominic's eyes returned to me, narrowed.

"You have company," he said tightly, as if Spencer were an intruder I hadn't noticed was in my cabin.

I nodded. "Camping rule number four: the smell of food will always attract animals. Apparently, that includes the ones who are also hungry teenage boys. Come on in and kill this bacon for me. It keeps spitting at me." I ignored the shadow on Dom's face and moved back into the kitchen, letting him choose whether he wanted to come in.

He came in and closed the door behind him. Spencer turned around, his face perfectly blank, and I glanced up from spearing strips of bacon onto plates to see that Dominic was wearing his usual cheery grin again. They exchanged a nod by way of greeting. I rolled my eyes.

I shoved a plate of bacon and grilled tomato in front of each of them, but Dominic didn't sit down at the breakfast bar. Instead, he moved around it and popped up onto the kitchen counter, balancing his plate on his legs. I scowled at him.

"Has nobody ever told you not to sit on the kitchen counter?" I asked, folding my arms over my chest.

Dominic grinned at me. "Nope. You forget, we're animals, Tilly. Rules of etiquette are different for us. We play with our food, we run around outside without a jacket on, we sit on kitchen counters."

He flourished a hand over himself to indicate his position on the worktop next to the sink, and I sighed, shaking my head in despair.

"Someone should teach you some manners," I said, crossing to the sink to turn on the taps. I squirted some washing-up liquid into the basin, covering my cereal bowl, a glass, and various pieces of cutlery in slimy green stuff that started to froth up with the water.

Dominic leaned over, and murmured, "And are *you* going to teach me some manners, Tilly?"

His voice was low, but I knew Spencer could hear it. I ducked my head, biting my lip. I whirled the taps until the water stopped; the basin was full of hot, bubbly water.

I took Dominic's already empty plate and said, "If I were to teach you manners, I'd use a dog whistle and bacon bits. I bet I could even teach you to sit where you're supposed to sit." I pointed to the breakfast bar where Spencer was sitting, snickering, but when he noticed me looking at him, his expression turned as fiercely blank as ever. I wondered what was going through his head. What was going through my head was a replay of the last time Dominic had been in the kitchen with me. I shoved the memory away before my face could flame.

With a good natured huff, Dominic slid off the countertop and shooed me out of the way of the sink, handing me a dishtowel.

I glared at him. "Hey!"

He smirked at me. "Hey, yourself."

"I can wash the dishes myself. I don't have a bandage this time!" I lifted up my arm to show him. I'd taken off the bandage that morning, because it had somehow gotten dirt on it, and the scrape I'd gotten when my wolf—when Spencer—had knocked me out of the way of Olivia's shot was almost healed anyway. There was just a patch of rough pink skin where the scrape had been.

Dominic just handed me a wet, soapy plate. I stared at it, then at him, and then turned to Spencer. He was scowling at the prongs of his fork as if he was trying to bend them with the power of his mind. I whistled sharply to get his attention. He glanced at me from under his dark brows, glaring, clearly not impressed by the whistle. I held up the dishtowel and threw it at him. He snagged it out of the air, and stared at it as if he had no idea what it was for. I laughed.

"You two can do the washing up," I said.

Spencer's expression darkened again, and Dominic looked at me over his shoulder, frowning.

"Where are you going?" he asked as I grabbed my trainers from near the front door. I sat down on the floor to lace them on, glanced up to see Spencer scrubbing a bubbly plate with the dishtowel, an expression of intense concentration—or intense annoyance—on his face. Dominic just looked like a wounded puppy.

I shook my head. "I promised Sarah I'd help her with something."

"What kind of something?"

I shrugged. "Girl stuff."

At that, the boys exchanged a glance and shuddered simultaneously. I grinned. With a rueful sigh, Dom turned back to the soapy water and handed Spencer another plate, muttering, "Girl stuff. The universal secret for scaring the hell out of guys."

I snorted. "That's right; we invented girl stuff exactly for that purpose. Now both of you be good until I get back. No chewing the furniture."

Spencer flipped me off as I went out the door.

** Spencer **

Once Tilly left, an awkward silence fell thick around the cabin. The only sounds were the splashing of the water as Dominic scrubbed dishes, the squeak of the dishtowel on a wet glass, and the boys' soft breathing. Spencer wanted to leave. He couldn't see a reason to keep hanging about since the only reason he'd bothered to come out of seclusion that morning was for Tilly, and she was no longer there. Except, he sensed that Dominic had something to say, and Spencer was curious to hear whatever that might be.

It took a long time for Minnie to work up the courage to ask what he wanted to ask, and he didn't look at Spencer as he asked it. He kept his eyes on the fork he was thoroughly washing. He cleared his throat, and Spencer glanced at him, waiting for him to be done drowning the fork.

"So, um…were you…I mean, did you…" Dominic stopped, his hands stilling on the piece of cutlery, and bit his lip. He stared into the soapy bubbles as if they held the answer to his unasked question.

Spencer snatched the fork from him. "Did I what?" he asked casually, though he knew exactly what Dominic wanted to know. He just wanted to make Dominic say it. It was a little bit cruel, but Spencer wasn't feeling too kindly toward his half-brother right then.

He wondered what Minnie and Tilly would have been doing if he hadn't shown up on her doorstep first. He got the idea that there would have been a lot more going on with those soap bubbles than just washing dishes. It was clear from their banter over the sink that Dominic had been round for breakfast with Tilly before, possibly more than once.

Here in a morning, leaving late in the evening. Oh, yes, I wonder what could possibly be going on with that, Spencer thought sarcastically, ashamed to admit he was a little bitter about it. He had no right to be jealous or bitter, except that he'd been the one to save Tilly's life—twice. He was also the one who was keeping her precious secret from the whole pack, including her curly headed BFF. None of that should have mattered though, because technically, neither of them could have Tilly. It was forbidden, but it didn't seem like Dominic was remembering that part, or maybe he just didn't care.

Dominic shifted uncomfortably, reaching into the sudsy basin and scrubbing at something under the water. He lifted one hand out of the water toward his hair, probably to tug on one of his curls, but then he realised his hand was wet and bubbly, and lowered it back into the water.

"Did you, you know, spend the night here?" he asked abruptly, his voice hard. It was clear from the thin press of his lips that the idea made Minnie very unhappy.

With a tiny, mirthless smile, Spencer slung the dishtowel over his shoulder and crossed his arms, leaning his hip against the cupboard under the counter. "Would it annoy you if I said yes?" he replied evenly.

Dominic glanced at him then, sharp green eyes under soft chestnut curls, and Spencer caught the glint of the wolf in his gaze. Oh yes, it would annoy him greatly if Spencer said he'd spent the night there.

All Dominic said was, "Plates go in that cupboard." He pointed to the cupboard Spencer was leaning against without looking up from the water again.

Spencer eyed the plates sitting, neat and clean, on the countertop, but didn't pick them up. "Is this where you kissed her? You said yesterday that you kissed her. Was it here in front of the sink, over soapy dishes? Or on the sofa in the living room? Or—"

Dominic slammed his hands down on the edge of the sink, the spoon he'd been washing clattering to the floor and leaking bubbles onto the floorboards. He glared at Spencer. "Why, does it annoy you?" he spat Spencer's own words back at him, startling him.

He'd never seen Dominic get quite so rattled over a little teasing—but, of course, it wasn't just a little teasing. There had been a vicious edge behind Spencer's words, and Minnie knew it.

Looking as calm as ever, Spencer bent to pick up the spoon from the floor and pretended to examine it for dirt. "I think you'll have to wash this again," he said blandly, tossing the spoon back into the water with a little splash.

Dominic's fingers tightened on the edge of the sink. "What kind of game are you playing, Spencer?" he asked quietly.

His shoulders shuddered, the hairs on his arms rising, and Spencer knew his brother's wolf was agitated. It was probably a good time to stop antagonising him, but Spencer wasn't quite done yet.

He shrugged, saw the way the nonchalant movement caused Dominic's jaw to twitch. Watching Dom's knuckles turning white on the sink, he said, "I could ask you the same thing."

"What is that supposed to mean?" Dominic snapped.

Spencer pulled the dishtowel from over his shoulder and tossed it onto the countertop. "You know relationships with outsiders are forbidden, and yet it's clear as day that you've got a thing for Tilly. I just hope you're not toying with her. I wouldn't want to be you if she ever found out that's what you were doing." He shook his head as if in disappointment, but in fact, the image of what Tilly might do to Dominic in that circumstance made him want to grin. The stupid boy didn't even know what Tilly was capable of—Spencer did.

With a sound awfully close to a growl, and his green eyes flaring, Dominic whirled on Spencer. "I'm not toying with her! And you're one to speak. It's not like you're as indifferent as you pretend to be, Spencer. Everyone knows you feel something for her!"

With a cruel half-smile, Spencer said, "Ah. Maybe I do, and maybe I don't. But I'm not the one who's been kissing her." He tried to keep the sour tone out of his voice and did it remarkably well. It didn't stop the anger he felt inside, though. He wondered how many times Dominic had kissed Tilly, if it had been more than once, if she'd let him do it or asked him to, if she'd liked it or regretted it. He wondered what it would be like to kiss her, if she'd be hesitant and shy or bold, if she'd like the taste of his lips more than Dominic's.

"Spencer," Dominic said, his voice surprisingly soft.

Spencer blinked and looked at him. There was no anger in his half-brother's face anymore, just a kind ruefulness that was much more his normal attitude. He sighed when Spencer met his gaze.

"I don't want to fight with you over this. You're my brother…whether or not you like it," Dominic smiled, a little wry,

206

"and I don't want to push you out because of a girl. You're right that it's forbidden. I know that. Really, neither of us should even think about—" He shook his head, curls bouncing. "So how about we make a deal? Neither of us is allowed to pursue Tilly. If she wants one of us, it's her choice, and we let her make it on her own. No persuasive action whatsoever." His mouth crooked into a thin, lopsided grin.

Struggling with his pride and his wolf, Spencer took a long moment to think before he answered. Dominic's deal made sense, it was fair, but it also felt like an order. Maybe it was just because Dominic was Frank's son as much as he was. Maybe it was because Minnie was the pack's second in command. Maybe it was just because Spencer didn't like the deal any more than he liked being told he had to ask permission before Changing, but the deal felt like a subtle command.

Slowly, Spencer nodded. "Fine. You've got a deal."

Dominic looked somewhat pleased as he returned to the sink to rewash the spoon he'd dropped, but Spencer could see from the tension in his forearms that he felt it was a hollow victory—and it was. Spencer had said they had a deal, but he'd lied.

** Tilly **

"So…" Sarah murmured, glancing up at me from where she was crouched at my feet, piling folds of fabric together, "What do you think of Spencer?"

207

I groaned aloud at the question, rolling my eyes. "Let's not go there." I shook my head.

 Sarah frowned at the hem of my dress, putting a needle between her teeth as she tried to tease the fabric into doing what it was she wanted. I stood rigid, but my muscles were growing tired. I'd been standing for over half an hour. My feet ached.

"Remind me again why I have to have a special dress? Can't I just wear my shorts?"

Huffing an indignant sigh between her lips, she took the needle from her mouth and stood up to look me in the eye, her dark green eyes narrowed. "Because," she said tightly, "it's the full moon. And you're the first outsider we've ever let watch us Change. The full moon Change is practically a ritual. So if you're going to be there, you need to be dressed for a ritual." With pursed lips, she glanced over my dress so far, and reached out to bunch the fabric of one of the shoulder straps.

I sighed. I looked down at my dress, and reluctantly had to admit it looked lovely. It was pure white, made of some light soft fabric, and it draped down over my body sort of like a Greek tunic, but all the way down to my toes. The collar was a V that dipped uncomfortably low, almost to my belly button, and the dress was cinched at the waist with a golden ribbon. The fabric swished gently against my legs and hips when I moved. Sarah muttered for me to stand still while she bound the shoulder straps into bunches with more gold ribbon.

"You haven't told me what you think of Spencer," Sarah observed, and I glared at her. She raised her eyebrows expectantly, unimpressed by my glower.

"And I don't plan to," I replied firmly.

She pouted at me. "Why not? I thought we were friends!"

I couldn't stand the way she was looking at me pleadingly, guilting me very effectively. So I sighed again. "Because I don't know what to think of Spencer," I said truthfully, fidgeting with the end of the ribbon around my waist. "He's...weird. I mean, sometimes he comes across as really antisocial and mysterious, but sometimes he's kind of..." I trailed off, unsure of the word I was looking for. I wanted to say *sweet*, but that wasn't it. Dominic was sweet. Spencer was...something else. Something I couldn't put a word to.

Sarah made a thoughtful noise, but she wasn't looking at me; she'd moved around to my back and was doing something with the straps of the dress. Her voice was cooler when she spoke again. "And what do you think of Dominic?" she asked.

I thought of him kissing me in my cabin kitchen, and blushed, glad Sarah couldn't see it. I ran the ends of the gold ribbon through my fingers as I spoke. "He's nice. He's kind of excitable, and fun. And I guess he's pretty cute." I chewed on my lower lip, trying to clamp down on a smile, but I could feel it spreading across my lips irresistibly.

Dominic made me smile, and I couldn't help it. There was just something about him. The same way that there was something about

Spencer that fascinated me. They were so different, so completely opposite to one another that it was hard to believe they were related—even if only by half. Dominic was all light and bouncy and Spencer was all dark and still.

Sarah made another thoughtful sound behind her lips, and I wished I could see her expression. "Honestly, if I were you, I'd go for Dom. He'd treat you right, and he's a good hunter. Spencer is barely even part of the pack, and I can't imagine him ever being boyfriend material. Well. I mean, not for a human anyway. He'd get bored of a human girl pretty fast— no offence. It's just how he is."

Sarah made an imperious gesture with her hand that I only caught out of the corner of my eye, and I turned to look at her. She eyed her work with a fingernail against her lips.

I didn't tell her that I wasn't *going for* anyone, because I didn't think she'd believe me, and I wasn't sure I would believe me either. I didn't tell her that I didn't care how good of a hunter Dominic was, or what his status in the pack was, because I wasn't part of the pack. I didn't tell her that I thought she was wrong about Spencer, that maybe she just didn't understand him, because that seemed presumptuous, and it wasn't my place to think I knew Spencer better than someone who'd known him his whole life. I didn't tell her that saying no offence didn't automatically take away the sting of her comments, because I didn't want to admit to myself that it stung in the first place. Why should I care whether Spencer would get bored of a human girl? I wasn't looking to *go for* him…and I wasn't exactly human anyway.

Chapter Twelve

That night, I dreamed of wandering the woods again, but I wasn't running.

I was walking, unstoppably, as if I were being controlled. I couldn't make my legs stop, couldn't lift my arms to grab branches to pull myself to a halt, couldn't even open my mouth to scream for help. Stones dug into my feet painfully, thorns bit at my skin, branches pulled my hair, and all I could do was keep on walking. I could roll my eyes around enough to see the black sky above me, the almost full moon frowning down on me sadly, and the towering trees reaching out to try to still my terrible, terrifying progress. I recognised the area around me, knew where my feet were taking me, but I had no idea why.

Voices, cold voices whispered through the trees to me, cruel laughter echoing from the darkness. I knew the voices, because I'd heard them most of my life, and they'd been haunting my nightmares long before that night. But the wandering nightmares were recent, horrifying in a new way. I could feel the energy of the woods pushing at me, pulling at me, trying to get in and break whatever was compelling me to walk ceaselessly toward the stream. I could hear it close by, a soft babble under the harsh whispers of threatening voices and the breathing of the trees.

My heart pounded rapidly, my breathing quick and frantic. My shut lips muffled a scream as my legs dragged me through a knot of thorns, scratching my bare skin and catching on my nightshirt. Cuts stung my legs and hands, and panic and fear clutched my chest with iron fingers. Ahead of me, I saw the glimmer of the stream, rushing and icy under the moonlight. Undeniably, my feet drew me toward the water, my toes scraping grass instead of dirt, squashing daisies and buttercups as I neared the edge of the stream, my toes curled over the bank...

I paused. My feet stopped pulling me forward to the glint of silver water, bright and menacing. A hesitant sigh of relief escaped my lips, my heart rate slowed as my muscles twitched, burning from the interminable exercise of my possessed body. I could feel goose bumps on my skin, a trickle of blood down my leg from a shallow gash, and wetness on my face from tears I hadn't realised I was crying. I felt the icy, moving water of the stream enclosing my foot, and I whimpered as my body struck into unwanted motion once again, pulling me into the stream.

It's just a dream, it's just a nightmare, it's not real. You're back in your cabin, in your bed, sleeping. This isn't real. *I told myself that over and over, but it felt so real. So real and so terrifying. I was a puppet with someone else pulling my strings. I was trapped inside my own body while—*

"Tilly! Tilly, wake up!"

My eyes flew open at the sound of someone shouting my name from a distance. I immediately jerked backwards because the person

212

shouting my name wasn't at a distance at all. He was right in front of me, gripping my upper arms almost bruisingly tight. Spencer's frantic blue eyes met mine, and I made a strangled sound of shock. His hair was a tangled wreck of black waves and rust coloured leaves, and he was naked. My eyes were drawn inexplicably to his left hip, where the jagged, curling black lines of a strange tattoo stood starkly against his white skin.

My mouth went bone dry, my heart did a funny little jig inside my chest, and my stomach curled up into a tiny, burning knot. I opened my mouth to speak, but no sound came out.
I licked my lips and tried again, my voice coming out as a croaking whisper.

"What's going on?" I asked, casting my eyes over his shoulder because it was easier to think straight when I wasn't looking at his face or, god forbid, his body. I wanted to close my eyes, so I could remember how to breathe, but I knew that would give me away. Instead, I stared fixedly at some blurred point beyond him, not really seeing whatever it was I was looking at.

Spencer released my arms, one finger at a time, and cleared his throat as he stepped back. I still didn't look at him, but I could feel him looking at me.

"You were sleepwalking," he said quietly.

I glanced at him then, startled, and realised that the thing I'd been staring at over his shoulder was a tree. I was outside, in the middle of the woods. Behind me, I could hear the babble of the stream. My feet were wet, and I was shivering. Looking down, I saw

I was wearing only my nightshirt. It came down to my knees, and I was wearing underwear, but I felt terribly exposed.

Stupidly, I said, "I don't sleepwalk." As if that negated the fact that I was undeniably standing outside in the middle of the night in my pyjamas.

Of course, Spencer gave me a look that indicated that he thought I was being intentionally dense, and that he found my denseness mildly amusing. He expressed that with just a slight lifting of his eyebrows and a twitch of his lips.

"Well," Spencer said in an even tone, "for the last four nights, you *have* been sleepwalking." There was concern in the flatness of his lips.

I really wished he'd put some clothes on. My focus was bad enough without the distraction of him being nude. Frowning, I shifted from foot to foot, feeling tiny stones and bits of leaves sticking between my toes. I hugged my arms around myself and shivered. Spencer smiled sympathetically, and I turned my attention to my dirty toes. "I thought you weren't supposed to wake a sleepwalker," I muttered.

He shrugged. "I thought the shock of the water would wake you up, but you just kept walking." He ran a hand through his hair, tousling it further. "The first night, I thought you were just wandering like you usually do, but you walked right past me, and I realised your eyes were closed. So...I've kind of been hanging out outside your cabin the last few nights, to follow you, make sure you didn't go too far or get into trouble. Usually, you would stop when you got to the stream, turn around and go back, but tonight..." He trailed off, face grim.

I nodded slowly. "Well, that explains the leaves in my bed, but I don't understand this. I really don't normally sleepwalk." Something in my head clicked, and I gasped. "The witches. They must have been using a Sleep-stalking Spell on me to lure me out..." His words caught up to me and I blinked. "Wait a second. You've been hanging around my cabin at night?" I didn't know how to feel about that. It was both creepy and kind of sweet, that he'd been looking out for me like that.

Spencer ducked his head, and I thought I saw a touch of colour spread across his cheekbones.

"I just wanted to make sure you didn't get lost or fall in a ditch or something," he said quietly.

I found it funny that he was standing there naked, but it was admitting that he'd been hanging around my cabin at night that had finally made him blush. It was the first time I'd ever seen him embarrassed, and I laughed. I almost didn't recognise the sound of it, too low and soft, sinking into the shadows around me.

As if he'd heard the difference in my laugh as well, Spencer tilted his head quizzically, an odd curve to his lips. His eyes glimmered with the reflection of the moonlight. Suddenly, the air around us felt charged with an unfamiliar energy. Spencer, with strands of black hair brushing his cheekbones, took a half step forward, toward me, and my stomach dipped.

"Matilda," he said my name, my proper name.

For the first time in my life, I didn't hate it. I liked the way it sounded coming from his lips, almost a whisper, almost a purr. My heart jerked, and I was painfully aware of my nightshirt flapping gently against my bare legs, the breeze sneaking under the shirt and moving across my stomach.

Spencer smiled, slowly, and it changed his whole face. He looked dark and seductive. He took another half step closer to me, and the spark of energy that touched my aura almost stung—but not quite. My breathing was shallow and uneven. Spencer's eyes flashed gold and blue. His wolf was awake and pacing inside him. I could sense it just under his skin, wanting to come out. It made me afraid, but at the same time, it gave me a thrill. He was close enough to touch, but I didn't dare move. He was a predator stalking his prey, and I was that prey.

Then Spencer raised his hand, and I stood unflinching as he drew his fingertips across my collarbone, just above the round collar of my nightshirt. Goosebumps lifted in the wake of his touch. He dragged his fingers lightly across my shoulder and down my arm, and gripped my wrist, reeling me in toward him. There were only a few inches of space between us, and I could feel the heat of his body beating against mine, feel his warm breath stirring my hair, and smell his skin—all stormy nights and burning wood. His hair was coal black, blacker than the sky above us. His skin was pale as the moon, and his eyes glowed blue, pale blue with gold around the irises. I couldn't look away from his eyes.

He was so close, his wolf was hungry, and the energy in the space between us sizzled so hot that it was flooding me with heat on the inside, even though my skin was prickling with goose bumps from the breeze. I knew that if I let him kiss me, it wouldn't end with just a kiss. The adrenaline was racing inside me, burning and reckless, and the night felt wild around me. His fingers on my wrist felt too warm and too intimate, his touch making things deep inside me tingle. There was so little between us, literally, only my nightshirt and underwear separated my body and his. I could feel the growling inside him, vibrating through my blood. I'd never felt desire like that, never known it could be so addictive, like a drug I wanted more of.

I stepped back. Spencer stepped forward. His fingers were still on my wrist, probably feeling the insane fluttering of my pulse. His eyes flashed gold again, before returning to blue more slowly. There was a power in his eyes that I could barely resist, didn't want to resist, but I had to.

I thought of Dominic, of his face when he smiled, of the tentative way he'd kissed me in a kitchen full of the smells of bacon and citrus shampoo. What would it do to him if he knew I was attracted to his half-brother? Would it be worse than if he knew I felt *more* than just primal desire toward Spencer? I didn't want to find out. I didn't want to lose Dominic, and I didn't want to lose myself to the dangerous friction dragging me further away from common sense and closer to Spencer's feral gaze. Digging my torn nails into my palms, I took a deep breath, turning my head away. I squeezed my eyes shut, feeling my heart drum on my ribs.

Then I felt Spencer's breath on my neck, his lips against my ear as he murmured, "Don't. Don't turn away from me, Tilly."

I dug my nails into my palms so hard, I was sure I was going to draw blood. The joints in my fingers turned white and sore. "I can't," I said raggedly, "Dominic…" I shook my head.

He growled, leaning closer, his bare thigh brushing mine. Fire shot through me, white-hot, and I lost my breath. Lost my thoughts. Almost lost my control.

"Forget Dominic. I know you want me," he purred, his voice thick with lust and the wolf inside him. His words made everything inside me turn to knots, a noise catching in my throat. "I can smell it on you. Your desire," he whispered it like a secret, like a promise, like a threat.

Drugged by his nearness, his scent, his touch, it took me an eternity to hear his words and not just the rough, dark tone they were growled in. Then a little part of my brain finally, finally kicked to life again through the haze, and I froze. Some of the heat drained out of me, the blood rushing to my feet, and then running back up into my face.

"You…what?" My voice came out heavy, as if I'd been breathing smoke.

Spencer's fingers stilled on my arm, where he'd been drawing teasing nonsense patterns with his fingertips.

I licked my dry lips, but my mouth was a desert. "You mean that literally, don't you?" I asked in a rasping voice, and my stomach sank as I said it, because I already knew the answer. Werewolf. Wolf. Animal. Animals could smell fear, predators especially, but they could smell other things too. Why hadn't I realised it before?

Spencer frowned, a line between his brows. "I..." His frown deepened, his mouth pressing into a line of frustration as he tried to work out what it was I wanted him to say.

There was nothing he could say. I closed my eyes, blowing out my breath as heat stung my cheeks. Embarrassed—I was totally, horrifyingly humiliated. He'd been able to tell all along how he affected me. Was that why he'd been hanging around me when he avoided everyone else? Did he think I would just...did he only want...I couldn't even finish the thought. I bit my lip.

"Tilly," Spencer said softly.

I felt his fingertips brush my cheek. I jerked away, opening my eyes to glare at him. He drew his hand back, looking as if I'd wounded him deeply. I tried to ignore the pang of guilt in my stomach. He sighed.

"Tilly, don't... it's not like that," he murmured, as if he could read my thoughts.

"Like what?" I snapped—or tried to. I wanted to lash out at him, but my voice came out soft and trembling, the voice of a hurt little girl.

Spencer looked down. "I'm not just...it's not...don't think so little of me, Tilly." He shook his head. "Don't think that just because

I'm part animal, I feel only animal needs. I'm as human as you are, I feel emotions the same way you do, and what I feel…" Pausing, he looked up again, his blue eyes meeting mine. "I feel like I *like* you, Tilly. No, don't look at me like that," he added.

I wondered what expression was on my face.

"I don't really like anyone, except maybe my half-brothers. I don't dislike people, but I don't generally like them either. But you're different, Tilly. You judge me for who I am, not for who my mother was, or what she did to my father. I like you, and I know Dominic likes you, too, and that drives me crazy. Wolves aren't known for temper control when it comes to females, but then neither are teenage boys." His smile was bitter.

"Spencer," I breathed, astounded. It was the most I'd ever heard him say at once, and what he was saying made my heart trip and my head spin.

He moved forward, so fast I didn't even have time to gasp, and his lips brushed my forehead lightly. Just the slightest touch of his mouth on my skin, but I felt it all the way to my toes.

"Just thought you should know," he whispered into my hair.

I drew a breath of his rainwater scent, lifting my face to his, but he was already retreating. He backed away from me, smiling wryly as my fingers trailed across his bare shoulder, my fingertips tingling. Then he was sinking into the shadows, disappearing, and I knew he was already a wolf again.

For a moment, I stood there, touching the spot on my forehead where his lips had brushed. I was trembling, and I didn't know if it was from the cold, the shock of waking up from a nightmare that wasn't just a nightmare after all, or the lingering adrenaline of desire.

Slowly, clumsily, I returned to my cabin, barely aware of where I was going. My mind was a mess, and I knew that I wouldn't be getting back to sleep with the scent of rainstorms and wood smoke burning in my nose.

Chapter Thirteen

** Tilly **

The final couple of days until the full moon passed in a blur. Dominic and Spencer joined me for breakfast the morning of the big event, which was about as awkward as it had been the first time. Then Dominic insisted on showing me the route the wolves would run that night, since I wouldn't get to run with them—obviously. I just got to watch them Change, and then I...I didn't know. Stood around until they came back? Returned to my cabin for a cuppa? I was hoping Sarah would give me a little guidance on what I was meant to do before the ritual started.

"So...looking forward to tonight?" Dominic asked, holding up a branch as I passed under it.

I gave him a swift, grateful smile and he let go of the branch, sweeping into a gentlemanly bow. I blinked.

"Shouldn't I be asking you that?" I replied.

I stepped over a raised tree root, only to slip on another one I hadn't noticed buried under some scattered leaves. Dominic caught my arm, steadying me. I frowned at my feet. I didn't usually stumble like that, the woods always steered me, guiding my feet. I wasn't focused on the energy around me. My mind was all over the place, distracted and flitting from worry to worry. The witches, the ritual later, the wolves being out in force with the hunters looking for them, the dirt I kept finding in my bed in a morning, and Spencer. No specific worry about him, just Spencer in general made me anxious. His sudden daylight appearances had me a little thrown and a tad spooked. He just popped up out of nowhere sometimes, and vanished again just as abruptly. I wasn't sure what he was doing, except for annoying Dominic.

"This is normal for me. Well, your presence excluded. We Change on the full moon every month. It's no big deal really." Dom shrugged, shoving his hands into his jeans pockets. "But it'll be a new experience for you. Are you scared? You don't have to be. Everyone is totally in control in wolf form. Nobody's going to hurt you."

I smiled softly. "I know. You've said that before."

He cut a glance at me from under his curls. His responding smile was shy. "I wasn't sure you'd still believe me, now that you know…" He looked away.

"Now that I know you're all werewolves? Of course, I still believe you. You were a werewolf when you promised me the first time, and nobody hurt me. The only thing that's changed is now I *know* you're a werewolf, so I don't expect anyone to hurt me any more than I did before."

I stepped in front of him, and waited until he met my eyes. His were a startling clear green, but if I looked closely, I could see flecks of gold in the green rings. "What you are doesn't make your promises mean less to me, Dominic. It's who you are that makes me trust you."

I don't know why I was suddenly feeling all sentimental. Maybe it was the bad feeling creeping up on me, or maybe it was just the way he looked at me with his bronze curls in his bright eyes, and his dimple a faint line in his cheek.

Sunlight falling through the gently waving leaves of the trees caught the angles of his face, lighting something in his expression that I couldn't define, but understood anyway. My stomach stirred with nerves, my heart tripped, but my hand was steady as I raised it slowly to touch his curls. His eyes didn't leave mine, but the green flared with sparks of gold as I tugged lightly on one of his loose auburn curls. His mouth twitched, but the rest of him was unnaturally still.

His voice barely audible, he whispered, "I'm glad you trust me."

My fingers tightened, wrapping his curls around them. I swallowed, taking a step closer. I kept my eyes on his face, not entirely sure what I was doing. I just felt like I had to do it.

"I'm not really used to this sort of thing," I said quietly, my voice rough.

His dimple flickered.

"I just…want to try something…" I checked his expression, making sure it was okay, that I had permission to try. The slight lowering of his lids, the flash of his eyes, let me know I did. Let me know I probably had permission to try anything I wanted right then.

Tentatively, I took another half step forward, until I had to tip my head back to look up at him, until I could smell leaves and oranges on him, until I heard his breathing hitch for just a moment.

His hair was silky in my fingers, soothing my nerves a little. Carefully, I raised myself on my toes, shutting my eyes, and pressed my lips against his.

My heart stumbled a little. Dominic stayed perfectly still, waiting, and I leaned into him slightly. He reacted, one hand lifting to touch my shoulder blade. His palm was warm against my back—warmer than the sunlight stroking the nape of my neck and the top of my head. I shifted, leaning back, and he let me go.

I lowered myself down so my feet were flat on the ground and stepped back. Biting down on my lip, I opened my eyes. Dominic was looking at me with yellow eyes, a slight smile curving his mouth. His curls were a little mussed from my fingers grasping them. I smiled back hesitantly.

"What was that for?" he asked, his soft smile cracking into a wider grin.

I looked down and shrugged. "Good luck?"

"For you, or for me?"

"Both, I suppose."

He paused, and then said, "Well. I feel luckier than a four leaf clover now."

He reached out and took my hand lightly in his, his dirt-smudged fingers enclosing mine. I smiled, the strange bad feeling that had been slinking along the edges of my shoulder blades disappearing. Maybe I would be as lucky as he felt, and nothing would go wrong later. Maybe.

Chapter Fourteen

** Tilly **

That evening, when it was time, I lifted my chin and stalked out the door in my bare feet and fancy dress, not bothering to lock my door. Sarah led me down the steps from the porch, the wood dry and rough under my soles. It was almost pitch black outside, but Sarah's hair was a bright beacon, so I followed her into the trees as that cold feeling knotted around my spine, gripping with icy fingers. I glanced up through the branches and spotted the moon, fat and round, shining in the endless expanse of charcoal sky. I didn't know if there was a moon goddess, but I prayed to her anyway, asking that nothing would go wrong.

When we reached the site of the ceremony, I was pleasantly surprised to see it was the clearing around the massive oak tree that Dominic had taken me to when I'd first arrived at their camp. Just like that evening, the tree was lit up with little hanging lanterns, making it glow like a great jewel. But this time, there was no picnic, and Dominic and I weren't alone. Everyone was there, even the infants. Ben and Polly were yipping excitedly, no noise I'd ever heard a toddler make before. Chris, in shorts with the batman logo printed on them, was racing Justin back and forth from the oak tree to the edge of the clearing. Annie was watching them with bright eyes, as if she wanted to join in. Bob and Greg were talking to Graham, and Frank was saying something to John, his face serious.

Reflexively, my eyes searched the crowd and found Dominic and Desmond both wearing just shorts, hanging about under the heavy boughs of the oak. Chewing my lip, I glanced around once more, looking for Spencer, but I couldn't see him. I wasn't entirely surprised, but I was a little disappointed.

Ever since the other night, when he'd admitted to liking me, he'd been…not avoiding me—not at all—but avoiding being *alone* with me. He was okay when there was someone else with me, even if it was Dominic. Though I kept an eye on him when they were in the same vicinity, after what he'd said about Dominic liking me driving him crazy, but the second it was just me and him, he made up an excuse to leave, or even just walked off without saying a word.

I tried not to be hurt. I knew I'd stung him the other night. I just didn't know what had really upset him: my assumption that he'd only been hanging after me because he wanted sex—although that had definitely made him angry—or that I'd turned away from him because of Dominic.

When I'd been able to snag a few minutes alone with him without him bolting, I'd tried to talk to him and apologise, but it was like talking to a brick wall. He just ignored me or shrugged and said it was no big deal. He was lying. It was a big deal, and we both knew it. I just didn't know how to get him to listen to me. I couldn't get through to him.

I understood, after that, what Dominic had really meant when he said Spencer was *distant*. I'd thought I understood before, when he'd just been a quiet shadow that only slunk out at night, but I realised that that had been damn near social compared to the Grim Reaper lurking silently and darkly around me the past few days. Distant? Even when he was standing three feet away, it was as if he was three miles away.

A low whistle startled me out of my thoughts, and I realised I was glaring darkly at my bare toes peeking out from under the excessively long hem of my dress. Trying to brighten my expression, I looked up to see Dominic and Desmond walking toward me. I guessed from his smirk that Desmond had been the one to whistle, his eyes darting up and down my body, taking in the dress. Dominic's green eyes were wide, almost awestruck, trailing more slowly over me.

I smiled shyly, touching the skirt of my dress, my face growing hot under the scrutiny. As slyly as possible, I returned the favour, intrigued. I'd never seen either boy shirtless before, and it wasn't a bad sight. Desmond was a little bulkier than Dominic, but they were both leaner than Spencer. I couldn't help but compare. Des had a little bit of hair on his chest, not much. Dominic had a birthmark just above his bellybutton, in the shape of an oak leaf. I wondered, helplessly, if Spencer had any birthmarks…he did have that tattoo…

A little distance away, Sarah turned, watching as the two boys gawked at me openly. Her mouth turned down at the corners. I lifted my hands in a semi-shrugging, semi-apologetic gesture when she caught my eyes. I felt uncomfortable, as if I was deliberately stealing the limelight, but she was the one who'd made the dress. I guess she'd just done a better job with it than she'd thought. That wasn't my fault.

"Wow," Dominic murmured, blinking as if someone had shone a bright light in his eyes. "Tilly, you look…" He shook his head, at a loss for words.

Desmond gave me a sly look. "Hot?" he put in.

Dominic nudged him. I looked down at myself, surprised. Did I look hot? I certainly looked different from when I was wearing my scrappy shorts and oversized hoodie. But hot? I suppose the plunging neckline probably had a lot to say toward Desmond's opinion. Self-consciously, I tugged at the fabric, pulling it closed over my chest and wishing fervently that I had at least worn a bra. But it really wasn't the kind of dress you could wear a bra with.

"I was going to say beautiful," Dominic said, glaring at Des, but there was colour on his cheekbones.

Desmond rolled his eyes and opened his mouth to retort, but someone else cut him off.

"Ravishing," a smooth, quiet voice said from behind me, dark and soft as velvet.

A delicate shudder ran down my spine, and I froze. I willed my expression to stay steady as I turned to look at Spencer, but when I saw him leaning casually against a tree right behind me, shirtless with his hands in his jeans pockets—of course he wasn't wearing shorts like the rest of them—I suspected my will failed me. Spencer flicked his eyes over me, swift and disinterested, but I thought I saw a glimmer of wolfy gold in the blue depths as he noted the V of bare skin exposed by the plunging neckline of the dress.

I felt someone step up close behind me, putting a hand somewhat possessively on my shoulder, and I knew it was Dominic. I glanced up at him, saw he was glowering at Spencer as if he'd said something to insult me, instead of complimenting me.

"What?" he asked, his voice strained with the effort of sounding at least partially civil.

I blinked. I'd never seen Dominic so riled before.

Spencer raised one eyebrow just a millimetre, the rest of him perfectly still...perfectly delicious to look at. I turned my eyes down.

"How she looks. She looks...*ravishing,*" Spencer said with deliberate slowness.

I could feel his eyes lingering on me, and I glanced up in time to catch his intimate smile, and looked down again hastily. My heart stumbled over an erratic, quick beat. Dominic's fingers tightened ever so slightly on my shoulder, barely noticeable if I hadn't been so painfully aware of his touch on my bare skin. Not the same way as I had been aware of my bare skin the other night with Spencer, when even his fingertips on my cheekbone had been enough to spark a fire inside me, and his thigh brushing mine had sent lightning through my body. No, I was aware of Dominic's touch, because I knew Spencer was, too. And I knew he wasn't happy about it, despite his calm demeanour.

Thankfully, Des stepped in to break the tension. He snapped his fingers. "Ravishing! Yes, that's the word I was looking for!"

I looked at him, giving him a knowing look. Over my head, I felt Dom giving him a glower.

With an unladylike snort that was at odds with my very feminine dress, I said, "Somehow, I don't think that was the word that you were really looking for, Des."

He just shrugged, unashamed. I put my hands on my hips, three pairs of eyes went to my breasts as the draping collar parted further, and crossed my arms instead, face burning. "Oh my God! Stop eyeing me like I'm a piece of choice meat!"

All three of them snorted in response. I glared at each of them in turn, Des first and Spencer last. Only Dominic had the grace to look even slightly abashed. He tugged on one of his curls, not meeting my eyes. Spencer's mouth twitched into a one-sided, and not entirely amused, smile.

"Trust me, if we were eyeing you like meat, you'd know the difference," he said, his tone unexpectedly serious.

I frowned and turned away from him, partly because looking at him shirtless made me feel funny and…melty. There was no other word for the strange feeling of my stomach slowly turning to warm mush inside me. Then Frank raised his voice, and I jumped.

"Attention please!" he bellowed.

We all turned to face him. He stood in front of the giant oak tree, the light of the lanterns haloing his large form, casting his stretched shadow across the clearing. Like Spencer, and unlike the rest of the pack, the alpha was wearing jeans instead of shorts. His broad chest was bare, though. He was a lot more muscular than I'd thought, but it was a kind of blocky musculature, nothing like his sons' lean and defined bodies.

Frank raised his thick arms, motioning for silence, and the crowd fell quiet. With a broad smile, he boomed, "Welcome, my friends and family, *my pack*, to the full moon of August!"

A cheer went up from the crowd, yips and howls joining the human roars of excitement. Frank grinned savagely, more a baring of teeth than a smile. He held his hands out for silence, and the group hushed so he could continue.

"I know that times have been trying lately. We have faced threats from the neighbouring pack, but we have concluded our differences peacefully! We have promised a joining of our two packs to come, which will bring us much strength, and I believe it will be good for us!" Frank roared, and yelps of agreement rose from his gathered pack members.

"We have also seen much happiness this month! Young Annie Changed for the first time at the beginning of the month! Laura, our sweet Laura, has turned fifteen!"

He pointed beefy fingers at the girls, and Annie shied into Sarah's legs as the crowd clapped proudly. Laura raised her chin, looking solemn and dignified. Frank waved for the clapping to subside, and then his eyes fell on me, steely grey-green eyes that pierced me uncomfortably even from across the clearing, with the whole pack between us. Behind me, I felt someone stiffen, and knew without looking that it was Spencer. Dominic, next to me, took my fingers slyly in his as I met Frank's stare across thirty feet of space.

"This month, we have welcomed someone new into our pack. She is not a wolf, like us, but she has proven herself trustworthy. She has saved one of our own, stood up for us against the human men who are now hunting us without knowing what it is they hunt!"

There were roars of outrage, and I gripped Dominic's fingers. When the roars died down, Frank met my gaze again, and I thought that I saw softness in his expression. A cold breath of air touched the back of my neck, raising the hairs there. Another hand slipped carefully into my free one, and I almost jerked in surprise. I cut my eyes to Spencer, but he was looking straight ahead as his fingers curled around mine. With my pulse pounding in my ears, I barely heard Frank continuing to address the crowd, his eyes still on me.

"Tilly has proven herself to be kind and understanding. She has kept our secret without disgust or fear of what we are! And for that we are thankful! Tilly," he paused, his voice softening.

He dipped his head once respectfully in my direction. All eyes turned to me, some wide and admiring, some narrowed but approving, all glowing reflectively in the moonlight.

"We welcome you to our pack," Frank finished.

For a moment, I saw him as a powerful leader—as an Alpha. My face blank, I nodded back, returning his respect. I didn't hold it against him that he'd wanted me away from the pack before he'd even met me. I understood why he'd thought I was a threat, and I thought I would have probably acted the same in his position. What mattered was that he'd let me stay and given me the chance to prove I wasn't a danger to his pack. What mattered was that I had friends, people I could trust—Sarah, Desmond, little Annie, motherly Jane, Dominic, and Spencer.

The alpha raised his voice again, lifting his palms toward the sky as if he was presenting himself as an offering. "My friends, tonight we forget our troubles and shed our human skins! Tonight, we offer ourselves to the moon, and we run as our true selves! Tonight—"

He paused, lowering his eyes to sweep over his pack. As if it were a signal, they all sank to the ground, kneeling, and bowed their heads, exposing the vulnerable backs of their necks to their alpha. It was strange and a little creepy, the way they moved seemingly as one. Even Spencer had let go of my hand and dropped to the ground, his inky hair falling forward over his face. I was the only one left standing, bright and obvious in my white dress.

With a sigh that I saw more than heard, Frank turned his face up to the sky. "Tonight, we are wolves!" he roared, his voice booming out over the treetops.

In an eerie, simultaneous movement, every one of the pack tipped their chins up to look at the full moon, glowing like a beautiful, luminous goddess in the ebony sky. As one, they all let out howls that rose and rose, piercing the nightly quiet of the woods, sending shivers racing up my spine, and goose bumps spilling over my skin. A deep, primal part of me, the part of the human brain that hasn't changed since the dawn of man, when wild things stalked the shadows beyond the mouth of the caves they lived in, screamed for me to run. I forced myself to stand where I was, listening to the beautiful and terrifying song of the wolves.

Then the howls died and were replaced by the sounds of crunching bones and snapping tendons as the pack members convulsed, twitching as they Changed. I covered my ears, unable to listen. It was like when Spencer had Changed in front of me, but multiplied by a dozen. I closed my eyes, not wanting to see the ugly contortions of their bodies as their skeletons shifted and grew, and fur swallowed flesh.

Through the fingers pressed over my ears, I could still hear the noises, whimpers and growls joining the horror movie soundtrack. I gritted my teeth, my stomach clenched with nausea, and I wished fervently that I'd stayed in my cabin, that I hadn't let Dominic coerce me into promising to be there, and that I….The sounds stopped.

Cautiously, I opened my eyes, peeling my hands away from my ears. There was silence for a moment, as grey dots dancing in front of my vision from squeezing my eyes shut so tightly. Then more howls split the stillness, and I saw a sea of fur glistening before me. The clearing was brimming with wolves, their sleek fur shining in every shade under the moonlight, from a grey so pale it was almost white, to russet brown and speckled auburn, to the darkest midnight black that only Spencer possessed. Long teeth flashed, animal eyes glowed, and sounds of snuffling and chuffing filled the air along with the pungent scent of something like dog, but far wilder.

I jumped as something brushed my ankle, and looked down to see a tail thumping against my legs. The wolf at my side was huge, the tips of its perked ears reaching almost to my shoulder. Its fur was a warm, woodsy auburn colour, and its lips were peeled back to show wicked fangs, but the expression wasn't threatening. Somehow, I knew it was a grin, and I smiled at the wolf that was Dominic. He yipped, playfully nudging my arm with his muzzle. Scorching breath puffed against my skin from his wide, rubbery black nose.

I looked out at the mass of squirming, snapping, yelping wolves and tried to identify each of them. There was a slender, red-brown wolf, I thought to be Sarah, and next to her, was a small, greyish wolf that was probably Annie, biting playfully at her sister's tail. The chocolate-brown wolf was Desmond. Up at the front, the massive black and grey brindled wolf was almost certainly Frank— judging by the way the other wolves bowed their heads submissively around him.

I couldn't connect any of the other wolves to their human selves, except, of course, Spencer, who stood out even amongst over a dozen other lupine bodies. Not just because of his jet-black fur and astounding size, but because there was, as when he was in human form, just something about him—the way he held himself, the way he stood somehow apart from the pack, the way his eyes were still fixed on the moon while everyone else was barking and nudging each other. He was a still, eerie shadow at the edge of the pack.

Then the huge black-and-grey wolf, Frank, the Alpha, made a long sound like a howl descending into a snarl. The wolves moved, an ocean of sleek fur, shining eyes, and graceful muscles. I watched as they flowed around the trees, escaping the clearing, and disappeared into the darkness of the night.

** Spencer **

Spencer ran along with his pack, ducking and dodging branches, diving over bramble bushes, and hurtling over fallen logs. Panting, yipping, and howling with the rest of them, he stretched his muscles and pushed himself faster, faster. The wind tore through his fur, warm bodies colliding with him, all pushing and shoving, made frenetic by the adrenaline of the Change and the excitement of the full moon. Everything was both crystal clear to his enhanced wolf eyes, and a blur going by in his speed. The air smelled of leaves, fur, and moonlight.

It was an incredible rush—running with his pack mates through the trees under the full moon. It was the only time they ever really accepted him, when who he was and who his mother was didn't matter squat. They were wolves, they were a pack, and they were together. *The only thing better than this*, Spencer thought, *would be to run on his own under the full moon.*

Of course, he'd Changed the other night, against Frank's orders, to better track Tilly as she sleepwalked through the woods—but this was different. Changing under the full moon wasn't as painful as it was every other night. It was real freedom.

The woods were alive with the sounds of panting and crunching leaves under large paws and enthusiastic yelps. The other woodland creatures scattered, hiding in burrows or up trees, as the pack flowed by, smooth and unstoppable as the stream. Moonlight poured through the branches, illuminating patches of dirt and flashes of fur, gleaming eyes and teeth, here and there. Everything was pumping muscles, pounding blood, and racing against the wind.

The pack broke into a clearing in the trees, running full tilt, knowing the route they had to travel…and suddenly slammed to a halt. Wolves crashed into one another, growls and snarls erupting, and teeth gnashing. Spencer dug his claws into the ground, sliding across the dirt and nearly joining the tangle of startled, angry wolves.

Nimbly, he scampered backward, away from the writhing mass of fur and claws, retreating to the edge of the clearing. Other wolves flowed past him, screeching to a halt or tumbling into the knot of abruptly stopped wolves. Confused and irritated, Spencer danced around the fray as wolves untangled themselves, looking for what had caused the sudden halt to their run. He was still circling, looking for a blockage or a threat, when he bumped, muzzle first, into an invisible barrier around the front of the group.

He snorted in surprise and backed up, shaking his head. He stepped forward again, and again met an invisible resistance as hard as a brick wall. Bristling, he tried to see what was obstructing his path, but there was nothing there but the air. Cautiously, he stretched out his muzzle and pushed at the barrier with his nose. It didn't budge, but once he was looking at it—or rather at where it was, since he couldn't actually *see* it—he noticed a faint blue shimmer in the air just where his black nose touched the barrier.

His hackles raised and a faint whine of incomprehension rose in his throat. He didn't understand what was going on. Looking around at his pack mates, some testing the invisible wall the same way and some watching with uncertain eyes, clearly none of them did either. Even the alpha, barking at them in a warning to step back and organise themselves, seemed puzzled.

Spencer slid back to the edge of the clearing, blending easily into the shadows of the trees, and pawed at the dirt uneasily. Something didn't feel right—no, something felt very wrong. He raised his muzzle, sniffing the air, and caught the scent of sweat, blood, and corruption. Humans. Spencer tensed.

The alpha seemed to catch the scent at the same time. He barked furiously, his hackles rising, and turned to face the direction the scent was coming from, his head swinging from side-to-side as he sniffed the air. The problem was the scent was coming from everywhere. All around them.

They knew they were surrounded, even before the hunters stepped out of the trees, ringing them and trapping them in the circle of the clearing. There were at least a dozen men, and the light glinting off dark metal meant they were all carrying guns. Enough of Spencer's human mind remained active in his wolf body to recognise the ambush.

The wolves pressed together, turning their backs to each other and baring their fangs at the hunters facing them. The men all raised their guns to their shoulders, aiming down the barrels to the trapped wolves. It would be like shooting fish in a barrel at that range.

Spencer crouched low to the ground, snarling ferociously, his muscles coiled to leap for the throat of the nearest man. He looked up past the barrel of the gun aimed at him and into the man's face. The hunter was smiling beneath an orange cap, and Spencer recognised his scent. It was the man who'd shot him. Spencer jerked forward, his teeth snapping, wanting to rip the man's body to shreds. He smacked into another invisible wall, and whined at the impact. Furious, he lunged again and again, slamming into the barrier he couldn't see. The man behind it laughed, showing tobacco stained teeth.

"Hello again, wolf. Remember me do you?" he chortled.

Spencer stopped trying to break down the invisible wall, his sides heaving from the effort, and his shoulder aching from the repeated impact. His lips pulled back from his teeth and he growled silently at the man.

Still grinning under his orange cap, the hunter adjusted his gun on his shoulder, his finger on the trigger. "Goodbye, wolf," he sneered, and then he pulled the trigger.

Chapter Fifteen

** Tilly **

I heard the gunshot ring out over the trees, and I was running before I knew what I was doing. The bad feeling that had been playing up and down my spine all day had crystallised in my bones, settling an icy knot in my stomach. All I could think about was Spencer, lying on the ground in wolf form, blood pouring from the gunshot in his side as the hunter in the orange cap vanished into the trees like a coward. My legs shook and I stumbled, got up and kept running. I gasped as I ran, telling myself that Spencer was okay, that Dominic, Desmond, and Annie were all okay. They had to be. If they weren't? Well, I'd find a way to make the hunters and witches, pay for every ounce of blood.

My blood was rushing in my ears, and I didn't know where the gunshot had come from, but my feet led me in what I hoped was the right direction. The trees whispered to me to hurry, their leaves bending to point the way, sucking in their roots so I wouldn't trip over them. I was running so fast that everything around me was just a blur of shadows, but I still couldn't get there fast enough. I was sure it would be only seconds before another shot fired and another wolf was hurt or maybe killed, because I was too stupidly, clumsily, humanly slow.

I burst into the clearing in time to see a startled looking man in an orange cap. The man who'd shot Spencer, I recognised him. He held a smoking gun, pointed directly…upward, as if someone had jerked his barrel up at the last second. But there was nobody near enough to him to have done it.

"Not that one," a cool voice instructed the hunter. I felt a shiver slither like slime down my spine, and turned my head, taking in the bristling, snarling pack of wolves encircled by men pointing guns at them. There, directly across the clearing from me, was the woman I'd known was there the moment I'd seen the guns. Olivia. Looking as coldly beautiful and pale as ever, she stood between two heavily armed hunters, her eyes glinting at me. She'd been expecting me as much as I'd expected her.

It took me only a second to piece together what was going on, and fear and dread strangled me. The hunters had been lying in wait for the wolves, and Olivia had been lying in wait for me. There we all were, unable to escape, and all I could do was stare at the woman who was going to kill my wolves.

"Matilda, how nice to see you again. I'd been hoping you would arrive in time for our little…party."

Olivia giggled, an infuriatingly girlish sound that attracted swift glances from the men around her. Even in a black trench coat and leather boots, she was stunning. It made me want to rip her face off.

Something brushed my leg, and I flinched, looking down. Glinting gold eyes looked up at me from a pitch-black wolf face, and I felt a wave of relief sweep through me. I hadn't realised how worried I'd been that he'd been shot, until Spencer was right next to me, clearly unharmed. He nudged against my legs, his eyes telegraphing that he recognised Olivia and her threat to me. I curled my fingers into his fur as his hackles rose, prickling. His muscles were tense under my knuckles, and he bared his teeth silently, but I held him back.

"Olivia. I'd say it was nice to see you, too, but you always taught me not to lie." I was amazed at how steady and calm my voice sounded, considering I was shaking apart inside. My brain was short circuiting, trying to think of a way out of the situation, a way to get everyone out unharmed. It wasn't the wolves' fight, it was mine, and I'd be damned if I let any of them get hurt because of me.

Olivia shook her head disappointedly. "Oh, Matilda. You say it as if it were a crime to want you to grow up to be honest and not a liar."

I twitched, my fingers tightening in Spencer's fur. At another time, I might have recoiled at the idea that I was essentially touching his hair, but at the moment, I needed the support of my wolf.

"It may not have been a crime to teach me to tell the truth, but I'm pretty sure what you did to me when I lied was a crime," I said tightly, remembering the birch cane, the Dark Room, and the stink of demons as they clawed at my mind with sharp, tearing laughter. I shuddered, and immediately regretted it, seeing the way Olivia's eyes narrowed, noticing my reaction.

"You were punished for misbehaving, as any child would be. We just had to punish you a little differently because of…" She smiled, but it looked like a sneer, "Because of what you are, of course."

I couldn't help it; I flinched. *'What you are.'* *What.* Like I was a creature, not a person. I gritted my teeth. I hated being a *what*, instead of a *who*. I hated it worse that she'd said it in front of the listening ears of the wolves. I glanced at them, trying to gauge their reactions to her words, but it was impossible to tell. They were all bristling and crouching, glaring at the hunters surrounding them. Only their swivelling ears, directed toward our conversation, let me know they were listening. How much they understood in wolf form, I didn't know.

Olivia noticed me looking to the wolves nervously, and her smile changed to something gleeful, cruel, and hard to look at. "Ooh," she said in a tone of delight, "Don't your little furry friends know? Haven't you told them your own secret? No? I guess we didn't beat the liar out of you well enough, Matilda." She clucked her tongue like a disapproving parent.

I bit my cheek hard enough that I tasted blood. Next to me, Spencer snarled, stepping forward. I kept my hold on his fur, gripping harder, trying to silently translate to him not to do anything. Olivia's icy eyes went to him, and I felt my stomach sink.

Please, don't hurt him. God, don't hurt him, I begged silently.

"Ah," the witch said, raising her eyebrows. "This one knows. This is the one who attacked me. Such a beautiful creature. Very protective of you." Her gaze cut to me again briefly, something horrible flashing in the green depths. "Been fornicating with the

animals, have you, Matilda? Disgusting perversion, if you ask me."
She made a noise of revulsion, turning her glare back to Spencer,
who barked viciously, pulling against my grasp on his fur.

He barely seemed to notice I was pulling out his fur. My
stomach churned with bright sickness, my face growing hot despite
myself, and I had to look down. I tried to breathe steadily.

In a thin voice, I said, "It isn't like that." I didn't know why I
said it, why it mattered what she thought, but then I realised I wasn't
explaining it to Olivia. I was telling it to the wolves around me, to
Dominic. I didn't know where he was amongst all the fierce lupine
muscle and fur, but I knew he was listening and watching.

Olivia scoffed delicately. "Oh, darling, I don't really care who
or *what* you want to screw in your spare time. I just want you to
come back home. If you come now, I'll even let you keep
your…pet? Boyfriend? Whatever you want to call him." She waved
a hand dismissively at Spencer.

He was hard as stone under my hand, but I could feel a growl
rumbling through his ribs. I willed him not to move. The men
gathered around us were starting to look confused, the barrels of
their guns dipping as their brows furrowed, trying to understand
what Olivia was saying. It was clear she hadn't told them the wolves
they were shooting weren't just wolves.

That was good, I supposed—good because it meant the men
couldn't scream werewolf to the town, good because they thought
they were just shooting animals, not monsters. If they didn't know
the creatures were half-man, they wouldn't grab pitchforks and

torches. It didn't seem as if it really mattered either way, because the wolves were going to die. Whether they died with their secret intact or not was sort of irrelevant to my panicked mind.

As if she knew what I was thinking, Olivia smiled thinly at me. "Don't worry. These men don't know anything more than they need to. Well, except Jack over there." She gestured to the man with the orange cap, the one who'd shot Spencer. "I believe you've met...twice, I think. I'm sure you recognise him. Your wolf certainly did. Anyway, he knows a little bit about you, now doesn't he? But even he doesn't know the whole truth. Come with me now, and I won't say a word. I'll even call off this hunt on your animal friends here."

The hunters all stared at Olivia with mixed expressions of confusion, irritation and awe. Some of them didn't seem to care what she was saying—they were either staring at her chest, or drooling down the barrels of their guns, bloodlust in their eyes.

"Now who needs to be punished for lying?" I spat, glaring. The sharp wind cut through the clearing, my power buzzing under my skin, and I knew I had to calm down before I did something I shouldn't—maybe accidental, maybe not.

Olivia's eyes narrowed to slits, and her mouth compressed. I'd pissed her off. I clamped my mouth shut, but it was too late. She smiled, and it was a hideously threatening expression.

"Well then. Maybe we should all just get our secrets out now, and stop lying altogether. What do you think?" she asked in a crisp, chiming voice.

I swallowed bile. She'd hit my weakest spot, and she knew it. The wolves around me whined fearfully, growled angrily. Surprisingly, Spencer was still and silent, but I could feel the tension under his fur.

Desperate, I pleaded. "No. Don't. Olivia, please. This isn't their fight. This is between you and me. Let the wolves go. I'm begging you, don't hurt them," my voice cracked.

My heart was thundering my chest. I couldn't let her do it. I couldn't let the wolves take the punishment for my mistakes. I tried to step forward, but Spencer rounded on me suddenly, snarling, and I stumbled back. My breath caught with fear, and he lowered his head apologetically, hiding his teeth. I knew he was just trying to protect me, but I couldn't let him do it.

I looked up at Olivia again and breathed, "Please, don't."

She shook her head and my heart sank. "No, you were right, Matilda. I shouldn't lie, and neither should you. I think everyone here has a right to know what's really going on. I'm going to use your little guard dog there as an example."

I felt the magic slam into Spencer before I could even blink. He fell to the ground on his stomach, growling as tremors wracked his body. I dropped down next to him, flashing back to the blood on my hands as I'd pulled the bullet out of him, and I pressed both my palms down on his side, trying to fight the magic Olivia was exerting on him.

It wasn't like the spell she'd been casting on him the night he'd chased her into the woods—it was different, stronger, more forceful.

247

I didn't know exactly what she was doing, until I heard and felt his shoulder pop, dislocating under my hand. I shrieked, and Spencer's growl cut off in a whine.

Writhing, he turned his head, looking up into my face, and I saw his eyes were agonised, panicked...and undeniably blue. Olivia was forcing him to Change, right there in front of the hunters. She was about to expose the wolves' secret to the stupid, heartless human men, who were gawking in astonishment and bafflement at the scene before them.

Utterly terrified and utterly panicked, I screamed at Olivia. "Stop it! Please, stop it! Don't do this!"

She only smirked back at me, callous and enjoying the pain she was causing. I couldn't break through the spell she was casting on Spencer. I couldn't do anything to help him fight it....but maybe I could stop her from casting it for long enough to get the wolves out of there.

Shakily, I forced myself to my feet, trying to ignore Spencer's high whine as my magic stopped dulling the edges of Olivia's. I knew it would be only seconds before he started to Change. Using all my fear, panic, and fury, I pulled together as much of my power as I was able to control, and I shoved my magic toward Olivia. It burst from my palms with such force that it knocked me backward, sprawling onto the ground. Blindingly bright and faster than I could blink, the power soared toward Olivia. I only saw her green eyes flash wide for an instant before the flare of light collided with her and sent her flying.

I reached out to Spencer, and instantly felt Olivia's spell snap, the pressure on his limbs vanishing. He was still fully wolf, but he was shaking. Gasping, I tried to get up, knowing Olivia wouldn't be down for long, but my arms and legs wouldn't obey me. I looked up, and saw every pair of wolf eyes on me, mistrustful and scared. Every single wolf, with the exception of Spencer, backed away from me, their hackles raised and teeth bared at me instead of the hunters now.

They knew what I was, and what I could do. I was the bigger threat. Only Spencer stayed by my side. Wriggling to his feet, he barked at his pack mates, pawing the dirt next to me, but they held their distance. Spencer growled sharply, a sound of frustration toward his pack, but I slid my hand across the dirt to touch his leg. He looked down at me, whined softly, nosing my fingers.

I smiled sadly. "It's okay. They have a right to be scared of me."

Spencer shook his head, snorting his disagreement, but I knew there was nothing he could do. The wolves knew my secret, and I hadn't expected them to accept it as easily as I'd accepted theirs. I was stung, but not surprised.

Around the clearing, the hunters stared at me in horror and shock, some of them rushing to Olivia to ensure she was still alive. I knew she was without checking. I'd given her a good jolt, but it would take a lot more to kill her. Slowly, the men seemed to come to a silent consensus, through glances, frowns, and brief nods. They raised their guns. Obviously, they had decided it didn't matter what was really going on there. It didn't matter that the woman who'd hired them clearly wasn't human, and neither was the stupid girl trying to protect the wolves. They were shutting out the things they couldn't explain with the conclusion that, whatever the issue was, they could get rid of it by shooting the wolves.

But the wolves were ready for them, and the men didn't even have time to put their fingers on their triggers before the wolves lunged. I didn't watch the men being torn apart, but I could hear the sickening sounds of human bones snapping, flesh ripping, and men screaming and gurgling. A few shots were fired, and a lupine howl was swallowed by the greater noise of snarls and gnashing fangs. I lay on the ground, focusing on breathing, while it happened around me. I felt someone stumble over my legs, but I couldn't be bothered to try to move again. Something hot and wet spurted over one of my arms and onto my dress. I stayed awake, but I really wished I hadn't.

By the time it was over, I had slipped into meditation and gathered enough energy to stand, though my legs wobbled under me. I didn't dare look at the carnage around me, positive my stomach couldn't take the sight of human body parts strewn across the dirt floor of the woods. I also couldn't look at the wolves, but I felt them backing away from me as I stood.

I was the only threat left in the clearing. I just hoped they wouldn't feel the need to tear me apart too. I turned my back on them, numb and cold with shock, and stumbled my way through the trees, almost blind in the darkness. I didn't care as I caught my dress on brambles, or when twigs prodded my bare feet. I just needed to get back to my cabin, even knowing it wouldn't be mine much longer.

Fumbling my way through branches, not paying attention to where I was going, it took me a while before I realised I was lost. Shock was starting to wear off, and I looked around me, unsure of how long I'd been walking, or even which direction I'd come from. The branches were so thick overhead that I couldn't see the sky, couldn't judge direction or time from the moon.

I was shaking. Nausea curdled in my stomach as realisation slowly broke over me, forcing me to think about what had happened. I looked down at my dress. For a second, I was disoriented, because I could have sworn my dress was white. I remembered Sarah draping white fabric over me to make it, but the fabric before my eyes was red. My mind clicked over, and I gasped. It was blood. There was a huge spray of blood staining my pretty white dress. It was smeared across my arms and chest too, sticky and cold, almost dry.

I bent over, retching, and fell to my knees. I was shaking so hard, my muscles hurt and a sweat broke out on my forehead. I crawled backward until my back hit a tree, and then I stayed there, rocking slightly as I cried—harsh and violent sobs tearing from my throat. Worried that the wolves might come after me, I stuffed my fist into my mouth to stifle the sobs. After a while, my sobs quietened, and exhaustion forced me under into a nightmare of blood, gunpowder, and dozens of sets of sharp wolf teeth tearing into my flesh.

The sound of someone whispering my name woke me up. I couldn't have been asleep for very long, and the coldness of the air on my bare skin startled me to instant awareness. My eyes flew open, and Dominic retreated, his hand falling away from my knee. His eyes were very bright in the darkness, but I couldn't read his expression.

With a flash of fear, I scrambled to my feet. Instantly, he sprang up too, holding his hands toward me defensively. Surprised by the gesture, I shrunk back with a bite of sadness, realising he was as scared of me as I was of him. Ironic, really. People always say that, '*They're* more scared of you than you are of them.' In that case, it might have actually been true.

Distantly, I noticed Dominic was dressed in jeans and a t-shirt, and he was free of blood. He'd obviously been home first, before he came looking for me. I didn't know if that was a good sign or a bad one. Surely if his intention was to kill me, he wouldn't have bothered washing up first.

I shook my head. I was being ridiculous. It was *Dominic* I was talking about. He wouldn't hurt me…would he? He'd promised he wouldn't. *Nobody will hurt you.* I doubted that still applied, considering how things had gone. He'd promised me that when he'd thought I was a helpless little human girl. Now he knew I wasn't. Did that mean our friendship was void? Would he be able to forget that he'd laughed with me, trusted me, and kissed me, in order to rid the pack of a threat in their midst—an unwitting Trojan horse that had led the witches to their pack?

I looked at him, trying to figure it out, but he just stood there, looking back at me. Slowly, his expression softened. I was sure mine was blank. My face felt stiff. He shoved his hands into his pockets, his shoulders slumping, and I relaxed slightly. He wasn't going to kill me. Not yet, at least.

Very quietly, he said, "You didn't come back to the cabins."

"I got lost." My voice was as flat as I thought my expression was.

He nodded, as if he'd guessed that. One hand came up to tug on his curls. "Yeah," he sighed. "That's what I thought. Maybe for the best. Everyone is pretty upset."

It was my turn to nod, unsure what to say. He bit his lip, his eyes flicking to me and away again, then back to me. He frowned, making the dimple in his cheek scowl at me. He rubbed his jaw with a clean, pale hand.

I'm covered in blood, I thought distantly. *Whose blood?* I didn't know.

Suddenly, Dominic spoke up again, his green eyes steady on my face, but his mouth was turned down gently at the corners. "Why didn't you tell me? Tilly, I thought we were friends…" He paused, frowning deeper. "I thought…we might be more than that."

The hurt in Dominic's voice stung me, and my anger flared in response, snapping me from my emotionless state. How dare he be hurt! How dare he act as if I'd disappointed him!

I laughed mirthlessly, and saw him flinch at my harsh tone. "Why didn't I tell you? Maybe for the same reason you didn't tell me you were a werewolf. Maybe because I was afraid of how you'd react. Maybe—" I stepped forward, my fists clenching.

253

A spark of gold shot through his green eyes, the wolf reacting to the threat I posed, but I didn't back off. I was too angry, too hurt to care if his stupid wolf instincts told him to rip me apart.

I glared him in the eyes, my voice hard and sharp as a whip. "Maybe because when you saw what I did to that witch, *you* backed away, just like the rest of them! You thought we were friends? So did I! So why was Spencer the only one who stuck by my side?"

Dominic shook his head, frustration and sadness all over his face. "Tilly, I didn't—"

I raised a finger, pointing at him. My hand shook I was so furious, and he took a step back, his eyes flashing gold again.

"Yes, you did! I didn't back away from you when I found out what you were. I didn't look at you with the betrayal and fear I see in your eyes right now! You can't hide it, Dominic! Your wolf, that thing that makes you different and makes you who you are, it gives you away!" my voice cracked, and I lowered my finger to my side.

My arms shook, and then my shoulders did too, and I realised I was fighting tears with all the will I had. I looked down, so he wouldn't see them shining in my eyes, refusing to let him see the hurt I felt. Only one person could be trusted with my weakness and it wasn't him.

When I spoke again, my voice was barely above a whisper, but it was steady. "I've never thought you were a monster, Dominic, and I don't need to hear it from your lips to know that's what you think of me right now." I sighed. "Correction. I've never thought you were a monster, until now." Before I could burst into tears, I turned and ran.

Chapter Sixteen

** Tilly **

Eventually, I found my way back to my cabin. I was cold and dirty, my feet hurt, my mouth tasted like bile, and I had leaves and blood matted into my hair. My hands shook so badly, it took three attempts before I could twist the handle, glad I hadn't locked it earlier. I doubted I could have handled putting the key in the lock.

I stumbled inside, collapsing against the door as it closed behind me. For a minute, I just stood there, leaning, breathing hard, and unable to move or think. Wetness touched my collarbones, and I felt the tears rolling down my cheeks, dripping off my chin. I hadn't realised I was still crying. It felt as if I'd been crying forever, but somehow, I just couldn't stop. My heart was slowing and the burning in my leg muscles cooling, so I pushed myself away from the door and padded unsteadily across the floor, leaving dirty footprints on the wooden floorboards.

I got to my room and pushed the door open, slipping inside with the desperate need to sleep for nine hours…or nine days. All I wanted was to crawl into bed, careless of my muddy feet or bloody dress, and pass out. I closed the bedroom door behind me, my vision blurring. The room was dark. I hadn't left any lights on before I left, and I didn't turn any on then. Sighing, my eyes still watering, I turned and reached behind me for the bow of the golden ribbon pinching the dress at my waist. I couldn't slip out of it with the ribbon tied, but my quaking fingers scrabbled uselessly at the tangled ribbon. It was double knotted, and my hands weren't steady enough to undo it.

With a rising feeling of despair and frustration, I made a choked noise, grabbing at the ribbon around my waist. I was ready to tear it apart to get the damned dress off, and then there were fingers over mine—light and steady, undoing the knot with ease. I gasped at the unexpected touch, jerking away and slamming my back against the door. My heart thundered in a panic, and it took my dazed, blurred eyes a long moment to work out who I was staring at in the dimness.

First, I saw the eyes, the crystal blue of the sea at sunrise. I paused, suspended in a state of warring emotions. I wasn't sure whether to relax or not. My fear vanished, but it was replaced with something almost like fear, something that made my heart stumble the same way. But I knew I was safe. If I was safe with anyone, it was with Spencer.

My eyes adjusted properly, and in the moonlight coming through the open window—I swore that window hadn't been open a minute ago—I saw he was naked, again, and covered in both blood and dirt as much as I was. I dropped my gaze, my breath catching raggedly in my throat. My nails dug into the soft wood of the door at my back. I was still crying, silently, almost absently.

"Tilly, it's okay. It's only me. It's okay," Spencer said gently, his voice near a whisper.

He took a step forward, and I flinched despite myself. He stepped back. I kept my eyes on my blackened feet. There was a shallow cut across the back of my left foot that ran up my ankle, visible through a rip in my dress.

"It's polite to knock first," I said, breathless and hoarse. I glanced at his bare feet, as filthy as mine, and felt a strange sort of comfort. Dominic had come to me, dressed and clean, frightened of me. Spencer came to me naked and dirty, nothing like fear in his blue eyes. "It's also polite to wear clothes," I added drily.

Spencer laughed roughly. "Yeah, sorry. I just…I was out looking for you after you ran off, and I didn't think before coming over here," he said, not sounding the least bit embarrassed about it.

I, on the other hand, even in my current state, felt heat rise to my face. It was dawning on me that there was a naked boy in my bedroom. The thought made me dizzy, so I slid down the door and sat on the floor with my knees tucked to my chest. I gripped my legs and leaned my forehead on my knees, breathing hard. *God, I'm a wreck*, I thought.

Spencer hesitated, standing in the middle of the room, and then grabbed a blanket from the bed, wrapping it around his hips. Then he sat down on the floor two feet away from me, facing me. The black ink of his odd, angular tattoo peeked out from the edge of the blanket. I couldn't read his expression, not because of the dimness, but because it was Spencer, and I had enough trouble figuring out his expressions when my brain was working properly. Right then, I could barely keep my eyes open. I hurt all over, including inside.

Why didn't you tell me Tilly? I thought we were friends. Dominic's voice, full of soft hurt, echoed in my head. The way he'd looked at me when he said it, the fear behind the hurt, the way he'd bristled at my nearness when I shoved my finger in his face, the way he'd backed away from me with all the others when I blasted Olivia...to keep *their* secret. Even the way he had bared his teeth at me, as if I was a threat, and he might rip me apart if I made one false move. All of it flashed through my head, every image like a punch to the gut or a spear to the chest.

My best friend was scared of me, maybe hated me. What was I supposed to do with that? What could I do? Nothing. I couldn't change who I was any more than he could change who he was. Who, not what, because my powers were a part of me as much as his wolf was part of him. So why was I automatically a monster and he wasn't?

A hand touched my arm, but I didn't flinch that time. I was shaking again, sobbing loudly into my knees. I lifted my head, tears falling onto the stained fabric of my dress, and leaned into Spencer. He put an arm around my shoulders, cradling me against him, and I cried into his chest instead. He was warm and solid, and still smelled like rainstorms and wood smoke, but he also smelled like sweat and coppery blood. I didn't care. I was just glad to have someone I could trust there with me. Comforting me.

Carefully, Spencer stroked my knotted hair, not snagging the gnarls or tangles. "Shh, Tilly," he murmured, his breath hot on the back of my neck. "It's alright."

I shook my head, gasping. "No, it isn't! They all hate me now! Dominic h-hates me! He's s-scared of me, they all are!" I forced the stuttering words out between sobs, shaking so badly I nearly bit my tongue. My chest felt tight, as if someone was crushing my ribs into my lungs, and my throat was full. My fingers were bunched in the blanket over Spencer's leg, my thumb brushing the skin of his knee, but I barely noticed. I was too terrified.

"They…they're going to kill me, aren't they? Now that they know wh-what I am, they're going to kill me! You saw the way they looked at me! They all think I'm a threat, that I betrayed them, that I-I'm one of *them*…" My words dissolved into harsh gasping, on the verge of hysteria.

Pushing me back, his fingers gripping my shoulders, Spencer shook me hard enough that my teeth rattled. "Tilly!" he snapped, not unkindly.

Through the blur of tears, I looked at him. His eyes were wide and startled.

"Tilly, nobody's going to kill you! I swear, nobody is going to kill you," he promised, his voice quiet but full of utter conviction.

He believed what he was saying, he meant it…but his words were so like the promise Dominic had made to me that I twitched. "You can't know that. Not for sure," I whispered.

He shook me again, just gently. "Yes, I can, and I do. Nobody is going to lay a finger on you, not a single member of the pack, no matter how scared or angry they are now. They'll calm down, and we'll talk to them. Both of us, together. And nobody will hurt you. I won't let them hurt you, Tilly, not for any reason."

The intensity in his blue eyes, the bright way he was looking at me, made me believe him. He was my wolf, even if he wasn't only a wolf, and he would protect me. My wolf would keep me safe.

Slowly, I nodded. "Okay," I rasped.

Spencer's grip on my arms loosened. He looked ruefully at the marks he'd left on my skin, mumbled an apology, and started to get to his feet. I grabbed his wrist, stopping him. He jerked in surprise, looking down at me. I peered up at him through lank, dirty strands of hair, my face tight and tear stained.

"Please," I whispered, "Don't go. S-stay here…with me. I don't want to be on my own. I won't feel safe. What if the witches come for me? Or what if they make me sleepwalk again? Or what if—"

Spencer ducked down beside me, putting two fingers over my lips to hush me. "I get it. I'll stay…if that's what you really want?"

It was almost a question, so I nodded, his fingers brushing against my lips. My lips tingled.

"Okay then. But maybe first I should…" He frowned, plucking at the blanket he was wearing.

I blinked. It took me a moment to realise what he meant, and I blushed. "Um, yeah. You should probably…" I swallowed, releasing his wrist.

"Yeah, I'll just go…get dressed." He stood, moving toward the window. He turned back, one hand on the sill. The moonlight threw sparks from his eyes. "I'll just be a couple of minutes. Will you be okay till I come back?" he asked, his face uncertain.

I hesitated, and then nodded. He sighed, then flung himself out the window, the blanket fluttering free as he disappeared into the darkness beyond the windowsill.

Shivering, I got up and shut the window, locking it. I'd have to let him back in, but at least nothing else could come in while he was gone. Well, obviously they could, but I just had to hope nobody was angry enough to break down the door to get at me. I wasn't sure I'd be able to put up much of a struggle, if any at all.

Safe in the knowledge that Spencer was coming right back, I fumbled my way into the bathroom and flipped on the shower. I didn't wait for the water to warm up before peeling off my dress—it stuck to my body where the blood had seeped through and had started to dry to my skin—and stepping into the shower. I had finally stopped crying, and my hands were steady enough that I managed to scrub most of the dirt and blood from my skin and hair. The crescents of my finger and toenails were still black, and there was a knot in my hair that I couldn't be bothered to wrestle with, but I was mostly clean. I couldn't do anything about the cuts or scratches, or about the bruises I was going to have the next day.

By the time I got out of the shower, I was feeling more stable. I wrapped myself in a towel and scouted out the walk-in wardrobe, pulling on cotton shorts and a t-shirt. I returned to my bedroom. It was still dim, lit only by the moonlight streaming through the window, but I could see well enough. A rapid tapping on the glass made me jump, and I looked up to see Spencer scowling on the other side. I went and unlocked the window, sliding it open. He climbed in.

"You locked it," he muttered accusingly as he closed the window behind him.

He flipped the lock anyway. Then he turned to look at me. I think I stopped breathing for a second. He was dressed in simple black jogging bottoms and a matching t-shirt, both somehow not as black as his damp hair. There were no signs of dirt or blood left on him either, so I guessed he'd showered too. His skin looked startlingly white against the black. In the dimness, he was an odd combination of shadows and light, charcoal and chalk. Except for the reflective shine of his eyes.

Knotting my fingers together, I said, "I was worried someone might come in while you were gone."

He frowned, but he just nodded, standing somewhat awkwardly next to my bed. Somewhat awkward myself, I recognised once again that there was a boy in my bedroom in the middle of the night. The fact that he was no longer naked and savage looking was little consolation to my nerves, but I knew it would be ten times worse for my nerves if he weren't here.

Clearing his throat softly, Spencer shoved his hands into his pockets. His head was bowed so I couldn't read his face. "Um. I can sleep on the floor...or in the other room, if you'd prefer?" He sounded as uncomfortable as he looked from his posture.

I started to nod, ready to agree, but then I paused. I glanced at the dark trees outside the window, the full moon hanging like a bulbous leering face in the sky. With something fluttering inside my chest, I moved to the bed and peeled back the covers, sliding in. I felt Spencer watching me, and I turned, raising my eyebrows at him expectantly. His eyebrows rose in response, surprise rather than expectancy. There was a question in his eyes.

I patted the space in the mattress next to me, shifting back against the wall. "Please?" I murmured shyly.

Spencer hesitated a moment, then nodded once sharply. I thought, more to himself than to me. Then he strode across the room, pausing only a split second before sliding into the bed next to me. He was as tense as a bowstring, and he relaxed only a fraction when I flipped the covers up over us and lay down. My back was pressed against the cool wall, my fingers secretly clenching the sheet under the pillow. Spencer's eyes were bright, locked on mine. He leaned over, eyes never leaving mine, and my heart slammed into my ribs— but he was only reaching up to yank the curtains shut over the window. Then he leaned back and my heart subsided, deciding to remain in my chest after all.

I'd thought I was exhausted before, but with Spencer lying next to me, I couldn't seem to close my eyes. I stared at him, watching the play of shadows on his face, the flickering of gold in his eyes, and he stared back. I wondered what he was seeing, what I looked like to him right in that moment. I felt raw and exposed, but I also felt alright with that, because I knew Spencer wouldn't hurt me, wouldn't judge me. I wished I knew what he was thinking.

"Tilly," he whispered suddenly.

"Hmm?" I murmured back.

He hesitated, as if he was considering what he was about to say very carefully, and I saw his eyes flicker. Then his mouth curved slightly, and he murmured, "Goodnight."

Smiling, I relaxed, leaning slightly away from the wall at my back. Spencer's knee brushed mine, the heat of his body warming me. His dark hair fell into his light eyes, tangling in his lashes. I closed my eyes.

Safe and warm with him lying next to me, I replied quietly, "Goodnight Spencer."

** Spencer **

He sensed someone was at the door before he heard the knocking echo through the cabin. Immediately alert, Spencer sat up in the bed, ears pricked to catch the sound of knuckles rapping on wood and boards of the porch creaking under nervously shifting feet. He knew who it would be, and grimaced.

Spencer looked down at Tilly, lying in the bed next to him, and for a moment felt dizzy. She was still asleep, pale morning light filtering through the closed curtains and onto her face. Her white-gold hair was rumpled, tossed across the pillow, her sugar-pink lips slightly parted as she breathed lightly. There were bluish shadows under her eyes, and there was a thin, red line of a scratch just above her left eyebrow. In sleep, she looked so young and fragile, and there he was, a half-feral half-wolf creature, in her bed while she dreamed on. The amount of trust she'd put in him, asking him to stay the night, was incomprehensible to him. It made something in his chest ache a little. He lifted a hand, his fingertips hovering over her cheekbone, desperate to touch…

The knocking came again, louder and more insistent, and Spencer jerked his hand back. With a muttered curse, he slid out of the bed carefully, not wanting to wake Tilly. She had been through enough; she deserved to sleep at least a little longer. He cast a glance over his shoulder as he slipped out of the room, seeing the soft shape of her body under the covers and the unguarded expression on her sleeping face, and then he closed the door and padded, barefoot, down the hall.

The person at the door started to knock again, and Spencer strode past the kitchen and living room. He let out a breath between his teeth, willing his expression to relax, and threw the door open. There, on the porch, as he'd expected, was Dominic. In the shadows under the awning, he looked worn and tired, with his curls all tangled as if he hadn't bothered to brush them when he rolled out of bed, and smudges under his eyes. His mouth was a thin line, and he looked surprised at first to see Spencer on the other side of the door, and then angry.

"What are you doing here?" Dominic snapped, his eyes narrowing.

Spencer looked his half-brother up and down, just slowly enough to let Dominic see the contempt in his eyes, and then leaned his elbow casually on the door handle.

Dominic tensed visibly, his jaw clamped. "Let me in," he commanded when Spencer didn't reply. "I need to speak to Tilly."

Without a word, Spencer stepped back, swinging the door open wider, a clear invitation to Dominic to come in, though what he really wanted to do was to send the curly headed tosser away and slam the door in his face. Glaring at Spencer, Dominic stepped over the threshold and looked around. Spencer closed the door quietly and turned to Dominic, who looked uncomfortable, standing with his hands in his pockets in the middle of the cabin, half-way between the living room and the kitchen. The boy's green eyes darted around the room, looking for Tilly. Spencer prayed his knocking hadn't woken her, that she'd sleep on until he could get Dominic to leave. He didn't want her to have to deal with her supposed best friend until she felt like it.

"Tilly is still asleep," Spencer informed him in a tone that dared the other boy to figure out how he came to know such information. He moved to the kitchen and leaned forward with his forearms on the countertop, steadily eyeing his half-brother over the low wall separating the breakfast bar from the kitchen.

As Spencer had intended, Dominic's cheeks flushed, and his eyes darkened. "What are you doing here?" he repeated, a mixture of anger and jealousy clouding his normally cheerful face.

Spencer wanted to ask him the same thing, but refrained because he thought he already knew Dominic's reason for coming over there first thing in the morning. Knowing it would infuriate the boy further, Spencer smiled—a wry and secret twist of the lips. The muscles in Dominic's arms tightened as he fisted his hands in his pockets, but his expression didn't change. Spencer had never seen his half-brother look so fierce. For a second, Spencer contemplated leaving it at his smile, without saying a word, letting Dominic make what conclusions he would. Then he remembered the last encounter they'd had in the cabin, and he couldn't bite his tongue on his next words:

"This time," Spencer said coolly, "I did spend the night here."

Dominic's face hardened. He looked outraged. "You took advantage—"

"No," Spencer snapped harshly, "I didn't." He shook his head, stalking away from his stupid half-brother. Of course he would think that was why Spencer had been there. He was so blinded by jealousy, he couldn't even consider the possibility that Tilly had simply *wanted* him here.

"I was here when she finally got in last night. Waiting for her," Spencer said slowly, ignoring the way Dominic bristled. "I was here when she came in, covered in dirt and blood, crying. And you know what she told me? She was terrified, Dominic, terrified that the pack was going to *kill* her! She was scared that *you* wanted her dead, because of what she is!"

"Liar!" Dominic barked, his eyes flashing. "Tilly knows I would never hurt her!"

"Does she?" Spencer replied calmly, watching Dominic shudder with the effort of holding his wolf back. "Because I seem to recall that you bared your fangs at her, just as everyone else did, last night when she showed what she could do. I was the only one who stood there next to her without fear, after she *protected* us! After she stood against a woman who terrifies her, the woman she ran away from! After she put herself on the line to keep our secret from the hunters!" Spencer was working himself into a rage, and he knew he should calm down, felt his wolf prickling under his skin. His voice came out half-growl on his next words.

"You say you have feelings for her, want to have her as your own. You're not even worthy to be her friend, let alone anything more!" A shudder cramped his spine, and the joints in his fingers popped. He clenched his hands in fists, fighting the Change.

He was so angry, furious. He couldn't believe Dominic had the nerve to show up there, as if he had a right to speak to Tilly after the way he'd acted, as if he could just assume she would want to see him, or that she'd forgive him. The part that really prickled, the part that killed Spencer, was that Tilly probably would forgive Dominic. If Dominic just said the right things, used his charm and his green eyes, Tilly would forgive him, and then...what of Spencer, the boy who'd stood by her and held her while she cried? Would she still let him hold her, or would she want Dominic to kiss her again? The idea sickened Spencer, and he felt his teeth grow sharp.

"You—" he started to go on, taking a step forward and seeing how it pushed Dominic's control.

The strain was written in the narrowing of his half-brother's eyes, and the tightness of his features. Spencer didn't care. He wanted to push until Dominic broke.

"Spencer, don't." The quiet, ragged voice came from the edge of the kitchen.

Spencer turned to see Tilly standing at the mouth of the hallway, looking exhausted and tearstained in her oversized nightshirt. She was leaning against the wall as if it were the only thing holding her up. There were scratches on her bare legs, and a bruise starting to show on her right knee. Shadows like more bruises were smeared under her eyes, which were fixed beyond him on Dominic. Spencer gritted his teeth.

"Tilly," Dominic sighed, running a hand through his curls. All the anger had drained out of him at the sight of her, his wolf retreating. He looked horribly ashamed, guilt like a pale mask over his face. "Tilly, I—" he started.

She shook her head, and he closed his mouth. Carefully, she pushed herself away from the wall and shuffled to the dining table, dropping into one of the chairs and putting her head in her hands, fingers buried in the mess of her hair. Spencer and Dominic exchanged a quick, conferring glance, before moving to sit down at the table with her. Spencer took the seat right next to her, and glared pointedly at Dominic until he sat on the other side of the table.

Tilly didn't raise her head as she spoke. "Why are you here, Dominic?" she asked in a slow, dispassionate voice.

Spencer wondered what her expression was under all that hair hanging over her face. He wanted to take her hand, but he knew she wouldn't like it with Dominic there, watching. He folded his hands together under the table, gripping his knuckles so he wouldn't be tempted to lunge across the table and throttle Dominic.

Dominic swallowed, his throat moving briefly. "I came to…apologise. For last night. For…" He shook his head violently, curls flying.

Tilly didn't see it, but Spencer suspected she sensed the boy's agitated motion. Minnie reached up and tugged on one of his curls, as was his habit. Spencer kept his eyes on him, narrowed in warning.

"I'm sorry, Tilly. Last night, I was a total jackass. I didn't mean to…I was just…" Dominic bit his lip, pulling on his curls so hard Spencer began to think he might pull his hair out.

"Scared?" Spencer pitched in unhelpfully, twitching one eyebrow. He folded his arms across his chest, leaning back in his chair.

Dominic bowed his head, wrapping a curl around his finger so he could better tug at it. The shame on his face was evident. It didn't soften Spencer's anger toward his half-brother. The way to avoid feeling shameful was not to act shamefully in the first place.

Tilly finally looked up. Her hair fell away from her face, and Spencer saw her expression; she looked miserable. He tensed, hating Dominic for making her look that way, but she didn't look at him. Her grey eyes were steady on Dominic's face.

"Is he right, Dominic?" she asked, not looking at Spencer. "Are you scared of me? You were last night. Are you still scared now, sitting at the table with me? If Spencer wasn't here, would you be able to sit there across from me and look me in the eye?"

Her voice was eerily flat, and Spencer thought she was doing that on purpose—either to try to provoke a reaction in Dominic, or so that her voice wouldn't shake. He could see the brightness of tears forming in her eyes, but then she blinked and the shine was gone. She was not the same broken girl that had sobbed into his chest the night before. She was the girl who'd jumped in front of a gun to save a wolf, who'd faced down the woman who'd tortured her since she was a kid, who'd pulled a bullet from his side, and hadn't run screaming when he'd become a boy from a wolf right in front of her. She was Tilly being strong, and for a moment, just a moment, Spencer felt something bright and hot flare inside him, something he didn't understand. It might have been pride…might have been something else. Either way, he looked down, fearing it would show on his face—he didn't want Dominic to see it, whatever it was.

Once the feeling had passed, Spencer looked up at Dominic across the table, searching the younger boy's face for some trace of fear. Tilly was watching him too, solemn and expectant. Inconspicuously, Spencer sniffed the air, but there was no tang of fear in it—just the stale dust of the cabin and the smell of lemon from the polish on the shiny dining table. It was so shiny the daylight pouring onto it through the window looked like spilled mercury, reflecting Tilly's grim face and Dominic's uncertain one like a mirror.

There was only a slight pause between Tilly's question and Dominic's answer, but it seemed to Spencer to stretch on forever, the air claustrophobic with a tension so thick, it made his nerves jangle and his wolf bristle inside him.

Dominic leaned forward, his elbows on the shiny table surface, his eyes wide and earnest under his unruly chestnut curls. "No. I'm not scared of you, Tilly," he said vehemently.

With a soft sigh, Tilly sat back in her chair, resting her palms flat on the table. Her expression softened, and she didn't look away from Dominic as she said, "Spencer, is he telling the truth? You said before you could smell—"

She broke off, hesitating only the slightest second, and he knew she was thinking of the other night, in the woods. When he'd wanted so badly to kiss her, when he'd woken her from her sleepwalking and seen the moonlight glow in her grey eyes like silver, and felt desire burning up in him like a desperate need. *I know you want me,* he'd said roughly, *I can smell it on you… your desire.* And he had. It had smelled like honey and cinnamon, sweet and spicy, overwhelming and intoxicating. He'd wanted so badly to feel her hair between his fingers, her lips on his, her skin against his…and she'd pushed him away. Because of Dominic. It was always Dominic.

Tilly finished her sentence, her pause barely perceptible except to Spencer because he knew what she'd been about to say and it wasn't, "…that you could smell—certain emotions. Can you tell if he's scared of me?"

Her eyes flicked to him, and he wondered if Dominic too could see the faintest blush of pink on her cheeks, see the slight darkening of her eyes at recalling the memory. A little of Spencer's bitterness drained out of him.

He nodded brusquely. "I can tell." He didn't elaborate.

Tilly frowned slightly, her pulse fluttering just under her jaw as he held her eyes. Then she looked away."Is he scared?" she asked, sounding a little exasperated.

Spencer's lips turned up at the corners, not quite a smile, and certainly not without malice. "No. He isn't scared…not right now, anyway."

Without looking up, Tilly nodded. Dominic shot Spencer a glare that she didn't see. He just stared evenly back at Dominic. As if sensing the silent hostility between the two boys, Tilly looked up at them both abruptly. Her cheeks reddened, her gaze falling on Dominic.

"Um…I don't know what Spencer told you about why he's here," she glanced at Spencer next to her, so swift it was barely even a glance, "but, um, it's not…what it looks like." She grimaced as she said it, and then groaned. "God that sounds lame."

She shook her head, and Dominic chuckled tentatively. Spencer clenched his fists under the table, hating Dominic right then, and for a second hating Tilly for her stupid need to clarify to the other boy, to let him know ever so subtly that she hadn't forsaken him for Spencer over one argument. Why didn't she just say, "No, I didn't sleep with your half-brother, and I'm still plenty available to you, Dominic, if you want to kiss me again"?

Dominic grinned, that goofy, annoyingly cheerful grin of his. The one that made Tilly smile back at him as if she just couldn't help herself. "It's okay. I...figured he was just here to keep an eye on you. Spencer might have the good looks, but he has none of the charm...and you've got better taste anyway, huh?" Dominic winked at Tilly as if he was sharing a secret with her. She giggled, and he glanced at his half-brother, undeniably smug. "Isn't that right, Spence?"

With an unconcealed glare in Dominic's direction, Spencer got up from the table, abruptly enough that his chair skidded backward across the floor, threatening to topple over. It stayed upright, but Spencer stormed past it.

Tilly jumped up with a cry of surprise. "Spencer! Where are you going?" she called after him.

He paused with his hand on the door handle, head bowed. He glanced over his shoulder at her. She stood next to her chair, looking startled and hurt by his sudden urge to leave, her grey eyes wide. Dominic, across the table, was still sitting, looking only mildly surprised and not at all upset about Spencer's aim to depart. Spencer bit his lip.

Raising his eyes to Tilly's, he said, "You know where." He opened the door and left, slamming it shut behind him.

** Tilly **

"What was that about?" Dominic asked as soon as Spencer was gone.

I stood and stared at the door for a moment, frowning. I hadn't expected him to react like that to Dominic's comments. Dom had only been teasing, after all. On the other side of the dining table, Dominic was frowning too, looking a little concerned. I felt slightly guilty about yelling at him like I had the previous night. I'd been too harsh, and he hadn't deserved it. He had just been surprised was all. In the middle of a circle of hunters aiming guns at him and his pack, I could hardly blame him for his reaction when I'd suddenly blasted Olivia with a power none of the wolves had known I had. Of course he'd been scared, maybe just not of me. And he *had* come looking for me afterward...

I shook my head, tearing my eyes away from the door. "I don't know," I muttered, only half lying. I thought I had an idea what it was about, and I knew where Spencer was going.

I had to talk to him. I looked at Dominic, who was watching me with uncertainty. If I ran after Spencer, he might get the wrong idea.

276

I had said that Spencer's being there wasn't what it looked like, but I didn't think Dominic entirely believed me, despite his joking. There was just something in the way he'd spoken to Spencer that made me think there was something going on between them that I didn't know about...but I may have been the cause of it.

Discomfited by the thought that I might have been the cause of discord between Spencer and his half-brother, one of the very few people Spencer did not seem to hold in contempt, I turned to Dominic."I should go after him. Find out what's wrong."

He frowned, displeased by the idea. "I'm sure he's just being Spencer. Moody and dark, as always. He'll be fine."

I shook my head. "I don't know...maybe I should just check and make sure. I kind of owe it to him, at least to check, after last night." I didn't wait for Dominic to reply. I turned and rushed down the hallway and into my room. Hastily, I yanked off my nightshirt and shorts, replaced them with jeans and a t-shirt, and returned to the main of the cabin.

Dominic was still standing by the table, scowling. I grabbed my trainers from where I'd left them by the door, tugging them on and lacing them up clumsily. I bounced to my feet, only to find Dominic was standing over me, curls shadowing his eyes. I hadn't even seen or heard him move. I gasped, startled, and he half-smiled.

The smile died a second later, and he asked, "How do you even know where he'll be? He could be anywhere by now if he's in wolf form. He's got a five minute head start."

I just smiled, shrugging. "I'll find him."

"But—"

"Just trust me, Dominic. I'll find him. But later, you and I are going to hang out, right?" I bounced from foot to foot impatiently, and he nodded slowly. "Good," I said, "'Cause you still have to beat me at checkers."

At that, he grinned reluctantly, and I leaned forward, placing a swift, chaste kiss on his cheek. Then I was out the door and racing down the steps, knowing exactly where Spencer would be, but not knowing exactly what I would say to him. I'd figure it out when I found him. Hopefully.

Chapter Seventeen

** Tilly **

Just as I'd expected, I found Spencer by the stream. Only, this time, he was on the other side of it, doing press-ups with his feet propped on a boulder. He'd obviously gone to his cabin to get dressed before going there, and his t-shirt hung loose, showing the flat hardness of his stomach. His biceps bulged with every press-up, and I was quite impressed by the ease and speed with which he did them. I watched for a moment, fascinated, and then I cleared my head and called over to him.

He didn't look up, but he stopped his press-ups and rolled over, kicking his feet off the boulder and lying with his arms spread on the grass. His chest rose and fell quickly, and his hair swept carelessly across his forehead until he ran a hand through it, tousling it.

"You know you're better than him, right?" Spencer said from across the stream, still without looking at me. He was looking up at the sky, his expression hard, and when I didn't answer, he turned his head, gazing across the water at me expectantly.

Startled, I didn't know what to say. "I…"

He made an impatient noise and rolled over again, pushing himself to his feet. Effortlessly, he leapt across the stream in one fluid motion and landed right next to me, close enough that I stumbled back in surprise.

He tilted his head, eyes fierce on mine. "You're better than him, Tilly. You deserve better than someone who's afraid of you–"

"You said he wasn't afraid," I said, confused.

Spencer laughed, a harsh sound more of contempt than humour. "He wasn't afraid then, with me there. He was too busy focussing on his jealousy. He wanted to prove a point to me, one up me, by having you forgive him in front of me. He's pathetic."

I shoved him. Impulsively, I slapped my hands against his chest and pushed him. He barely stumbled, and even then I think he only stumbled because I'd caught him off guard. I glowered up at him, and he blinked.

"Don't talk about Dominic that way! He isn't pathetic! How can you say that? He's your brother; I thought you two got along."

"Half-brother," Spencer corrected tightly, his eyes narrowing. "And we did get along. Until he figured out that I like you as well, and he tried to make a deal with me to… never mind. It's not like he would understand how I feel about you anyway. He probably doesn't think I'm even capable of loving someone, let alone that I could love you like I do, but—"

My lips parted. He was still talking, looking darker by the moment, but I wasn't really listening. *Did he just say what I think he said?* I stared at him, unsure what expression was on my face. *Let alone that I could love you like I do…* Yeah, he'd said what I thought he'd said. For some reason, it surprised me. It probably shouldn't have, after everything—him saving my life, me saving his life, our quiet meetings by the stream in the middle of the night, him spending the night in my bed. That one made me blush, though I knew nothing had happened. Still. He'd been in my *bed*.

No, the fact that he liked me, the same way Dominic liked me, hadn't surprised me at all. The fact that he *loved* me, though…that surprised me. Maybe it was just because he was *Spencer*, dark, quiet, and detached, and I didn't really expect him to feel that way about anyone. Or maybe it was just hearing him *say* that he loved me that surprised me. Or maybe it was the realisation that I'd begun to possibly love him, too. Whatever the reason, I was surprised, and it must have shown on my face, because Spencer stopped talking abruptly and frowned at me with concern.

"Tilly?" He eyed me warily.

I tilted my head quizzically, the way I'd seen him do so many times. "You l-love me?" my voice was soft and shy.

Spencer blinked at me, his eyebrows rising as if that wasn't what he'd expected me to say. Looking confused, he nodded. "Yes. Of course. I thought you knew that."

He sounded so genuinely puzzled by my reaction that I laughed unexpectedly. I hadn't meant to laugh. I put a hand over my mouth, afraid he'd think I was laughing at him. But he just continued to stare at me with that baffled expression, and I laughed again. Slowly, his confusion mixed with amusement and he raised one eyebrow.

"Am I missing something here?" he asked.

Still laughing, I shook my head. Taking deep breaths, I got my giggling under control, but I couldn't look at him, sure that if I did,

I'd start laughing again. "No, you're not missing anything exactly. It's just…" I shook my head again, biting my lip.

He did that quizzical head tilting thing again. "Just what?"

I considered my words, trying to figure out how to explain to him why I was laughing. "It's just that…you're…*you.*" I made a noise of frustration, knowing I sounded ridiculous.

He stared at me blankly, assuring me he didn't get it.

I thought again. "Um…what I mean is…Spencer, has anyone ever told you that you're really *distant* from other people?"

He seemed to consider for a moment, then shrugged. "Not to my face, but I know what they think," he said it with a casual sort of disinterest.

I stared at him, wondering if he even realised how he sounded. It was the tone he always used when he was talking about other people. I stared, but he just stared back, clueless. I stifled the urge to giggle again, this time in amazement. He was totally oblivious.

"Spencer, sometimes talking to you is like talking to someone who's only half here. I'm surprised to hear that you…feel that way about me because…. Well, I'd sort of thought you only talked to me, because I happened to keep showing up to save your life." After I said it, I blushed, regretting it.

A strange expression came over his face, one I couldn't identify, and then he was gripping my arms. I gasped, but he didn't let go. He pulled me closer, until I had to look up to see his eyes. His blue gaze burned into mine, and I felt my heart splutter.

"Tilly, I don't spend time with people because they treat me nicely, or they fancy me, or even because they save my life. I spend time with people only because I want to. I spend time with people because they make me smile, because I enjoy being around them, because they understand me…" His voice was low and intense, and he bent his head closer to mine, so close I could see the gold flecks in his eyes.

"You understand me, Tilly. You might not even realise it, but you understand me better than anyone else I've ever met." He laughed, only slightly bitterly. "Ironic, isn't it? That I've spent my whole life with people like me, werewolves, but yet, none of them are really *like* me. None of them would sit down on a rock and talk to me in the middle of the night about anything I would be interested in. None of them would look at me and see anything but a sulky boy with a pretty face, whose mother ran away from the pack." His lips brushed my ear, his breath warm on my neck, and my eyelids fluttered.

He sighed softly. "None of them would fascinate me the way you do."

His hand came up, fingertips caressing the back of my neck, and I shuddered. His other hand went around my waist, pressing against the small of my back, so I was plastered against him, not a millimetre between us. His body was hard and hot underneath his t-shirt, and his hair tickled my temple. His breath on my neck was burning. I flashed back to the other night in the woods, when I'd wanted so badly to kiss him, and I raised my arms around his neck. I didn't care about Dominic

I should have, but I didn't. Not after how he'd reacted to me the night before. I'd forgiven him, but I didn't trust him as I had before. I trusted Spencer. Dark, mysterious Spencer who'd protected me again and again, who'd never once looked at me with fear, who'd spent the night in my bed next to me because I was frightened. Spencer, and who *loved* me.

I turned my head slightly, and then Spencer was kissing me. It wasn't at all how I'd thought it would be. I'd expected him to be rough and impulsive, all burning passion and hunger. Instead, his lips were gentle on mine, warm but careful. His fingertips brushed against the nape of my neck, light as a feather, and I found myself digging blunt nails into his shoulders in response.

My skin felt hot and tight, but inside, I felt as if I was full of melting honey. Where Dominic's kisses had been chaste and comforting, Spencer's was anything but. It was slow, and so thrilling, my toes curled inside my trainers. He flicked his tongue against my top lip, teasing, and I gasped. I felt him shiver, and I was unsure if it was with desire, or if he was fighting his wolf. Tenderly, playfully, I bit his lower lip, hoping nervously I was doing it right. Besides Dominic, I'd never really kissed a boy, and I'd never in my life kissed a boy like *that*. But Spencer made a low sound deep in his throat, and his hands tightened on me, so I guessed I was doing okay.

As if biting his lip had snapped his careful control, he kissed me harder, wilder, more the way I'd expected him to. Expecting it, though, didn't dim the sensational fireworks that sparked through my nerves, sweeping me up in a wave of molten flame. I clung to him, half-afraid I'd be burned away in that fire. His hands slid down my body, rough and desperate, over my breasts and down my waist, burning through my t-shirt. Suddenly, he spun us, backing me against a tree. I made a muffled sound of surprise, but his mouth muted it. My fingers were knotted in his inky hair, my heart hammering against his, every cell on fire, and I didn't want it to stop. The desire pulsed through me, intoxicating, burning, and aching. I wanted more, I *needed*—

"What the hell!"

I jerked away from Spencer with a gasp, only succeeding in putting about an inch of space between us, thanks to the tree at my back. Spencer just sighed, like he wasn't surprised in the least to see Dominic standing glaring at us, looking more outraged than I'd ever seen him. Guilt twanged in my chest, way down deep, and I dropped my hands from Spencer's shoulders quickly, curling them against my chest and bowing my head. My face flamed with embarrassment and shame at being caught, not just kissing Spencer, but kissing Spencer *like that*. Like I was drowning, and only his lips could save me. Like I was on fire, and only he could quench the flames.

Oh god, what Dominic must think of me. My eyes filled, but I blinked back the tears.

"Dominic," Spencer said evenly, but his eyes were locked on the other boy, blazing blue and gold, half-feral. He didn't move away from me one bit, didn't let go of my hips, only turned his head so he could see the boy who'd interrupted us.

I really wished he'd let me go. With his hands still on me, my body continued to burn and ache for his kisses and touches. It was hard to concentrate, but I had to, because Dominic wasn't looking at Spencer. He was looking at me, with wide, angry, hurt eyes. I couldn't hold his gaze.

Dominic made a small noise, half bitter chuckle and half hurt sigh. His voice was as hard and cold as shards of ice, each one leaving a gash in my heart, making me feel sick. "So this is why you wanted to come find him so badly, huh? This is how you make sure he's okay? By making out with him against a tree and letting him put his hands—"

"Dominic," Spencer snapped. "That's enough!"

The bitter laugh that escaped Dominic's lips sent a shiver down my spine.

"Is it? It doesn't look like she's had enough."

I couldn't believe it was Dominic, sweet cheerful Dominic, my best friend, the boy who'd kissed me so softly in the kitchen, who was saying those things. I stared at him, so aghast, my throat locked.

"Shut up, Dominic!" Spencer barked, his eyes turning yellow. He snatched his hands off me, though, turning to face Dominic fully. His muscles were taut, fists clenched. Spencer was really angry. "Don't blame Tilly just because you're jealous! It isn't her fault. *I* kissed *her*. She told me not to, told me she didn't want to hurt *you*, but I didn't listen."

I knew I should say something, shouldn't let Spencer take the whole blame, because I was just as guilty as he was. I'd wanted him to kiss me. I'd let him, and I'd kissed him back, and I hadn't wanted to stop. I'd entirely forgotten about Dominic for those moments, lost in Spencer's lips and hands. Lost in his admission that he *loved* me. I could hardly believe it. *I should explain to Dominic somehow...*but I couldn't.

My mouth was dry, my throat was full, and I was afraid that if I tried to speak, I'd burst into tears because of the way he was looking at me. Not as if he were scared of me, not then, but as if he was disgusted with me. As if he'd thought me better than that. Truthfully, I'd thought myself better than that too.

Tossing his head in agitation, Dominic growled, and it wasn't the sound of an angry boy, but that of an irritated wolf. I started fearfully, shocked at the sound escaping Dominic's throat, but Spencer didn't even flinch.

"I thought we had a deal, *brother?* What of that? What of family and loyalty? Have you forgotten what that means to our kind?" For the first time, Dominic spoke like an authority figure, like someone who felt responsibilities and respect for rules, like...like the Second in Command of a werewolf pack.

I wasn't even a werewolf, and I could feel the power of a leader crackling in the air. It was clear from the way Spencer was gritting his teeth that he felt it too, and he didn't want to bend to it. I wondered if Spencer had ever bent submissively to the leaders of his pack. Somehow, I couldn't imagine that he had. No matter how weakly he was tied to the pack, Spencer was not a follower. That much I was certain of.

"Don't speak to me of family, Dominic," Spencer said, his voice quiet and as black as night, a threat of its own that made me take a step back from him. "The pack has always been your family, but it has never truly been mine. You and Desmond are the closest I have to family. The only ones I regard that way. But even you would dismiss me and cast me aside, because it's how our dearest father treats me, because my mother betrayed the pack when she left Frank."

Spencer took a step forward, just a tiny step, and Dominic's eyes flared green-yellow. He shifted, his chest swelling just enough to make him seem somehow a lot bigger, more commanding, more threatening. He was trying to glare Spencer down, obviously not happy that a lower member of the pack was openly challenging him. I swallowed, taking another step back carefully, trying not to attract their attention to me. It looked as if there was about to be a fight, and I wondered if I could get to the cabins and get help in time to stop it. Sarah, Jane, or Graham—someone who might be able to calm them down.

Spencer went on, sounding as calm and as dangerous as Dominic looked unstable. There was the barest of smiles on his mouth. Not really a smile, I realised, but he was baring his teeth, just slightly. As with everything Spencer did, the subtlety of the expression gave a lot more impact than if he'd been full out snarling in Dominic's face. It scared me.

"And as for loyalty, *Minnie,* you can't say jack to me about it after the way you turned on Tilly last night."

Nervously, I half-raised a hand for attention, unable to resist putting in, "We've already talked about that. It's okay—"

"No, it isn't, Tilly!" Spencer whirled on me, and I jumped. His expression softened, apology in his eyes, and he sighed. "It isn't okay, Tilly. You don't understand. Loyalty is more than a word to our kind. It's practically law. And just because you're not one of us, it doesn't lessen the intensity of my wolf's need to protect you. *My* need to protect you." he explained.

Spencer looked as if he wanted to have the conversation in private rather than in front of Dominic, whose eyes were returning to their normal green, but he still looked furious.

"Is...is that because I saved your life?" I asked hesitantly. I had to know.

Spencer frowned, nodding. "Yes. That's part of it. But only part, Tilly."

"Enough!" Dominic snarled suddenly. His glare fixed on Spencer again. "You know what this means, Spencer. You know it's forbidden to have a real relationship with anyone who isn't wolf, honorary member of the pack or not. If Frank finds out—"

Spencer was abruptly right up in Dominic's face, his eyes glowing with anger, his lips peeled back from his teeth. "Frank won't find out," he spat, his jaw clenched.

Dominic's eyes narrowed, but he looked calmer, eerily so. He opened his mouth to say something, but his words had cut me and sprung a leak in my chest.

"Forbidden?" I said quietly, and both boys looked at me with faint surprise on their faces, as if they'd forgotten I was even there. "It's forbidden…for a werewolf to be with someone outside the pack?" My heart curled in on itself, my face heating with anger, embarrassment, and shame. Of course it was forbidden. I had been an idiot to allow myself to think, even for a moment, that maybe Spencer and I could be…

Dominic was looking at me with wide, pained eyes. Spencer stepped toward me, reaching out a hand as if to comfort me, but I jerked away.

"Tilly.""

"Don't," I snapped, glaring at him. "Don't say a word. Don't even try." I turned on my heel and walked away into the trees, hearing him call after me, praying he wouldn't follow.

when I was deep enough in that I was sure he couldn't see me, I broke into a run. I'd been running a lot lately, running away from my crappy adoptive family, running away from the truth of what Dominic and Spencer were, and I was running away from the pain and hurt as the small blossom of hope I'd begun to feel was crushed under the heel of pack rules, running as if I could really escape it.

I ran hard and fast, my legs burning and lungs puffing, tears rolling down my cheeks, and branches whipping at me furiously. I ran, and I wished that once, just once, nothing bad would catch up to me.

Chapter Eighteen

** Tilly **

I don't know how long I ran for, but I didn't stop until I was well and truly lost. I bent over, bracing my hands on my knees, lungs heaving. My legs ached and trembled, and I was gasping like a fish out of water. I slumped to the ground at the base of a birch tree, and leaned my head back against the rough trunk. My forehead and back were sweating, but my eyes were dry. Despite the lancing pain of a stitch in my side, I smiled. The adrenaline felt good. Sure, I'd probably never find my way back to my cabin on my own, but at the moment, that didn't bother me.

For a while, I just sat on the ground, sprawled out tiredly, and considered not going back at all—just up and leaving. There was no reason to stay there. Dominic was a douche, the werewolves probably hated me, and the witches knew where I was back there. If I moved on, nobody would expect it. It would take the witches a while to figure out I was gone, and hopefully by then, I'd be far enough away that they wouldn't find me. Leaving only made sense, except for one thing. There *was* a reason to stay, and that reason was tall, dark and handsome, with mysterious blue eyes, a body I couldn't stop thinking about being pressed against mine, and a mouth I wanted to taste again.

I smacked my head against the tree trunk in frustration, closing my eyes. *Dammit!* If I'd found out the day before that the werewolves were forbidden to have relationships with outsiders, I'd have had no problem in leaving. I'd have upped sticks and vanished. *But now...*I shook my head. *Now there's Spencer*, I thought with both a mental and an audible sigh. Once I knew he loved me, once he'd spent the night in my bed, and once he'd *kissed me*, I couldn't just leave. No way.

It was probably the stupidest decision of my life, but I wasn't leaving.

I raised my hands and pressed my palms to my eyes until I saw grey dots against the darkness, heaving a sigh that would have knocked over anyone standing in front of me. *Boys*, I thought. *They are so much trouble.* Werewolf *boys? Beyond trouble.* And yet, somehow, I couldn't bring myself to regret my decision, couldn't bring myself to regret kissing Spencer either. I played it over in my head, feeling a blush stain my cheeks and my body grow warm and tingly at the memory of his lips on mine, his hands roaming the shape of my body...

Someone cleared their throat suddenly, and I jumped guiltily. I looked up, sure my face was scarlet, and winced, wondering if it was possible to get any redder. Spencer was standing over me, leaning against the tree, looking down at me with one eyebrow raised. His lips were twisted in an amused, knowing smile, and I wondered if he could actually read my mind.

"Can you read my mind?" I blurted without thinking, then clamped my hands over my mouth and looked down, hiding my face under my hair. *Whoops.*

Spencer chuckled, and I hunched my shoulders up higher, wishing he'd go away again. Hearing him laugh like that, warm and smooth, did absolutely nothing to banish the images in my head and the heat in my stomach. I pulled my knees to my chest and rested my forehead on them, breathing steadily.

Think of something else, think of something else! But I couldn't. I groaned with humiliation.

"No," Spencer said, still chuckling, "I can't read your mind. I'm a werewolf, not a psychic. Why? Was there something particularly interesting going on in your thoughts?"

His voice was mocking, but not in that way that made me feel like he was laughing at me, Well, he *was* laughing at me, but it wasn't condescending. I was blushing so much, I felt like my ears would burst into flames.

With my forehead still against my knees, I shook my head. "No, nothing interesting at all."

Spencer made a thoughtful noise, and I heard him move away from the tree to stand in front of me. "Hmm," he murmured. "Are you sure about that? Because your heart's going awful fast. Sure you weren't thinking something...exciting?" I could hear laughter in his voice.

I looked up and glared at him, praying he'd think the redness of my face was from the exercise. "I just ran like three miles or something. Of course my heart rate's a bit elevated."

He raised both his eyebrows in a look of comical surprise. "Oh, *elevated.* Fancy word for a girl who was just thinking about doing very primitive things with me."

"Shut up! I was not!" I covered my ears with my hands, but I could still hear him laughing. I scowled at the dirt on my trainers. *Remind me why I like this guy? Oh, yeah, because he saved my life…and he's a hell of a kisser.*

All of a sudden, he was kneeling right in front of me, leaning in. With a choked noise of surprise, I jerked backwards, my hands sliding on the leaves on the ground under them. Spencer grinned, and for the first time, I noticed he had a faint silvery scar just under his lower lip. Then I realised I was looking at his lips and moved my gaze back to his eyes, but it didn't help one bit.

His eyes were so *intense*; it was like staring into radioactive pools of blue liquid. Something inside me quivered in delight, and I thought of him kissing me there and then, on the ground, far away from anyone to interrupt us. I let out a jagged, shuddering breath.

Spencer's mouth turned up at one corner wryly, his lids half-lowered, and he leaned back. "Primitive things indeed," he murmured.

Desperate to change the direction of the conversation, I asked, slightly breathlessly, "How did you get that scar? On your lip? I thought werewolves could heal things like that?"

Looking surprised by my question, Spencer lifted his fingers to his lip, touching the faint scar. His eyes took on a distant glaze, as if he weren't seeing me anymore. "It was inflicted with silver. When I was very little, so little I only barely remember it. I was playing with a knife in my mother's kitchen, reaching for it on the countertop, and when my fingers touched it, it burned. I yanked my hand back and the knife fell. It cut me, and I must have wailed like a banshee, and my mother was so upset. She blamed herself for leaving the knife lying around. She picked me up and cradled me, wiping away the blood and tears, and she sang to me. A lullaby...I don't...I can't remember the lullaby anymore..."

There was something suddenly so raw and vulnerable in Spencer's expression that I had the urge to put my arms around him and comfort him. I didn't move, fearful that if I did, it would disrupt his memory. I had never seen him look like that before—as if there was something, some*one*, he really *cared* about. Someone he truly loved with the kind of love one could only feel for family.

He blinked and half-gasped as if he'd been jolted back to the present by a punch to the gut. He stared at me for a long second before recognition flashed in his eyes, and his throat moved as he swallowed, his vulnerable expression hardening. I could practically see the cold, hard armour he had around himself being built up again link by link, brick by brick. It was amazing and terrible at once, seeing him withdraw into a skin made of ice, distancing himself from the world like a tree pulling its roots from the earth and shrivelling.

I wondered, if a person separated their self from other people for long enough, did they shrivel? If they kept everyone away, hiding, shielding their self from possible love and friendship, did their soul become weak and dry?

"Spencer," I murmured gently, leaning toward him.

He got to his feet hastily, brushing off his jeans with brisk, sharp movements. "We should get back to the cabins. We need to talk to Frank about what happened last night, and we'd better do it before Dominic changes his mind about keeping his mouth shut about what he witnessed."

What he witnessed? You mean, you kissing me? I got to my feet slowly, hiding my face so he wouldn't see I was stung by his brusqueness. "Okay," I said, nodding.

Spencer glanced at me, a fleeting glance, and his expression flickered for a second, but I couldn't read it. Then he jerked his head once and said, "Follow me, or else you'll be lost out here for days."

He turned and started walking quickly through the trees, his back to me. I watched his tense shoulders receding between the branches, and sighed softly before hurrying to catch up with him. I made a decision, though, as I walked. I decided that, no matter what it cost, I would find a way to make Spencer let love in through that hard armour. I would not let his soul shrivel.

"No, there is no way that is happening!" Frank boomed, shaking his head. His lips were pressed flat beneath the bristles of his moustache.

I shrunk back, wishing I hadn't opened my mouth and suggested it. Spencer, next to me, was stock still and taut.

Frank turned his steely grey eyes on me, and his grimace deepened. "No. What are you thinking, girl? And Spencer, I thought you knew better. I thought you knew the laws of the pack!"

Spencer opened his mouth to say something, shook his head, and closed it again, speechless. Honestly, I was pretty much speechless too. This was not the reaction either of us had expected when we'd come to talk to the alpha.

Frank rubbed his prickly jaw, and said, "No, there's no way you're leaving, Tilly. I don't care why those witches are after us. I don't care why they're after you. They picked a fight with us, and we're not going to back down. You saved us when you didn't have to. You didn't have to come running at that gunshot, and didn't have to stop that witch from exposing Spencer. You could have saved your own skin, and you didn't. That means something to us, and I'm not letting you walk away from the best protection there is around here. A strong werewolf pack. That's the end of it." He shot Spencer a meaningful glower, which I couldn't decode, and then turned and walked away.

Spencer turned to me and raised one eyebrow slowly. "You just had to suggest leaving, didn't you?"

I couldn't tell from his voice what he thought of that, the idea that I'd be willing to leave. I wasn't willing, but I thought I'd throw it out there, just on the off chance that my going away would mean the wolves wouldn't decide to *make* me go away. Turned out, the wolves didn't want me gone after all. Well. Frank didn't. I suspected I was still going to be a pariah among the pack, but at least I'd be a well-protected pariah.

I shrugged. "I just thought he should know all the options. I was sort of expecting him to call me wolf chow, and you know, eat me." I shuddered dramatically, and grinned at him, but Spencer didn't grin back.

He had that brooding look again—eyes narrowed, brows pushed down, staring at me as if he was trying to see inside my skin. "Would you really have left if he'd told you to?"

With a sigh, I shrugged again. "Yes, I would have left. If I thought it would keep the pack safe, and if I thought I might become doggy snacks if I stayed, I'd go." *But I'd pray for you to come with me*. I didn't say that bit out loud, and I kept my head bowed, so he wouldn't read it on my face. He didn't need to know he was the only thing keeping me there, protected or not.

Unexpectedly, Spencer snorted. I looked up in time to see him rolling his eyes. "You're more loyal to the pack than I am," he muttered.

He turned, motioning for me to follow him, and I did. We started to wander off toward the stream. It wasn't hard to guess where we were going. Spencer shoved his hands into his pockets, his narrowed eyes scanning the bushes as we walked. I wasn't sure if he was looking for threats, or if he was just always on his guard.

We came to the stream, and he sat down on his boulder, stretching his long legs out in front of him. I hesitated, my gaze flicking to the tree he'd backed me up against earlier. I felt heat stain my cheeks, and then felt Spencer's gaze on me, no doubt noticing. I turned around, making it look as if I was just casually strolling up and down the edge of the stream. His gaze rested heavily on my back, but I refused to turn around. I watched the clear water of the stream bubbling and swirling over rocks, leaves, and the algae clustered at the edges.. I realised it had been days since I'd meditated.

"What are you thinking about?" Spencer asked suddenly, his voice quiet.

I glanced at him over my shoulder, lounging on that rock as if it was a perfectly comfortable piece of furniture. Somehow, he still looked graceful, sprawled out like that. I didn't know if it was a werewolf thing, or a Spencer thing.

"Meditation," I answered simply, continuing to walk with my back to him.

He grunted. "Mh. You meditate?"

"It helps me focus, helps me control my temper and my power. I can feel the energy of the woods around me. It's like a living, breathing creature, with thoughts and feelings. It's just that most people don't have the ability to feel it, to sense its thoughts and emotions, the way I do," I explained.

There was a thoughtful silence for a moment, and then Spencer asked, "Is that something all witches can do, or just you?"

Absently, I said, "Some witches can, some can't. It's part of what makes me so weird. Different from normal witches, I mean. I have certain powers that shouldn't reside together in one witch." I shrugged, as if it was no big deal, but it was. I waited for him to ask me what I meant or what my powers were, but he didn't.

I turned to him, and changed the subject. "Thank you, by the way…for…staying last night," I murmured, hugging my elbows. I was embarrassed I'd broken down like that, but I'd been so scared and exhausted. And I'd been so angry at Dominic. I didn't know what I would have done if Spencer had left me alone in that room all night. I know I wouldn't have slept.

Spencer blinked, evidently surprised by my thanks. He stared at me blankly for a second, as if he didn't understand the words I was saying, and then he smiled, a stunningly sweet and shy smile, just a little lopsided. "No problem. You seemed like you needed it."

I nodded. "Yeah, I sort of did. Sorry, though…for the crying. I'm not usually…I don't normally go off like that." I grimaced. "I guess I was worried about the witches coming to kidnap me, or making me sleepwalk again, or something." I wondered why my personal wardings didn't prevent that, the sleepwalking. It was definitely an issue, but I had no idea how to fix it. I'd sort of skipped over the Sleep Summoning part of my witch approved learning curriculum.

Spencer made a low, concerned sound, frowning. "Yes, the sleepwalking is a problem. Much as I'd like to spend more nights in your bed," he flicked me a mischievous glance, and I looked away, "it's hardly practical. Plus, someone is bound to catch on, make assumptions, and tell Frank I've been fraternising with an outsider, and then we're both royally screwed." He shook his head in frustration. "So, what we need is help. Help from someone not interested in pack laws or politics. Someone who has power of her own." He tapped his chin with a forefinger in a mockingly thoughtful pose, and I scoffed at him.

"And you happen to know someone like that?" I asked.

He grinned. "As a matter of fact, I do."

Chapter Nineteen

** Tilly **

"So this is where your witchdoctor lives?" I eyed the crumbling, leaning shack sceptically. It was small, rickety and looked sort of like it had just grown out of the ground and been forgotten about. Moss crawled up the walls, leaves piled around the porch, and cobwebs smothered the cloudy, darkly curtained windows. It seemed to be slumping down on one side, the rotting porch steps twisting like a frown at the front of the shack. It was only a fifteen minute walk from my cabin, and I was surprised I hadn't come across it in my wandering before.

"She's not a witch doctor; I said she's a witch, who happens to be the pack's doctor. A Healer. Since, obviously, we can't really go to a normal doctor without them figuring out there's something wrong. I mean, besides, undoubtedly, a shard of metal sticking out from one's ribs. We come to Jasmine," Spencer explained, but he was giving the twisted porch steps and sagging, lichen coated roof the same wary look I was.

"Well," I said, "do we go in? Or do we need to make an appointment first?"

Spencer cut a sideways glance at me with a silently laughing smile. "You're a real cutup. No, no appointment needed. In fact, she probably already knows we're here," he said, gingerly loping up the steps.

The old wood groaned miserably under his weight, and even creaked under my slighter body. I shuddered. Creaky old cabins like that were always the setting for gory horror movies. But then, I supposed, my life had been pretty much a horror movie since I was six, and the past couple of weeks hadn't changed that one bit.

How much worse could it really get?

Swallowing that thought before Fate picked up on it, I asked, "Your witchdoc— Healer woman is clairvoyant?" One of the witches I'd lived with was clairvoyant, but only weakly. Naomi, the youngest, and possibly the kindest, if you could call any of them kind in any way, had occasional visions. Of course, she'd used demon blood to strengthen her powers.

After a long pause, the door started to crack open with a weary whine. A puff of cool, lavender and sage scented air swept out onto the porch. I grabbed Spencer's hand nervously, gripping his dry fingers tightly. Out of the corner of my eye, I saw Spencer cut me a quick, surprised glance, his eyebrows rising, but I kept my gaze straight ahead on the widening gap between the door and the wall— only darkness showing beyond it. I was suddenly terrified. The only witches I'd ever met were the sisters who'd adopted me. I didn't know what to expect of this one. Would she be as cold and dark hearted as Olivia, Naomi, and Gwen? Would she take one look at me and know I'd dabbled with demons, and banish me from her cabin in horror?

Slowly, the door peeled back to reveal a woman much younger, and much less creepy, than I had expected. I took a second to be ashamed of myself. What had I been expecting, an old lady with warts on her nose? Some of the most beautiful people I knew were witches, and the woman behind the door, maybe twenty-five at most, was no exception.

She was lovely, with smooth hair the colour of autumn leaves cut into a stylish bob, and skin as fair as mine. Her full lips were as red as rose petals, and curved in an amused smile. Though she was half a foot shorter than me, she had a figure so slender, I was jealous. The only thing that struck me as odd about her was her eyes. They were wide and bright, but every time she blinked, they seemed to change colour—brown to green to blue to grey and back to brown.

I wondered if it was a side effect of seeing different futures as a clairvoyant. Naomi's eyes didn't do that, though. The woman must have been a particularly strong seer.

"Well, well," the woman said, her strange colour shifting eyes resting on Spencer. "Look what the wolf dragged in." She leaned against the doorframe, giving Spencer a sultry kind of look.

I glanced at him, expecting his usual blankness in response, but he was smiling. Actually smiling, fondness for the woman written in the cheekiness of his grin. I felt a spark of something nasty and pushed it down. *Is there something going on between these two?* I pushed the thought down, too, and hard. I didn't know what the witch's powers were; if she might be a telepath as well as a clairvoyant.

"Afternoon, Jazz." Spencer ducked his head briefly in greeting.

I pursed my lips at the nickname. Obviously they were very familiar. I tried not to wonder just how familiar they were. Spencer had said relationships with outsiders were forbidden—he hadn't said anything about casual sex.

Spencer waved a hand, drawing the woman's attention to me. Her eyes, an eerie shade of green, fixed on me and widened, lightening to hazel.

"Jasmine, this is—" Spencer started.

"Matilda," Jasmine breathed.

I flinched. I got a sinking feeling in my stomach. *Oh God, what if she knows the witches? What if she's helping* them? I began to panic internally, my fingers tightening on Spencer's, so suddenly, that he cast me a concerned look. But the witch went on, her voice low and strange, the way I'd heard Naomi talk when she was in the midst of one of her visions.

"The Leyland Sisters' adopted child. The one with the double powers. I've been waiting for you."

I swallowed, putting my free hand into my pocket, so she wouldn't see how badly I was shaking, unnerved by how much she knew about me. *The one with the double powers.* That was one way of putting it, and only 'the Sisters' knew about my unusual combination of powers. Not even Spencer knew exactly what my powers were, though I had told him they were not normal for a single witch.

"Tilly," Spencer said quietly, reassuringly.

Jasmine blinked and her eyes, now a dark shade of blue, flicked back to him, and then to our joined hands. I was squeezing his so hard, his knuckles were white, but he didn't show any signs that it was hurting him. There was only worry in his voice, no pain.

Abruptly, Jasmine smiled, a pleased and self-satisfied kind of smile. Spencer noticed and blushed. I was startled out of my panic for just a moment. Spencer did not usually blush, not easily, but there was definitely a smear of pink across his cheekbones and he was looking down at his feet.

Jasmine giggled. "And you said it would never happen! Ha! I told you, I'm never wrong, Spence baby, never!" She clapped excitedly like a little girl.

Spencer's blush darkened. He muttered something, so low even I couldn't hear what it was.

Jasmine leaned forward, cupping her hand around her ear. "What was that, Mr. I'd Never Fall For An Outsider?"

He lifted his gaze, glowering at her, and bared his teeth. It was a look scary enough that I wanted to take a step back, but the witch just continued to grin at him smugly.

"Nothing," Spencer growled between his teeth. "But if you're so all seeing, Jazz, I guess you know why we're here?"

Jasmine nodded, stepping back from the doorway and gesturing for us to come in. Spencer ducked in the door, and I had no choice but to follow. The door closed behind us, and the room became so dim, it took my eyes a moment to adjust. All the curtains over the windows were closed, the only light provided by large, fat candles

307

scattered around on desks and bookshelves and hanging in sconces on the walls. The smell of lavender and sage was much stronger inside, though not unpleasant.

Jasmine skipped past me to touch a spot on the far wall, flipping a switch. Suddenly, the electric lighting flared to life, and I squinted against the brightness. Once it was properly illuminated, I could see the shack looked bigger from the inside, and not nearly as run down as the outside. There was a door in the wall next to the light switch, presumably leading to a bathroom or private bedroom, and another in the adjacent wall that was flung open, so I could see inside. Beyond it was a pale, bright room that seemed to be some sort of sickbay, with a clean, neatly made bed, a metal cabinet, a red plastic bucket with a grey cloth hanging out of it hiding in a corner, and a comfy looking chair like the kind you might find in a hospital. Obviously, that was where she did her doctoring for the wolves, and maybe other supernatural creatures too.

She danced past me again and started to shuffle papers around on a large wooden desk. The whole room was scattered with books of all sizes, some with leather covers and ancient looking yellow pages, some with shiny metal buckles attached. Books were piled on the floor, spilling off the bookcases, towering on the desk. *It has to be a fire hazard*, I thought, *with all those candles around.*

Even as I thought it, Jasmine began going round the room, blowing out the candles.

Then she turned, hands on hips, and looked at me with those restless eyes. "So, you're here for a Protection Charm. Something that'll keep the Leyland Sisters at bay and out of your pretty little head."

Startled by her assumption, I stammered, "I– um…it…"

Spencer rubbed his thumb across my knuckles, and I shut up, mostly because my mouth went suddenly dry. "Yes, that's why we're here," he said steadily, though I noticed a hint of amusement in his tone, no doubt at my expense. I scowled.

With a knowing smirk in my direction, Jasmine made a faint, approving noise. Turning her eyes back to Spencer, she asked, "Have you got something to use as a Charm? Something she can keep on her at all times, preferably."

I pondered why she was asking him, as if this Charm weren't for me, but Spencer stuck his hand in his pocket and brought something out, and I guessed she'd already known he had an object for her to Spell.

Without looking at me, Spencer stretched out his hand over Jasmine's palm and let something drop from his fist into her hand. I only caught a glimpse of it, small and white with a chain attached, and wondered what it was. Jasmine closed her fingers over it quickly, wandered to her desk, and sat down in the chair behind it.

Humming to herself, she dug around between the stacks of books and pulled out what looked like a mortar and pestle of black stone. She took the pestle and laid it aside, then dropped the Charm Spencer had given her into the bowl. From apparently nowhere, she produced a sachet of some herbs—I assumed protection herbs—and tipped the contents into the bowl, sprinkling it over the Charm. She pulled another sachet from somewhere, and did the same, though I had no idea what herbs were in that one.

I watched, fascinated, as Jasmine bent her head, her fingers cupping the bowl, and closed her eyes. She spoke an incantation in Latin, one I recognised well, because I'd used it myself a few times. I didn't doubt her protection magic would be stronger, though. She invoked the elements, the power of the sun and moon, and sea and sky, asking them to protect the Spell-Bearer from harm. I thought she was done, for there was no more to the incantation that I knew of, but she continued in a slower, almost husky voice, as if she were trying to seduce the Charm.

Mentally translating her words, I blushed fervently, and Spencer shot me a sideways, questioning look. I kept my eyes on Jasmine as she spoke the second incantation. I knew what it meant. *I call upon the power of the fire and the moon to help the passion of new love bloom, and aid the moon's child in keeping his loyalty strong.* The extra herbs she'd added must have been for that part of the incantation.

As soon as she spoke the last word, the contents of the bowl burst into brilliant purple flames with a sizzling pop. They subsided quickly, leaving behind only the Charm. She held it up, clean and untouched by the magic fire, and I gasped as I recognised it. It was a white pebble, swirled with blue and gold—the pebble I'd found in the stream during one of my late night meetings with Spencer. Only, it had a gold chain glued onto it, turning it into necklace. Jasmine handed it to me, and I stared at it in my palm, then up at Spencer. He smiled at me shyly, and shrugged.

"How…when…?" I stammered, amazed. I'd forgotten completely about the pebble. I'd left it in the drawer of my nightstand in my cabin, and hadn't even looked at it in a week. I couldn't imagine how he'd gotten hold of it, or why. Had he known somehow that I'd need it for a Charm?

Looking a little uncomfortable, he said, "You dropped it the other night when you were sleepwalking. I picked it up and thought I'd hold on to it, put a chain on it so you could wear it. That way you wouldn't drop it again…" He shrugged again.

I bit my lip, looking back down at the beautiful, shiny pebble in my hand. It was such a sweet, thoughtful thing for him to do, but I couldn't imagine why I would have been carrying it when I was sleepwalking.

I slipped the chain over my head and the pebble rested against my chest in the narrow valley between my breasts, cool, smooth, and tingling slightly against my skin from the freshness of the magic put on it. Tentatively, I touched it and smiled. *My Protection Charm…*I wasn't sure if I meant the pebble, the boy standing next to me, or the wolf who had protected me from the start.

Carefully, Spencer took a step closer to me and lifted his hand, brushing the magically enchanted pendant. His fingertips drew a tiny blue spark from the stone, and he jerked his hand back. I laughed under my breath, glancing at him through my lashes. He met my gaze with intense blue eyes, and my stomach fluttered.

Jasmine cleared her throat, and I looked quickly away from Spencer.

Jasmine, her red hair shimmering under the bright light, had her hands folded elegantly in her lap and her thin brows were raised expectantly. "Now, if you two are quite done with your moment," she snickered, "I believe there's something you'd like to ask me, Tilly."

I blinked. "There is?"

She nodded. I thought about it for a second, but nothing came to mind. I shook my head.

Jasmine just smiled. "Wouldn't you like to know why it is that you have the powers you do? Wouldn't you like to know *what you really are?*"

"I…" I licked my lips nervously. "You…you know what I am?" My voice was almost a whisper. My heart pounded and my stomach felt as if it was full of cold, wriggling worms. Could she really know what I was? Could the odd, pretty woman tell me why I had the ability to raise demons from the Underworld, something only a Dark witch or a Shaman could do, and still held the power to do Light Spells? Maybe if I knew what I was, I could find a way to get rid of my Dark power. I'd never have to feel the touch of a demon's mind in mine again, and the Sisters would have to leave me alone. I'd be no use to them without that power.

"I can tell…if you give me your hands." Jasmine closed her eyes, nodding, and held her hands out to me.

Hesitantly, I put my hands in hers, and her soft fingers enclosed mine. I glanced at Spencer, who looked both confused and fascinated. I gave him a smile that was meant to be reassuring, but he didn't look reassured. Taking a deep breath, I turned back to Jasmine and closed my eyes.

A shock of energy, like electricity, shot through my arms from our joined hands, and the darkness behind my lids flashed into colour. Strange, meaningless patterns shifted across my eyes, changing colours the way I'd seen Jasmine's eyes do. Psychedelic shapes bubbled across the blankness, lime green and hot pink to cyan blue and butter yellow to chocolate brown and chalky grey.

The energy flowing from Jasmine into me subsided, and I gasped as my eyes flew open. Jasmine released my hands, her own eyes opening. *Slate grey*, I noted, *eerily similar to my own*. Her mouth was pressed into a thin line, and she blinked twice, focus coming into her eyes. She fixed her gaze on me intently, and I bit my lip.

"So, do you know what I am?" I asked anxiously. I felt Spencer move up behind me, and I reached blindly behind me for his hand. His strong fingers closed around mine, easing the knot in my stomach.

Jasmine made a soft sound between her teeth, a noise of surprise. She blinked, and her eyes turned a disturbing shade of indigo. *"Candesco Venefica,"* she whispered with a strange combination of fear and awe.

313

I swallowed, the bitter taste of having confirmation of what I'd always suspected sitting thickly in the back of my throat.

"*Cande*-what?" Spencer asked, his brow creased with incomprehension.

Still staring at Jasmine, I murmured, "*Candesco Venefica*. It's Latin. It means…Grey witch."

Half Light witch and half Dark witch, with all the powers of both, and the weaknesses of neither. A Grey witch was the most dangerous kind of witch, with access to both the Underworld and Earth's power. A Grey witch had the power to raise hordes of demons and bind them to This World, so no other witch, except another Grey witch, could banish them back to the Underworld. *I* had the power to do that…if I wanted. I didn't. I really didn't. I had one foot in the Dark World and one in This World, and I wanted to have both my feet in This World.

"Is that…bad?" Spencer was eyeing me warily. It wasn't fear *of* me, but fear *for* me.

I felt oddly disconnected, sort of relieved to finally know for sure why I had the power I did, but there was a sharp edge of horror creeping up on me under the numb relief. I pushed it away. I didn't want to deal with it just yet, didn't want to think about what it meant for me and for my— *No. Don't think about it. Not yet. Just get out of here.*

Seeing I wasn't in any state to answer Spencer, Jasmine spoke up, sliding her hazel eyes from me to him. "As far as possible outcomes go, this is a good one. With Tilly's combination of powers, she could have been some sort of Dark Fae or even part demon. A Grey witch can be either Dark or Light, depending on how she chooses to use her powers. She's actually pretty lucky, to have a choice like that. But she has to be careful. With the kind of power she has, it's easy to lose sight of what is right and wrong. The lines become fuzzy, and morals become…grey."

Spencer was still looking at me with some measure of concern, trying to read my expression, and I knew that he was going to ask why I looked so unhappy when that was good news.

I wasn't ready to be having that conversation, not there and not then, so I nodded my thanks to Jasmine and said, "Thank you, Jasmine, for the Charm and…the information. But I need to track down my idiot best friend and have a talk with him, so I'll be going now. It was nice to meet you."

If Jasmine was insulted or surprised by my blunt goodbye, she didn't show it. She just smiled brilliantly and waved as I turned for the door. Spencer followed me out the door onto the creaky porch, pausing to say something in a low voice to Jasmine. I moved down the rotting steps, stuffing my hands into my pockets, and started walking back in the direction of the cabins. Spencer caught up with me, and I sensed the questions forming in his mouth, so I hunched my shoulders and refused to look at him, hoping he'd get the hint that I didn't want to talk. Thankfully, he did. We walked back to the cabins in silence.

We were almost back to the cabins when Spencer touched my elbow, drawing me to a halt. Expressionless, I looked up at him, willing my eyes not to betray what I was feeling. I needed just a little time to myself to think about things first—then I'd tell him what was going on. I'd tell him what Jasmine had deliberately and tactfully not mentioned when she explained to him what a Grey witch was and why they were so rare.

For a moment, Spencer hesitated, his fingers still light on my elbow. Shadows of the leaves alternated with splashes of light on his face, and the breeze blew his hair across his forehead, lifting it out of his eyes. His dark brows were furrowed. "Are you okay?" he asked.

Mechanically, I nodded. "I'm fine. But I really should go and find Dominic."

I turned to go, but Spencer tugged at my elbow again, turning me back to face him, gently but firmly.

His eyes narrowed to sharp blue slits. "You're lying. Don't lie to me, Tilly. I expect it from everyone else, but not from you." His mouth thinned.

I dropped my gaze, unable to hold his stare, while I pretended to misunderstand him. "No, really, I need to talk to Dominic about earlier. I was kind of harsh, and I didn't even give him the chance to try to explain, and I know what he saw…us kissing…it must have hurt him, and I…"

My voice trailed off as my throat closed up, partly because thinking of the look on Dominic's face when he'd interrupted me and Spencer earlier made me feel horrible, and partly because I could feel Spencer's glower burning holes in the top of my head. He knew what I was doing, and he wasn't happy about it. I wasn't particularly happy about it either, sure that of anyone I knew, Spencer would understand...

But first I had to make sure *I* understood.

I wasn't sure I could.

I was a Grey Witch. The part that Jasmine had tactfully left out in her explanations was that a Grey witch could only be the product of a union between a Light warlock and a Dark witch. Never a Dark warlock and a Light witch—for some reason, that only ever produced stillborn babies. Only a Dark witch could carry a Grey witch foetus the full nine months without a miscarriage. And then, in one hundred per cent of cases, the Dark witch mother died in childbirth. Every. Single. Time.

I'd had a mother. My mother had died in a car crash, with my father, when I was six.

That meant the woman I'd thought was my mother was not my biological mother, and I didn't know how to handle that just yet.

"Tilly," Spencer said softly, and I blinked. I looked up at him, so darkly handsome in the shadows of the trees. "You know you can tell me anything, right?" he murmured, his fingers sliding up my wrist.

A shiver ran through me, my skin tingling under his butterfly-light touch. I pulled my hand back carefully, nodding without breaking his gaze. "I know," I whimpered. "And I will. Just...not yet."

317

Spencer dropped his hand, nodded once in understanding. "You know where to find me when you're ready to tell me." He leaned forward swiftly, placing a feather-soft kiss on my forehead, and then turned and strode quickly away into the trees.

I watched his tense shoulders disappear between branches, and then I let out a sigh that made my ribs ache. I turned toward the cabins reluctantly. I had to find Dominic, and I had no idea where he was or if he would even want to talk to me, but there was one person who might be able to lend me a hand.

Chapter Twenty

** Tilly **

"Desmond," I said, and he lifted his head, looking distinctly surprised to see me. I found Dominic's brother outside his father's cabin, chopping blocks of wood and hefting a heavy steel bladed axe as if it weighed nothing. He was shirtless, his lightly bronzed skin covered in a fine sheen of sweat, and I got the impression he'd been at it for a while. Considering there was a good supply of firewood stocked up against the back of every cabin, I assumed he was chopping wood recreationally, rather than as a chore—the werewolf version of a gym workout.

When he looked up, resting the long wooden handle of the axe against his shoulder, I saw his wavy brown hair was damp and sticking to his forehead and temples. His eyes, so like Dominic's, lit with not-unwelcoming surprise at the sight of me. His mouth quirked into a narrow half-smile.

"Hey there, Tilly."

I lifted a hand in a wave. "Hey. Have you seen Dominic?"

Desmond shook his head, pushing his hair back from his face with the hand not holding the axe. I kind of wished he'd put it down, it was making me nervous.

"Not since he ran through here in a huff a couple hours ago." As if he'd sensed my nervousness Des smiled ruefully at me and dropped the axe next to the pile of wood he'd hacked up.

"Ugh," I groaned, imagining Dominic taking off furiously. He could have been miles away by then if he wanted to be. I'd probably never find him, if he didn't want to be found. "Do you know where he might be?"

Picking up his discarded t-shirt from the ground, Desmond wiped his face, and then his hands. He blew out his cheeks and shook his head again. "Not a clue. Somewhere he could blow off steam, probably. In which case, *you* should stay away." He gestured at me with his t-shirt.

I blinked. "Me?" I squeaked, "Why should—"

"A: because you're human...mostly. And an angry werewolf is not something you want to face, especially when it's Dominic having a tantrum." Des snorted, rolling his very green eyes. He slung his t-shirt over his shoulder, his fingers picking idly at the collar of it as he spoke. He tilted his head down, giving me a disturbingly canny look. "And B," he added, "Because he likely isn't going to want to see you for bit. Better to let him calm down first, and he'll come to you, probably bubbling with apologies." He raised an eyebrow meaningfully, folding his arms across his bare chest.

I stared at him for a second, and then looked down, ashamed and embarrassed. "He told you what happened?" I asked softly. No doubt half the pack would know, and God, what would they think of me? What would happen if they all knew Spencer and I had feelings for each other? Would they keep us apart? I didn't know what I'd do if I didn't have Spencer to talk to. And if Dominic didn't forgive me, I wouldn't have him either.

With a short chuckle, Des said, "I guessed."

I had to repress a sigh of relief. So the pack didn't know. Only Desmond did. Startled, I asked, "How?"

"I know my brother," he said with a half shrug. Then with a wry smile, he added, "And believe it or not, I know a little bit about Spencer too. It's obvious to anyone paying attention that Spence likes you. I've never seen him spend so much time around anyone else before. And the whole pack knows Dom has a thing for you... except Dad. He'd freak if he knew." Desmond grimaced, his gaze turning inward somewhat.

I wondered what he was thinking of. Eyeing him with cautious suspicion, I muttered, "Your dad's not real tolerant of relationships, huh?" My tone wasn't *that* bitter. It was just that I was maybe a little peeved at the idea that Spencer should be forbidden to be with me, just because I wasn't a werewolf. I was an honorary member of the pack, shouldn't that count for something? I'd saved his life more than once, saved all their lives. Surely *that* counted!

Surprisingly, Des made a bitter sort of noise too, and scowled. "Oh, he's big on relationships. As long as they're between a boy wolf and a girl wolf. Anything else is..." He made a vague, dismissive gesture with his hands, but there was a sour twist to his mouth.

"You said it's obvious that Spencer likes me...but I didn't know until he told me." I chewed my lip, my fingers going reflexively to the Charm at my neck. The cool stone still hummed with magic.

"That's because when a guy like Spencer likes a girl like you, the girl is always last to notice," Desmond said quietly, smiling.

I looked at him, pursing my lips uncertainly. "What's that supposed to mean?"

"Don't worry, it's a compliment," he said.

I remembered the last compliment he'd given me, before the running under the full moon. *Ravishing! Yes, that's the word I was looking for!* Remembering the way he'd eyed me, I bit my lip, wondering...

Hesitantly, I asked, "And you're not...*bothered*...by any of this? I mean, it kind of seemed like..." I shrugged, twisting my fingers together. I felt my brows draw together and tried to smooth them out. It wasn't that I wanted him to be bothered by my...whatever it was I had with Spencer. I was just worried that maybe, knowing what I'd done to his brother, and what his half-brother had done to me, he'd think of me badly.

His even gaze wasn't full of disgust or contempt, just comprehension. "It seemed like I was into you, too?" he said flatly.

I scrunched my nose, shrugging. "When you say it like that, it sounds really...conceited."

Desmond was silent for a few seconds, his expression unreadable. Then he said carefully, "It's okay. I'm not bothered.

You're really not my type." He glanced at me, a thin sad half-smile on his mouth.

I blinked, confused. "Then why were you…?"

"Because I need everyone else to think you're my type, so they don't say anything to my dad." The bitterness in his voice was pronounced, and he glared at a spot on the ground, looking both defiant and uneasy at once.

I opened my mouth to ask why he'd need his dad to think I was his type, and then something clicked. *Oh, he's big on relationships. As long as they're between a boy wolf and a girl wolf.* The words clicked in my head.

"Oh," I muttered, staring at him in surprise.

He seemed to realise I'd caught on, and hunched his shoulders, bowing his head. He was bulkier, more muscled and rough edged than his brother, with a faint graze of stubble across his set jaw. Looking at him, I'd never have guessed.

"*Oh.* You're gay?"

He winced at the word, and nodded. "Yeah." The word was glum and quiet. He cast a look around, as if ensuring nobody else had heard, and then lowered his gaze again.

I got the impression it wasn't something he admitted easily, and I felt a pang of sympathy for him. Hesitantly, I asked, "And your parents don't know?"

He shook his head, nudging a piece of wood with his toes. "My dad would have a fit. And if he knew I've got a boyfriend, too…he'd go nuts."

I tried not to look too surprised that he had a boyfriend. Instead, I asked gently, "Does Dominic know?"

His shoulders slumped, and he huffed. I really did feel bad for him. Nobody should have to hide who they really were from the people they loved, from their family. It wasn't right.

"Dominic...doesn't know yet," he said, kicking the chunk of wood with a sudden, forceful movement. It sailed into the trees, crashing through leaves, and disappeared. "I've been meaning to tell him. Actually, aside from you, the only person who knows is..." He paused, his eyes meeting mine briefly.

"Spencer," I said, understanding. Of all people, of course Spencer would be the one Desmond could trust. Even more than his full-blooded brother.

Des smiled thinly. "He'd never tell the pack. He's good with secrets that way."

I nodded. "Yeah, I know."

Desmond looked up at me quickly, green eyes flashing as if he'd just remembered something. "He knew about your witchy mojo, right?"

I tried not to wince and failed. There was no condemnation in his voice or his expression, and no fear or repulsion either. Just curiosity.

"Yeah," I sighed gloomily.

Spencer's voice echoed in my head: *I won't let them hurt you, Tilly, not for any reason...You understand me, Tilly...I know you want me...* Absently, I touched my lips, feeling the phantom warmth of Spencer's mouth on mine.

There was a pause, and then Desmond broke into a grin. Knowingly, he asked, "So, you and Spence, huh?"

Startled, I dropped my hand from my lips hastily, feeling my face flush. I shrugged, and chuckled.

"Wow. The guy's only had one girlfriend that I know of, and that didn't last long. I was starting to wonder if he was..." He trailed off, looking uncomfortable.

"Like you?" I put in. Desmond made a face, but nodded. I looked down at my hands, unsure what to say. Changing the topic, I asked, "Who was Spencer's one girlfriend? Jasmine?" *It would explain their overtly friendly manners toward each other*, I thought, though the idea did give me a strange, hollow feeling in the pit of my stomach.

Desmond's eyebrows went up sharply in surprise. "Huh? You know Jasmine? Well, I suppose, she's a witch, you're a witch."

"No, I don't know her, really. Spencer just took me to see her earlier..." I reached up and touched the Charm around my neck again.

He shook his head. "No, not Jasmine. She just flirts with everyone. Although, she does have a special fondness for Spencer, so maybe they did hook up at one time or another. I don't know." He shrugged casually, disinterested.

"So who?"

"Sarah," he said, and I felt my eyebrows shoot up. He made a face, nodding. "A couple of years ago. He was seventeen, she was twenty two. It was...weird. Everyone knew she was crushing on him, even though he was younger, and I think Spence only agreed to go out with her because he thought it would get him into the pack more. Like I said, it didn't last. Spence was just too distant, and Sarah was too pushy. The ending of the story is that *she* broke it off, but personally I think Spencer did. He just let her tell everyone it was the other way round, so she wouldn't have to be humiliated, telling everyone a seventeen year old kid from the bottom of the pack dumped her."

I gaped, amazed. "Wow. That's..." I pressed my lips together, unsure exactly what it was. Desmond might have nailed it with *weird*. It also kind of made sense...kind of. "That might explain why Sarah was so adamant I go out with Dominic. She said Spencer wasn't boyfriend material. Not that I was even looking at him like that at the time."

Desmond arched his brows wryly. "At the time? So now, you're...?"

I scowled. "Now, I'm...*confused.* Just shush." I waved a hand at him, and he grinned. Having officially reached the maximum amount of blushing I could withstand for one day, I cleared my throat and made a vague gesture over my shoulder, saying, "I should...go."

Des shifted uneasily, looking down. "You know, what I told you?"

"Don't worry. Your secret's safe with me. I promise," I assured him, and he smiled gratefully. "If you see Dominic, tell him I need to talk to him, will you?"

Desmond nodded. "Sure."

"Thanks." I turned, shoving my hands into my pockets as I walked away. I chewed my lip thoughtfully. I was having a really interesting day so far.

Chapter Twenty One

** Tilly **

By the end of the day, Dominic still hadn't shown up. I wasn't really surprised. I hadn't expected him to just swing by to play checkers like everything was still alright, but I was disappointed. I'd hoped he'd at least come by in order to yell at me some more. At least then, I could have apologised, explained to him that I hadn't meant to kiss Spencer, hadn't meant to hurt him. Guilt was gnawing at me, and it didn't look as if I was going to get the chance to relieve it. I figured I probably deserved to live with the shame for a while, until Dominic deigned to talk to me again. After all, he had caught me kissing his brother—half-brother. Yeah.

I sighed, putting my head down on the dining table. Words played through my head, taunting me, berating me, haunting me. *He'd get bored of a human girl pretty fast…I'd been hoping you would arrive in time for our little party…I can smell it on you. Your desire…You're better than him, Tilly…so this is why you wanted to come find him so badly? This is how you make sure he's okay? By making out with him and letting him put his hands on me.*

"Do you regret it?" The sudden, quiet voice came from behind me, and I nearly jumped out of my chair. With a gasp, I twisted in my seat and saw Spencer standing by the door, watching me with an unreadable expression in his eyes. I hadn't even heard him come in.

I cleared my throat. "Do I regret what?" I asked. My voice was a little hoarse, and my eyes felt sore and tired, but I was glad to see him. My heart rose just a little inside my chest at his presence.

He frowned at me, tilting his head in that quizzical, thoughtful way of his. "Do you regret kissing me?" he asked tonelessly.

I flinched as if he'd snarled the question and shook my head slowly. "No, I don't regret it." I tried to read his expression, and couldn't. I whispered, "Do you?"

His mouth curled up at the corners, and he moved toward me across the floor, his footsteps eerily silent. He didn't stop until he was right beside my chair, and then he took my face gently in his large hands and bent to place a swift, chaste kiss on my lips. He stepped back, breaking into a grin.

"No. I never do things I think I'll regret. I just wanted to make sure you didn't, because of Dominic."

At the mention of his half-brother's name, I winced. Spencer saw it and his eyes narrowed. I sighed again.

"I don't regret the kiss. I just feel bad about hurting him. I mean, I knew he liked me, I think I even led him on, letting him kiss me before, but I didn't mean to hurt him. I thought maybe I…but I didn't realise…" I shook my head, frustrated that I couldn't get the words out. I was trying to say that I'd thought I did like Dominic the way I liked Spencer…before I realised I was falling in love with Spencer. I couldn't say it, not to Spencer. I didn't want to admit to him that I maybe sort of did like Dominic that way, still, and I wasn't bold enough to admit, out loud, in real words, that I loved Spencer.

Spencer sat down in the chair opposite mine, across the table, and looked at me evenly with those sharp blue eyes. He folded his hands neatly together on the shiny table surface, his gaze so intense I started to squirm.

Everything about Spencer is intense, I thought, *from the way he looks at a person, to the way he speaks, to the way he moves.* Nothing he did was without focus, without consideration. Every movement, every action, was contained and purposeful. Like he was a predator who was always tracking his prey.

Eventually, he said evenly, "You said you wanted to talk to me." He blinked, once, briefly breaking his intense gaze.

I let out a breath I hadn't realised I'd been holding and nodded slowly. I opened my mouth to explain, felt the words dry up in my throat, and turned my face to the window. Outside, it was dark, the black sky flickering between the swaying tops of the trees. Faint silver stars speckled the area around the milky white moon. It was still full, but Spencer had explained that the running only took place the first night of the full moon. The other two nights, the wolves could Change and run as they pleased. Beyond the glass, I could hear howling and barking.

Sideways, I glanced at him, but he looked perfectly patient, waiting for me to talk. I fixed my gaze on the window again, and decided the best way to explain was quickly, like ripping off a plaster. So I sucked in a deep breath, and said, "The woman I thought was my mother, who died in the car crash, wasn't my biological mother." The words burned my throat, and tears seared the backs of my eyes. I felt sick. The woman I'd loved till I was six—still loved, despite the years that had gone by—wasn't who I'd thought she was. Was the man I'd called Daddy my real father, or just another liar? Had I ever had a real family at all? Had my biological dad just dumped me off on some poor, unwitting couple after I killed his wife in giving birth to me?

The darkness outside the window blurred, and I was looking at my reflection in the glass, seeing tears streaking my cheeks, my grey eyes wide and scared. Then there was another reflection behind mine. Spencer leaned over the back of my chair, his hands reaching to clasp mine, his cheek resting on the top of my head. I closed my eyes, feeling the reassuring strength of his fingers and the warmth of his cheek against my hair.

He whispered, "I'm so sorry, Tilly."

I knew he meant it. It made me cry harder. He let me cry; he didn't try to soothe me, didn't tell me it would be okay, or that it wasn't the end the world. He just held my hands and hummed softly into my hair until stopped shaking. Then he let go of me, moved around my chair to face me, and knelt on the floor at my feet, looking up at me with gentle blue eyes. Lightly, he rested his hands on my bare knees under the hems of my ragged denim shorts, and despite my tears, I shivered at his touch.

His thumbs rubbed over my skin, and he said quietly, "You figured it out when Jasmine told you that you're a Grey witch. How?"

Swallowing the lump in my throat, I whispered, "You know how Jasmine said Grey witches were rare? Well, that's because they can only be made by a Light warlock and a Dark witch, and being on opposing sides, they don't often get together. And when they do, when they create a Grey witch…the mother dies giving birth to it. Every time." my voice cracked, and I took a breath to steady myself. Spencer was still rubbing his thumbs against my knees, which wasn't really helping my stability any.

He frowned. "You mean, the odds—"

"No. I mean, *every* time, Spencer. Every single recorded birth of a Grey witch has killed the mother."

Spencer blinked. His thumbs stilled. He pursed his lips, apparently at a loss for words. I didn't think I'd ever seen him speechless before—not when he didn't want to be silent. Normally, when he was silent, it was simply by choice. Then he laid his head down against my legs, and I almost choked on my next breath. He rested his forehead against my knees, his breath hot against my legs. I looked down at him in surprise and confusion, a jittery feeling racing around and around in my stomach.

His lips brushing my skin, he murmured, "I'm sorry, Tilly."

I shuddered. "You said that already," I observed, curling my fingers into my palms so I wouldn't reach out and twine them in his dark hair as I wanted so badly to do. My concentration on the conversation was wavering. Having him so close, breathing against my bare skin, was throwing my focus in other directions, and I was having trouble pulling it back to one place.

He looked up, putting his chin on my knees instead, and I saw his pupils were slightly dilated. I knew he could tell my mind wasn't all in the right place.

"I mean it, Tilly. I know what it's like to lose your mother when you're young, and it's even harder when you feel like she betrayed you," he said softly.

I blinked. I'd almost forgotten his mother was dead too. She'd stolen him away from the pack, from his father, and then died and left him on his own when he was just a toddler. That was why the pack didn't accept him, and probably never would, because his mother had betrayed the alpha.

I felt suddenly sorry for him, but I didn't dare show it. Instead, I lifted my hand and touched his cheek. His eyes flickered at my touch, and he leaned his face into my hand. With a watery smile, I whispered, "Thank you."

He covered my hand with his and turned his head, brushing a kiss against my palm. I felt the sensitive shock of it through my hand and wrist and all the way up my arm. My breathing hitched, and he glanced up at me, his eyes suddenly very dark, irises ringed with gold. His nostrils flared, and he stood up so abruptly I flinched. He strode around the other side of the table and stood facing out the window, his hands clasped tightly behind his back. I chewed my lip nervously, wondering if I'd done something wrong.

He half-turned his head and said over his shoulder, "It's not your fault."

I didn't know if he was talking about my biological mother's undoubted death, or about his odd behaviour, so I just nodded, knowing he could see my reflection in the glass.

He sighed. "Maybe you should go to bed. You've had a rough day."

I nodded again, but I didn't move, staring at his back. After a moment, I asked, resigned, "You're not leaving, are you?"

Without turning around, he shook his head. I shifted in my seat and caught a glimpse of his reflection in the window, his mouth curled in a wry smile. "No. Not until I'm certain that Charm of yours works. I'll stay here tonight, just in case."

He motioned vaguely toward the sofa, and I pursed my lips. Carefully, I slid out of my chair and rounded the table to stand behind him. I reached out and brushed his hands, still folded behind his back, with my fingertips. He tensed.

Licking my dry lips, I said shyly, "You don't have to sleep on the sofa, you know. You could…sleep in my bed…" I blushed as I said it, knowing how it sounded.

I heard his breath catch in his throat, and he spun away from my touch quickly, putting his back against the wall. He groaned, throwing up a hand over his eyes. Startled, I stepped back. A shudder ran through him, and I opened my mouth to ask what was wrong, but he spoke first. "God, Tilly, you shouldn't say things like that," his voice was rough, and he clenched his fist over his eyes.

"Why not?" I asked quietly, watching the muscles cording tightly along his forearm. He shook his head, pressing his lips together. I stepped forward, closer to him, and he stopped shaking his head. "Why not?" I pressed again.

When he still didn't answer, I took another step forward and put my hands flat against his chest. His skin was burning hot against my skin, even through his t-shirt. His jaw was tight, nostrils flaring.

I asked again, "Why shouldn't I say things like that, Spencer?"

He groaned again, lowering his arm from his face. His eyes were closed. Blindly, but without fumbling, he grasped my wrists and pulled my hands off his body, closing them inside his own fingers, so I couldn't touch. "Because," he said, his voice lower than I'd ever heard it before, "You are vulnerable right now, and I'm...not entirely in control."

He leaned his head back against the wall of the cabin, opening his eyes. He looked straight up at the ceiling, but I could see his eyes were burning molten gold. He blinked once, twice, and again, and I finally saw a flicker of blue in the gold.

Butterflies beat at my stomach, trying to fly out my mouth, and I blushed hot. He was still clasping my hands in his, and I bowed my head so he wouldn't see me smile. "Spencer, do you remember what you said to me earlier?" I asked, slightly breathless. I felt him look down at me.

"Yes."

He didn't say anything more, so I rolled my eyes and prompted, "What did you say to me?"

Silently, he stared at me until I glanced up. His eyes were shifting from blue to gold and back, his expression unreadable. He released my hands slowly, one finger at a time. I swallowed, afraid he was going to turn away, or act as if he didn't understand what I wanted to hear.

He took my face, very lightly, in his hands and rested his forehead against mine. He kept his bright, shifting gaze on mine as he murmured, "I said I love you."

My heart jumped, and I curled my fingers into his forearms. "Did you mean that?"

His answering smile was delicate and beautiful as gossamer, lighting his eyes to a breathtaking blue, filled with sparks of gold. "I don't say things I don't mean," he said quietly.

My heart lodged in my throat, and I had to close my eyes against the intensity of his gaze. I felt as if he was searing me all the way down to my soul.

My voice a ragged whisper, I said, "Then kiss me. Please."

He sucked in a sharp breath, and I felt the shudder that rolled through his body. Voice rough with equal parts regret and desire, he growled, "I can't."

"You can," I insisted. "Kiss me, Spencer. Just one kiss."

He made a choked noise, and I realised I was dangerously close to pleading, but I didn't care. I wanted to finish what we'd started earlier, forbidden or not. I was burning with the need to feel his lips and hands on my body like before. He was the only one I could truly trust, he was the only one who understood, the one who could make me forget what I was, who I was, and what I'd done.

But he didn't want to. He loved me, but when I wanted him to kiss me, needed him to distract me, he refused. He let go of my face and pried my hands gently off his arms, stepping back. I stood for a moment with my eyes closed, and bit my lip, unwilling to let him see the tears building behind my lids.

In a cracked voice, I asked, "Why?"

Spencer blew out his breath. "I can't." he said again.

I turned away, opening my eyes to glare at the floor. My vision blurred as tears clung to my lashes. I hugged my arms around myself and shook my head. "Why not? You did earlier."

I sounded petulant to my own ears, pathetic, and I felt the tears begin to slide down my cheeks. I bit my lip so hard, I tasted blood on my tongue, trying to stifle the whimper rising in my throat. He sighed, and I felt him move up behind me. He tried to put a hand on my shoulder, but I ducked away from it.

He said softly, "Earlier, you weren't upset about finding out your mother wasn't your real mother. Earlier, you hadn't just lost Dominic. You want me to kiss you now, so you don't have to think about it, to take away the pain. But it doesn't work like that. It'll take away the pain for a while, but it'll come back. I'm not going to take advantage of you when you're upset, Tilly."

A tear fell off my chin, and I watched it hit the floor. I hugged myself tighter. He was right, of course. But it didn't mean it hurt any less to be rejected. I should have been glad he had the decency a lot of guys wouldn't, but I just felt stung instead.

Carefully, ignoring the way I flinched, Spencer put his hand on my shoulder and turned me to face him, wrapping his arms around me gently. I stood stiff, but unresisting, in his arms, until he started humming into my hair again, a tune I didn't recognise. Slowly, I relaxed against him and laid my head on his shoulder. He stroked my hair soothingly, his fingers untangling the snarls in it.

"I will kiss you again, Tilly, I swear. Just not right now. Make up with Dominic tomorrow, let me see that you're okay, and then I'll kiss you until you're dizzy." There was a lilt of amusement in his dark voice.

I buried my faint smile in his chest. "You promise?" I murmured, my voice muffled against his collarbone.

"I promise."

With a sigh, I pulled myself away from him. His fingers clung to the ends of my hair, a smile hanging on his lips.

"Fine," I grumbled sulkily. "Tomorrow. I'm going to bed now."

He grinned, dropped a light kiss on my forehead, and shooed me off toward my room. "Goodnight, Tilly. Sweet dreams."

I flipped him off as I closed my bedroom door, and heard him chuckle on the other side. I undressed, slipped into my pyjamas, and brushed my hair before getting into my bed. I left the Charm necklace on, curling my fingers around the Spelled pebble as I lay down. It was warm and alive in my hand. My pillow still smelled faintly of Spencer from the night before. I snuggled into it, and fell asleep smiling.

** Spencer **

Unable and unwilling to sleep, Spencer lay sprawled on the sofa in Tilly's cabin, staring at the rays of moonlight crawling along the shadowy beams holding up the roof. If he listened carefully, he could hear her steady breathing in the room down the hall, hear her whimpering as nightmares plagued her. He knew by then, from standing watch outside her cabin for several nights, that she often had nightmares. They weren't what he was looking out for, he was just there to make sure she didn't sleepwalk into the witches' clutches.

Okay. That wasn't the *only* reason he was there. That was just his excuse. He wanted to be there…well, not that spot specifically, on the sofa. But he'd meant what he'd said to Tilly. He wasn't entirely in control of himself. He hadn't been all day. That much had been obvious when he'd kissed her by the stream that morning, kissed her almost desperately. He'd *felt* desperate. He'd felt breathless ,too hot, and hungry. He'd kissed her as if he was starving for the taste of her lips…after telling her he loved her.

With a groan, he tossed his arm over his face, pushing away the memories of Tilly's body pressed flush against his. He couldn't believe he'd told her he loved her. He hadn't meant to, not like that and not yet. It had just slipped out, and it wasn't the kind of thing he could just take back. Not that he would if he could. It was true, he loved Tilly. It seemed insane, so insane he hardly believed it himself. Two weeks. He'd only known her for two weeks, and already the thought of giving her up, holding her at a distance because what he felt was forbidden, it made him feel sick.

The fact that she hadn't said it back, hadn't told him she loved him too, should have made him nervous. It didn't. He didn't expect her to say it back, not yet. She'd had so much to deal with, between him admitting his love for her, to the falling out with Dominic, to her realisation about her mother. She needed time to figure things out, and he understood that. She would tell him how she felt eventually. He could wait.

He could also wait until she was less vulnerable to kiss her again. He *would* wait, even if it took days, or a week, or a month. Even if he wanted nothing more than to go into her room, wake her up, and kiss her until she was dizzy as he'd promised her, as she'd asked him to do. He wanted to taste her lips, feel the softness of her body, the heat of her skin, and smell her desire for him.

Rolling over sharply, Spencer buried his face in the sofa cushions and growled, his hands fisted over his head. No, he was *definitely* not in control of himself. Restless, he shoved himself off the sofa and paced the cabin silently. He opened a window to let in the cool night air, hoping it would help cool his burning skin. The sun was starting to come up, staining the tops of the trees amber. The air coming in the window smelled fresh, damp and green, and he sucked it into his lungs.

Deciding it was probably safe to leave, because if the witches were able to Summon Tilly, they'd have done it by then, Spencer hunted around the cabin until he found a pen and paper. He scribbled a note and left it on the dining table for Tilly to find when she woke up. Then, with the Change already biting at his heels, he threw himself out of the window and hit the ground running, with his front paws sliding on the dewy leaves.

Spencer ran fast, exhausting the burning in his body, running out his most primal instincts. He ran until he reached the edge of his pack's territory, the border between Their Land and the Other Pack's Land. He ran along the border until he reached the stream, far deeper and rougher than it was nearer the cabins. Then he followed the stream back to base, and slunk through the trees to his cabin. Sides heaving, he padded up to his porch, claws clicking on the warped, aging wood, and he Changed back. Sweat coated his human skin, and the cool late summer breeze lifted goose bumps on his arms and legs. Panting, he fumbled with the door handle, his hands shaking from the exertion of the exercise and the Change.

Before he could get the door of his cabin open, someone called his name, and he froze. With an internal sigh, he turned. At the bottom of the steps, Frank stood with his thick arms crossed over his wide chest, looking up at his son with cold grey-green eyes. Faint lines rayed out from the corners of his eyes and mouth, and formed wormlike grooves across his forehead as he scowled. Spencer wasn't worried—his dad always wore that expression around him.

"Frank." Spencer dipped his chin in a respectful greeting.

Frank's lips tightened under the bristles of his thick moustache. Spencer never called him *Dad* to his face, and he didn't call him *Sir* like some of the other pack members.

With a jerk of his chin, Frank grunted, about the most civil greeting Spencer warranted. "Get dressed," the man said gruffly. "We're meeting with the other pack, and you need to be there."

At that, Spencer blinked in surprise. "Why do I need to be there?" he asked, not defiantly, but with real curiosity. Normally, Frank barely allowed him to meetings within their own pack, let alone a meeting with another pack. It made Spencer suspicious. Something was up.

As if to confirm Spencer's unease, Frank smiled at his least favourite son. It wasn't a pleasant smile, nothing like the proud looks or amused grins he gave his other sons. It was more…vindictive. If it hadn't come from the alpha, Spencer would have bristled. As it was, he got a nasty acid feeling on his tongue and swallowed it.

With narrowed eyes, Frank said with deliberate distinctness, "You need to be there to meet your future mate."

Expressionless, Spencer waited for the punch line. He waited eight heart beats, nine, ten… Frank was still watching him with that unpleasant smile. Slowly, it sunk in that Frank wasn't joking just to piss Spencer off. He was serious. Spencer's hands curled into fists, knuckles cracking as his nails lengthened into claws.

Through sharpening, gritted teeth, he ground out, "What do you mean…my *mate?*" His voice was as quiet as ever, but a guttural growl rose from his throat.

Frank's smile widened, a sign of cruel amusement. "To end the territory feud with the other pack, we agreed to join with them. You know that. A pack joining can only be facilitated by the joining of one pack member to a member of the other pack. The other pack has too many females and not enough males. As one of our strongest young wolves, you were the obvious choice for the joining." It might have sounded like a compliment, but it was a stab in the back.

Nostrils flaring with rage, Spencer felt his jaw pop. His claws sliced gouges in his palms, and his finger joints crackled. A growl rose from the depths of his gut, rumbling through his ribs and rattling his teeth. His ears lengthened and pressed flat against his head. He bared his teeth, eyes flashing gold.

"You used me. You sold me off to securrre the pack's terrrritorrry! You bastarrrd!" Red mist descended over his vision. His spine arched, and he shut his eyes, fighting the Change. Spencer couldn't remember the last time he'd been so furious, the last time he'd felt so betrayed. Anger was burning a hole in his gut, his growling shredding his throat.

Frank just stood there, watching with a cruel gleam in his eyes. Spencer had never hated his father as much as he did right then.

"You've been promised to a very attractive, healthy girl. She'll be turning eighteen in a couple of months, and then you and she will be mated, and the packs will join. Call it taking one for the team, if you must."

Promised? Mated? Promised to a girl he'd never even met. Promised to be *mated* to her. Wolves mated for life, and it was meant to be the same for werewolves. That was why it was such a big deal that Spencer's mother had left Frank. Spencer could not— *would not*—be forced into a relationship he didn't want. Especially not when he was just starting a relationship he did want—with Tilly.

Oh God. Tilly. How was he supposed to tell her about this? How could he possibly explain it? He *loved* her. He wanted to be with *her*, whether or not it was forbidden.

"I won't do it," Spencer hissed. Then louder, he snarled, "I won't do it, Frank. I'm not going to be married off to some girl I've never even met, not for the pack and not just because you say so! Dammit, Frank, I'm your son, whether you like it or not. I'm not a chess piece you can just make do whatever you want!"

"Actually," Frank said evenly, "as your alpha, I can make you obey commands. If you won't do what's best for the pack, I will order you to."

Spencer glared, his muscles spasming as he tried to hold off the Change. "You'll have to order me, Frank. Because I'll leave the pack before giving myself up for the good of people who don't understand me."

Frank shook his head, grimacing. "I know you would. That's why I waited until now to tell you. And that's why I'm ordering you not to leave this pack, Spencer. You will not abandon this pack the way your mother did."

"My mother didn't abandon the pack! She abandoned *you*! She was running away from you, because she didn't love you anymore, because you're a heartless bastard when you want to be, and because you're the kind of man who puts his pack before his own son!" Spencer roared.

He didn't see the way Frank flinched, because he abruptly burst out of his human skin, losing the fight against his inner wolf. In his rage, he Changed so fast, he barely felt the agony of his bones snapping and muscles ripping. Everything went red, for a second, then white, then black. The next thing he knew, he was lunging for Frank's throat, a savage snarl tearing from his elongated wolf jaws.

Puffing up his chest and growling back, Frank didn't move a muscle as his son flew at him—all teeth, claws, and murderous rage. Raising his voice above the sound of Spencer's snarling, he said one word, "Stop!"

The full will of the alpha crashed down on Spencer, and he fell to the ground inches from ripping Frank's face off. He hit the dirt, belly touching the ground, and his vicious snarling choked off into a pathetic whine. He struggled against it, the alpha's voice of command, but it hurt. It hurt like the Change, to fight his alpha, and he was worn out from his run, from not sleeping the previous night, and from suddenly bursting out of his human skin.

Looking down at him with those steely, merciless eyes, Frank said firmly, "You will not leave this pack. You will meet this girl today. When the time comes, you will marry the girl you are promised to. You will do what is best for this pack, Spencer."

Each word, in each command, hit Spencer like a brick, breaking a little more of his will and shattering his ability to resist.

Frank's face softened and his voice lost the tone of command. "I'm sorry, Spencer. But this is how it has to be. It had to be you." Frank turned and walked away, leaving him whimpering on the ground.

Spencer laid his head on his paws, unable to ask why, why it had to be *him*. He didn't have to ask. He already knew. It had to be him, because if it were Dominic or Desmond, they would never forgive their father for taking away their choices. Frank had never cared whether Spencer forgave him for the things he did to him or not, which was just as well, because Spencer had never forgiven him for any of it. Not for ignoring him when he was a kid, not for whipping his big hand across his face when Spencer did something wrong or talked back, not for treating him like crap because his mother had broken the man's heart and wounded his alpha pride. He would never forgive Frank for taking away his freedom and his choices by taking away the possibility of Tilly and what he could have had. What he had to say goodbye to before it had even started.

Because he couldn't be with Tilly, not when he was doomed to be married off to another girl. If he even clung to her for the few months he had, it would only be worse. It would only make it harder when they had to end it. He'd be breaking her heart, while he broke his own, and that was something he wouldn't do. That was something he still had the power to avoid. He could make her hate him again. Just thinking about doing it made him want to throw up, but he'd do it to save her the pain later. He would do anything to save her.

Chapter Twenty Two

** Tilly **

Spencer was gone when I woke up, and morning sunlight shone through the windows onto the note sitting on the dining table. The cabin was bright and warm, the floorboards smooth under my bare feet as I padded across to the table. Smiling, I picked up the note and unfolded it. I was unsurprised to find Spencer's handwriting was neat and careful.

> Tilly,
> Went for a walk. I'm probably at the stream as you read this note. Come find me when you're ready for that kiss I promised.
> Spencer.

Folding the note, I tucked it into the waistband of my shorts, grinning foolishly. Deciding to skip breakfast, I found my trainers and pulled them on, knotting the laces quickly. Then I was bouncing down the porch steps and heading for the stream, eager to see Spencer. I felt so much better than I had the night before. A good night's sleep had done a lot to refresh my weary body, and even the nightmares hadn't been so bad. My Charm bumped against my sternum as I skipped through the trees, hopping over a patch of nettles and snagging a handful of bluebells on the way. When I could glimpse the clear, glinting water of the stream just ahead of me, I stopped and tucked one of the bluebells into my hair. Then I stepped out of the trees and turned, smiling, toward where Spencer usually sat, but he wasn't there. I frowned. He'd said he'd be there, and so far, I hadn't known Spencer to lie to me. Something must have kept him—maybe he'd run into Dominic and wanted to talk to him. I was sure he'd turn up soon, so I sat down and started plucking daisies for a daisy chain. Half an hour later, I'd denuded the area around my side of the stream of daisies, and made four long daisy necklaces and a bracelet. I was on the other side of the stream, and I was working on a daisy headband. My fingertips were stained green, and there was daisy gunk under my nails, and my stomach was rumbling, since I'd skipped breakfast. I was starting to think Spencer wasn't just being held up—I was being stood up. It was so hard to believe he'd do that to me after what he'd said. So I stayed a little longer, completed my daisy headband and replaced the bluebell in my hair with the floppy flower crown. Then I slung the necklaces around my neck, tore the bracelet off my wrist, and stood up. The daisy bracelet fell apart on the ground, and I stomped on the delicate little flowers. I hopped over the stream, flower chains swinging around my neck. My Charm bumped my sternum, and I tucked it into my sky-blue t-shirt. Halfway back to my cabin, someone caught my arm from behind, and I spun, thinking it was Spencer, or maybe Dominic. Sarah flinched back from my fierce glare, her eyebrows rising into her perfect red hair. She took in my interesting jewellery and smiled.

349

She was wearing a lot of real jewellery, including a shiny toe ring and bright rings on each of her fingers. Her white skirt swished at her ankles, and she jangled when she moved thanks to her excessive bracelets. "Wow. Are you starting a jewellery company out here?" she teased, toying with one of my necklaces.

I just stared at her. Her smile fell.

"Okay. Tough crowd. What's wrong with you? You look more sour than Spencer at a wedding party." I flinched at his name. Then I sighed. "It's nothing." She gave me a look that said she didn't believe me, but she let it go. "Okay then. Let's go join the others." She took my arm and started dragging me. "The others?" "Yeah, I was coming over here to find you. We're having lunch with the other pack, and Frank wanted you to be there. Just so the other pack knows what it's getting into. That we've got a human here," she explained.

I opened my mouth to tell her I wasn't human, but she waved a hand dismissively at me.

"We're not going to tell them about your little secret. That's your thing, not ours. They don't need to know." I shut my mouth and let her haul me through the trees. After a moment, I asked "Why are you guys meeting with the other pack exactly?"

"Since our packs are going to be joining together instead of fighting over territory, we thought it best to get to know one another first. Make sure there aren't any problems," she said.

I bit my lip. *Maybe that's what Spencer got held up by, helping out with this meeting,* I thought, though it seemed unlikely. Since when did Spencer take an interest in pack business, especially when there were lots of other people involved?

"It's pretty important," Sarah added.

I sighed, trailing after her reluctantly. I really would have rather hid out in my cabin all day. I wasn't in the mood for talking to strangers, or really anyone for that matter. Of course, Dominic was bound to be at the lunch thing. *This*, I thought with an internal groan, *is going to be awkward.*

As it turned out, it wasn't awkward. It was so much worse. Tables and chairs had been set up in a clearing in the trees, and the barbeque was puffing out smoke signals while Graham tended to the huge quantities of meat. There were too many people crowding the small area, most of whom I knew, but several of whom I didn't recognise.

Chris and Annie were talking to a girl who looked about ten, and Laura was reading a magazine with a pretty blonde girl. Dominic was indeed there, talking animatedly to a very attractive blonde. The girl laughed, and Dominic grinned, his eyes lighting up in that way that meant he was pleased. Then he seemed to feel me staring, and his eyes flicked to me. He blinked, his smile falling. I couldn't read his expression, but I lifted a hand in a cautious wave. He didn't wave back. The girl he was talking to turned and saw me, and I heard her ask, "Who's that?"Dominic shook his head and said something back in a voice too quiet for me to hear, and turned away. I swallowed the lump rising in my throat, and looked away, searching the crowd for someone else to talk to. Sarah had vanished into the hustle and bustle as soon as we'd arrived. When I scanned the teeming mess of people, I saw a flash of white of her skirt, and saw she was chatting easily with a young man, maybe in his early twenties. He was handsome enough, with messy, sandy blonde hair, a bit of stubble, and the naturally lithe body all the wolves seemed to have. He was smiling, clearly enthralled by Sarah, and I pursed my lips, looking around again. I spotted Desmond standing in the shadow of one of the cabins, leaning against the wall of it with his arms folded sulkily over his chest, and I started toward him until I saw a shadow opposite him move. He wasn't alone after all. Standing just a few feet away from him, there was another boy. They didn't appear to be talking, but as I watched, curious, I noticed something in their body language. I realised that it was the boyfriend Desmond had told me about.

With a faint smile, I started to look away, but Desmond's eyes flashed up as if he'd sensed me watching—the same way his brother had. Catching my eyes, he lifted a hand. I waved back, grateful someone was being cooperative. I gave him a faint, knowing smile, and he ducked his head, grinning. His boyfriend stepped forward, saying something to him, and I backed away, leaving them to their privacy.

I wondered if Frank would really be upset if he found out his son was gay, upset enough to forbid his relationship. Surely he wasn't that heartless? No parent could be, could they?
But then, what did I know about parents. I had none.

Tired of wandering around on my own, I retreated to the edge of the buzzing crowd and leaned against a tree, watching everyone getting acquainted and setting up lunch on the tables. I really didn't know why Frank had insisted I be there. I was out of place—the 'human' girl among the wolves. I might as well have been invisible, but I was okay with that, though. I didn't want to be seen, didn't want to have strangers asking me why I was hanging around a pack of werewolves, or how I'd become an honorary member of the pack. I just wanted to go back to my cabin and mope for a while.

Then, as my eyes roamed the crowd absently, they fell on a shadow lurking nearby. I looked up, and saw Spencer, hanging back near the trees just a few meters away from me. Seeing him, even after he'd stood me up, my heart did a little flip. I supposed it wasn't really his fault, he'd been roped into being there, no doubt, by his father. He could make it up to me, I was sure.

Before I could even think of taking a step toward him, he broke into a smile, and I blinked, surprised. He wasn't looking at me, though. He was smiling at a cute brunette girl standing in front of him. Wearing an orange tank-top and matching sandals, she was definitely pretty. The girl, a little older than me I was guessing, was blushing at something Spencer had said, and he was watching her with amused, hooded eyes.

Something in my gut twisted, and I fought for breath as Spencer reached out for the girl's hand, rubbing his thumb intimately across her knuckles. The girl giggled, fluttering her lashes at him. I wanted to puke. Then I noticed Spencer kept looking off to one side, and I followed his gaze. A little distance away, talking to a man I'd never seen before, Frank was keeping an eye on his son. My chest loosened, and it felt as if I could breathe again. Of course, Frank was watching, so Spencer had to act appropriately. He wasn't flirting with that girl because he wanted to. He just needed to, so his father didn't get suspicious.

I blew a sigh of relief. As if I'd called his name, Spencer's head jerked up, and his eyes fixed unerringly on me. I saw a flash of something cross his face, and then he shut it down, expression blank. I smiled at him, and he just stared back for a moment. The girl next to him scowled, looking putout that his attention was being taken from her.

She asked him, in a decidedly unpleasant tone, "Who's she?"

I was getting tired of people asking that already. Dropping my smile, I jerked my head, motioning for Spencer to follow me. He glanced at the girl clinging to his side, said something softly, and pried her off. With a nod at me, he slunk into the trees, leaving the girl glaring at me. I gave her a friendly, apologetic wave, and ducked into the cover of the trees to talk to Spencer.

I found him not too far in, standing under a beech tree, frowning. His hair was falling into his eyes, which were dark and brooding, his brow furrowed. I smiled when I saw him, but he didn't smile back.

Crossing his arms unhappily, he said, "What do you want?"

I blinked at his tone. Quietly, I said, "You weren't at the stream this morning. I wondered where you'd gotten to." He wasn't looking at me. His eyes were riveted on some point over my shoulder, and it was making me twitchy. It made me feel as if there was someone behind me. I shook off the feeling.

With a casual shrug, he said, "I got caught up."

Strike two. His voice was flat and hard, his eyes like ice. It stung me, and I frowned. What was wrong with him? He was acting like…like a total dick. Like he had the day I'd met him. I'd thought we were past that, but apparently not.

"Got caught up with what?" I asked.

He shrugged again. "Stuff."

"*Stuff?*" I curled my hands into fists, resisting the urge to punch him.

Another shrug. If he shrugged one more time, I was going to dislocate his shoulder.

I took a breath and counted to ten, calming down, and then I smiled hopefully up at him. He glanced at me when I took a step forward, putting my hands on his chest. I looked up at him through my lashes.

"Well, I can think of a way you can make it up to me," I murmured, lifting myself on my toes. He turned his head away, and I sank down again. My heart and stomach sank too. Confused and hurt, I snatched my hands off his chest and took a stumbling step backward.

"I…" I blinked back the burning in my eyes and looked down. "But…you promised," I whispered, feeling my face grow hot with humiliation. Why did he keep rejecting me? What was his *problem*?

He didn't shrug again, but his tone was as dismissive as if he had. "I lied," he said bluntly.

I choked, sucking down a breath to cool the burning in my throat. "Why?" I asked softly. Tears were starting to dampen my lashes, making the ground and Spencer's feet look blurry. I couldn't stand to look at his beautiful, cold face. I wanted to know why he was doing this to me. After he'd been so sweet, after he'd said he *loved* me. What had changed to make him suddenly act like that?

"Why do you think?" he said sharply, a mocking edge to his voice.

That sharp edge cut me like a knife. I was gritting my teeth so hard, I thought my jaw might break, trying so hard not to cry. Why did I think he was being a prick? I thought he was toying with me, like a cat with a mouse.

"But...you said..." My throat closed up briefly, and I paused. I couldn't say it, not with him standing there looking at me with those cold, blank eyes. "What you said yesterday, what about that?" My voice wobbled, and a hot bead of water slid down my face. I turned my head to the side, so he wouldn't see it.

He grimaced. "I–"

Whip sharp, I looked up at him, glaring. "I swear to God, Spencer, if you tell me that was a lie too, you're going to find out exactly what a Grey witch can do with her Dark side," my voice cracked.

More tears spilled, but I didn't lift a hand to wipe them away. My gaze was steady on his, and then he looked away, uncomfortable, and my heart broke. A small sound like a whimper escaped my lips before I could clamp down on it. I put a hand over my mouth, closing my eyes. I felt as if he'd punched me in the gut, thought I might be sick, but I breathed around the pain and forced myself to look at him again.

Swiping the tears off my face, I drew a deep breath and levelled a glare at him. He stared at a spot on the ground next to me.

"I see," I said, proud of how steady my voice was. "So. That's how it is then. It wasn't Dominic who was playing games with me after all. It was you. And I was stupid enough to fall for it, just because you saved my life. Silly me."

I saw a muscle twitch in Spencer's cheek, hoped I was annoying him. I was one shrug away from neutering him. I waited for him to do it. He didn't. I was slightly disappointed.
I shook my head, watching him.

"You're not going to say a word, are you? You're just going to stand there like a heartless statue."

This time, he did shrug again. My nails cut into my palms hard enough to draw blood, and I knew I had to get away from there before I did something I'd regret—like blasting him into a tree. I could feel the power to do it bubbling up inside me, with my fury, hurt, and humiliation.

Evenly, he said, "Men are animals?"

A bitter laugh burst from my mouth, and I saw him flinch. I was glad of it. I couldn't believe he was that heartless. Distant was one thing. Cruel was another, and nobody had ever warned me Spencer was cruel. Maybe they hadn't spent enough time with him to know, but I knew.

"Yes," I spat. "Clearly. Well, you don't have to worry about saving my life again. I can take care of myself." I reached behind my neck and undid the clasp of my Charm necklace. It slid from around my neck, and I tossed it to the ground at his feet. He closed his eyes as if he couldn't stand to look at it…or at me.

Furious, I started to walk away. I glanced over my shoulder once, saw him staring at the pebble lying in the dirt. He looked up at me, his eyes unfathomable.

With a cold smile, I spat one word at him. "Fetch."

I walked away with tears in my eyes.

I returned to the gathering, already having wiped the tears from my eyes and pasted on a fake smile that hurt to wear. I was hunting for one person, whether he wanted to talk to me or not. I got jostled in the crowd, people bumping into me, and Sarah snagged my wrist at one point, her green eyes large as she took in my face. I hoped I wasn't all blotchy and tearstained.

"Whoa. Tilly, what's wrong?" she asked with more sympathy than she had earlier.

I shot her an impatient look. "You were right," I said. "I should go for Dominic." I snatched my hand back and slid away, determined to find Dominic. I didn't care if he didn't want to talk to me. I'd make him talk to me. I'd apologise, beg for him to forgive me if I had to. Anything. I'd been such an idiot, believing Spencer's act. Sarah had tried to warn me, and I hadn't listened. I'd stupidly imploded my friendship with Dominic before I'd even given it a chance to turn into something else.

When I finally found him, Dom was still talking to the pretty blonde girl. He looked startled when I marched up to him and, muttering an apology to the girl, snatched his arm and dragged him away from the crowd. He let me tow him until we got into the trees, and then he tugged me to a stop, and I whirled. His expression surprised me. He didn't look angry, like I'd thought he would. He looked concerned. So sweetly concerned, even after our argument the day before. It made me feel even guiltier."Tilly, what's going on? You look like you've been crying. What happened?" He reached for me, his thumb skimming my cheek, and I grabbed his wrist, pulling his hand away from my face. Instead, I put his hand on my hip, and leaned into him. He took a step back, surprised, and I snaked my arms around his waist, holding him there."What's going on is your half-brother is being a heartless bastard. So I owe you the biggest apology ever. I'm sorry. About everything. About letting him kiss me, about yelling at you, about…about believing his stupid lies."

I laid my head on his shoulder, and Dominic's hand came up reflexively to stroke my back soothingly. His touch didn't make me quiver and burn the way Spencer's did, but it was light and pleasant, comforting. And I really needed comforting right then."Shh, Tilly.

Slow down. Tell me, what happened with Spencer? What did he do?" Dominic asked softly.

I shook my head against his chest, and whispered, "I don't want to talk about it. Just…tell me you forgive me, Dominic. Please. Tell me you forgive me for being an idiot, a bitch, and a terrible friend. I shouldn't have trusted him. I trust you. I don't want to lose that." My eyes were burning again, and I willed the tears to stay back. My fingers were knotted in Dominic's t-shirt, and I could feel his muscles were tense. He was silent for so long, I was sure he wasn't going to answer, wasn't going to forgive me. Then he relaxed a little, his other arm coming around me. He hugged me gingerly, laying his chin on the top of my head.

"Of course I forgive you, Tilly. Of course I do," he murmured, one hand stroking my hair.

Relief swept through me, making my knees weak, and a few tears escaped from under my lids. I squeezed him tightly. Carefully, I tilted my head and touched my lips to his collarbone.

He froze. In a tight voice, he asked, "What are you doing, Tilly?"I smiled against his skin. He smelled like green leaves and oranges. "Thanking you," I said, placing another kiss on his neck. I heard his breath catch, the steady rise and fall of his chest against mine pausing. I kissed him again, just under his ear, his curls brushing my face. He shuddered, arms tightening around me."Tilly, I don't think—" his voice was rough, and his hands were balled into fists against my spine.

I pulled back, glancing at his face. His eyes were closed, his mouth thin. Fighting for control—fighting to do the decent thing and push me away. I didn't want him to push me away, didn't want him to do the decent thing the way I'd thought Spencer had done. I wanted Dominic to kiss me.

I brushed his ear with my lips, feeling his heart pounding through his shirt. "Good," I breathed. "Don't think."

I unlinked my arms from around his waist and moved my hands up his back, over his shoulder blades. I nuzzled at his neck, feeling his pulse flutter against my lips. He shuddered again, and then he tilted his head down. I skimmed my mouth across his cheek to the corner of his mouth, pausing there, teasing. Lightly, I brushed my mouth across his. His fingers touched a slice of bare skin on my back between the waistband of my jeans and the hem of my t-shirt. My daisy chains were getting crushed between us, and my daisy crown fell off. I barely noticed, didn't care. Dominic held me tighter, and done with the teasing, he covered my mouth with his. It wasn't like the light, chaste kisses we'd shared before. I was glad. I let him pry my lips apart gently, let him slide his tongue into my mouth. He tasted like apples and sunshine, and he groaned against my lips. His hands didn't wander the way Spencer's had, and his lips were softer, less demanding.

When I finally pulled away, we were both breathing hard. Dominic's pupils were dilated, the green iris so dark, it was almost black, flecked with gold. His mouth was darkened too, and his cheeks were pink. I knew I probably looked even more telling.

Stepping away, I reached up to fix my hair, smiling. Dominic blinked a couple of times, his eyes flickering gold, and then blew out a long breath.

"Holy…" he muttered, shaking his head as if to clear images from it.

My smile widened, and I bit down on it, blushing. I looked down at my daisy chain necklaces, and saw they were all but flattened. I ripped them off and dropped them to the ground carelessly, kicking dirt over them.

Then I looked back up at Dominic, who was watching me with a dazed sort of fascination. I beamed. "I think we should get back to the group, don't you? Wouldn't want to miss lunch." I winked.

Dominic broke into a grin and laughed. We made our way back to the crowd, and took seats at one of the tables. I sat next to Dominic, and Desmond settled on my other side. He cut me a look sideways, one eyebrow subtly raised. I made a face and shook my head slightly. He seemed to understand. He turned to his other side, and I saw he was sitting next to the boy he'd been talking to earlier—his boyfriend.

The guy was cute, I supposed. Shoulder length brown hair tied back in a loose ponytail on the nape of his neck, sharp features that made him look somewhat dangerous, and gorgeous dark brown eyes framed by thick lashes. He wasn't quite handsome, not quite pretty, but somewhere in between. I had yet to see an ugly werewolf. I wondered if they were all naturally beautiful, because wolves were naturally beautiful creatures.

At one point, while Dominic was talking to the red-haired girl I'd dragged him away from before, Desmond leaned over to me. "You know Spencer's staring at you, right?" he muttered, so low I barely heard him.

Startled, I looked up and saw Des was right. Sitting two tables away, almost as far away from me as he could get, Spencer was watching me with an intensity that made me want to shiver even at that distance. I clamped down on the feeling and glared at him for a second before turning back to Desmond. I could still feel his gaze on me like a laser. Not so quietly, I said, "He can stare all he wants. As long as he stays the hell away from me."

Des blinked, looking half-surprised and half-confused. But I felt the laser glare drop, and I knew Spencer had heard me. I smiled victoriously, but all I really wanted to do was cry.

Chapter Twenty Three

** Spencer **

Desperate to be alone, Spencer escaped the gathering as soon as he possibly could. He'd spent the whole afternoon talking to Lilac—the girl he was destined and doomed to be with—even though every word, every smile, every breath of her scent made his gut twist and his heart ache. She was a nice enough girl, pretty he supposed, smart enough, but she didn't fascinate him. She was bubbly, uncomplicated, and seemed to enjoy his company, while he was putting on a show, playing his part. If he showed her how he really was—*distant*, as Tilly had described him—there was no doubt she would lose interest in him. It was only fair, he supposed, since he had no interest in her to begin with.

The gathering was coming to an end, just as it was starting to get dark. As much as he wanted to lose himself in the sweet oblivion of his wolf and sink into the freedom of running under the sunset and through the trees, he refused himself the pleasure, the escape. He was disgusted with himself, sick with himself. After the way Tilly had looked at him earlier, he knew he deserved it. Inside him, his wolf whined at the thought of Tilly, and he mentally snapped for it to shut up. He was stomping his way viciously through the trees toward the stream, needing to hear the soothing babble of the water, as if it would help ease the hurting in his chest. He reached the bank, looking around frantically, half-hoping and half-dreading that she was there. She wasn't. Of course she wasn't. She was probably with Dominic, playing some stupid board game.

And that's where she should be, he thought to himself. Still, the thought made his lips curl back from his teeth, a growl threatening in the back of his throat. He shook his head violently. He stalked across the grass, the joints in his fingers popping as he worked his hands in fists, pacing. His feet crushed a patch of torn daisies, and he paused, looking down at the broken chain of little white flowers. He remembered the daisy chains around Tilly's neck and circling her head when he'd stood in front of her and told her he didn't want her, didn't love her. When he coldly lied to her face, he'd seen how it made it her crumble, seen tears rise to her pretty grey eyes. It was such a mess, like the mess of trampled, broken daisies under his feet. Carefully, he knelt, picking up the chain of ruined flowers. It fell apart in his fingers. Such an innocent and beautiful thing, a daisy chain. Innocent and beautiful like her, and as he had the chain, he'd crushed her.

Tossing the daisies into the water, Spencer thumped to the ground, cradling his head in his hands, his fingers tugging at his hair. He leaned his elbows on his raised knees, head bowed, breathing hard around the sick feeling crawling up his throat. Over and over, his mind replayed the image of Tilly's face as she'd thrown her Charm to the dirt at his feet. She hadn't just been throwing away her protection, he knew. She'd been throwing away *his* protection, the thing he'd given her all along. She'd been tossing *him* and

365

everything he'd said to her, done for her, to the dirt. The pebble was just a symbol.

His nails turned to claws as the animal inside him roared, angry and confused, unable to comprehend the complex swirl of emotions making the human boy gasp like a wounded doe. Spencer was stunned and scared by the strength of feeling within him, something crippling, something he didn't have a name for any more than his wolf did. It was almost as if despair, rage, guilt, jealousy, and sorrow had all been bundled up in one poison and had been injected into his veins to tear him apart. His knuckles cracked, and his toes popped inside his trainers. Savagely, he yanked them off without unlacing them, chucking them across the stream. One of them landed in the water, and he didn't bother to fish it out. He didn't care—he wanted out of his clothes, out of this skin.

He was already pulling off his t-shirt when the breeze blew the scent to him from behind, and his arms seized up. Slowly, he lowered his t-shirt back down, and glared into the water at his rippling reflection, hands in clawed fists at his sides. His face in the darkened water was pale, his black hair mussed, and his eyes dark and wild, burning blue and flashing gold as he fought the Change. He looked feral, half-mad. As the cooling breeze whipped around him, he caught the scent again and saw his eyes flare pure gold.

Tilly. He waited, tense, for her to come closer, to yell at him, hit him, or slam him with that bright power of hers. Part of him longed to turn around and go to her, explain to her why he'd acted like he had, tell her he truly did love her, and apologise with all the words he knew. Part of him trembled to do it, and his wolf whined eagerly. The other, less selfish part warned him he should leave before his will broke and he gave in to the temptation to try to fix things. Maybe he couldn't save her this time, not from himself. Maybe he was selfish enough not to want to. Maybe, like his mother before him, he was willing to betray the pack for what he really wanted.

** Tilly **

I don't know how I ended up at the stream. I'd only been walking back from Dominic's cabin to my own and, somehow, had gotten sidetracked. My feet had brought me there, while my mind was elsewhere, lingering on the make-out session Dominic and I had just had on the sofa in his cabin. It had been pleasant, exciting, interesting, until Desmond had walked in the door and let out a long whistle of surprise, his eyebrows rising into his wavy dark hair.

Dominic and I had sprung apart like scalded cats, both blushing, and Des had just chuckled. While Dominic bowed his head in embarrassment, Desmond shot me a bright glance with a question in his eyes. His lips turned down at the corners. I read the question easily enough. *What are you doing?*

I shook my head in response, an apology in my eyes and on my lips. *I don't know.*

Desmond had scowled, a silent warning, and I looked away, announcing that it was time for me to leave. Dominic had kissed me lightly on the cheek at the door and watched me walk away into the trees.

Then I was standing twelve feet away from his cruel bastard of a half-brother with my heart in my throat and tears in my eyes. Shame and guilt warred with anger inside me. After how he'd treated me earlier, I should have hated Spencer. I didn't. When I saw him sitting by the stream, I should have wanted to go over and scream in his face. I didn't. Seeing him there, curled up with his head in his hands, clutching his hair as if he was in pain, I just couldn't hold on to my fury and hurt. I'd never seen him so discomposed, so rattled. It shook me, and I wondered what had him so upset. Was it me? Was it because of me? Or was it egotistical, maybe even stupid, of me to think that? To hope for it? Abruptly, he started pulling off his shoes and threw them carelessly, one landing in the stream. He shot to his feet, tugging off his t-shirt, and I bit my lip gingerly. The breeze swept a few strands of hair into my face, and I brushed them back absently, but I saw Spencer freeze, tensing. He lowered his t-shirt back into place and stood, strung tight as a bow, staring into the water. I waited for him to do something else, to turn and walk away, or to Change and vanish into the trees to prowl the night. He just stood there. Waiting. He knew I was there. He was waiting for me to make a choice. I could walk over there, or I could turn and leave. I started to turn, my feet muffled on the dirt and moss, and then I paused, thinking of the way he'd been clutching his hair, growling, and muttering to himself. I hesitated, uncertain.

Words fought in my head *You understand me, Tilly...I said I love you...I don't say things I don't mean...I lied. I lied.* He lied.

He'd lied to me, but I was starting to wonder, watching him then, which time he'd really lied. I needed to know. I stepped out of the trees. Spencer didn't turn, though I noticed his head tilted ever so slightly in my direction, listening. For a moment, I just stood and stared at his back, the tight set of his shoulders, the curled weights of his fists at his sides. And then he spoke."What are you doing out here?" he asked, his voice flat.

I recalled he'd asked the same thing in the exact same tone the first night I'd found him by the stream, chucking pebbles into the water. It felt like an eternity ago, though I knew it had only been a few weeks. Hell, the day before felt like an eternity ago. Everything in my head was blurred, confused, and jumbled. I rubbed my forehead, trying to focus, but all I could think of was Spencer's eyes when he'd promised on the night of the full moon, after the attack, that he wouldn't let anyone hurt me for any reason. He'd said so many things like that, been my saviour so many times. How could one day and a handful of cruel words negate that?

"I could ask you the same thing," I said coolly, moving past him to the rock he usually sat on. I slid onto it, my eyes on the grass. My torn daisy bracelet from that morning was gone, only a couple of crushed daisies were left lying in the dark blades like fallen stars.

Spencer grunted. "How long have you been standing there?"

I shrugged, knowing he sensed it even though he was refusing to look at me. His eyes were riveted on the water.

"Long enough to be curious as to what you're doing here," I replied casually. He wanted to play at indifference and mystery? Two could play that game.

"What does it look like I'm doing?" he snapped, exasperated and irritated.

I tilted my head, pursing my lips. I stated, "It looks like you're avoiding my questions."

He shot me a glare, then turned his eyes back to the water. "Go away, Tilly," he said in a hard tone.

"No," I said, just as stubborn.

"No?" he repeated, as if he were surprised I'd refused him.

I snorted. "Yes."

He turned his head toward me and blinked, confusion shadowing his eyes. "What?"

With an internal smile, I asked, "Are you done?"

"Done with what?" He scowled, looking more confused than before, and more annoyed.

"Being an ass."

"What do—" he started to ask, and I held up a hand, silencing him. His eyes narrowed in response, his mouth thinning. I ignored the glare.

"Stop asking questions and answer one of mine for once, Spencer. It's the least you can do." I saw a flicker of something in his eyes, and he turned away sharply.

His jaw was clenched, and he hissed through his teeth, "Which question would you like me to answer?"

"That's another question. And the first one. What are you doing here?"

He shrugged. I was so sick of that motion.

"Nothing," he said, sounding bored.

I glared at him. "Funny. It looked a lot like you were stressing out about something."

"Yes," he spat, "I was wondering why you keep showing up when I've made it clear I don't want to see you."

I felt the sting of the sarcasm and pushed it aside. "Maybe I just like annoying you," I said with a smirk.

Spencer scoffed. "Maybe you're just obsessed with me."

I snorted. "Get over yourself."

"You're the one who seems to think I'm in love with you, even though I told you I was lying

when I said that."

Ouch. "I think a lot of things," I muttered.

He looked at me sideways, hands in his pockets. His brow furrowed under his sleek black hair. His face was mostly in shadow, since the sun had gone down and the moon had yet to rise. His eyes seemed to gleam from the darkness.

"What is that supposed to mean?" he asked, disgruntled.

I just smiled blandly at him, enjoying his bafflement. It was his turn to be confused, and my turn to be mysterious. Maybe he'd finally get just how frustrating it was, how annoying his cryptic answers and unfathomable expressions could be.

He scowled at me. "I don't understand you," he grumbled in a tone of utter frustration, shaking his head again.

He stared at me, as if trying to read my thoughts on my face. I kept my expression carefully blank. He made a noise of irritation.

With a shrug, I said more quietly, "I guess I don't understand you either."

His jaw tightened, a muscle flickering in his cheek. But all he said was, "I guess not."

"And yet..." I tilted my head, looking at him thoughtfully.

"Yet what?" he barked, his patience fraying.

I was getting to him. That was exactly what I wanted. I wanted him to react. I wanted him to get pissed off. Because if he got pissed off, he wasn't indifferent. If he wasn't indifferent, the chances he'd lied to me earlier, not the night before, were much greater. If he was truly indifferent to me, really didn't care what I thought of him, didn't care what I felt, he wouldn't look so damned twitchy. Like I was coming dangerously close to saying something he didn't want to hear.

So I just shrugged, agitating him further. He twitched again. A growl escaped his lips, rolling up his throat and over his tongue.

"What? *What are you thinking?*" he snarled.

I smiled, this one more genuine. I answered honestly, "I'm thinking that you're a bad liar."

He blinked. "I'm not—"

I shook my head, cutting him off. "I might have believed you...if it weren't for the fact that you've got my Charm in your pocket." I motioned toward his left jeans pocket. I knew he had it, because I could sense the buzz of its power. Jasmine had put a strong Spell on it. Somehow, I knew it was what had drawn me there, led my feet there before my mind knew that was where I needed to be. Maybe it was that second Enchantment she'd put on it at work.

Help the passion of new love bloom, and aid the moon's child in keeping his loyalty strong.

Looking stunned, Spencer reached into his pocket and pulled out the Charm. With the chain looped around his fingers, the pebble swung free, flashing white, gold, and blue. "How did you know?"

"I can feel the magic," I said, wiggling my fingers at him playfully.

He snorted and muttered something under his breath, scowling at the grass.

"What was that?" I asked, raising my eyebrows expectantly.

He shook his head. His expression hardened, and he closed his fist around the pebble. "Nothing. What do you want me to say, Tilly? What do you expect me to say to you?"

I sighed. "I want to know the truth," I said quietly. "I want to know why you tried to push me away...and then nearly pulled your hair out because of it." A wry half smile tugged at my lips.

He made a last ditch attempt at whatever game he was playing. He glared at me, and snapped, "I was *not* stressing out because of *you.*"

It was a lie. I noticed what I hadn't earlier—he had a tell. When he lied, his shoulders twitched. It wasn't quite a shrug, but awful close. I'd seen it before, but I'd mistaken it for an actual shrug. He was trying not to hunch his shoulders, because he didn't like lying. Not to me, anyway.

He muttered, "I don't care what you do, so long as you quit stalking me."

"Oh?" My eyebrows went up, and I called his bluff. "Then I guess you don't care that I was just making out with your brother. For the record, he's a lot gentler than you are. He knows just exactly what to do with his tongue."

He growled, a dark sound that rose from his gut and rumbled through his chest. I saw his eyes flash gold, his possessive wolf instincts snapping to alertness. I hid my smile.

"Ah. So you do care."

A look of exasperation and agony crossed his face, so fast, I hardly saw it. I didn't understand it.

"Why are you doing this to me?" he asked, his voice half-snarl and half-pleading.

"Why are *you* doing this to *me?*" I retorted, sliding off my rock. I stormed up to him, looking up into his face with determination, trying to read his eyes.

He turned his head away. Softer than before, he muttered, "Go away, Tilly."

"Give me an honest answer, and I will." I folded my arms stubbornly.

He ran both his hands backwards through his hair, tousling it. He sighed, but it rumbled into a growl in his agitation. "You are the most frustrating, most stubborn girl I've ever met."

"And you're the most irritating, unfathomable guy I've ever met. So we're even," I shot back.

He frowned. Very quietly, so quietly I almost didn't hear it, he said, "No. We're not."

I puzzled over what he could possibly mean for a moment, confused, and then let it go without an answer. It wasn't important. I tried to steer the conversation back on topic to get the answers I really wanted.

"Spencer, why did you lie to me?"

"Tilly…" he started, his eyebrows pushing down over his darkening eyes.

I set my feet a little wider apart, glaring up at him. I wasn't budging. "I want an answer. I won't leave you alone until I get one," I warned.

Suddenly, his expression broke and turned into something softer. There was something almost vulnerable in the shape of his mouth, and in the pleading in his eyes. "Tilly, please, don't make me explain," he murmured, his gaze not quite holding mine.

My worry and curiosity both rose, and I frowned at him. "Why not?" I asked, gently.

He shook his head, his hair flopping into his eyes. "Just…please go, Tilly. It's better if you do. Just accept that I can't be with you."

"*Can't* is different from *don't want to*," I pointed out.

He groaned at my insistence, shutting his eyes, and shaking his head. A totally inappropriate butterfly of warmth fluttered in my stomach at the sound. I remembered how he'd groaned the night before, when I'd said he could sleep in my bed, the desperate longing in the sound, the hunger in his blazing gold eyes even as he refused my request to kiss me.

Blinking away the memory, feeling my face already growing hot, I forced my mind to stay on topic. I asked, "So why can't you be with me today, when you could yesterday? What changed overnight?"

He stared at me expectantly until the obvious answer smacked me in the forehead.

"The gathering. It's something to do with the gathering, isn't it? And Frank?"

He didn't answer, and a thought struck me.

"Oh, god, did he—" My eyes widened as I considered the possibility that Frank had seen Spencer leaving my cabin that morning. If my face hadn't been red before, it was then, imagining what Frank would have thought.

Spencer shook his head, reassuring me. "He didn't find out. That's what makes it worse. He wants to hurt me, and he doesn't even realise how well he's achieving his goal." He choked on a bitter laugh.

I frowned, becoming more confused and more worried. He wasn't making sense to me, and I needed real answers from him. "Makes what worse? Spencer, what are you talking about?"

His sour, mirthless smirk died away, replaced with an expression that broke my heart. It took me a moment to identify it as I'd never seen it, and had never expected to see it, on Spencer's handsome face. It was despair. Dark and sucking, turning his eyes to bottomless pools of the most glacial blue.

"The packs are joining, Tilly," he said in a ragged murmur. "Two packs joining together...there are certain rules for such things. Old rules." His sigh seemed to hurt him, dragging up from the depths of his lungs, and his eyes darted away from mine to the round coin of the moon hanging solemnly in the sky above us. "The only way two packs can join together is when a member of one pack marries one from the other pack."

At first, I didn't understand what that had to do with us, our conversation, or our relationship. I stared at him, at the raw pain and anger in his eyes, at the flickering muscle in his clenched jaw and his flaring nostrils. Then it clicked, and I understood. My mouth fell open, a gasp strangling in my throat. Spencer's lids fluttered down in shame as he realised I'd finally caught on.

Feeling as if someone had their hand around my throat, I choked, "And...*you're*...?" I couldn't even finish the question, but he knew what I meant.

Grimly, his mouth a thin white line, he nodded. "I'm the lucky groom," he said it as if it was a death sentence.

I made a small, breathless sound—a whimper that escaped my mouth as his words hit me like a blow to the chest. "Oh."

Turning away from me, he clenched and unclenched his fists. His nails were long, curved into claws, stained with dark liquid. Blood dripped from his hands, through his fingers, and I reached to make him stop gouging his palms, but he snatched his hands away from me.

"In less than two months, I'll marry Lilac. *For the good of the pack*," he spat.

I recognised that he was quoting what he'd heard—what Frank had undoubtedly told him.

I caught my lower lip between my teeth, plagued by doubt as I remembered the way he'd smiled at the brunette girl—*Lilac*. Of course she'd have a pretty name to match her pretty face. Weakly, I squeaked, "But...you don't...you don't *want* to, right?"

With a sharp scoff, he turned his face away from me, so I couldn't see his expression. His back to me, he shrugged. "It doesn't matter what I want. I don't have a choice." His voice was flat, matter-of-fact.

I shook my head and stepped toward him, taking his hand. He tried to yank it away from me, but I held tight, and he subsided. He let me pry his clawed fingers out of a fist, and I watched the cuts in his palm slowly stitching themselves up. Blood coated his hand, and I knelt, tugging him down with me. Reluctantly, he sank to the grass by my side, and I drew his hand into the stream, letting the cool water wash away the blood. His claws sank away, becoming blunt, dirty fingernails once more.

Softly, as I rubbed my thumb between his knuckles to scrub away the blood, I said, "We all have choices, Spencer. You don't have to do it just to earn Frank's respect."

Gingerly, he pulled his hand out of mine and wiped it thoroughly dry on his jeans. His hair shadowed his face. "No, Tilly," he said. "I *literally* don't have a choice. I've been ordered by the alpha to do it. I can't fight that command. Some commands I can fight, but he put his whole will, the full force of his power into this one. There's nothing I can do."

I put a hand over his to stop him from rubbing it raw against his jeans. He paused, looking at our overlapping fingers, and his shoulders slumped.

Very gently, he said, "I had hoped that, if I could make you hate me again, it would be easier for you to let me go, when the time came, than if I let your feelings for me grow."

Tears stung my eyes, and I pulled my hand away from his, leaning back. My mouth felt dry and my eyes wet. There were a hundred things I wanted to say, all crowding on my parched tongue, sticking there. Eventually, I managed to push back the tears, and anger welled up.

Fury at Frank spilled across my tongue, hot and acidic as bile. "He can't do that!" I snapped, my own hands balling into fists on my knees. I slammed my fists against my legs hard enough to bruise myself.

Spencer sighed. "He can and he is. He's selling me out for the good of the pack."

"But you're his *son!*"

"It doesn't matter," Spencer muttered.

I gaped at him, astonished at the way he was acting—as if he was accepting the order, as if he'd already given up hope of fighting it. "Yes, it does, Spencer! It matters!" I yelled, lunging to my feet. "He can't just treat you like that! He can't...he can't just take away your freedom like that!" I threw my hands up, stomping my foot like a child pitching a tantrum. "Dammit!" I snarled.

That dangerous sparkling feeling, the feeling of my magic reacting to my rage, crackled along my nerves and filled my skin. Gritting my teeth, I sucked in deep breaths, pushing the Dark part of me that fed on my nasty emotions back down.

Startled by my vehemence, Spencer stared up at me, blinking. The way his black hair fell across his wide eyes made him look younger, innocent—too young to be forced into marriage to a girl he didn't love.

My lips trembling, I crouched next to him, putting a hand on his head and tangling my fingers in his soft hair. Leaning in so we were nose-to-nose, I looked intently into his eyes, so blue under dark lashes. "Forget about Frank, the packs, and the other girl for a minute. Tell me the truth. Do you love me?" I asked quietly. My heart pounded in my throat as I watched his pupils dilate at my nearness, waiting for his answer, praying I was right.

Slowly, his hand came up and cupped the back of my neck, his forehead leaning against mine. He blew out a gentle sigh that brushed against my lips. Unblinking, his eyes flickered with sparks of gold. "Yes," he breathed, "I love you."

A smile trembled across my lips, and I closed my eyes briefly in relief. Then I looked at him again, my fingers curling tighter in his hair. "Then promise me, *promise me*, Spencer, that you'll fight this. I don't care how strong Frank's will is. Yours is stronger, I know it. Promise me, if you love me, you'll at least try. Not just for me, or for us, but for yourself. You deserve to be happy, Spencer, even if it isn't what Frank wants for you."

For a moment, he just stared at me, our noses pressed together, breathing each other's air, lips barely a centimetre apart. His eyes sparkled with shifting swirls of gold. "I'll promise," he said carefully. "I'll do whatever I can to fight the commands, whatever it takes to be with you…" He paused, his brow furrowing. "I'll promise, if you tell me one thing."

Very slightly, I nodded. "Anything."

His voice soft as a breath, never breaking his intense gaze, he said, "Tell me you love me, too. Tell me that, and I'll promise you anything."

My breath caught in my throat, and I bit my lip. My heart thrashing an erratic rhythm inside my chest, I fought to hold his gaze, fought to make the words come to my lips. They were there, on the tip of my tongue, in the shape of my mouth, but they were silent. I couldn't say it. It was true, but I couldn't say it. Why couldn't I say it, when it mattered most, when he was staring at me with the bright light of hope slowly dying out of his mysterious eyes?

He was already drawing away, his expression shutting down. Desperately, I opened my mouth and closed it again silently as tears flooded my eyes. I choked on the horror rising in my throat as I realised why I couldn't say it, why I couldn't tell him I loved him, even though I knew I did. *Dominic*. His face flashed behind my lids, flushed and smiling, curls tousled after I'd kissed him earlier in a misguided and desperate attempt to push away the pain of Spencer coldly telling me he didn't love me, lying to my face.

Part of me, a part much larger than I'd realised, cared about Dominic too much to tell Spencer how I really felt. I didn't *love* Dominic, but what I felt for him was almost as strong. I couldn't hurt him again, not after kissing him as I had earlier, after making him believe I was done with Spencer. I'd thought I was finished with Spencer, I'd thought Dominic would be better for me. If I told Spencer I loved him, I'd lose Dominic. If I didn't tell him, I could risk losing Spencer. Either way, I lost someone I cared about too much to lose.

And I had no idea how to sort that out before it was too late.

Through blurry eyes, I looked pleadingly up at Spencer as he pulled away from me and got to his feet. His face blank, he brushed grass off the knees of his jeans, not looking at me.

I stumbled to my feet. "Spencer, please," I begged, not sure what I was asking him for. Not to leave me, maybe. Not to give up his freedom just because I couldn't say three little words.

He was already walking away. Terror wrapped around my heart like crushing tentacles. Desperate, I called, "Spencer, I…" He paused, his back to me, waiting. Breathing hard, I tried to force the rest of the words out. Tears spilled down my face. "Please," I whispered, my voice cracking.

Silently, he shook his head, and walked away into the trees, a shadow blending into the darkness. I stood where I was, unable to force my feet to follow him, and I pressed a quaking hand over my mouth. I squeezed my burning eyes shut. I wasn't sure what scared me most anymore—the witches hunting me, or my own heart betraying me.

Chapter Twenty Four

** Tilly **

"Tilly? Earth to Tilly?"

I blinked sluggishly, my blurry eyes focussing on Dominic's concerned face hovering in front of me. He was standing opposite me, leaning over the low wall that separated the kitchen counter from the breakfast bar. Sitting on one of the tall chairs at the breakfast bar, I dropped my gaze to yesterday's newspaper resting on the counter. Dominic had brought it over and read it nervously. The headline read, "Hunters Found Massacred in Woods," and underneath, in smaller print, it said, "Reported wolf sightings lead local police to believe this was a savage animal attack."

I turned the paper over and looked down at my bowl of untouched cereal, half surprised I hadn't completely passed out and dunked my head it—yet. I slid it away from me, just in case, and laid my head down on the counter, my arms forming a reasonable pillow.

I was exhausted. I hadn't slept at all. Without my Charm, and without Spencer, I couldn't dare. So, all night, my brain kept whirring, while my heart kept tearing. I couldn't stop thinking about Spencer, what he'd told me, and his face when I couldn't tell him I loved him. No matter how I'd reworked the conversation in my head, no matter how many different ways I'd tried to justify it, it always ended up the same—with me saying nothing, because my heart was in two places at once.

I'd imagined Spencer with the brunette girl, Lilac, imagined him kissing her the way he'd kissed me the other day at the stream, and every time it had made me feel sick and made my chest ache. I'd imagined Dominic kissing the blonde I'd dragged him away from, and found it hurt too, though not as much—but still too much. Lastly, I'd imagined Olivia coming for me and dragging me, kicking and screaming, from my cabin. As loud as I had screamed, nobody had come to help me. Not Spencer, not Dominic, not anyone. Olivia had laughed as she stole me away into the darkness and thrust me to the ground at the feet of the hunter with the orange cap. The man had raised his gun to my head, and that time, he'd pulled the trigger.

That image had terrified me until my heart pounded in my ears and my chest felt tight, and I couldn't stand to close my eyes. I laid on my back, grasping the covers, staring at the darkest shadows of the room and squealing at every rustle beyond the window, until the sun had begun to rise.

I'd been up since six am, and Dominic had come knocking at a little before nine. I had been expecting him anyway. It was nearly ten o'clock, and I was barely even able to keep my eyes open. I couldn't think straight. Just trying to think made my head hurt, and I put my arms over it, resting my forehead against the cool surface of the breakfast bar. I heard Dominic move around to my side, touching my arm lightly in concern.

"Are you okay? You look shattered," he said gently.

I almost wanted to laugh at how appropriate his word choice was. Shattered. I was shattered, and it went beyond the exhaustion. My heart was shattered, or at least cracked.

Without sitting up, I mumbled, "Didn't sleep well."

"Nightmares?" he asked.

"Something like that." I sat up slowly, my head flopping on my neck, and groaned. The light was too frickin' bright. I squinted. Then I was overcome with a yawn, and covered my mouth with my hand, almost tumbling backward off my chair. Dominic caught me as I started to slide, his mouth pulled down in a worried frown.

"Come on," he said softly, "I think you need some fresh air. It'll help wake you up, and you can do that meditating thing you do." He laced his fingers through mine, and opened the door, pulling me out onto the porch.

The sun was shining strong, and the breeze was unseasonably warm for late August. It breathed across my face and neck, lifting strands of my hair and rustling Dominic's curls. The woods looked very green, the hazy sunlight beaming through the leaves tinted with colour as it fell to the dirt.

I didn't resist as Dom tugged me after him into the trees, not caring where he was taking me. I blanked out for a while, my body operating on autopilot while my mind took a short vacation to nowhere in particular. When I regained my senses, I found Dominic had taken me to the clearing where they'd had the full moon ritual. The giant oak tree was still hung with lamps and ivy, and the mossy space under the expansive boughs looked cosy and comfortable.

I settled down between two thick roots, curling my back against the tree, and Dominic sat next to me, perching on a root. In my sleepy spot at the base of the old oak, with Dominic watching out, I finally relaxed. I shut my eyes, leaning my head back against the bark. The energy of the woods around me flooded in, welcoming me back like an old friend. It sparkled, flowed through my veins, and under my skin, revitalising me and sweeping away my worries. I let it soothe me, letting go of myself bit-by-bit, until all I could hear and feel was the trees, birds, and flowers.

I was startled awake by the sound of a crow cawing close above me. In a panic, unsure where I was or what I was doing there, I jerked upright, looking around. Slowly, I recognised my surroundings, and remembered why I was there. Beside me, Dominic was grinning at me, his chestnut curls bouncing carelessly into his sparkly green eyes.

"Hello there, Sleeping Beauty. Did you have a nice nap?" he teased.

I rubbed my eyes, pulling myself into a less tangled position in the nook of the tree roots. I really hadn't meant to fall asleep, but I did feel a great deal better, refreshed and energised. My head felt clearer, though my heart was still confused. The way Dominic was smiling at me really wasn't helping that.

Stretching my sore spine, I decided the moss wasn't as soft as I'd thought before. "Mh, were you watching me sleep?" I mumbled, suddenly worried I'd been drooling. I swept a hand across my chin, but it was dry.

With a chuckle, Dominic shook his head. He rose to his feet easily and stretched too, raising his arms over his head. Then he shook out his curls like a dog shaking out its coat. "No, I didn't watch you sleep. I've kept occupied with other things." He shrugged.

"Like what?" I asked curiously, trying to get my numb legs under me.

He reached out, and I took his hands, letting him haul me to my feet. I stumbled, and he steadied me with a hand on my elbow.

"Okay?" he asked, and I nodded. He grinned again. "Well, I've been busy with various things. I spent a while trying to catch a butterfly with my hands, I annoyed a caterpillar that decided to crawl on my leg, I Changed back and forth a few times chasing rabbits...oh, and I tried to make one of those daisy chain things you were wearing yesterday. I failed miserably. I couldn't work out how you make the daises stay together." He shook his head, scowling.

I laughed. "That's because the art of daisy chain making is a secret for females only," I joked, smiling.

He laughed, his dimple flickering. Then something in his eyes changed, and he took a half step closer to me, his fingers still resting on my elbow. I blinked, noticing the shift, and knowing what it meant. Cautiously, I bit my lip, my head suddenly spinning again. My heart gave a dull thud-thump, turning over slowly as if time had slowed down. Dominic leaned over me, bending his head so his curls brushed my face. His lids half-lowered, I could tell he was looking at my lips. His fingers grasped my elbow more firmly, his other hand coming up to stroke my cheek.

I had a moment of panic as he lowered his head to brush his mouth over mine. Something in the back of my mind rebelled, telling me it was wrong, and another part whispered that it was right, and that Dominic was what I needed. Sweet, kind, uncomplicated Dominic. In my already strange and dangerous life, wasn't that what I really wanted? Someone who would be gentle with me, who didn't make me nervous as much as he intrigued me, who would always be there when I needed him?

I realised then that yes, that was what I wanted. That was what I needed, from a friend, not from a boyfriend. That sense of comfort I got from Dominic wasn't anything more than friendship. The butterflies I got when he kissed me weren't a sign of desire, but of nervousness, because some part of me understood it wasn't him I wanted to be kissing. I did love Dominic, just not the same way I loved Spencer. I loved Dom as a friend, someone who'd been nothing but good to me since I had been brought into the midst of the pack.

It was a realisation that arrived too late.

Dominic bowed his head to mine and covered my mouth with his before I could protest, his lips confident and sure—and why not? After the way I'd kissed him the day before, he had every reason to believe I wanted him. His mouth pressed on mine, pulling my lips apart, and his fingers curled around the back of my neck. He tugged me closer, and I stood unresisting, unable to push him away for fear of hurting him, but unable to kiss him back. I waited for him to realise I wasn't returning the kiss, and to notice that I didn't smell of desire any more than the trees around us did.

Abruptly, his mouth stilled on mine, and his fingers tightened on my elbow. Feeling my eyes burn behind my closed lids, I willed him not to hate me for not wanting him. I prayed he would understand, that he would still be my friend, even after I'd led him on. Surely he would understand I'd been confused and uncertain, and I hadn't meant to hurt him. Surely—

What he whispered against my lips was not what I'd expected. "He's watching us," he murmured, still holding me close.

I froze as dread knotted sickly in my stomach. I didn't need to look to know who he meant, didn't need to open my eyes to feel the piercing gaze burning holes in my spine. I took an unsteady breath and pried my eyes open. Dominic lifted his head, glaring over my shoulder. His hands were still on me. With my throat constricting, I pulled out of Dominic's grasp and spun.

A spear of pain and horror shot through my heart at the sight of Spencer. He stood not ten feet away, indeed watching us. His glare, resting on Dominic, could have cut steel, and there was a faint rumbling working its way up from his chest. I put my hand over my mouth as if to erase the taste of Dominic's lips on mine, and the movement drew Spencer's glare to me.

I flinched back under that powerful glower, and just for a second, I saw the flicker of both understanding and betrayal in his eyes. He knew why I hadn't been able to tell him I loved him. With tears in my eyes, I wanted to explain to him what I'd just figured out, that I didn't want Dominic at all.

He'd already returned his glower to Dominic, and his lips peeled back from inhumanly long teeth. I gasped, afraid, and heard the popping of his knuckles as his nails grew into deadly claws. Behind me, there was more cracking, and I spun around to see Dominic raising hands that didn't quite look like hands, tipped with claws like Spencer's. His nose was scrunched up, his jaw shifting, chest puffing out. Panicked, I realised there was going to be a real fight, and there was nobody else around to stop it.

Without time to think, and unsure what else to do, I jumped between the two shuddering, snarling werewolves and held my hands out. I swung my gaze from one of them to the other as their attention fixed on me and their growls dimmed. "Stop it! Both of you, stop it! This is stupid, you hear me? It's ridiculous! You both need to *back the hell off!*" I yelled, my heart thrumming so fast, I couldn't tell one beat from the next.

For a moment, I saw surprise cross Dominic's face, and a note of something like respect flash across Spencer's, and I thought I might have gotten through to them. Then Dominic's expression twisted, and he made a move as if to lunge for Spencer. Instinctively, I threw myself backward, wrapping my arms around Spencer protectively. Spencer tensed all over, as if I'd shot him, and then relaxed slightly, putting his hand on my back. I heard a small, choked noise from behind me, and glanced around. Dominic stood there with hurt and anger all over his face, and I realised what I'd just done.

Pulling myself away from Spencer, I frowned, reaching out. "Dom, please…"

He turned his head away. "Don't," he snapped. He cast Spencer a hostile glare and his lip curled. His eyes fixed on me again, colder and darker than I'd never seen them. "I see what's going on here. It's him. All this time you've just been playing me, haven't you? Acting like my friend, acting like you wanted more ,and all the while, you've been screwing my half-brother behind my back."

"Dominic, no, it isn't like—"

"It isn't like that?" he barked, "Then how is it? And what was that little act about yesterday, huh? You had a fight with your boyfriend, so you kissed me to, what, make him jealous?"

"No, that's not—"

"Then *tell me* how it is, Tilly!" He spun on me, pressing so close we were nose-to-nose. His eyes were blaring the gold-green of his wolf, roiling with anger and hurt.

I whimpered in fright, and the gold in his eyes dimmed. He stepped back with a sigh.

"Tell me how it is, because I honestly don't know anymore. Did you feel anything for me at all? Anything other than *friendship?*" he spat the word like a curse.

I felt my eyes prickle and bowed my head. "I…I thought I did," I said carefully.

He made a strangled sound, and I looked up in time to see a bitter smile cross his lips. It looked unnatural on his normally cheery face. He started to turn away to leave, and I caught his arm. He tried to shake me off, but I tightened my grip.

"Dominic, no. You're going anywhere until I explain. I need both of you to understand. I *need* you to know why I acted the way I did."

He paused, considering. I chewed my lip, waiting. Then he sighed again, shoulders slumping, and I cautiously let go of his arm. He turned back, but he wouldn't meet my eyes. Instead, he stared at the ground, shoving his hands into his pockets. Tears stung my eyes, but I blinked them back.

"Dominic, I wasn't just toying with you, I swear. I was just…confused. I-I've never been around guys much, I've never even had a boyfriend before. I was brought up apart from that sort of thing. I thought what I was feeling toward you was more than friendship. I thought that…I mean, it's just that I knew you liked me like that, and I guess I let the attention get to me." I shook my head, pausing so my voice wouldn't crack.

He stood there, still as stone, and just as expressionless.

Quietly, I went on. "It wasn't until the other day, when Spencer kissed me, that I realised how I felt about him. I guess it had just sort been creeping up on me, and then…I was already so sure I wanted you too. I didn't want to hurt you." Even to my own ears, it sounded like the most pathetic excuse. *I didn't want to hurt you.* But that was exactly what I'd done, and I couldn't undo it.

For a second, Dominic was silent. I couldn't see his expression because he'd bowed his head and his curls were shadowing his face. Softly he said, "What about yesterday?"

I opened my mouth to explain, and couldn't. I tried anyway, because he deserved some sort of an answer. "Yesterday…yesterday was…" I just couldn't think of the words. How could I possibly explain that I'd kissed him on some sort of vicious impulse to push away the pain of Spencer telling me he didn't love me? At the time, I'd thought he meant it, and it hurt like nothing I'd ever experienced before.

Desperately, I looked to Spencer. He was scowling, but when he noticed me looking at him, his expression softened. He sighed almost inaudibly. Then he stepped forward, and said, "Yesterday, I told Tilly I didn't love her. I told her I'd only been being nice to her, acting like I liked her, so I could get…s-something from her…" I noticed the way he stumbled over his words for a moment, the flash of shame in his eyes. "I hurt her. And she went to you, Dominic, because you're her best friend. Whether you like that title or not, that's what you are. Tilly went to you when she needed comforting. If I were you, I wouldn't take that lightly."

He glanced to me, eyes catching mine and lingering for a moment. "Even if Tilly didn't feel about me the way I feel about her, I'd be pretty lucky just to be her friend."

I smiled shyly, and Spencer smiled gingerly back.

Dominic was silent as the grave. In fact, he was so quiet for so long that I started to think he wasn't ever going to talk to me or

Spencer again. Then he lifted his head, and his expression was not what I had expected. There was no anger or disgust on his face. Hurt? Yes, there was that. Disappointment? That, too. But there was also understanding, and most importantly, *forgiveness*. The sight of that forgiveness in his eyes made my knees weak and my lips tremble.

He only looked at me for a moment before moving his gaze over my shoulder to Spencer. His eyes narrowed, thoughts flickering behind his green irises. But all he said was, "You love her?" There was nothing accusing in his voice, just a question tinted with surprise.

I swallowed and turned, glancing at Spencer. He didn't look at me, his eyes held steady on his half-brother, but he knew I was watching him. He nodded slowly.

"Yes," he said.

To my surprise, his voice wasn't as steady as his gaze.

"I love her, Dominic."

The raw honesty in his face made me look away, even as my heart fluttered.

Dominic simply nodded. He turned his curious gaze to me. "Do you love him?"

My heart lurched into my throat, and I looked down at my feet. I could feel Spencer's gaze burning hot into the side of my head. Dominic had asked the question Spencer most wanted answered, the one I hadn't been able to answer before. Choking on the words, I nodded. I didn't have the courage to say the words aloud, but the nod was admission enough. Beside me, Spencer drew in a sharp breath.

"So," Dominic said.

I looked up at him. He looked confused, his eyes on Spencer again.

"So why would you lie to her? Why would you tell her that bull yesterday and hurt her? You *don't* lie, Spence. You work around the truth sometimes, but you rarely outright lie."

That time, Spencer was the one who didn't seem to know how to explain. He shifted his feet, a line forming between his eyebrows.

I answered for him, "He was trying to protect me. He thought it would be easier on me if he…broke up with me sooner rather than later." I hesitated over the term because, well, it wasn't like we'd officially been going out in order to officially break up.

Dominic's brow creased. "But why would he have to…" He paused, his eyes widening and swinging back to Spencer. "Oh. The pack joining ceremony. Dad chose you?"

Spencer didn't say anything, but the look on his face was enough to give Dom his answer. Dominic grimaced, reaching up to tug on a handful of his curls. "Damn, Spencer. I'm sorry. I knew about the ceremony, but I figured it was such an old rule, dad wouldn't bother using it. That's…" Dominic shook his head, sympathy written in stark lines on his young face.

With a brutally blank expression, which I had learned was his shield to keep people from seeing what he didn't want them to see, Spencer said, "Of course he's using the rule. Frank loves his bloody rules too much. He chose me to make a point…and then ordered me to go through with it, for the good of the pack, when I refused. He *ordered* me, Dominic." Spencer's voice was hard and cold as steel.

I saw shock softening Dominic's expression. Whatever anger and jealousy he may have harboured toward his half-brother over me was already being forgotten, pushed aside. I was glad, so glad, that Dominic was as kind-hearted and forgiving as he was. Otherwise, I'd have lost him, and I wasn't sure I could have let go of my best friend.

"God, I can't believe he'd do that to you, Spence! But…you *can't* go through with it!" Dominic yanked on his curls, his eyebrows shooting up.

Darting a glance at me, Spencer's expression turned wry. "Obviously."

Dom's eyebrows pushed back down over his eyes, his grimace so deep it made his dimple scowl. "So what are you going to do?"

Spencer shrugged. "Fight it. If I can."

"But it's an order from the alpha. You can't fight it," Dominic pointed out.

A dark smile spread across Spencer's mouth, and a flicker of something dangerous flashed in his eyes. "Being on the edge of the pack has its benefits. I've fought commands before and broken them. I can certainly try with this one. It'll just be a bit tougher."

Dominic smiled knowingly at his half-brother. "Uh-oh. He's got that look again," he muttered, and slid his gaze to me, stage whispering, "Never tell Spencer he can't do something. It never goes down well. He takes it as a challenge every time." He shook his head, and I laughed.

"I'll keep that in mind," I said, grinning.

Suddenly, Spencer was right behind me, his breath hot on my neck as he murmured in my ear in a suggestive tone, "You can *challenge* me any time."

I swallowed as heat flooded my face.

Dominic snorted. "Yeaaah…I'm going to take that as my cue to leave." He turned on his heel, and flashing me an uncertain smile, strode off into the trees, leaving me and Spencer alone.

We stood for a long moment in silence, me staring at the ground while Spencer stared at me. Then he said, "I think we need to talk." I nodded and he paused. "But it can wait a while," he added in a whisper, lifting his hand to cup the back of my neck and bringing his mouth down on mine.

Chapter Twenty Five

** Tilly **

The minute we got back to the cabins, we were attacked. Not by the witches or hunters, but by Frank. He was waiting outside Spencer's cabin, with Dominic lingering nearby, looking concerned and agitated. As soon as we came into his view, Frank exploded into a fit of rage, most of which was directed at Spencer.

He stormed forward and grabbed Spencer by the back of his collar, and growled, "You! You punk ass little runt! What do you think you're doing?"

Startled and a little scared by the man's outburst, I stumbled backward into Dominic, who steadied me absently as he rushed toward his father and half-brother.

"Dad! What are you doing!?" he cried, looking shocked.

Spencer, though, didn't look shocked in the least. He stood in the alpha's grasp and stared back into those steely, angry grey eyes with obvious loathing and contempt. It was easy to believe, right then, that Spencer truly hated his father. I found I couldn't blame him in the least. The man might have been a powerful werewolf, but that wasn't what made him a monster; treating his son the way he treated Spencer did.

"I think," Spencer said slowly and clearly in that quiet, dark way of his, "that you should let me go."

Frank stared at him for a moment, snarled, and threw him viciously to the ground. I gasped and rushed forward, but Frank whirled on me and his eyes flashed gold. Whimpering, I flinched back. Dominic grabbed my arm and pulled me back against him protectively.

"Dad!" he snapped, "What the hell!? What's going on?"

I'd never heard Dominic take that tone with his father before, and judging by Frank's expression, he hadn't either. He looked momentarily taken aback by Dominic's obvious anger and disrespect. The gold in the man's eyes dimmed, and he took a step back, straightening up. He ran a hand through his red hair and cleared his throat. He looked at me and I sank further into Dominic's safe embrace.

"I apologise, Tilly," he said formally.

I just nodded carefully. Frank's eyes went to Dominic, whose jaw was set and his eyes were narrowed to gleaming slits, glaring at his father.

"It's okay, Dom. I'm not going to hurt her. I just…I don't want her near Spencer."

The alpha's gaze travelled back to his eldest son, who was pushing himself up from the ground, looking at his father with such hatred that it sent a shiver down my spine. He was shuddering, trembling with the Change in his fury, but he hardly seemed to notice, even as his knuckles and the vertebrae in his spine started to crack and shift. He leaned forward, inhuman fangs bared, eyes furious pools of molten gold. I'd never seen Spencer so angry. It was frightening. He looked…savage…feral…*bloodthirsty.*

"What?" I squeaked. "Why? Why can't I be near him? He's not going to hurt me any more than you will." I winced. I'd said *will* when I'd meant to say *would*, because he was going to hurt me when he forced Spencer to marry another girl. He was already hurting me, I supposed, because just knowing our time together was limited made something inside me crumple.

Frank eyed me for a second, as if he'd noticed the difference and knew what it meant. Carefully and soothingly, he said, "It's not your fault, Tilly. You didn't know our rules. But Spencer did, and once again he has disobeyed them. I'm sorry for that."

My heart clenched tighter than my stomach, anxiety rushing up to capture my lungs, and I suddenly understood what was going on. I turned panicked eyes to Spencer, and Frank followed my gaze. He sighed very softly, almost regretfully. Spencer was on his feet, but he was twitching with the Change, breathing past it to calm himself before he did something stupid. I almost wished he would, wished he'd do something that would stop Frank's next words.

Glaring at his eldest son, Frank said, "I hear you and Tilly have gotten rather close, Spencer. Too close. You know the rules! Relationships with outsiders are forbidden. Completely and utterly, in the strictest sense! And you, Spencer, you are formally promised to another girl! This is unacceptable! I don't want you near this girl again, you hear me? End it, Spencer, or you know what I'll have to do. I won't have you ruining this pack for a girl. A witch!"

401

His face turned red with anger, and I felt Dominic's arms squeeze me tighter, as if he could block Frank's words if he just held me close enough. Spencer's face was entirely blank—scarily blank. The kind of emptiness that reminded me of a sheet of ice over a raging river; Spencer looked calm, but underneath, in the current of his eyes, there was a thrashing torrent of fury waiting to be let out. It wouldn't take much more to make him crack.

All he said, in an eerily soft voice, was, "Somebody told you. Who?"

Frank barked. "It doesn't matter who told me! It's forbidden all the same! I'm warning you, Spencer." The alpha strode to his son and grabbed at the front of Spencer's t-shirt, dragging him closer, until they were nose-to-nose and eye-to-eye.

I whined. I could practically feel the waves of menace rolling off Spencer, could see the wolf snarling behind his eyes. Either Frank didn't see it, or he just didn't care. He should have cared. "I'm warning you, *boy*, do as you are goddamn told for once in your miserable life. I won't order you this time, but I'm only giving you one chance. Leave the girl alone, or I will make you. You got me?" Frank snarled, shaking Spencer by the shirt.

For a second, I was certain Spencer was about to wolf out and tear his father to shreds. I could see the longing to do it in his eyes, the fearless, wild rage. Then Frank shoved him, sending him stumbling, and marched away into the trees. Spencer got his footing before he fell, and stood for a moment, glaring into the trees where his father had stormed away.

I started toward him, but Dominic grabbed my arm to keep me back. He turned me and tucked my face into his chest, just as I heard the sound of clothes shredding, bones snapping, organs bulging. A terrible howl ripped apart the quiet woods, scaring shrieking birds from their nests and sending small animals scurrying into their dens. It was a long, ululating sound of rage that sent shivers tumbling, icy-cold, down my spine. Dominic kept me locked against him until the howling ended.

When he let me go, Spencer was gone. I didn't want to know where he'd gone or what he planned on doing. I stared at the ground, at the scattered shreds of what had been Spencer's clothes, and tears sprang to my eyes, leaking down my face. Why was it all so difficult? Why couldn't Spencer and I just be together without all the drama and complications? Why did Frank have to *forbid* us from loving each other, as if our feelings for each other were somehow wrong, just because I wasn't a werewolf?

"Shh, shh, Tilly. God, don't cry. Don't cry," Dominic hushed me gently, wrapping an arm around my shoulders. He pulled the cuffs of his jumper down over his fingers and mopped away my tears as if I was a child.

I sniffled. Distantly, I had to wonder who had told Frank. Dominic and Desmond were the only other people who knew about me and Spencer, and it was obvious Dom hadn't told. Considering Des had his own secret, I doubted he'd tell. Nobody else could possibly have known, unless they were spying on us awful closely.

"There we go. That's better," he murmured, and I smacked his hand away sulkily. "Come on. We'll give Spence time to chill out, and in the meantime, you can hang with me and Des. He said something yesterday about needing to talk to me, but I figure anything he's got to say, he can say it in front of you."

I frowned, and shook my head. I knew what Des wanted to tell his brother, and I didn't think I should be there when he did. "No, it's okay. I think I'm just going to go back to my cabin and take a nap. I'm exhausted, and I feel a headache coming on." That much was actually true. So much had already happened, even my nap under the oak tree that morning felt as if it had been days ago, not hours.

Dominic frowned. "Are you sure?"

"I'm sure. I'll be fine. I just need to lie down for a while and…think about things." I shrugged, hoping he'd understand.

He nodded slowly, his green eyes showing a little concern. I gave him a small, reassuring smile, and he gave in with a reluctant sigh.

"Okay," he sighed. "Go lie down. And Tilly?" he added as I started to turn away.

I glanced at him over my shoulder. He looked sad.

"I'm sorry about my dad. Really. As much as I hate to admit it, if Spencer makes you happy, you should have a right to be with him." Putting his hands into his pockets, he looked at the ground for a moment, and then slouched away with his curly head bowed.

I watched him go, feeling a stab of guilt. But I was far more worried about Spencer, and what he might be doing, and what was going to happen between us. It seemed like there was no choice, really. We couldn't be together.

Feeling my lips tremble, I shook my head, pushing away the thoughts before I started crying again. It hurt my heart to think that Spencer and I had barely had a chance to be together, and we were already being torn apart. It hurt worse to think of him being ordered away from me, physically unable to be near me because of the will of the alpha. Worst of all was knowing that in less than two months, Spencer would be partnered to another girl—a *suitable* girl. A werewolf. He'd promised to fight it, to fight Frank's orders, but just how much good would it do? If he couldn't break the orders…

I wiped at my watery eyes and started back toward my cabin, desperate to lie down and lose myself in sleep for a while. Maybe when I woke up, my heart wouldn't hurt so much. Halfway back to my cabin, I bumped into Sarah, almost literally.

I'd been walking with my gaze downcast and my shoulders hunched as I tried miserably not to worry where Spencer was, and Sarah leapt into my path out of nowhere, startling me. I jumped, gasping, my hands flying to my chest to hold my thudding heart behind my ribs.

"Jeez, Sarah, you scared me!"

The smile she turned on me was less than pleasant; there was sharp edge to it. I blinked, surprised. Had I said something wrong?

She flipped her red hair over her shoulder, her smile growing, only making me more uneasy. Her green eyes flashed.

"Oh, hi there, Tilly," she said sweetly, as if she hadn't noticed me, until I'd spoken.

Unnerved, I frowned. "Is something wrong, Sarah?" I asked.

Her strange smile expanded into a full on grin, and she laughed. It was a sound like tinkling glass, jagged and cold. "No, nothing's wrong. Not now anyway." She looked at me through narrowed eyes, and flicked her fingers on her hip. Then she abruptly turned and sashayed away, hips swaying.

I stared after her in confusion, my stomach a writhing knot of discomfort. I couldn't think what I'd possibly done to upset her like that. And what did she mean, *not now anyway*?

A dull thumping in my head reminded me I needed to sleep. Shaking off the discomfiting encounter with Sarah, I put a hand to my head and groaned. Somewhere nearby, a bird twittered, its song piercing my eardrums. I started walking again, determined to escape the noise. I'd figure out what I'd done to piss off Sarah later. Then, maybe a miracle would happen, and Frank would stop being an ass and free Spencer from his obligation to put the pack before his own happiness.

I woke up groggily on my bed, and stretched as I rolled over. The light coming through the closed curtains was dim, and I twitched the fabric aside to see that it was getting dark outside. I glanced at the clock on the nightstand, and its little ticking arms informed me that

I'd been asleep for a couple of hours—it was just after eight in the evening.

My stomach growled as I swung my feet out of bed, putting a hand to my head. I'd missed dinner, no doubt, but at least my headache was gone. I still felt miserable, and my mouth tasted like dry paper. I ran my rough tongue over my teeth and tried combing my fingers through my hair. With a sigh, I decided it was time for a shower.

Figuring I wasn't going anywhere else, I gathered some clean pyjama shorts and a t-shirt and made my way to the bathroom. I flipped on the light and took a hesitant look in the mirror. The redness of my eyes startled me, as did the paleness of my skin under the harsh lighting. I looked positively corpselike. I felt almost as bad. My sleep-sluggish thoughts kept dragging me back to Frank's angry, gravelly voice and the barely contained seething fury in Spencer's glinting eyes.

I'm only giving you one chance. Leave the girl alone, or I will make you. You'd have thought that a man who knew the pain of heartbreak as well as Frank did, who had felt it so intensely that he lashed out at his eldest son because of it, would have more compassion toward our situation.

I suspected that his injured pride and feeling that his first wife had betrayed him by leaving was exactly why Frank was doing this to us—to Spencer, really. He was punishing Spencer with heartbreak, the way his mother had done to him, by keeping his son away from love. Even before he knew about our relationship, Frank had already pushing Spencer toward a relationship he didn't want by forcing him toward a girl he couldn't possibly love—precisely *because* he was forced to her.

In the mirror, my reflection's eyes grew bright and shimmery with unshed tears, and I took a deep breath. Shaking the thoughts away, I stripped and stepped into the shower. I stayed there for a long time, sitting with my knees tucked up to my chest while hot water cascaded down on me. My wet hair dripped into my face, streams running over my closed eyes. I sat until the water started to turn cold on my skin and the mirror was completely fogged with steam.

It was with great reluctance that I eventually exited the spray of not-so-hot water, and only did so because I was developing goose bumps and my teeth were starting to chatter. Turning the water off, the silence of the misty bathroom made the sounds of my damp footsteps seem loud. I dried off and slipped into my shorts and t-shirt, scrubbing my wet hair with a towel so it fell in an unruly mess around my face and shoulders.

I swiped my hand over the mirror, clearing the fog, and took another look at myself. I didn't look quite so corpselike. My cheeks were flushed from the heat of the water, my eyes were still a little pink, and my fair hair was a shade darker with being damp. The knot in my stomach had eased too, and the kinks in my muscles had relaxed. I still looked about as happy as if a judge had just sentenced me to death row.

With a sigh, I left my damp towels on the bathroom floor and returned to my bedroom. I pushed the door to my room open, and found Spencer sitting on my bed, shirtless. My mouth dropped open, and my stomach dipped as my heart lifted. Seeing him, I suddenly felt lighter, and my lips spread into a helpless smile. His head was bowed, and lost in his own thoughts, he didn't seem to have noticed me standing in the doorway yet. He was leaning forward with his elbows on his knees, his feet and chest were bare and his ebony hair was tousled and falling over his face.

Behind him, the window was open, once again. I was sure it had been closed when I went for my shower. The light was fading from the sky, turning the treetops gold and the clouds black, throwing Spencer's shadow onto my bedroom floor. He looked like a beautiful marble statue poised on the edge of my bed, deep in thought. I admired him silently for a moment, before the breeze swirled in the window and around the room, and Spencer's head snapped up as he caught my scent. In the dimness, his eyes shone with silvery reflective light.

"Tilly," he whispered in a rough tone that took me by surprise and made a slow blush crawl up my face. He blinked, and the reflective light in his eyes vanished, leaving human blue orbs.

Shyly, I grinned at him. "Do you have some aversion to clothing?" I asked pointedly, trying not to drool as I looked at him.

He broke into a smile and stood up, hooking his thumbs in the belt loops of his jeans. My eyes strayed over him, and I bit my lip. His teeth flashed white as he chuckled. Taking a step toward me, his eyes roamed my body. I felt his gaze stroking my figure and caressing my bare legs. Slowly, he returned his gaze to mine and twitched one eyebrow.

"You're one to talk," he murmured, taking another step closer.

Cautiously, I closed the bedroom door behind me and leaned against it, watching him as he stalked closer to me without taking his gaze off mine for a second. I could feel a shiver building in the base of my spine and heat spreading through my body from low in my stomach. All he was doing was *looking* at me. No, not quite looking, it was more like he was undressing me with his eyes.

He slunk up to me until he was close enough to touch, close enough that I could smell the wild stormy scent of his skin, and feel his body heat. I tipped my head back to look up at him, his eyes glimmering somewhere between the dark cobalt blue of the human and the golden shine of the wolf. His head bent to mine until we were breathing the same air, and his starlit eyes filled my vision. His lips were just an inch from mine, torturously close. He lifted his hands and placed them flat against the door on either side of my shoulders, blocking me in, so I had nowhere to run. Not that I wanted to run. I doubted I even could. My legs felt like jelly, barely holding me up as it was.

Somehow, I managed a semi-coherent thought. In a breathless whisper, I said, "You shouldn't be here. If Frank finds out—"

Spencer snarled. The sound should have scared me, but it didn't. Instead, it had the opposite effect, and I curled my fingers into my palms, my nails scratching at the door. I willed my knees not to give out.

Spencer pressed even closer, his nose touching mine, his eyes blazing. In a ragged voice, he growled, "Screw Frank. I'm not letting him take you away from me. Whatever it takes, Tilly. I'll break every order he sets on me and we'll leave. We'll run away. I don't care where, so long as you're with me. I want to be with you, more than I've ever wanted anything in my life. And nobody, not even my father, is going to deny me that."

My heart stumbling, I whimpered, "But what—"

He slid his hands from the door to my shoulders, slipping his fingers down my arms and lacing them through mine. He pinned my hands to the door and I forgot what I'd been about to say. Whatever it was, it couldn't have been important. Nothing was important— nothing but Spencer, and the way he was looking at me and making me melt inside.

With a soft growl, he leaned into me and murmured roughly in my ear, "No buts. I love you. That's all that matters."

He drew his mouth lightly across my cheekbone, and my eyes fluttered shut. I exhaled a shaky breath, only his weight pressing me against the door keeping me standing. With his body crushed against me, and his heat burning me through my t-shirt, I could hardly keep a thought straight. I could feel his heart pounding through his skin, rapid and fierce as a war drum. But one thought whispered through my head, and I managed to cling on to it for long enough to say it aloud.

When his lips paused at the corner of my mouth, I finally said the words that had been sitting on my tongue for two days. I told him, very softly, in a whisper against his mouth, "I love you, Spencer."

With his body as close as it was, I felt the shudder that ran through him and heard his breath catch in his throat. The small sound rolled into a low, rumbling growl, and he released my hands, so he could wrap his arms around me. He kissed me, and lightning exploded through my body, every inch sizzling with the sweet shock of it. His mouth was brutal on mine, demanding, excited, *hungry*. I could taste the wildness on his lips, the moonlight on his tongue.

With a moan, I sank my fingers into his hair, clutching at him and wanting him closer even though we couldn't possibly get any closer with clothes on. Violent waves of desire rushed over me, smothering me and tossing me, and I was completely at their mercy—completely at Spencer's mercy. And he was entirely at mine. I'd never felt so vulnerable or so empowered, especially when I scraped my nails lightly down the back of his neck, and he made a helpless noise of desire, somewhere between a groan and a growl.

So fast it made me dizzy, he lifted me and spun, dropping me on the bed. Panic skittered through my head, making my muscles tense, and he paused, sensing my anxiety. Tearing his mouth from mine with some obvious difficulty, he pulled back and stared down at me. His eyes were hooded and stormy, the blue a dark ring around his dilated pupils, sparkling with gold glitter. We were both panting, both trembling, both *wanting*. Spencer's hands were half-curled into the mattress on either side of my body, and he hovered just slightly over me. The breeze blew cool air over us, but I still felt far too hot.

Quietly, his voice so ragged I could barely understand his words, Spencer murmured, "Tilly, it's okay. We don't have to…"

His mouth made a funny shape, and I was sure I blushed, but I was already burning all over, so I couldn't feel it. He saw it, though, and lifted one hand off the mattress, holding and balancing himself on the other. He touched my face very gently, a stark contrast to the way he'd been kissing me. The wildness in his eyes softened a little.

"We can wait, Tilly. This is all so new to both of us. Give it time. Give *us* time." He smiled, a fragile thing as tender and mysterious as the moonlight stroking through his midnight-black hair.

Slowly, I nodded, relaxing. I raised my hand and brushed dark strands out of his eyes, watching them flicker blue and gold under his lashes. It was a constant fight against the wolf, instinct pushing and the boy resisting. I knew it couldn't be easy for him to wait when his every animalistic impulse was snarling for him not to. I knew he wanted me, and damn, did I ever want him. But he was right—always, he was right. I wasn't ready. It was too much in too short a time. We'd known each other less than a month, and while that must have felt like months to his wolf, which had already chosen me and wasn't changing its mind, it was hardly any time for two people to fall in love.

With a cheeky smile, I said, "We're still going to make out, though, right?"

413

He shifted to lie next to me instead of hovering over me, and I suspected it was because the way we were slotted together was way too provocative. He laughed, and I felt the sound rumble through his chest. His smile was blinding in the darkness, and he nodded.

"If that's what you want, it's fine by me."

He leaned in, sweeping his mouth over mine gingerly. He took his time with this kiss, *really* took his time, even as his left hand coasted down my side to the hem of my shorts and slid down my bare thigh, drawing circles on my skin. I let my own fingers roam his body, his biceps to his bare chest to his solid abs.

I traced the curve of his hipbone and suddenly remembered something I'd noticed before. I was kind of ashamed to admit I'd noticed, but it was a little hard not to have, considering how often he showed up naked in front of me.

I broke the kiss and asked, "What's your tattoo of?"

He stared at me with dazed, golden eyes for a moment. Then he blinked, and his eyes were blue again, the gears in his head slowly churning to life again. "My tat? Oh, the one on my hip?" he said in a tone of dawning realisation.

I raised my eyebrows at him. "What, you have more than one?"

His answering smile was the definition of wicked. "Actually, I do."

I opened my mouth to ask where it was, then shut my mouth without saying a thing, feeling colour rise to my cheeks. I decided that if I hadn't seen it, it was probably somewhere I had deliberately not been looking, and I didn't want to know.

Instead, I simply said, "Yes, the one on your hip."

He grinned, and I bit my lip. He rolled onto his back and peeled back the waistband of his jeans, and I averted my eyes, blowing out an unsteady breath as I fixed my gaze out the window. He chuckled and I was sure he rolled his eyes.

"It's okay, you can look. I'm not getting more indecent than that. But you can see the tat."

Hesitantly, I looked down to his hip, catching his eyes briefly on the way. There, against the fair skin just under his hipbone, was a strange symbol like shape permanently inked. It looked like an X cutting through an M. Curiously, I reached to touch it, and pulled my hand back shyly, glancing at him for permission.

His expression answered mine, and I hesitantly traced the shape of the tattoo with my fingertips. Spencer made a soft sound—so soft I almost didn't hear it. I heard the stifled moan of delight, and I took my hand away quickly. I glanced at him again, under my lashes, and saw his eyes were closed. His chest rose and fell rapidly. Clearly, he was having self-control issues. I decided not to push him, and sat up, folding my legs modestly under me.

Tucking my hair behind my ears, I asked, "So, what is it?"

After a second, Spencer let his waistband fall back in place, covering most of the tattoo and allowing my heart to stop trying to pound its way out of my chest. Carefully, he sat up, putting his back against the wall and turning his face to the cool breeze coming in the window. His eyes were still gold, and his voice low, but he seemed to be better in control without me touching him.

"It's a rune," he said, flicking his gaze to me sideways, "Well, technically it's two runes, from the Elder Futhark Alphabet. An old Norse alphabet, I think. The X is *Gebo*. It means *Gift*. As in, the wolf is my gift. The M is *Mannaz*, and it means *Man*. It reminds me I'm not just an animal, although sometimes I wish I was. The tattoo is a symbol of what I am, both man and wolf." He touched his hip with an absent gesture, his eyes sliding from me to the moon hanging just above the treetops outside, a mysterious ghost against the black, starry sky.

Fascinated, I asked, "What's your other tattoo of?"

Turning back to me, he smiled and lifted the hem of his pant leg, showing a little black shape on his ankle. That would explain why I hadn't seen it before. It was so small, no one would never notice it, if they didn't already know it was there. It looked like a squared off, upside-down U, with one arm shorter than the other.

"*Uruz*. It's a strength rune. I think, in some obscure way, it also means *Rain* in Icelandic." He explained with a shrug.

I laughed, and he gave me a strange look, folding down the leg of his jeans again.

"What's funny?" he asked. I shook my head, but he pressed, "Come on, explain why you're laughing. You don't believe in the runes?"

I shook my head again, this time in negation to his assumption. "No, no, that's not it. I'm a witch, remember? Of course I believe in the power of runes. I was just thinking it's funny that your tattoo means *Rain* because, well…" I hesitated, feeling silly and embarrassed, but he gave me that intent stare and I sighed. "Well, because you smell like rain."

I hunched my shoulders, bowing my head. My ears burned. Would he think I was weird for noticing how he smelled? I hoped not. I mean, come on, he was a *wolf* for God's sake, he could tell from my scent when I was feeling *things*, sinful things. *That* was weird, and yes, a little embarrassing. Maybe more than a little.

Spencer blinked. "I smell like rain?" he asked, sounding both surprised and curious.

I nodded. "Rain and burning wood."

"Hmm," he murmured, looking thoughtful.

Abruptly, he leaned forward and I tried not to flinch. He sniffed my hair, and I laughed quietly. He leaned back, his lids half-lowered.

"Mmh, you smell like wild roses and freesia. Delicious." He hummed in delight.

I blushed. I'd never been called delicious before.

Aware that it was getting late, and that the conversation had strayed, I started to worry. "Spencer?" I said cautiously.

His smile faded as he registered my tone. His eyes darkened to their usual blue, and his eyebrows pulled down.

In a whisper, I asked, "What's going to happen?" I wasn't sure if I meant what was going to happen with our relationship, since Frank had found out and essentially banned us from seeing each other, or if I meant what was going to happen with the witches and their attacks on the wolves.

With a grim expression, Spencer lay down and patted the space on the mattress next to him. Obediently, I lay down next to him, and he looped an arm around my waist, pulling me against his chest. I rested my forehead against his collarbones, breathing in his rainwater-and-bonfire scent.

"I don't know, Tilly," he admitted quietly. "I really don't know."

I sighed and closed my eyes, snuggling against him. Despite the breeze fluttering the curtains, I was perfectly warm in his arms. "Will you stay?" I asked, hoping I didn't sound needy.

Spencer kissed the top of my head. "Of course," he whispered into my hair.

I felt myself already starting to slip away, safe and drowsy with him next to me. The last thing I heard before falling asleep was Spencer's voice warm in my ear.

"Sweet dreams, Tilly."

Chapter Twenty Six

** Tilly **

I woke up alone, with warm sunlight pouring onto my face through the open curtains over the window. The space in the bed beside me was empty and cool, letting me know that Spencer had left some time before. He'd closed the window, but not the curtains, which I suspected meant he'd actually gone out the window and closed it from the outside. A little part of me was sad that he'd left, but I understood why he had. He hadn't wanted to get caught leaving my cabin, so he'd slipped out early enough that nobody would be hanging about to see him.

With a sigh, I rolled over and stretched all the way to my toes, groaning appreciatively as my spine cracked, relieving an ache in the small of my back. The sheets were blissfully soft and cool against my skin, and the pillow still held Spencer's rain storm scent. I smiled, rolling back over and burying my nose in the pillow.

Memories of the previous night flashed through my head, a tumult of emotions and sensations accompanying the images, and I laughed quietly, slightly giddy. Despite everything—the witches, Frank, and all the complications—I felt *good* about me and Spencer. Even if we couldn't be together publicly, we could still secretly be together in private. The idea gave me a thrill, and made me feel wicked.

Eventually, I got the energy to pull myself out of bed, and almost skipped into the bathroom. The first thing I did was look in the mirror. My hair was a wreck, and my lips looked darker than usual—tender from the wild kissing the night before. I grinned at my bright eyed reflection.

Wrinkling my nose, I noticed a mark on my collarbone, and tugged down the top of my t-shirt. My face turned pink as I realised I had a love bite. The grey eyes in the mirror widened with surprise. I'd never had a hickey before. I couldn't even really remember getting it, but things had been a little out of control. My cheeks went from pink to red as I remembered just how unruly it had gotten.

Just thinking about Spencer's hands on my bare thighs and his breath hot on my lips, I saw my pupils in my reflection expand into big, round, black holes. Blowing out a breath to calm myself, I blinked and pushed the memories away. Slowly, my pupils dimmed to their normal size, and the achy heat in the pit of my stomach dissolved. I turned away from the mirror and hit the shower, more because I needed the cold water, than because I was particularly dirty. After all, all I'd done between my shower the night before and that morning was sleep—and make out with my hot werewolf boyfriend. Yeah. I cranked the temperature dial on the shower all the way to the blue, as low as it would go, and stepped into the freezing spray.

After my shower, I grabbed a quick breakfast of chocolate cereal, eating it as I danced around the cabin to Billy Idol's '*Dancing With Myself*', which was blaring from a radio I'd found hidden away in a closet in the spare room. The thing was ancient and dusty. I hadn't been sure it would even work, but when I'd plugged it in, I'd been pleasantly surprised to find it picked up four different stations. I was sticking with the 80's station because it sure beat the hell out of the techno crap on the others.

I didn't want to leave my cabin, knowing that if I did, I'd have to avoid Spencer every time I saw him. So I stayed inside all morning, dusting and washing the floor and such, while listening to the radio. Nobody, not even Dominic, bothered me. Well, not until around lunchtime. It was just a little after one in the afternoon when someone finally came knocking on the door and interrupting my housework. While Steppenwolf's '*Born To Be Wild*' poured out of the radio, I danced to the door of the cabin and flung it open, wielding a fluffy blue ledge duster like a sword, pointed right at Desmond's face.

Jerking back in surprise, Desmond's green eyes widened, and he held up his hands. "I surrender! Please don't dust me to death!" He grinned cheekily.

I jabbed him in the chest with the end of the duster before lowering it to my side. "What are you doing here?" I asked, baffled to find the other brother standing on my porch in ratty jeans and a faded green t-shirt that matched his eyes.

Desmond snorted and rolled his eyes. "Yeah, afternoon to you too, Tilly," he muttered.

I realised how my question had sounded and felt slightly ashamed. I bowed my head, duly chastised. "Sorry. I'm just surprised. I was expecting Dominic." I wasn't sure what it meant that Dominic hadn't come to see me yet. Was he sulking with me, or mad at me after the day before? I mean, he'd seemed okay with me and Spencer once I'd explained everything, but still. Maybe he'd had time to think about it and decided he didn't want to be my friend anymore. Maybe he didn't want to be friends with someone who'd lied to him and snuck around with his half-brother behind his back.

"Sorry to disappoint you, but Dom's busy dealing with Spencer, so all you get is me." Desmond flashed his cheeky grin again, and the breeze blew a few wavy strands of hair into his eyes. He pushed them back absently, tucking them behind his ear.

I blinked. It was the most feminine gesture I'd ever seen him make, and I wondered for a second just how often he had to stop himself from saying or doing something that would him give him away to his father or the pack.

Before thinking about it, I said, "You told Dominic, didn't you? About…being…" I hedged around the word, remembering the way he'd winced when I said it before.

He looked down, his smile fading. He nodded. "Aye, last night. That's actually sort of why I'm here. I was kind of hoping…I could just hang out with someone who knows. Take a break from…acting." A splash of red bloomed across the tops of his angular cheekbones, and he shifted uncomfortably.

I opened the door wider, silently inviting him in. He slunk in with his shoulders hunched, giving me a quick, grateful smile. I frowned.

"Dominic didn't take the news well, then?" I asked, concerned. I hadn't thought Dominic, sweet and understanding as he was, would have a problem with his brother being gay.

Des shook his head, tapping his fingers nervously on the back of a chair at the dining table. "No, it wasn't like that exactly. It was more that he was hurt I hadn't told him sooner. And when he asked who else knew, and I said Spencer...well. He kind of flew off the handle."

He glanced at me, and I felt the worry on my face.

He misread it and said, "It's okay, I didn't tell him you knew. He won't be mad at you. But he was seriously pissed that I'd told Spencer before him. He said something about Spencer knowing everything and stealing everything that he wanted." Desmond gave me a canny look from under his lashes. "He stormed out after that, but I gathered there was more to his hissy fit than that."

I sighed and gestured toward the sofa. I sat, and Desmond sat next to me, an expectant look on his face. I rubbed my hands over my face, my good mood deteriorating. *'Born on a Bayou'* came on the radio, and I got up to turn it off.

When I sat down again, I asked, "How mad was he at Spencer last night, exactly?"

Des made a face, which wasn't reassuring. "Pretty damn mad. Mad enough that he sprouted fangs and claws and had to go for a run. I don't think I've seen Dom so mad since we were kids, and me and Spence tied him to a tree for a joke." He smiled faintly at the memory.

I almost asked why they tied him to a tree, but then I figured it was just the sort of thing boys did to each other.

Feeling guiltier by the second, I said, "You said Dominic was 'dealing with Spencer'. What does that mean precisely?" I was worried there would be another fight, and after what I'd witnessed in the clearing, I was scared someone would end up with missing parts.

"Don't worry, Dominic was calmer this morning. I think he just went to talk to Spence." Des paused and grimaced at me, linking his hands together on his knees. He tilted his head down, still looking at me with eerie focus. Quietly, he asked, "What happened yesterday, Tilly?"

I blew out my breath, slumping back against the sofa cushions. I rolled my eyes toward the ceiling, staring at a nest of cobwebs hanging in the corner of one of the rafters. What happened? A lot happened. I didn't even know where to begin, how to even start to explain it all to Desmond.

"It's complicated," I muttered, hoping he'd drop it.

Des just sat back and waited patiently. "I've got time."

I sighed again and spoke while still staring at the ceiling, because it was easier that way. "God, Des, it's such a mess. I made a mess of things." I shook my head, trying to figure out where to start. I bit my lip. "Spencer caught me kissing Dominic," I said softly, and saw Desmond's eyebrows shoot up. I groaned at his reaction and went on, "They nearly got into a fight, and I…I had to explain that I'd realised I didn't love Dom the way I love Spencer, and…" I rambled until my throat closed up suddenly, cutting off my words.

Des stared at me for a long time. He let out a breath. "Wow. Okay. So…you chose Spencer."

I nodded.

He frowned. "No wonder Dom threw a fit."

Unsure what to say, I just nodded again, feeling miserably guilty. Then I said, "Not that any of it matters, because Frank found out about me and Spencer, and he forbid us from being together." My voice cracked, and I swallowed.

Des sighed, putting his hand over mine sympathetically.

With a bitter laugh, I said, "That's not even the worst of it. You know about the ritual for the pack joining?"

He hesitated, and then nodded. "I know there's supposed to be some sort of marriage thing, but it's an old rule. I don't think—"

"Well think again, because your dad is implementing the rule…and he's making Spencer the groom," I said angrily, and a spike of ice went through my heart. I closed my eyes, trying to unclench my jaw. Just thinking about the stupid pack joining, Frank's anger, and Lilac's pretty face, it all made me want to scream.

For a long moment, Desmond silently stared at me, and then he practically leapt to his feet, so quickly and violently that I yelped in surprise. He strode to the fireplace and slammed his hands on the mantle.

"Dammit!" he yelled.

I almost smiled. I'd said the same thing when Spencer told me about Frank's plans for him. I hadn't expected Desmond to be so furious on our behalf, though. The brunette boy shook his head, and I saw his knuckles turn white from gripping the mantle so hard.

"I knew my father was capable of being a dick, but I didn't think he could be plain cruel. He's gone too far this time. Him and his damn obsession with the rules, with having only *pure* relationships," he spat the word pure with bitterness and contempt, and made a noise of disgust.

He turned his head, and I saw a mix anger, sadness, and sympathy in his eyes.

"It's not right, Tilly. This isn't how the wolves are meant to be. Our kind aren't all like Frank. It's just…he's so blinded by what happened with Spencer's mother, he loses sight of the boundaries when it comes to Spencer." He sighed.

I heard the disappointment in his father in the sound. There were tears in my eyes, and I whispered, "Frank's *ordered* him to marry the other girl."

For half a heartbeat, Des said nothing, and then he said, "If you ask me, Spencer would leave the pack in a heartbeat…if he had a reason to. And now you're his reason. The orders are Frank's way of making sure that doesn't happen."

I nodded. "Spencer said he'd try to fight the orders."

At that, Desmond whistled, a low, impressed sound. "Well, if anyone can fight the alpha's will, it'll be Spencer. But God knows what it'll cost him to do it. Frank could have him banished or beaten for disobeying the alpha's orders. Or worse, he could find a way to force Spence to stay with the pack, and kick you out instead." With a heavy sigh, Desmond put a hand on my arm and squeezed. "I'm sorry, Tilly. I really am. But if anyone can find a way out of an arranged marriage by alpha's orders, Spencer can. And no matter how angry my brother might be with Spencer, Dom cares about you too much to let anyone make you unhappy. Even if what makes you happy is another guy."

After the serious conversation, Des and I finished the chores, with him laughing while I sang along to classic rock songs on the radio. He was apparently more of a country kind of guy. We played a game of Chess, and then Annie and Chris came along to ask if we wanted to play Stick-in-the-Mud with them. We ended up spending the rest of the afternoon playing games with the kids.

After that, I spent the rest of the day trying not to think about Spencer. I collapsed onto the sofa in my cabin, fully dressed, at a little after nine pm, exhausted from all the running around, and quickly tumbled headlong into a heavy sleep plagued by dreams of Spencer's blue eyes and his lips on mine.

Chapter Twenty Seven

** Tilly **

"Tilly! Tilly, wake up! Please, Tilly, get up!"

I jerked awake at the sound of someone shouting my name and a rapid pounding on the door that echoed loudly through my dark cabin. The abrupt movement landed me facedown as my elbow smacked the floor I yelped, pushing myself to my feet, and rubbing my elbow. Looking around dazedly, I realised I was in the living room, and I must have fallen asleep on the sofa. It was no wonder my neck ached when I turned it to look at the clock in the kitchen to see it was half past two in the morning. *Ugh.*

The rapid pounding on the door came again, and a frightened sounding voice called my name. I stumbled to the door and threw it open. Sarah was standing on my porch, looking panicked. Her red hair was a tangled mess, as if she'd been running through the trees and had snagged it on branches, and there was a scratch on her cheek. Her eyes were wide, and she was pale. She grabbed my hands as soon as I opened the door, and began dragging me out.

"Oh my God, Tilly, you have to come with me! Dominic's in trouble! We went out for a run, and he…. There was a trap or something…. And the witches…. And Dominic's hurt! Come on! I need your help!" She spoke so fast, her words blurred.

I had to focus to make sense of it. "Whoa, Sarah, slow down! Calm down and tell me, what's wrong with Dominic?" I asked, but she was already pulling me down the porch steps.

Her grasp on my wrist was tight, and she was too strong for me to fight, so I stumbled to keep up with her as she dragged me into the trees, gasping and half-sobbing. My heart hammered fearfully, worried about Dominic.

Panting as we ran, and I asked breathlessly, "Sarah, what happened to Dominic? How badly is he hurt? Shouldn't we get Frank or Kat?"

I didn't know why she would need my help if Dominic was hurt. I wasn't like Jasmine. I wasn't a healer. Maybe it was just that my cabin happened to be closest, but then, Spencer's cabin was only another hundred yards away, and surely he'd be a lot more useful than I would. I hadn't the first clue about werewolf first aid. And if Dominic was hurt badly enough to need help, if he couldn't heal himself.... But if it was silver, nobody else would be able to touch it.

"Sarah," I gasped. "Sarah, is it silver? Is he hurt with silver?" I stumbled over a root, and nearly fell, but Sarah's hand yanked me back up viciously, pulling me on. "Ouch! Sarah, you're hurting me!" I cried, but she didn't stop.

We emerged into a clearing I recognised, the one where the hunters and Olivia had ambushed the wolves the night of the full moon. Finally, Sarah stopped pulling me along. She jerked my wrist hard, and I fell to my knees, scraping them on the rough dirt. With a cry of protest and pain, I looked up at her and my stomach flipped over nauseatingly.

She was *smiling*. No, *laughing*. Cold, harsh laughter that made the hairs on the back on my neck stand up. There was a wild look in her eyes, replacing the fear and worry I realised had been faked.

Behind me, a voice rasped my name, and I whirled. At the edge of the clearing, Dominic was slumped on the ground, thin silver chains binding his wrists and ankles. There was blood leaking from under the chains, tinting the shiny metal red. There was also a streak of blood running down the side of Dom's face from a head wound, but the wound seemed to have healed. His hair was a mess, some of the curls matted to his head with sweat and blood. Lines of pain etched themselves into his face, making his dimple stand out like a deep gash in his cheek. There was fear in his eyes, turning them to the gold-green of his wolf.

With a cry, I started toward him, but Sarah brutally pushed me down. I hit the ground hard, a twig digging a gash into my arm, and I was knocked breathless. While I was down, gasping for air, she launched a savage kick into my side. I tried to scream as I rolled over, clutching my side, but all that came out of my mouth was a thin whistle. I heard Dominic call my name in an agonised voice, and Sarah laughing loudly over me.

Lifting my head, I glared up at her through strands of hair darkened by dirt. "Sarah, what's going on? What do you *want*?!" I rose to my hands and knees, one hand still gripping my bruised side. God, it hurt.

Sarah looked down at me with a smile like a knife's edge, her eyes wilder than her hair, and she tilted her head. "What do I want?" she sneered. "I want to hear you scream, bitch." She kicked me again.

I did just what she wanted—I screamed. A second too late, I bit down on my lip, not wanting to give her the satisfaction. From the other side of the clearing, Dominic growled and thrashed. When I glanced over, I saw him shaking with the Change, but the silver was preventing the transition.

My head spun, and I felt like puking. Struggling for breath through the lancing pain in my side, I turned my attention back to Sarah. "I don't understand, Sarah!" I choked, feeling tears rolling uncontrollably down my cheeks.

Standing over me, she looked terrifying and beautiful at once, haloed from behind by the moon hovering in the black sky just above the jagged treetops. With a snarl, she swiftly slapped me across the face. So hard my head snapped aside, and I saw stars in front of my vision.

"Don't lie to me, you stupid little bitch! I warned you!" she yelled, pulling back her foot to kick me again. I whimpered and fell to the side, and she scoffed. "Pathetic," she spat, curling her lip. Under it, her teeth were long fangs. Her eyes glinted yellow, and when she raised a hand to push back her hair from her face, I saw her nails were claws.

Terrified, I whimpered again. Curling in on myself in case she decided to land another kick, I rested my forehead against the dirt, trying not to heave up the contents of my stomach. Almost without meaning to, I whispered, "Spencer." Where was he? Where was my wolf, my protector, this time?

Sarah suddenly grabbed a handful of my hair and wrenched my head back, snarling right in my face. Her eyes glowed with primal rage, and her voice was thick with a growl. "Don't you darrre say his name! I warrrned you to stay away from him! He's mine! Spencerrr is mine!"

She tore her hand free of my hair, pulling out strands by the roots, and she kicked even harder. I swore I felt a rib crack, and I screamed in agony. I tasted blood in the back of my throat, and then bile. I rolled over just in time to throw up, shuddering and heaving.

Suddenly, everything made sense. Sarah's warnings about Spencer, her glares the night of the full moon when Spencer had called me ravishing, the way she'd snapped at me the other day, maybe even the way Olivia had stopped the hunter from shooting Spencer on the full moon. I glowered up at her, tasting the salt of my tears and the coppery tang of my own blood.

"You told Frank about Spencer and me," I hissed.

She smiled viciously. "I did." Her smile turned into a grimace, and she bared her teeth. "But that wasn't enough, was it? He was at your cabin last night. He was in your bed, wasn't he? Did you have fun? Did you let him screw you, like the filthy little slut that you are? I bet you did. Was he good, Tilly? Did he make you *scream*?" She lashed out with the back of her hand, her claws slicing across my cheek.

I bit my lip so hard, I tasted a fresh wave of blood and gagged. But I swallowed it and the cry of pain rising in my throat. I refused to let her hear it.

I looked over at Dominic, who had gone scarily silent. He was still, but his eyes were open, locked on me and blazing purely green. When I met his eyes, he looked away, and I couldn't stop the whine that escaped my throat.

"Dominic, I didn't–" I started, not sure why it even mattered what he thought of me anymore. I was pretty sure Sarah was going to kill me. She had a murderous light in her eyes, and I could sense her wolf howling for more blood.

She laughed again, looking from me to Dominic. "Aww. Didn't you want him to know you were banging his brother? Oh, sorry, half-brother. Wait. Were you banging Dom, too? Oh, you really are a dirty little slut. I know you were playing with him. I saw you making out with him at the pack gathering. Hell, I'm sure you would've gone after Desmond too if he wasn't batting for the other team." Sarah shook her head, a look of disgust and contempt crossing her face. I stared at her and she caught my expression. "Oh, yes, I know all about Des and his dirty little secret. It's a shame really. He'd be hot if it weren't for that. Waste of a good looking guy, if you ask me."

I hadn't thought I could hate her more, but right then, hearing the revulsion in her voice as she spoke about Desmond as if there was something horribly wrong about him, I hated her with an intensity that took me by surprise. It was toxic, and I felt the

Darkness inside me boiling up like acid, crawling over my skin and flooding my veins with a feeling of power that was both repulsive and wonderful at once.

I knew it was wrong, that I shouldn't let it take me over, but it felt so good. It made me feel stronger than I ever had, as if I had the power to crush Sarah like a beetle with just a flick of my wrist. I pushed it down, fighting the Darkness. No matter what, I would not be Dark.

In my head, I heard Jasmine's voice from the day Spencer had taken me to get my protection Charm. *She's actually pretty lucky, to have a choice like that. But she has to be careful. With the kind of power she has, it's easy to lose sight of what is right and wrong.*

I had the choice. And I was choosing to be Light, whatever it cost.

"Spencer. Doesn't. Love you," I ground out between clenched teeth. Every breath I took was agony, sending bolts of pain up my side from my cracked rib. "He never did," I spat.

I watched Sarah's face transform into something not entirely human, but not entirely wolf. There were horrible cracking and popping noises as the bones in her face shifted. Her nose stretched flat and wide, her jaws extended, and her eyes changed shape. A low growl rumbled from between large, ivory fangs, and her joints dislocated as she leaned down onto her hands, snarling foul, hot breath in my face. Her saliva dripping fangs were inches from my nose, and she twitched and twisted as her limbs lengthened, her ribs expanded, and her ears grew long and pointed.

Then there was a soft laugh from the trees, and Sarah dug her claws into the dirt, sticking somewhere between human and wolf. I twisted around in time to see Olivia sweeping out of the shadows of the trees, smiling delightedly, as if she was witnessing two children playing a game, instead of a psycho werewolf threatening to rip me apart. The sight of her made everything inside me turn cold with fear and loathing, and my stomach turned over so violently, I nearly threw up again.

"Sarah, tut-tut. Remember what we talked about," Olivia said gently, but reprovingly, like a mother chastising her child, and Sarah growled. "You wouldn't want to break our deal, now would you?" Olivia pursed her lips.

Sarah, reluctantly, backed off. Her eyes came back to me, though, and stayed there, glaring and full of a thirst for my blood. It wasn't just homicidal rage, but jealousy. She was jealous of what I had with Spencer, and she'd tried to ruin it, and she'd failed. If I hadn't been so afraid of her right then, I might have felt a little pity for her. She was clearly in love with Spencer, probably had been for a long time, ever since they'd gone out. She'd never gotten over him, but he just wasn't interested in her. Then I'd come along and stole what she thought should have been hers—Spencer's attention. It was all very sad, in a way, and completely twisted, of course.

"Your deal?" Dominic croaked from the other end of the clearing.

I'd almost forgotten he was there. He looked livid, and was shaking so badly, I thought he might Change despite the silver.

"You made a deal with them to make sure they didn't kill Spencer. And what did you do in return, Sarah? You sold out the rest of your pack? Fed the witches information? Lured Tilly here for them?"

There was hurt in his voice as much as anger, and I realised this must have been even harder for Dominic. He'd known Sarah for years. They'd been friends and pack mates, and she'd turned him over to the witches to be killed, just so they wouldn't kill Spencer. Everything was about Spencer.

Sarah looked at him and a flicker of remorse showed in her eyes before she clamped down on it and sneered. "All of the above. I'd do anything for Spencer. He doesn't care about the pack anyway. He probably hates you most of all, Dom. And once Tilly is out of the way, I'll be the one who's there to comfort him. He'll fall in love with me, just as he should have two years ago."

Dominic turned his face away from her, from both of us, but not before I caught sight of the pain on his face. The pain had nothing to do with the silver chains, and everything to do with being betrayed, his life traded for his half-brother's. Guilt sprang up inside me. Sarah wasn't the only one who'd chosen Spencer over Dominic.

I glared at Sarah. "And what about Frank's orders? He commanded Spencer to stay with the pack and marry Lilac, the girl from the other pack. Even if he ever did fall in love with you, not that he ever would, but if he did, he couldn't really be yours, could he?" I was plunging the knife into Sarah as much as twisting it in my own heart.

Sarah just smiled at me, cruel and condescending. "Once Olivia kills Frank, the alpha's orders no longer apply. The orders die with him. And then it'll just be me and Spencer, and we'll start our own pack. Our own family." A slightly dreamy look came over her face.

I stared at her. I decided that, as much as I hated her, I could still feel pity for her. She was out of her mind. Full on crazy, and completely delusional.

"Oh, come on now, pet. Don't look so scared." Another voice I recognised floated out of the darkness, and I whipped my head around. A woman who looked like Snow White made real stood next to Dominic, her pale fingers buried tenderly in his curls. Her red lips spread in a soft smile, and she shook out her shoulder length black bob. Her eyes were as black as her hair—eyes that sometimes saw the future.

Naomi was by far the kindest of the witches who'd adopted me, but she could be just as cruel as Olivia when it suited her. She gave me fond smile that was almost sisterly, as she wound Dominic's curls around her finger. "Sarah's just a little naïve. I'm sure your boyfriend will be just heartbroken when he finds out you're gone."

Panic rushed up inside me, my gaze darting from Sarah, to Olivia, to Naomi. Dominic had fallen silent under Naomi's touch, his eyes wide and blank, lips parted. I glanced at Naomi's hand on his head. I'd forgotten she could do that, make a person see something that wasn't there just by touching them. She could put them in a dream or a nightmare, and it would feel utterly real until the second she took her fingers away.

I knew because she'd done it to me once or twice. Dreams mostly, to keep me docile, but a nightmare occasionally, at Olivia's command. It was Naomi's first innate power, and her strongest. I hoped she was putting Dominic in a dream and not a nightmare.

She saw my look, and winked at me. "Don't worry, he's enjoying this. You should see some of the things he thinks about doing with you." She clucked her tongue, and I might have blushed under different circumstances.

Sarah made a rough sound, glaring at Naomi, but Naomi ignored her. Someone put a hand on Sarah's shoulder and snorted. Ironic silver nail polish glittered on the nails of the hand, and Sarah moved aside to reveal the final Leyland sister.

Taller and meaner than Naomi, but not as slender and cold as Olivia, and not as pretty as either of them, Gwen was the middle sister in every way, from age to height to the strength of her power—except her cruelty. She was the cruellest of them all. Her black hair was knotted in a thick plait over one shoulder, and her hazel eyes stared mockingly down at me. Gwen had always seemed to hate me in a more personal way than Olivia or Naomi. She'd always taken pleasure in my pain, where Olivia had only thought it was necessary to get what she wanted from me, and Naomi had found it distasteful to punish a child so helpless. Olivia was about mental pain. Gwen was the one who liked the birch cane…and fists.

"Don't lie to the girl, Naomi," Gwen sneered. "After we kill the wolves, Matilda's little mutt will probably be humping Sarah here by the end of the week. Men are such animals, don't you think?"

She laughed harshly, and Sarah's grin grew wider over pointed teeth. My stomach spasmed, and I gagged. I was determined not to throw up again, but I was so scared and so angry, I was shaking with it. If I'd been a werewolf, I'd have Changed, but I wasn't. I was just a pathetic little witch trying not to get sucked under by her Dark side.

I needed my Light side. I needed to tap into it. So I closed my eyes, and desperately grabbed for the energy around me. The energy of the trees, the earth, and the plants, of the sky, the stars, and the moon; I could feel it all, gathering and hovering just above my skin. I could feel my Light magic rising up, swelling under the Dark, breaking through to reach out to that soothing, powerful energy.

"Uh-uh-uh. Not this time, Matilda," Olivia said, stepping toward me.

I flinched back, and then gasped in pain as the motion sent jolts of white-hot agony searing from my cracked rib. Faintly, Dominic moaned. Whether in pain or pleasure from whatever nasty dream Naomi was using to keep him docile, I couldn't be sure. I didn't look over to check. I kept my eyes on Olivia as she stalked closer to me.

She loomed over me, as tall, beautiful, and cold as an ice queen. Then she put a hand on my head, lightly, as if to stroke my hair soothingly. A pounding, sharp pain filled my head, and my vision went white. If I screamed, I couldn't hear the sound of it over the roaring in my ears. Another hand fell on my shoulder, and another on my back, and the pain in my head tripled. It made my cracked rib feel like a little bruise. It felt as if my skull was going to crack open from the pressure inside. The pain ripped through my whole body, as if it was stripping away my skin.

Then it stopped, and the hands lifted off me. My vision was black, and I felt empty and raw—as if I was missing something vital. There was still a roaring in my ears, high-pitched and crackling, and it took me a long moment to realise it was coming from me. I was still screaming, and I couldn't seem to stop until I ran out of breath and the noise choked off into harsh sobs that scraped my torn throat. Slowly, I opened my eyes, and all I saw was black and brown, blurring in front of my eyes. I blinked a few times, tears streaming down my face, and the black and brown smears resolved into dirt. I was lying down, with my cheek pressed to the ground.

Gasping, I tried to sit up, but my muscles were shaking so badly that my arms buckled under me, and I nearly ended up with another mouthful of dirt. I could feel the dirt sticking to my cheek, clinging to the wetness of my tears, and taste it in my mouth. Turning my head to the side, I spat, but it didn't help. A fresh wave of blood coated my tongue, and I coughed it up, shredding my burning throat even more. Red splashed onto the brown of the dirt as I coughed, drops splattering my white, white hands. I felt dizzy.

"What... what did you... do to me?" I rasped. My sides heaved, and my cracked rib protested, but after the blinding agony of whatever they'd done to me, it suddenly didn't feel quite so bad. My vision blurred again, dizziness swamping me, and I closed my eyes, so I could focus on not puking again.

Olivia answered me, but her voice sounded slow and echoing in my ears. I wondered distantly if I had some sort of brain damage.

"We just put a *Debilitas* Spell on you to temporarily paralyse your powers. Couldn't have you trying to blow us up before we get you back home," she said. "And don't worry about your little wolf friend over there. We're taking him with us...to keep you company, I suppose."

I groaned, a brief thought passing through my mind. *This wouldn't have happened if I'd been wearing my Charm.* But I'd thrown my Charm at Spencer when he'd tried to make me hate him. He probably still had it. I never should have taken it off. *God, Spencer.* A spike of terror ran through me and clamped around my chest. *Before we get you back home.* The words bounced around my head, making me want to scream again.

I had sworn that I'd kill myself before I let the witches take me back, and the idea flashed across my mind quick and sharp as a razor. I could do it. I could attack Sarah and her wolf instincts would kick in, and the odds were she'd rip me apart, no matter what Olivia wanted. I could pick up a jagged rock from the ground and cut my wrists.

But I couldn't do any of that. I couldn't kill myself, no matter what I'd sworn, because the witches had Dominic too. I couldn't leave him alone. He'd promised me nobody would hurt me, and he'd kept that promise as best he could. Now it was my turn to protect him and keep him from getting hurt as best as *I* could.

Together, we'd get through this, and we'd get out of it.

The time for running was over.

It was time to fight.

10114933R00244

Printed in Great Britain
by Amazon.co.uk, Ltd.,
Marston Gate.